Jami Dutton

FALSE ACCUSATIONS

FALSE

ACCUSATIONS

ALAN JACOBSON

POCKET BOOKS

New York London Toronto Sydney Tokyo Singapore

Quoted text [on page vii] from Vernon J. Geberth, Practical Homicide Investigation, Second Edition, Copyright 1994 by CRC Press, Inc., Boca Raton, Florida. Reproduced by permission of publisher.

POCKET BOOKS, a division of Simon & Schuster Inc.
1230 Avenue of the Americas, New York, NY 10020

Copyright © 1999 by Alan Jacobson

Library of Congress Cataloging-in-Publication Data

Jacobson, Alan, 1961–
    False accusations / Alan Jacobson.
       p.   cm.
    ISBN 0-671-02678-X
    I. Title
    PS3560.A2585F35   1999
    813'.54—dc21   98-51983

First Pocket Books hardcover printing March 1999

10 9 8 7 6 5 4 3 2 1

POCKET and colophon are registered trademarks of Simon & Schuster Inc.

Designed by Elliott Beard

Printed in the U.S.A.

RRDH/

For my parents, Florence and David, who provided me with the persistence and fortitude necessary in undertaking anything worth accomplishing in life

The homicide crime scene is, without a doubt, the most important crime scene a police officer or investigator will be called upon to respond to. Because of the nature of the crime (death by violence or unnatural causes), the answer to "What has occurred?" can only be determined after a careful and intelligent examination of the crime scene and after the professional and medical evaluation of the various bits and pieces of evidence gathered by the criminal investigator. The crime scene . . . provides an abundance of physical evidence that may connect a suspect or suspects to the crime.

—From Vernon J. Geberth
Practical Homicide Investigation

CHAPTER

I

THE DARK BLUE car snaked around the curve, its headlights slicing like razors through the dead air. It slithered through the neighborhood, hunting for food, sniffing out its prey. With one punch, the large engine muscled up from thirty-five to sixty in less than three seconds, its hunger for speed ravenous.

The man crossing the street caught a glimpse of the looming vehicle and twisted backward, shoving his companion toward the sidewalk—

But there wasn't time.

The car's bone-crushing impact threw the woman onto its hood, then tossed her aside . . . while the engine yanked the man underneath its front end, swallowing him whole.

The dark vehicle lurched slightly as its tire ran over the fallen prey. It then sped off down the street, hung a sharp left, and slipped into the pitch of night.

11:59 P.M.

THE MAN'S TORSO was twisted, his head a bloody mess, with bits of brain tissue scattered around his crushed skull. The woman's body was much more intact, having slid off the side of the car's hood after being thrown up into the air by the initial impact. Her legs appeared to be broken and were bent into an unnatural position, the way a rag doll sometimes lands when a child tosses it aside after she has finished playing with it.

Most of the available officers in the City of Sacramento that night had been diverted to the minority neighborhood of Del Morro Heights to contain an escalating battle sparked by a broad crackdown on gang-related activities. When the call came in to investigate the discovery of a possible hit-and-run several blocks away, the two officers who responded anticipated more of the same, an offshoot of the hostilities.

But they were wrong.

Officer Larry Sanford slammed his car door and ran over to the woman, who was lying faceup in the street; the other victim was obviously deceased. Both were black, he noticed. Sanford pulled a hand out of his leather glove and felt her neck for a pulse. "Shit," he said, the vapor that emanated from his mouth tailing off into the cold night air. He looked up and down the street, but saw no one. He glanced over to his partner and shook his head.

"Dispatch, this is Unit Nine," the other officer said. "We've got a Code Twenty on San Domingo Street. Notify homicide. Securing crime scene."

"Roger, Unit Nine."

"She's still warm," Sanford said. "Let's get this area secured." Using a roll of yellow warning tape, he established the boundaries of the crime scene while his partner blocked off the street and its adjoining arteries with traffic cones. Although out of the academy only six months, they both knew the routine: quick response, safeguard and preserve. That is, secure the crime scene to protect all materials in the vicinity because everything was considered evidence until proven otherwise. No one—not even another police officer—was to enter the crime scene until the detectives arrived. One of the most significant threats to a homicide investigation was the disruption of physical evidence: nothing in the scene was to be disturbed, moved, stepped on, or contaminated in any manner.

With the thermometer at 33 degrees, Sanford rolled up the fur collar on his standard-issue blue nylon jacket and shoved his hands into his pockets. He sucked a mouthful of damp air into his lungs: rain was on the way. He sent his partner back to the gang-related conflict while he stood watch over the crime scene.

In his boxing days, Detective Bill Jennings had a flat, rock hard gut. Some thirty years later, the musculature was stretched thin by the ravages of abuse, resulting in a bulging beer belly. Nevertheless, he carried his weight well and never hesitated to throw it around, both literally and figuratively . . . sometimes for the better, and sometimes for the worse.

By the time Jennings arrived at San Domingo Street, his partner, Angela Moreno, was already there surveying the scene. Moreno, thirty-five years old with short-clipped brown hair, nodded at Jennings as he approached.

"Long time no see," he said.

"Yeah, what, three hours?"

"What've we got here?" he asked as they walked over to the two bodies.

"Looks like a hit-and-run. Got two of 'em," she said, kneeling down in front of one of the victims. "And we've got some broken glass. A headlight," she said, turning over a large fragment and looking through it.

"Don't touch it," Jennings said, grasping her arm. "Saperstein should be here in a few minutes."

"You called Saperstein again?"

"He was the one on call."

"You haven't even looked over the scene. It's just a hit-and-run. We don't need a criminalist poking his nose all over the damn street to tell us what we already know."

"The man single-handedly saved my career, Angela."

Moreno waved a hand. "I read the reports, Bill. It was a clean shoot."

"Of course it was. But a white cop had just shot and killed a black kid. The media had a juicy story and took it for a ride. And with the election and all, I was a fucking political hot potato . . . people were tossing me around like I had the plague or something." Jennings shook his head. "I was guilty before the body was cold. Everyone bailed out on me except Saperstein."

"I heard all about it. Don't you think I checked you out before I took this assignment?"

"You never told me that," he said. "You checked me out?"

"I vaguely remembered reading something in the paper about it. Then my Vice partner started getting on my case, telling me I should look into it." She placed the glass fragment back where she had found it. "The comments you'd made back in eighty-seven with Stockton PD didn't help any."

"Yeah, well those were taken out of context—"

"You don't have to explain," Moreno said. "I checked into it."

Jennings stood up, his five-nine frame putting him eye-to-eye with his partner. "When Saperstein took the stand and started explaining that the shoot happened the way I said it did, I felt vindicated. He had all these formulas that showed I was standing where I said I was, and that the perp had turned to fire on me." He pulled a pair of crumpled leather gloves from his pocket and struggled to insert his pudgy fingers. "Without Saperstein's analysis of the physical evidence, those accusations would still be hanging over my head. So don't give me shit about using a criminalist. I'm gonna use one anytime I can. And if you're smart, when you're primary, you will too."

"But this just looks like a simple hit-and-run," Moreno said.

"I don't care. What it looks like and what it turns out to be may be two different things. I'm not taking any chances."

With the assistance of several other officers who had just arrived on the scene, they quickly canvassed the surrounding blocks to try to ascertain if anyone had seen or heard anything relative to the murders. Thirty minutes had passed when a car drove up to the yellow police tape half a block away. Out stepped a man in his mid-forties, his hair an uncombed mess, his suit coat creased and covering a severely wrinkled shirt.

Stuart Saperstein exchanged pleasantries with Jennings and received a cold reception from Moreno, who was apparently silently protesting his need to be there. No doubt sensing the tension, the criminalist excused himself and began the task of documenting the scene by arranging a handful of halogen floodlights a short distance from the bodies.

He opened his field kit and within a couple of minutes was on his hands and knees, examining each of the bodies. He measured distances and calculated angles, dictating his findings into a microcassette recorder. Steam was rising off the hot floodlights against the cold, damp December air.

Squinting at the ruler through his reading glasses, he motioned for the identification technician who had just arrived to photograph and document the scene. "As soon as I mark this, let's get a series of shots. When you take the midrange shot, I want to be in it."

"You're so vain," Jennings said, leaning over his shoulder.

"It helps for the jury to see me at the crime scene examining the physical evidence. It gives me an advantage over the defense's expert—"

"I know, I know. Just giving you shit."

Moreno shook her head and walked off down the block in the direction of an officer who was approaching with a man at his side.

Saperstein stood up and faced Jennings. He tilted his head back and looked at the detective through his reading glasses, which were resting on the tip of his bulbous nose. "You look like shit."

"Thanks. So do you."

Saperstein smiled. "Yeah, but I always do." He motioned to Moreno, who was nearing the officer down the block. "She doesn't like me."

"Nothing personal. She just didn't think a criminalist was needed here."

"She's new to Homicide, huh?"

"Transferred in from Vice three months ago."

"Well, I guess I'll have to prove her wrong. Teach her a lesson." Saperstein bent down to measure again. He was a perfectionist, and with good cause: when there were no obvious suspects, homicide detectives often relied heavily on the criminalist's interpretation of the scene. If he could accurately ascertain what had happened, he could then surmise *why* it happened—which could help determine the sequence and mode of death, the victim's position at the time of the deadly blow, or how many shots were fired in a gun-related homicide. Often, the physical evidence the criminalist gathered at the crime scene was enough to narrow the field of suspects, help locate the perpetrator, or obtain a confession from him.

Jennings looked up and saw that Moreno was talking to the man the officer had brought over: a witness. As he made his way toward his partner, he rubbed his gloved hands together to bring blood and warmth to his numb fingertips.

"What do we got?" he asked as she flipped her notepad closed.

Moreno nodded at the man to her left. "This is Clarence Hollowes. Says he heard a big bang around eleven-thirty, ran out into the street, and saw a car leaving the scene."

"I don't want to get involved with no po-leece," Hollowes said, jawing on a piece of gum. He was dressed in clothing that was even more wrinkled than Saperstein's. He was unshaven and his hair was peppered with gray.

"Is that right," Jennings said. "Why not? Got something to hide?"

"Po-leece mean trouble. That's just the way it is. You get involved, you get in trouble."

"We're not going to cause you any trouble, are we, detective?" Jennings glanced at Moreno, who frowned at him. More fallout from having called Saperstein. He turned back to his witness. "What can you tell me about the car?"

"Well, as I was telling this lady here, it was dark colored. A fancy one, real shiny, kind of like a Mercedes."

"Was it *like* a Mercedes, or *was it* a Mercedes?"

"I'm not an expert or nothing on fancy cars, but it was a Mercedes. I'm pretty sure."

"He got a partial plate," Moreno said.

"Oh. You saw the license plate, sir?"

"Yeah, like I told her, I saw two numbers. A two and a *C*."

"Did you get a look at the driver?"

"Looked like a white guy. Wearing a baseball hat."

"Did you see a logo or anything on the hat?" Jennings asked.

He hesitated a moment. "Maybe there was something on it, I don't remember."

"What'd the driver look like?"

"You know, a white guy."

"Old or young?"

"Neither."

"Beard?"

"Uh, no beard, I don't think."

"Any distinguishing marks?"

"Just a white guy. Didn't see his face. Drove by me real fast."

"Did you see what color hair he had?"

Hollowes shrugged. "Nah, too dark. Too fast."

"What about the car? Any dents, broken lights or windows?"

"Man, I don't know. It happened fast, you see? Bang, boom, I ran over and saw the car leaving. Then I saw them bodies in the street."

"I'm gonna give you my card," Jennings said as he pulled a wallet out of his jacket pocket. "Call me if the car comes by here again, or if any of your friends say they saw something, okay?" He looked at Moreno. "You got his address?"

"Ain't got no address," Hollowes said.

Jennings had already guessed the man was homeless—which made him very grateful for the information he had provided. In his experience, the homeless tried not to get involved, preferring to function outside of society.

"In that case," Jennings said, "call us collect."

Hollowes took the card and studied it.

"Oh," Jennings said. "One last thing. Did you touch the bodies?"

"Touch them?" he asked, looking down at the ground. "Now why would I do something like that?"

"You know, to get some change, a buck or two for food."

"I just took the cash, that's all. Gotta eat, you know?"

"Did you take anything else? It's important that we know," Jennings said.

"You see? Talk to the po-leece, get in trouble."

"No trouble, Mr. Hollowes. We're not gonna arrest you. It's just that we have to know if you took a wallet, or anything like that. We'd need the identification to tell us who these people are."

"No. Just the money. There was eight bucks in his wallet, twelve in hers. They were dead. They ain't gonna miss it."

"Did you move the bodies in any way?"

"No. I didn't touch no dead bodies. Just took their money."

Jennings nodded. "Thanks again for your help. We'll be in touch."

"They good people," Hollowes said.

"Who are?" Moreno asked.

"Them," Hollowes said, nodding at the bodies.

"You know who they are?"

"Can't remember their names. They help us get a place to stay on nights like this when the cold go way down to your bones."

"You mean they did this for the homeless, like it was their job?" Moreno asked.

Hollowes nodded. "Yes, ma'am."

"Is there anyone who'd want to hurt them?" Jennings asked.

"None of us, that much I can tell you. They been good to us."

Moreno nodded. "If there's anything else you think of, please give us a call."

Hollowes turned to walk away. "Them rich people think they can flash them fancy cars in our neighborhood . . . " he said as he walked off out of range of the streetlight's glow and into the shadows of a nearby tree.

"I was wondering the same thing," Jennings said to Moreno. "What the hell is a white guy doing driving a Mercedes in Del Morro Heights at eleven-thirty at night?"

"Taking a shortcut?"

"A shortcut on life, you mean. The guy's lucky they didn't catch him."

"They?"

"The neighbors," Jennings said as they walked back toward Saperstein. "It would've made our job easier."

"How so? We'd have three murders to write up." They exchanged a smile as Jennings fastened the top button of his overcoat.

"You know, this could've been personal," Jennings said. "Something related to their work with the homeless."

Moreno nodded. "Possibly."

"Detective!" yelled an officer who was jogging down the street toward them. "We just got a call from someone with a partial plate on the car."

"Another witness?" Moreno asked.

"Don't know," said the man, who was heaving mouthfuls of fog into the air. "It was an anonymous call. The desk sergeant thinks it was a female voice. She said she saw a dark Mercedes sports sedan," he said, looking down at his notepad, "with a license of two, *C,* and *O* or *U.* Couldn't see the driver's face. Driver was wearing a baseball hat, and was weaving a bit about a block away from where we found the victims."

"Did she say where she witnessed it from?" Moreno asked.

"No."

"Have them run a voice print analysis on the tape. I want to know more about this caller," Jennings said. "Anonymous tips are bullshit."

"Can't get a voice print."

"Why the hell not?"

"Call didn't come in on the 9-1-1 line. She called the division directly. They don't record incoming calls. She was in a real hurry to get off the line. Didn't want to get involved."

They headed back toward the bodies as a light rain began falling.

"So what's the story?" he asked Saperstein, who was placing a couple of plastic bags filled with specimens into a nylon duffel bag, out of the drizzle.

"Hit-and-run. The car left with a broken left headlight."

"That's it? A broken headlight?" Moreno shook her head. "I already knew that."

Jennings, ignoring Moreno's comment, reached into the male victim's coat and removed a wallet. "What about the speed of the car?" he asked Saperstein.

"Judging by the damage to the bodies and the tire marks down the street, the driver must've been accelerating. He came off that curve," he said, nodding to the area down the street, "and brought it up to, oh, about fifty, maybe sixty, would be my preliminary estimate, at the time of impact."

Jennings looked over at Moreno, as if to say *You wouldn't have known that.* She threw him a look that had daggers attached to it.

"What else can you tell us?" Jennings asked, moving over to the woman's purse and examining its contents.

"It doesn't appear as if the windshield was broken," Saperstein said. "But I bet there'll be clothing fibers on the wipers, and probably on the bumper or fender area."

Jennings nodded.

"Oh, there's something else. We can probably get a partial tire print for you off the blood around the male victim."

"What about the woman?"

"Judging by the position of her body, it appears that she was thrown onto the hood of the car. Probably died from internal hemorrhage."

"Are there any other tire marks in the street?"

"Aside from the one around the male and the one down the block, none that I've seen, but I haven't had a chance to fully survey the entire roadway yet. Judging by the bloodstain patterns around the male victim, I'd expect to find some blood on the underside of the suspect's car, near the left front wheel."

"So it doesn't look like the driver made any attempt to avoid them," Jennings said.

Saperstein removed his glasses. "Based on what I've seen so far, I'd say he wasn't trying to get out of their way. If he had, we'd see tire marks consistent with a swerve or intense braking.

No, your driver either never saw these people step off the curb, or—"

"He meant to hit them."

"Exactly."

Jennings nodded, thanked him, and asked for his report as soon as possible.

As they walked away, Moreno was the first to speak. "I still don't see his conclusions helping us much."

"We'll see. We know more about what happened now than we did before," he said. "Maybe the fact that the guy was accelerating and there are no skid marks supports the theory that it wasn't an accident. Let's do a background check on the victims. Could be there was someone who had something to gain if either of them wound up dead. Maybe there's no homeless connection at all. Maybe one of them had a kid in a rival gang. *Maybe* the driver never did see them until it was too late, and it was just an accident."

"All right, all right," she said, followed by a slight pause. "*Maybe* Saperstein was helpful."

Jennings walked over to his car and spoke to the desk sergeant via radio, requesting assistance on locating the Mercedes with the partial license plate they had obtained.

"I also need a background check on two people." He opened the victims' wallets. "An Otis Silvers, and an Imogene Pringle." He removed a small piece of paper and studied it. "Pringle was carrying around a pay stub for the Homeless Advocate Society. It's possible Silvers was with them too. See if we've got anything on this homeless group while you're at it."

"Anything else?"

"Yeah, which judge is on call tonight?"

The sergeant leafed through some papers on a clipboard. "You're not gonna be happy."

"Don't tell me it's Ferguson."

"I hear he's a bear when he gets called in the middle of the night."

"Just find me the owner of the car and I'll worry about the damn warrant."

Jennings hung the mike on its receptacle in his car and turned to Moreno. She threw a hand up to her mouth to stifle a yawn.

"Oh, c'mon, these hours can't be worse than Vice," he said.

"No, Vice is worse. A couple all-nighters a week. But I haven't been on Vice for three months. My body's not used to it anymore."

"Better snap out of it. It's gonna be a long night."

CHAPTER
2

AT 4:12 A.M. on the morning of December 2, all was quiet in the pristine pocket of rural Carmichael where long driveways wound their way up to five-thousand-square-foot mansions built out of brick, granite, and cedar. One of the older sections of Sacramento, the area had made a gradual transformation from small one-story ranch houses built on one-acre lots to an affluent person's dream: rather than erecting a large home on a small plot of virgin dirt, it provided them the opportunity to raze an old structure and replace it with a luxury-filled two- or three-story centerpiece on acreage studded with ancient, large-trunked, wide-canopied oaks.

Four speeding police cruisers suddenly appeared, screeching around the gentle curves of the narrow streets. The cruisers's tires violently kicked up dirt and loose rocks, shattering the serenity of the lush green lawns and intricately shaped shrubbery. Their swirling red-and-white lights threw splashes of color onto the tall hedges and stone walls that lined both sides of the street.

As the cars converged on the home of Dr. Phillip Madison, the officers exited their vehicles, the chatter of the various police radios creating a primitive form of multiple-speaker stereo surround-sound. A few barking dogs could be heard in the distance.

Bill Jennings climbed onto the hood of his car and looked over the hedges and beyond the stone wall. After a quick scan of the grounds, he jumped down off the hood. "Seavers, take two men and search that semidetached garage to the west of the house," he said, pointing off to the left. "I'll take the others and hit Madison with the warrant. Manheim, grab a muzzle in case he's got a dog."

Six men ran in tandem toward the house like a small contingent of Marines just landing on shore. A KMRA-12 news helicopter was approaching in the distance, its spotlight trained on the ground below.

Jennings looked up at the approaching helicopter. *The damned radio. They heard it over the damned police radio.*

Seavers and his two men arrived at the massive five-car garage and blasted open the side door with their shoulders. Against the wall was a large, midnight blue Mercedes S600. "Don't touch anything," Seavers said as they swarmed over the car.

"Engine's still a little warm," Officer Leary said, his left hand hovering in front of the grille. "Left headlight's busted and there's a dent on the front fender."

One of the other officers craned his neck under the car and pointed his flashlight. "There's some blood, I think . . . hard to tell."

Seavers walked over to view the front end of the vehicle and saw the license plate: 2CUTWEL. He smiled. "Looks like we got our man."

At the house, Jennings was pounding on the door; he had already rung the bell five times in frantic succession. The front porch light snapped on. An eye could be seen peering through the lens in the middle of the large, ornately carved wooden door. It opened six inches and a powerfully large black Labrador poked his snout through, growling, fighting against his owner's knee to get out.

"Phillip Madison?" Bill Jennings asked.

Their suspect was a shade over six-foot-two with dark, slicked-back hair and broad shoulders. He was dressed in jeans and a UCLA alumni T-shirt. "What's going on?"

"Sacramento City Police Department," Jennings said. "Please get hold of your dog and move aside, sir; we have a warrant to search your premises."

"A warrant?" Madison slipped his hand under the

Labrador's collar and moved back a step. Jennings entered and Officer Manheim, wearing thick leather gloves, grabbed the dog by the nape of the neck and strapped a muzzle on him. The animal bucked and swung his head wildly, slamming into Madison and throwing him against the wall.

"What are you doing? What the hell's going on here?"

Manheim slipped a pronged choke collar over the dog's head and tied the leash to the iron railing outside the front door. The Labrador yelped and dropped to the ground, writhing while pawing at the restraint secured to his snout.

Three police officers followed through the door and fanned out inside the home. "I have a search warrant for your premises," Jennings repeated amidst the commotion.

"For what?"

"Where were you around eleven-thirty last night?"

"Where was I? Home, in bed, watching TV. Why?"

"Anyone else here? Wife, kids . . ."

Madison clenched his teeth. "My wife and kids are . . . away. No one else is here."

"So you were alone?"

"Yeah. Look, what's the problem? I don't—"

"Did you lend your car to anyone today?"

"No. Would you just tell me what's going on?"

As they spoke, Seavers walked in through the open front door. He nodded to Jennings. "We've got him."

Jennings stepped toward Madison. He spun him around and placed his arms behind his back, shoving him up against the wall. Snapping handcuffs on his wrists, he said, "Phillip Madison, you're under arrest for the murders of Otis Silvers and Imogene Pringle. You have the right to remain silent. Anything you say can and will be used against you in a court of law. You have the right—"

"This is insane! I want to talk to my attorney!"

"You'll get your chance. If you can't afford one, which I doubt judging by the spread you've got here, one will be appointed for you."

He escorted Madison out of his house and down the marble steps, where a police car was pulling up.

"Get in the car," Jennings said as he opened the rear door.

As he placed Madison into the backseat of the cruiser, Seavers took Jennings aside.

"We found a busted headlight, a dent in the fender and grille, and probable blood spatter around the left front wheel. Hood's warm."

An officer walked into the hallway and presented Jennings with an empty bottle of 1994 Fetzer Merlot. "Found it on the table in the kitchen." He was holding it with a handkerchief so as not to smudge the fingerprints.

"Mark it and get it to Saperstein for dusting." Jennings turned to Seavers. "I want a PAS before you pull away," he said, referring to the Preliminary Alcohol Screening test. "After this many hours, I'm sure everything'll be out of his system. But do it anyway, just in case. And get me every pair of shoes the good doctor owns. Even though our witness didn't see it, he might've gotten out of his car at the scene, or even a few blocks away. I want the soles analyzed. If there's anything on his shoes that's indigenous to that area, I want to know about it. And see if you can find that baseball hat."

Madison watched from the car as a couple of officers walked into his house with boxes. He overheard "busted headlight," and "blood." He couldn't hear anything else they were saying, but one thing was clear: he was in deep trouble.

CHAPTER
3

THE SACRAMENTO COUNTY JAIL, a curving, eight-story concrete monolith, was designed to make the experience of staying there quite undesirable. With gray, echo-inducing walls and fifteen hundred inmates bulging from its claustrophobic six-by-ten cells, it was another California jail stocked beyond capacity.

Phillip Madison had never seen the inside of such a place. Like a scared animal, his eyes darted into every nook and corner of each corridor and room he passed through. The cold, tight handcuffs were squeezing his wrists so hard that his hands were going numb. As if that was not enough, both shoulders ached.

He was taken into the central processing and booking area, where a desk sergeant sat behind a large wire mesh cage. Rusted metal file drawers sat on the worn gray tile floor behind him. There were various signs with instructions pinned and stapled to the walls around him. He saw a CPR poster, a placard informing employees what to do in case of a work injury, and a list of twenty or so rules of conduct.

The sergeant behind the wire screen handed a manila envelope to Officer Leary, who stood with Madison. "Put your rings in here, along with any other valuables you want to have returned to you or your family," he said.

Madison hesitated and turned to Leary with a blank look on his face. "What?"

"Your rings, doctor. Take them off and give them to me. I'll put them in this envelope for you."

Madison, still handcuffed, struggled to remove the jewelry.

"You have any other valuables on you?"

"I was fast asleep when you came to my home, for Christ's sake."

"Just answer my question, sir."

"That's it, just the rings."

Leary sealed the envelope and listed the items on the Prisoner Inventory Form. Madison initialed the bottom of the document, and the materials were handed to the desk sergeant for storage.

Madison was handed a pair of orange overalls, the letters *CJ*, for County Jail, emblazoned across the back in large black letters. His handcuffs were unlocked, and he was given strict orders not to make any unnecessary or sudden moves. He took his new clothes and changed into them under Leary's guard in a small room off to their left. He was then rehandcuffed and his clothing was cataloged.

Madison was led into another small room where a taupe-colored machine resembling a copier sat atop a counter. Cables snaked around the back of the scanner and plugged into a computer. The officer lifted the top of the unit. "Put your right hand on the glass and keep it still," he said. A few keystrokes later, a green light was passing beneath Madison's hand, making a digitized copy of his fingerprints. The procedure was repeated on his left hand.

"It's come a long way since the old ink pad, huh."

"You've been printed before?" Leary asked.

"When I got my medical license, eighteen years ago."

"What kind of doctor are you?"

"Orthopedic surgeon."

"Guess I should be careful with these hands then."

The last time Phillip Madison had his picture taken it was for the California Medical Society's Surgeon of the Year Award eight months ago. Standing in the cold room against a wall that was incrementally marked with vertical numbers denoting feet and inches, he realized that posing for mug shots was a far cry from the glamour of Dean Porter Studios. The plac-ard hung from his neck, his name and number lettered in white against a black background. The camera clicked, he turned, it clicked again, and then again. Pictures that would never find their way into the family album. Photos and memories he would keep from Elliott and Jonah, his young children.

The holding cell was encased with steel bars; blotches of black dirt were permanently ground into the gray cement floor, on which hundreds of accused offenders had stood and paced, urinated and spat while awaiting their release or trans-fer to a shared six-by-ten living space. Several prisoners sat along metal benches that lined the walls. Some of them smelled of alcohol, a couple of urine. One man had an over-grown beard and an anger in his eyes Madison could tell was deep-seated, and dangerous. He'd stay as far away from that one as possible.

The other men no doubt sensed that Madison was not one of them . . . a criminal of a different sort. Of course, the clear nail polish and well-manicured, callus-free hands were defi-nite indications, but it was more than that. The way he car-ried himself and held his head distinguished him from the others.

Madison counted sixteen prisoners in the cell, all staring at him, all resenting him because they probably could tell that he possessed the very things that had eluded each and every one of them: money and success. He wondered if they could sense the fear seeping from his pores.

Half an hour later he was removed from the cell and led down the hallway to a pay phone on the wall. Still in a daze, Madison had difficulty recalling the phone number of his attorney and longtime personal friend, Jeffrey Hellman. He called information after having been assured it would not count as his one call, but the number was unlisted. He paced the floor, trying to clear his mind, trying to focus. A moment later, he flashed on the number and made the call.

The phone rang four times and an answering machine

clicked on. "You've reached the residence of a famous attorney. If this is business related, call me at the office at 555-9800. If you're calling for one of the family, leave a message and we'll call you back if it's constitutionally required."

Madison cursed under his breath, then left a message. "Jeffrey, it's Phil. I'm in trouble. A lot of trouble. It's about six in the morning, and I'm at the county jail. No, I'm not making a house call. Please get your butt over here as soon as possible and get me the hell out of this godforsaken place."

Madison was returned to the cell, where he sat down on the hard metal bench. After an hour of desperately replaying the events of the past three months in his head, he finally succumbed to fatigue and closed his eyes.

"—a visitor. Madison, did you hear me?" a sheriff's deputy was saying.

Madison sat up abruptly. "Huh? Are you talking to me?"

"You have a visitor. It's your attorney."

Douglas Jeffrey Hellman was pacing the floor, running his short, stubby fingers across his full head of dark brown hair. He stopped and glanced around at the sparse interview room. He'd been here many times before, consulting with countless clients over the years . . . some guilty as hell, others—a substantial minority—incorrectly accused. But for some reason, this morning the room stirred the buried feelings of solitude and depression he'd experienced three years ago when his wife passed away. After her death, he had spent a little time with the bottle, a few weeks in psychotherapy, six months swallowing Prozac, and then some more time recovering from all the medication he'd consumed.

Hellman's lingering thoughts were disturbed by the sudden metallic click of a steel door opening.

"Jeffrey—"

"Phil, what the hell happened?"

"What do you mean, *what the hell happened?* You make it sound like—"

"Okay, okay. I'm sorry. Just tell me what happened," he

said, softening his tone and motioning his client to the chair that was positioned in front of a square metal table. As they sat down, he pulled out a small pad and was ready to take notes.

"What's there to tell?"

"I want to hear all of it."

"There's not much to it. I was fast asleep when all of a sudden these cops were at my door asking me where I was tonight. I mean last night."

"And . . ."

"And what?"

"What did you tell them?"

"I told them that I was at home watching television."

"Were you?"

"Jeffrey—"

"I'm sorry. I have to ask these questions. Just answer them and don't take any of them personally."

"Fine. Whatever. Yes. I told them the truth."

"Did they ask you that before they read you your rights?"

Madison hesitated. "Yeah."

"Okay, back to last night. Did you go out at all?"

"No, I got home around nine, ate dinner, and took a shower. I got into bed, started to watch the news, and fell asleep."

"That's it?"

"Yeah, that's it."

"Did you hear anyone out in the garage? Strange noises around the house? Anything?"

"No. And Scalpel didn't hear anything either. At least, he didn't bark or get all worked up."

"What about while you were in the shower?"

"I don't remember."

"Phil, I need to know. Think. Did he bark while you were in the shower?"

"No. I don't think so. I don't remember, Jeffrey."

Hellman sighed.

"Look, even if he was barking, if he was downstairs, I might not have heard him. You know the layout of my house."

"Yeah, yeah, all right." He tapped his pen on the pad for a moment. "Did you have anything to drink last night?"

"Some wine with dinner. Why, what've they got on me? What's this all about? I didn't kill anyone."

"They're saying you ran down two people last night, around eleven-thirty. They have a witness who provided a description of your car and a partial license plate—"

"My car?"

"Yes. That's why I was asking—"

"It was obviously stolen. Did they find it?"

"Yeah. In your garage."

"Oh, come on. That's ridiculous."

"Why?"

"Somebody stole my car, killed two people, and returned the car to my garage? That's insane."

"Don't knock it—that's our story," Hellman said.

"Our *story?*"

"Well, the cops have another version, and believe me, you'll like ours a whole lot better."

"They think I did it?"

"There was an anonymous caller. She said she saw some-one in a car of your make and model swerving across the road about a block from the accident scene. She said the driv-er was wearing a baseball cap."

"Anonymous tip?"

"Yes."

"Female?"

"Yes."

"Jesus, Jeffrey. We both know who that was."

"Yeah, but that doesn't help us right now."

"What do you mean?"

"I mean I don't like the case they have against you."

Madison slammed a hand on the table. "But I'm innocent, Jeffrey!"

"I know . . . but it's up to us to prove it."

"I thought I was innocent until proven guilty."

"Technically, that's correct. The burden of proof is on the prosecution."

"Yeah, so?"

"The evidence is damning. I'd say they could very possibly make a case of it."

"What evidence?" Madison asked, leaning forward and cocking his head.

"Your car. I don't have anything official yet, but I hear that the left headlight is broken, there are bloodstains on the front end, the grille is dented, and there are clothing fibers on it. The lab's running tests on it as we speak, but it doesn't look good." He studied Madison's blank face for a moment. "Can you explain the damage to the front end of your car?"

"No. It wasn't there when I got home. At least, I don't think it was."

"Are you sure?"

"I don't know, Jeffrey." He shook his head and leaned back in the hard plastic chair. "I don't inspect the exterior of my car every time I get in or out of it."

Hellman sighed. "We need a plan. First of all, I'm going to get you out of here. Second, we need help. I'm going to get a private investigator on this and see what he can dig up." He flipped his notepad closed.

"Great. Let's get this thing out of the way. I've got enough problems without a hit-and-run hanging over my head."

"Right now, Phil, this hit-and-run *is* your problem. All the other things are secondary. This is not a joke, and it's not to be taken lightly. You're the prime suspect in a double murder case. We're talking serious jail time here. And at least for now, the evidence points undeniably to you. You're in deep shit."

"Great."

"But we haven't gone to work yet. They haven't seen my fancy footwork. And you've got one of the most important things going for you: you're innocent. We'll just have to prove it, that's all."

Madison was looking down at the table. He kept hearing Hellman's voice repeating itself like a record with a bad groove. *You're in deep shit. You're in deep shit.*

". . . Phil," Hellman was saying. "Phil, listen to me."

"I'm listening, I'm listening."

"We're going to get you cleared, okay?"

"Call Ryan Chandler."

"Who?"

"Ryan Chandler. A former patient of mine. He used to be a cop with the Sacramento Police Department. You won't find anyone better."

"Phil, no offense, but this is my area of expertise. Let me handle who we choose as the PI. We need someone good, someone I know I can trust."

Madison locked eyes with his friend. "Jeffrey, just call him."

Hellman sighed and opened up his notepad again. "All right, all right, I'll call him."

"He's in New York, you'll have to get his number."

Hellman stopped writing and looked up. "New York? You're kidding, right?"

"No, I'm serious. Trust me. Get him on the case."

"But Phil—"

"Call him. Do it for me."

"Fine. But if he doesn't measure up, he's outta here."

CHAPTER
4

THE SACRAMENTO MUNICIPAL COURTHOUSE was housed in a modern complex of attached buildings on H Street in downtown Sacramento. Arranged around an adjacent three-level parking structure, it occupied an entire city block. People scurried in and passed through the metal detector, where two guards stood properly accoutered with sidearms, primed to act in the event of a crisis. Hellman took the elevator up to the third floor, where he met Madison in a private cubicle near the courtroom.

"All we're here for is the arraignment. He'll read the charges against you, and we'll discuss bail. Then we get a date for the preliminary hearing."

"Sounds like a party," Madison said wryly.

"Phil, no matter what you're feeling, you have to remain calm and look confident."

"Easy for you to say. You didn't just spend a day in the county jail."

"When you're in that courtroom," Hellman continued, ignoring Madison's comment, "don't look down at the table and don't act depressed. Keep your head up, seem interested in what's going on, and look the judge in the eyes when he addresses you. Got it?"

"Got it."

They walked into the courtroom, which was well lit, with several rows of movie theater–type spectator seats crammed close together.

The Honorable Leonard Barter strode into the courtroom

from a door off to the side of the bailiff's desk. "All rise," the bailiff said. "Court is now in session."

The judge took his seat, pushed aside a few files, and gave the bailiff a short, almost imperceptible nod.

The bailiff began reading the first case from the docket. Hellman's mind snapped out of his preparatory stupor once he heard Madison's name. Standing across the aisle was Timothy Denton, the seasoned prosecutor who had made a name for himself over the years with the best conviction record in the DA's office. Never one to turn down a challenge, he seemed to thrive on high-profile cases.

Barter glanced over at a document, then looked at the defendant. "Mr. Phillip Madison—"

"*Doctor*, Your Honor," Hellman said.

Barter removed his glasses and glared down at Hellman. "*Doctor* Phillip Madison. Detectives Jennings and Moreno have supplied me with the charges against you. Have you reviewed them with your attorney?"

"Yes."

"You're charged with two counts of vehicular manslaughter, which resulted in the death of Imogene Pringle and Otis Silvers. If convicted, the sentence would be a two- to six-year term for each victim. You're also charged with two counts of hit-and-run, and one count of failure to render proper roadside assistance."

"Your Honor," Hellman said, "Dr. Madison requests bail."

Barter turned his gaze toward the prosecutor. "Mr. Denton?"

"Your Honor," he said, shaking his head, "this is a double murder. The defendant is accused of running down two people in cold blood. The woman was a single mother of two. Further, the defendant, a physician himself who could have rendered emergency medical assistance, left the scene of the accident. The people ask one million dollars."

Madison leaned forward, his eyebrows rising with his voice. "A million dollars?"

"Mr. Hellman," Barter said, "please ask your client to keep his remarks to himself."

Hellman was already admonishing Madison in his ear by the time the judge had spoken.

"Sorry, Your Honor. Dr. Madison is . . . a little out of his element. The figure took him by surprise."

"Well, make sure he doesn't have any more surprises. Your job is to prepare your client so that he knows what to expect when he walks into this courtroom. I trust you'll be more thorough next time."

"Yes, Your Honor," Hellman said, clenching his jaw. "I will."

"Now, do you have an opinion on bail?"

"Yes sir, I do. Dr. Madison is a respected member of the medical community with a reputation that many physicians never achieve. He's saved countless lives over the years, and is well rooted in the community. He serves as president of the Consortium for Citizens with Mental Retardation and has responsibilities to that agency. Dr. Madison has a wife and two children and does not pose even the slightest of flight risks. We request bail in the amount of two hundred and fifty thousand dollars."

"Very well, Mr. Hellman, Mr. Denton. I see no risk of flight. There is no prior history of criminal activity, am I correct?"

Denton and Hellman nodded.

"Very well. Bail is set at five hundred thousand dollars."

"Thank you, Your Honor," Hellman said.

He rapped his gavel on the desk and moved the next file in front of him.

Hellman gathered his papers together. "Now what?" Madison asked.

"Now we get to work."

CHAPTER
5

"STOP IT! Cut it out, Noah! Noah, I asked you not to do that!" Ryan Chandler yelled across the room.

"Ryan," Denise said, "get off your butt and do something about it. He's just ignoring you."

"Denise, I *am* doing something about it."

She looked up from her law book and removed her glasses. "I meant something effective," she said as Noah, the four-year-old bundle of energy, ran by with the golden retriever plodding after him.

"You're the one who wanted a kid," he said as he walked into the adjacent playroom and started the VCR.

A ball flew by his head; he ducked and it hit the armrest of the couch next to him. "Look, Noah—*Aladdin,*" Chandler said, pointing to the television where the Disney logo had appeared.

"Saying I wanted a kid is a distortion of the facts," Denise shouted from the other room. "You're the one who jumped on top of me in the Caribbean. I told you I was ovulating."

He walked back into the bedroom. "And I'm not sorry I did," he said.

"Me neither. But—"

"But our lives have never been the same," he said, locking the door. "Time to start trying for another one."

"Sorry, wrong time of the month."

"So? Then just for fun."

"Not here—not now—" she said, motioning toward the playroom.

"*Aladdin*'s on. He'll be busy for at least a half hour. He won't even remember we're home."

"But I've got to get my outline done—"

"Law school can wait." He took her hand and led her over to the bed. He began stroking her shoulder-length chestnut hair as his lips trailed down her neck and—

The phone rang.

"Shit."

"Just let the machine get it," she said, taking his face in her hands and moving her lips toward his.

The phone stopped in the middle of the second ring. "Noah got it," he said.

"Oh well," Denise said while planting little kisses on his cheek. "Hope he takes a message."

Chandler rolled over and groped for the phone on the night table. "Hello—Hello—Noah, hang up, buddy. Daddy's got it." But Noah was busy talking, telling the caller he was watching *Aladdin* and playing with his dog. Just then, Chandler heard the phone drop on the wood floor. It made an ear-deafening thud as it bounced a couple of times.

"Can you hold on a minute?" Chandler yelled into the phone as Denise took off toward the playroom.

"Daddy's trying to talk, sweetie-pie. Let's hang up now," Chandler heard her say on the other end as she placed the handset on the receiver.

"Sorry about that."

"No problem. I'm looking for Ryan Chandler."

"Who's this?"

"Jeffrey Hellman. I'm an attorney in Sacramento, California. I'm calling about a case that you'd probably be interested in working on—"

"Mr. Hellman, let me stop you right there. Since you called *me,* you probably realize that I now live in New York. I don't work on cases in California."

"I understand that, Mr. Chandler. But this one's urgent, and you might want to make an exception for it."

"I doubt it. I'm pretty firmly entrenched here. I can't really get any time off work, I've got a wife and kid . . . it's just not possible."

"Okay, I figured that'd be your response, but he insisted. My client's very persistent."

"Who's your client?"

"Phillip Madison."

"Phil? Mr. Hellman, what kind of law do you practice?"

"Criminal defense."

"And Phil's your client?"

"Yes."

"I see why you've called me," Chandler said as he stood up and walked over to the adjacent rolltop desk. Denise had returned to the room and sat down next to him. She mouthed, *What's wrong?*

Chandler held up a hand and turned his attention back to the phone. "What's he accused of?"

"Double homicide. Hit-and-run."

"Phil Madison?" he asked, his voice rising an octave.

"Their case is pretty tight. It doesn't look good."

"I feel strange asking this, but did he do it?"

"He insists that he's innocent. I've known Phil a long time and I believe him."

"I understand, I know what kind of man he is."

"In any case, I'm sorry to have bothered you. Enjoy the rest of your weekend."

"Hold it—Mr. Hellman?"

"Yeah, I'm still here."

"Give me a couple days to get things in order. Can you pick me up at Sacramento International Monday morning?"

"Name the time. I'll be there."

CHAPTER

"I SPENT SEVEN YEARS with the Sacramento Police Department, as well as two years as a special investigator with the county district attorney," Chandler told Hellman in the car on Monday morning. He laughed. "I feel like I'm on a job interview."

"Go on," Hellman said as he negotiated the jug-handle on-ramp leading into Interstate 5.

"I blew out a disc in my lower back and that was the end of my career. And the beginning of a long depression," he said, staring out the side window at the empty fields that surrounded Sacramento International.

"That's when you moved to New York?"

"More like wandered the country until I found myself in New York. My father lives there, so I figured at the time that it was as good a place as any to wind up. But just like when I was younger, he had a definite opinion on what I should do with my life." Chandler chuckled. "Seems he's got an opinion for improving everyone's life, except his own. Messed that one up pretty good, actually." He paused for a moment. "Anyway, I went back to school and ended up in forensic science."

"You like it?"

"It's not the same as being out on the street, but it's as close as I can get given the circumstances."

"Your dad a cop?"

"Judge. *Was* a judge. Past tense."

Hellman sensed that there was a story associated with that

comment, but he wanted to broach the topic of Madison's case. "The police are still gathering evidence on Phil. They've been through his house, his car, and just about everything else he owns with a fine-tooth comb. Whatever they've found is being processed at the lab. If things turn out the way they look like they will, you're going to have to perform some magic to get him off."

"Getting him off is your job, Mr. Hellman. Mine is finding the evidence that'll help you help him."

"How long do you have out here?"

"Don't know yet. My boss is pretty tough about time off in the middle of a murder investigation. No one ever wants to ask him for it. He gets all upset, his face turns red, and he yells a lot. People are afraid of him."

"Except you."

"I've been through enough shit in my life not to let old Hennessy bother me. I just roll with the punches. I try not to take advantage of the situation."

"What situation?"

"I'm the best forensic investigator he's got. Best east of the Mississippi."

"Oh yeah?"

"I bet you think I'm a pompous ass."

"You must be a pretty damned good mind reader too," Hellman said, wondering why Madison was so insistent on hiring this guy to work his case.

"I just thought I should be up front with you. I hope we don't get off on the wrong foot," Chandler said.

"Not at all. You can say anything you want. Just do your job well and we'll get along just fine. Like brothers. Do a shitty job and I'll kick your ass the hell out of California. A man's life is on the line."

"Not just a man," Chandler said. "Phil Madison."

They arrived at the Madison home at half past nine. As they parked in the circular driveway, Hellman informed Chandler that he was going to be staying in the Madisons's guest suite— and that it was not up for debate. "Phil insisted. He's asked me to arrange for you to have a car, plenty of cash to cover expenses, as well as anything else you'd need . . . you'll be well taken care of."

"I've no doubt."

As Chandler opened the car door, Hellman took hold of his arm. "He's been through a lot. Don't be surprised by his appearance."

"Being arrested for a double murder is a harrowing experience."

"There's been a lot of other shit too. This was just the crowning jewel. His life has been a shambles the past few months."

"Oh."

"I'll let him tell you all about it."

"Aren't you coming in?"

"I've got to get to the office. Besides, I know the whole story—I've lived it with him. Here's my card. Call me any time—day or night," he said as he wrote his home number on the back.

Chandler watched Hellman's Lexus disappear out of the driveway. He turned and took a sweeping look at the large Tudor-style brick and granite home. "I should've been a surgeon," he said as he walked up to the door.

He rang the bell: chimes sounded up and down the musical scale. The door opened and revealed Phillip Madison, dressed in jeans, a flannel shirt, and no socks. "Ryan!" he said, smiling widely and extending a hand. "How've you been?"

"Not too bad, Phil, not too bad at all. I've had an eventful life since we last spoke."

"Good things?"

"Oh, some good, some very bad. Let's just say it's been an adventure."

"An adventure?"

"I got married again."

"Is that the good part or the bad part?"

Chandler smiled. "The good. And I have a four-year-old son. He's quite a handful."

"Just like his father, I bet."

"He's got a little bit of both of us in him."

"Jesus, a four-year-old . . . how long has it been?"

"About seven years, I think."

"Seven years . . . yeah, I guess that's about right. I have two kids myself. Elliott just turned five and Jonah's three."

"Leeza okay?"

"Fine, fine." He pointed to Chandler's back. "How's it doing?"

"It hurts. There are things I can't do. I've learned to live with it."

"I wish I could've done more for you, Ryan."

"Despite what others may think, you're only human, Phil."

They both laughed. "Yeah, well, some people may not even afford me that distinction anymore. My reputation isn't what it used to be. The last few months have been very . . . turbulent."

"Your attorney mentioned something about that."

"That's why I had him call you."

"He said it was urgent. What the hell's going on, Phil?"

"Urgent's a good word." Madison motioned for him to sit down on one of the living room chairs. It was royal blue and gold velvet, woven into an intricate paisley pattern, matching the large L-shaped sofa. He brought in a can of Sprite for himself, a can of Coke for Chandler. "Want a glass?"

"Can's fine."

He sighed deeply. "Well, where to start . . . I guess it all began about three months ago. God, there's so much to tell you."

"I've got nowhere to go," Chandler said, taking a sip of Coke and leaning back in his chair.

CHAPTER
7

ALL HELL was breaking loose. Out of desperation, Phillip Madison finally put two fingers in his mouth and whistled loudly. The dog turned and looked at him, Elliott was shocked into attention, and Jonah stopped screaming.

Leeza came running down the steps of the three-story home, her wavy brown hair bouncing wildly above her shoulders. Dressed in a pearl-colored silk shorts outfit, she walked into the kitchen with a look of concern on her face. "What's going on down here?" she asked.

"Scalpel saw a cat in the yard and began barking," Madison said. "Elliott wanted to go to the zoo, and Jonah wanted to watch *Beauty and the Beast*. I said no, and they both threw a fit simultaneously."

"In other words, a normal morning in the Madison household," she said with a smile.

"Exactly," he said, smiling back. He leaned over, gave her a kiss, and then tickled her ear with his lips. "You look very hot," he whispered. "I love that outfit on you."

Just then, the pager that was clipped to his belt sounded a series of shrill beeps. Madison glanced at the number and sighed. "It's the hospital."

"That's a surprise," Leeza said.

He walked over to the phone on the wall above the highly polished, black-and-white-speckled marble kitchen counter and dialed the number.

"Janet, this is Dr. Madison. What's up?" He stood there and avoided Leeza's angry stare. He nodded. "Uh-huh. How much was he given? Uh-huh . . . And he's still in pain? Okay, have them run another EMG— He did? What were the results?" Madison ran his fingers through his hair. "Damn." He listened for a moment, then shook his head. "No, I don't agree with Dr. Rinaldo. If we wait, he may never regain feeling in his leg, and his drop foot won't resolve. He'd have a permanent motor deficit." Madison sighed. "Page Dr. Oliver and prep the patient. I'll be right over."

Madison hung up the phone and looked at Elliott and Leeza. Leeza's arms were crossed over her chest; Elliott was resting his head on his hands. Even Jonah understood. "Zoo. I want the zoo," the three-year-old said, his large brown eyes focused on his dad's face.

Madison sighed. He sat down at the table next to Elliott, looked at his son's delicate, nearly perfect features—a dead ringer for Leeza—and brushed back the boy's thick black hair with his fingers. "I know I said I'd take you guys today, but there's a patient—"

"A patient," Leeza said. "There's always a patient. When do we count? When do you drop everything for us?"

"Leeza, please—"

"That's what I keep saying. Please make time for us. Please cut back. We need you. Your kids need their father. I need a husband, a husband who's home some of the time."

"What am I supposed to do, turn my back on my patients?"

"Why can't somebody else do this surgery? I thought there's a doctor on call . . . John Ingersoll. It's his weekend, isn't it?"

"Leeza, this is a highly specialized procedure. The surgeon on call can't do it—"

"They're all special procedures."

"Yes, they are. That's why I am who I am. That's why we live in the house that we do, the neighborhood that we do. Live the lifestyle that we live. There are only a few surgeons in northern California who can do what I do. When I get a case like this, there's no one else who can take over for me."

"And who takes over for you with your family? Am I supposed to?"

"I haven't figured that one out yet. I'm working on it. I'm trying to schedule things differently. I thought this guy could make it till Monday, but he's already had more morphine than he should've had, and his EMG has degraded—he's going to have permanent nerve damage if we don't operate soon. We can go to the zoo another time. But for this patient, delaying his surgery another couple of days will have long-term effects on his life."

"How long will this surgery take?"

"Probably twelve hours. It's a bad one."

"Twelve hours," she said. "There goes the whole day. And evening. We had plans with the Fentons tonight."

"Honey, I'm sorry. I don't know what to say."

"Daddy, you're going to work again?" Elliott said.

"There's a man who's sick and I have to take care of him."

"My tummy hurts. You have to stay home and take care of me."

Madison felt a punch of guilt slam him in the stomach. He took Elliott's small hand in his own and squeezed gently. "I promise, champ. Tomorrow we'll do something very fun. Marine World or something like that, okay?"

"That's what you said the other day," Elliott whined. He looked over at Leeza. "Mom, will you take us somewhere today?"

"Sure, honey. We'll go to the zoo, okay?"

Elliott leaned against his mom's shoulder. "Okay."

"You keep making promises you can't keep, Phil. It isn't fair to the kids."

"Look, I would hope that if one of you were seriously ill and I wasn't around, that your doctor would put you first and come in on his day off—just like I'm doing for this patient."

"You know as well as I do that all he'll say after the surgery is how high your bill is. You think that once he's up and walking again he'll care that he ruined your day off, a rare day off you were supposed to spend with your kids?"

Madison shrugged. "I can't think about it that way."

"Do you realize that you spend more time in meetings for the Consortium than you do playing with your kids?"

"I'm going to cut back as soon as we get the staffing situation straightened out."

Leeza sighed. "One day the kids will be grown up and you'll say 'where have all the years gone?' You can't get back these times. Once they're gone, they're gone." She looked at him, awaiting a response. He just sat there and nodded.

"And you see all these great things we have? This house, our Mercedes, the stocks, the furniture, the artwork . . . none of it's going to matter, because when you have a heart attack and die from working too much, I'll collect the two million in life insurance and enjoy all of it with another man—one who'll put me and the kids first and his career second. *We'll* be playing with the money and material things *you* worked so hard for, because you won't be around to enjoy them."

"I'll only die from the heart attack if the cardiologist on call decides to spend the day with his family and not answer his page to report to the hospital."

"Phil, you're impossible."

"That's why you married me."

She sighed, stood up and walked over to him. "One day," she said, wrapping her arms around his waist, "you'll realize how important we are. I just hope it won't be too late by then."

CHAPTER
8

MADISON WALKED OUT of the operating room, the perspiration from his chest drenching his blousy maroon hospital scrubs. He had removed his latex gloves and was stretching and exercising his hands. He rubbed them together, dispersing the white powder that had been deposited across his palms.

"Great job, Phil," Fred Oliver said, patting him on the back.

Madison rolled his head around and stretched his shoulders back. "My neck's killing me."

"After fourteen hours, everything aches."

"I'm glad that EMG was run this morning. The MRI didn't show nearly that much encroachment."

"All that scar tissue," Oliver said, shaking his head. "It was wound around that nerve like a sheath. And that disc fragment. You did a good job fishing it out. I took one look at that and I knew twelve hours wasn't going to be enough."

Fred Oliver was Madison's most requested assisting surgeon—particularly in difficult cases such as this one. He had hands of stone—with dexterity that professional basketball players would envy. And, like most neurosurgeons, he was somewhat eccentric.

"I'm absolutely exhausted," Madison said as he flopped onto the bench in front of his locker. "If breathing wasn't reflexive, I'd have definite cause for concern."

"I know the feeling. As soon as I change I'm gonna call a cab, go home, and nap for the next few days."

"Can't. You're scheduled in surgery at eight Monday morning."

Oliver's shoulders slumped. "Eight?"

"I saw it on the schedule on my way in."

"Shit, the L5 discectomy."

"That's the one."

"Totally forgot."

"Don't complain, at least you'll have a day to rest. I've got a trip to Marine World with the family tomorrow. If I can drag myself out of bed."

"At least you have a family to go home to," Oliver said, pulling his shirt over his head. "I've got a quiet house and a maid who comes once a week."

"I've got to figure out a way of spending more time with them. I'm in meetings more often than I'm with my wife and kids."

"Bad sign, Phil."

"So I've been told," he said, walking toward the showers.

Madison dressed, gathered his energy, and went out to the waiting suite, where he met with the patient's family. Three of them were asleep, slumped across a row of padded chairs, but the parents were awake, if a bit dazed after the fourteen-hour wait. They jumped up as Madison walked through the door.

He informed them that the surgery was successful, and that their son would be able to walk again without a deficit. It was a particularly grueling surgery, but he had a very competent neurosurgeon assisting him. He briefly explained why it had taken longer than anticipated, and they nodded as if to indicate that they understood. They didn't, but it did not matter as long as everything was going to be all right.

A nurse walked by and smiled, telling them that Dr. Madison was brilliant in the OR, and that had another doctor performed the surgery, their son's chances of walking again would have been significantly less.

"That's very kind," Madison said, "but we don't want them to think that I paid you to say that." They all laughed. The family was relieved. Madison was again the hero.

King of Sacramento General Hospital.

*　*　*　*

The ride home was only about fifteen minutes, and a relatively straightforward route down the freeway. At two o'clock in the morning, he was glad that it was a such an easy drive. He could have made it with his eyes closed . . . which almost occurred on several occasions.

Madison parked his car in the semidetached garage and entered the house via the back door, trying to be quiet so as not to wake the dog. Fortunately, Leeza had thought of it, and as usual whenever he had a late or emergency surgery, she left him in the kitchen so he would not bark from upstairs and wake the children.

Madison received a few slobbery licks from Scalpel and pacified him with a couple of pats to the head. Sitting down at the table, he began to leaf through his mail, which Leeza had evidently picked up from their post office box while she was out. There was a reminder notice about a leadership retreat for the board of directors of the River City Theater Company, and a letter signed by him to the board members of the nonprofit Consortium for Citizens with Mental Retardation, or CCMR, informing them of a date change for their meeting. *Leeza's going to love this. Another two meetings.*

The theater company retreat he could probably skip, but the CCMR meeting was a different story. CCMR, which helped people with mental retardation assimilate into society, also provided resources to parents who needed to understand the law or navigate government bureaucracy. But most importantly, it supplied programming so adults with special needs could socialize in a positive environment.

Madison initially became involved with the consortium when he brought his younger brother, Ricky, who had been born with Down's syndrome, to one of its programs eight years ago. Over the course of several months, it had helped instill the social confidence Ricky needed in order to function in society, and it educated him and his parents on the various agencies that offered job training and placement for adults with disabilities. As a debt of gratitude, Madison agreed to serve on its programming committee. That was followed by a seat on its board of directors, which led to his acceptance three years later of the vice presidency and then, two years after that, the presidency.

He put the meeting notice off to the side and continued with his mail. There were bills from Pacific Bell and AT&T, and one from the American Heart Association reminding him of his thousand-dollar pledge. At the bottom of the pile was a catalog from Hammacher Schlemmer. As usual, Leeza had filtered out the junk mail. He had too little time to bother with get-rich-quick schemes and the endless stream of low-interest credit card offers.

He shoved the pile of papers aside and removed his shirt. Even though it was the middle of the night, the temperature outside was still around 80, which meant that it must have climbed near 110 in the late afternoon. With a separate central air-conditioning unit for each floor, Leeza often raised the ground floor thermostat to 80 during the night. He opened the refrigerator and closed his eyes for a moment. The cold air felt good.

He pulled out a couple of cartons of Chinese food—Leeza must have ordered in—and he popped them into the microwave. He really didn't feel like eating—the cozy sheets and Leeza's body beckoned—but he knew if he didn't put something in his stomach, he would awaken with a splitting headache. As it was, he would probably feel awful in the morning, but he did not want to compound it.

After eating, he went upstairs without the assistance of the three-story staircase elevator—it would make too much noise and wake everyone—as much as he could have used it. His knees felt like they needed a quart of oil, and his arches ached.

He stopped by the boys' rooms as he walked down the hall, and peeked in on them. He planted a kiss on their cheeks, tucked them in, and trudged into his bedroom. Throwing his clothes in a pile by the bed, he glanced at the clock: it was 2:31. He half fell onto the mattress, rolled onto his side to give Leeza a kiss, and was asleep before he reached her lips.

CHAPTER
9

As Madison slept, he dreamed of being devoured by a giant whale. His face was soaked, he was engulfed in water, and he found it difficult to breathe. Finally, shaken from his sleep, he realized it was Scalpel licking his face with a huge, slobbering tongue. He threw a hand up and swatted the dog away as Elliott jumped in the bed and shouted, "Daddy!"

"Wake up, sleepy head," Leeza said. "What time did you finally get home last night? I waited up till about eleven-thirty. Fell asleep after the news."

His eyes were plastered closed. As he struggled to pry them open to snatch a look at the clock, Elliott sat down on his stomach. "What time is it?"

"Seven-thirty."

He moaned. "Seven . . . "

"You're lucky. I let you sleep. The kids had me up an hour ago."

He rubbed his eyes. "I didn't get to bed until two-thirty."

"Two-thirty? Why so late?"

"Where's Jonah?" he asked, moving Elliott off him.

"In front of the TV, watching *Sesame Street*."

Madison closed his eyes. Leeza picked up a pillow and hit him. "Get up! We're going to Marine World today, remember?"

"Yeah, Marine World!" Elliott yelled.

Madison rolled out of bed, feeling like a stiff board, and lumbered over to the shower. The cold water would wake him up. He had done it many times before in medical school and during his internship at Sacramento General.

Everyone dressed quickly while Leeza reheated the pancakes for Madison for breakfast. He sat down at the kitchen table and pulled a copy of the *Sacramento Herald* in front of him. He scanned the front page and shook his head. "Remind me to cancel this rag. The *Bee*'s a lot better."

"Surgery go well yesterday?"

"It was a bear, but the guy will be able to walk, probably pain free. Fourteen long hours. My feet still hurt."

"You're not Superman anymore."

"Shhh . . ." he said, bringing an index finger to his lips and smiling. "Don't tell anyone else that."

He finished breakfast, they loaded the van, grabbed the camera, and made it into the garage.

"I can't believe we're actually going somewhere as a family," Leeza was saying as she strapped Jonah into his car seat.

As Madison sat down in the van and reached for his seat belt, the phone rang. She clamped a hand down on his shoulder. "Phil, don't answer it."

"It could be important." He jumped out of the van and snatched up the phone. "Oh, hi, Ma."

Leeza rolled her eyes toward the ceiling. "Great." She cursed herself for agreeing to put a phone jack in the garage.

"Look, Ma, let me call you back tomorrow. I've got the kids in the car—yes, I know it's been a couple of weeks, but I've been busy . . . No, I think talking to you is important. I didn't mean I was too busy to call you, I meant, well, I haven't even seen the kids, Ma. I've really been swamped . . ."

Leeza was throwing dirty looks at Madison faster than an automatic weapon fires its rounds. He threw up his hands, mouthed *I'm sorry* to her, and turned away.

"What kind of problem is Ricky having? . . . So what, what's that got to do with his job? . . . Okay, okay, put him on. I'll talk to him."

Elliott shouted from inside the car: "C'mon, Dad, talk to Uncle Ricky later. We have to go! You promised!"

Madison sat down on the workbench and nodded at Elliott.

Ricky had been institutionalized at birth upon his pediatrician's recommendation. It was the doctor's opinion that with another young child at home, trying to deal with the burden of a son with mental retardation would deprive the other child of important attention and time. Reluctantly, the Madisons agreed and Ricky was sent away.

For ten years, they wondered if they had made the right decision. The nagging concern that they had taken the easy way out weighed heavily on the Madisons until a week before Ricky's eleventh birthday. At that time, new research was released indicating that institutions were not only ineffective but unnecessary because individuals with mental retardation could largely care for themselves and be contributing members of society. Shortly thereafter, Ricky was deinstitutionalized, an event that brought tremendous joy to the Madison household. He returned home and was immediately enrolled in a special-education school within the local public school district.

Instead of resenting Ricky's presence, Phillip immediately took to him, and often assisted his parents with his brother's care. As the years passed, however, Ricky's caseworker, who had been present regularly in the early going, was increasingly less available. To fill the gap and to solve problems, the Madisons turned to big brother Phillip—but the call usually came when his own wife and children needed his time. This created a great deal of friction with Leeza, but deep down she understood and felt sorry for Ricky. She would voice her complaint and then let it pass.

Madison was shaking his head. "I got it, Ricky, don't worry. I'll call tomorrow and take care of it . . . It'll all be okay tomorrow, all right? . . . Now put Mom back on the phone. . . . I love you too."

After telling his mother that he would straighten everything out tomorrow, he explained to her again that he had to go, and hung up.

Leeza was waiting in the van. She would not look at him, artfully avoiding his gaze in such a manner as to communicate her feelings to him without verbal or visual means.

"I'm sorry," he said. "Ricky had a problem at work—"

"Let's just go," she said.

"Yeah, Dad," Elliott said, "let's just go."

After ten minutes' travel down Highway 50, Leeza turned to Madison. "So what's wrong with Ricky?"

"He had a problem with his boss at work. No big deal. Just a misunderstanding and Ricky doesn't know how to express himself and give his side of the story. I'll resolve it tomorrow."

"Sometimes I feel like your life's not your own. You give everything you have to help people get better and improve the quality of their lives. You give your time and money to several charities, you-name-it to your brother . . ." She threw up a hand. "You're always doing for others, do you realize that?"

Madison shrugged.

"It got worse when you became vice president of the Consortium five years ago. And then when you took the presidency—"

"I'd rather not go through all this again, Leeza. Please."

"I know, honey. I'm sorry, I don't mean to keep beating the dead horse. It's just that your life hasn't been yours ever since. It hasn't been ours either."

Madison sighed. "As soon as Donna returns my time should free up."

"Donna, at the Consortium? I didn't know she was out."

"She was having some psychological problems, and it kind of got out of hand."

"What kind of problems?"

"Irritability, forgetfulness . . . sometimes she just seemed to be spacing out. The last week or so it seemed to worsen. I don't know if she's having problems at home, or if it's a delayed reaction to the death of her sister, but she's taken time off to get her head together."

"How long is she going to be out?"

"Who knows. With this kind of situation, she could return in a couple of weeks—or maybe never. Murph's looking into it. He said he was going to call me tonight to discuss it."

"Who's gonna handle the fund-raising?"

"Donna's assistant. Murph just hired her a few weeks ago. I've never even met her. Her name is Brittany . . . Brittany something. She was originally hired to help with the backlog of membership accounts receivable collections. Then, when we had that glitch with the licensing board, Donna had to free up some time. She gave Brittany some of the fund-raising duties. Good thing, because at least she had some idea as to what Donna was doing, and how she was doing it. *Harding,* that's her name. Brittany Harding."

"Phil, you can't continue to carry the organization on your back. It's time for someone else to run the agency. You've given it everything you've got, and it's time to pass the baton."

Some time ago, he had realized that Leeza was right, but he had held off telling her that there was no one else who was ready or competent to assume the presidency. Having a brother who benefited from the assistance that the Consortium currently provided to hundreds of area children, youth, and adults, he felt committed to the organization. He couldn't leave it without adequate leadership firmly in place.

"I'll look into it," he said. "Just don't count on anything changing in the near future."

"I gave up hopes of that a long time ago," she said, punching him playfully on the shoulder.

They made it to Marine World by eleven; Jonah had fallen asleep on the way, but awoke when they arrived. The crowd was large, the weather beautiful but unseasonably chilly. Although the dinosaur and shark exhibits fascinated Elliott, they scared Jonah, and he ended up clinging to his father until they moved on to the petting zoo.

The boys spent the next four hours running, yelling, feeding the animals, and eating corn dogs and ice cream before finally collapsing in the back of the van on the way home. All in all, it was a good day outdoors with the family.

When they drew close to town, Leeza called Bruce's Pizza on the car phone and ordered dinner. It was ready by the time they arrived, and Leeza held the warm cardboard boxes on her lap until they made it home a couple of minutes later.

The phone was ringing as they headed into the house. "The machine will get it, Phil. We're gonna eat dinner first."

"But—"

"The machine will get it," she said, taking him by the arm and steering him toward the kitchen.

The pizzas were devoured in a matter of twenty minutes. The answering machine had a message from Michael Murphy, the regional executive officer of the Consortium for Citizens with Mental Retardation. Murphy was hired eleven years ago by the Consortium. Based in San Francisco, he would make weekly trips into town to touch base with staff and monitor administrative matters. Murphy's job was to play watchdog over the other two offices in northern California. He had been personally responsible for hiring Donna, the Sacramento administrative officer, ten years ago.

Madison took his handset over to the family room lounger and punched Murphy's number into the keypad. The phone was answered two rings later with a boisterous "Hellllooo—," Murphy's trademark.

"You always sound so damned energetic, Murph. Makes me feel like a wretched old man."

"Positive mental attitude, Phil. Gotta live and breathe it twenty-four hours a day, or it doesn't work. You can't turn it on only for business meetings or staff conferences."

"I'll remember that," Madison said. "I got your message."

"Good, good, Phil. Thanks for calling me back."

"Anything new with Donna?"

"Nothing. I spoke with her husband. He said she's seeing a shrink, but he hasn't seen much improvement. They were taking her to an internist to check for other causes. Other than that, he didn't say much, and I didn't want to pry. I think we'll just have to wait and see."

"How is what's her name—Brittany—doing?"

"Fine, as far as I can tell," Murphy said. "She's still getting her feet wet. It takes a while to learn all the procedures. She really wasn't here that long before Donna started having problems."

"Do you think she'll be okay?"

"Yeah, she's got all the tools—she's a meticulous organizer, good with details, and quite attractive."

"Murph . . ."

"In the short term, I think she'll do fine. With a little training here and there, she should pick it all up without a problem. Kind of like panning for gold—you have to sift through all the sediment to find the value. I just wish I knew how long Donna was going to be out. It's hard to plan things when you don't know who to plan them around."

"Tell me about it. I have a board meeting in a week and I've done very little to prepare for it. Donna usually took care of all that."

"Let me know if I can be of any help."

"Count on it," Madison said.

CHAPTER
10

THE CONSORTIUM occupied what was essentially an old car dealership building. It had been renovated and remodeled by a construction contractor whose son had suffered a severe head injury as a result of a motorcycle accident. In appreciation for all the assistance the CCMR had provided his son, the contractor transformed the building into a respectable facility that proudly housed the services and offices the CCMR required to run their operations. That was fifteen years ago, and the structure had an outdated late seventies–early eighties look to it. Still, it was functional and served its purpose.

His conversation with Michael Murphy eight days ago still occupying his thoughts, Madison entered the building and walked down the corridor to the office of the administrative officer. There, he found Brittany Harding sitting behind Donna's desk with the phone pressed against her ear. She looked up, saw Madison, and motioned for him to sit down. She continued her conversation.

He had not yet met her in person; he had only spoken to her on the phone five or six times during the past couple of weeks. She was much more attractive than he had envisioned. She had long, lustrous auburn hair that was blown back and loosely permed, giving it a playful lift and fluff. High cheekbones of Asian ancestry showcased large brown and gold-highlighted tiger eyes. Her makeup was understated.

Harding's desk was meticulously arranged, with a blotter in place and messages and notes tucked neatly under the edges. There was an in box, an out box, and a neatly stacked pile of opened mail. There was even a coaster under her can of opened Diet Coke.

She sighed and leaned back in her chair. ". . . Yes, Mr. Ivy, I'll take care of it. I've already told you that I'll look into the matter . . . Yes, I will. As I already said, I'll call you once I have an answer for you . . . Uh-huh . . . Uh-huh," she said, opening a paperback novel to a bookmarked page. Her eyes began moving across the lines of text. "Yes, Mr. Ivy, I'm here . . . I understand. Okay, okay, right. 'Bye."

She hung up the phone, closed the novel, and sighed heavily again. "Some people . . ." she said, her voice trailing off. She arose and extended a hand toward Madison. She squeezed his hand. It hurt. "And you are . . ."

"Phil Madison."

"Oh, Phil. Glad to meet you in person. Or I guess you prefer 'Dr. Madison'?" she asked.

"No, Phil's fine. I try not to be so formal here. I'm called 'Doctor' all day. It's kind of nice to hear my real name sometimes. I actually forget what it sounds like," he said, smiling.

She took a swig of Coke. "Want some soda?"

"Sure," he said. "I haven't had anything to drink all day."

She walked into the adjacent room and pulled a can from the compact refrigerator.

"Sorry I'm late," he called to her, "but I had a patient with complications."

"I thought you flaked out on me. I was gonna leave, but then I got this call and the guy kept me on the line for twenty minutes. All he did was complain." She walked in and handed him a can. "Do you want a glass?"

"No, can's fine. I never bother with glasses."

"Me neither," she said, settling back into her chair, crossing her long, slender legs in front of her. She pulled another coaster from her drawer and handed it across the desk to Madison.

"I did call, by the way, from my car. I left a voice mail."

She glanced over at her phone and noticed the red light blinking.

"You said this guy was complaining. About what?"

"Nothing important," she said, brushing the long, thick locks off her face. "We've only got a little while before the board meeting. If there's anything you want to review before we go in . . ."

"I thought we'd go over the agenda together to make sure we're on the same page." She nodded but did not say anything. "How's everything been since we spoke? Holding your own?"

"'Holding my own' would be a good way of describing it."

"Good. I know it's tough trying to learn everything in a crash course, picking up someone else's work in midstream . . ."

"Well, that's not the hard part."

"What do you mean?"

"I feel like I'm constantly putting out fires. Everything's a mess. I'm sure I'm not telling you anything you didn't already know, but Donna wasn't the greatest organizer. When I first started working with her, I noticed some inefficiencies, but I didn't realize the scope of it all until I took over."

"We never seemed to have a problem before," Madison said. "Her last couple of weeks aside, I always considered her to be a consummate professional and quite well prepared." He glanced at Harding's desk again, the extreme degree of neatness placing her comments about Donna in perspective.

"Anyway," she said, "I got your fax on the agenda. Why don't we go through it."

He sat back, a bit put off by her attitude. He pulled out his CCMR folder from a leather briefcase and found the agenda. He would have to be understanding. She'd had a difficult day. He certainly hadn't noticed indications of an attitude problem during their prior conversations. On the other hand, they were just quick calls to inform her of things that needed to be done, to touch base on board matters, and other items of that nature that did not allow much independent expression of thought.

They discussed the agenda, matter-of-factly covering each topic in a swift but thorough fashion. For the most part, he was educating her on what he was going to be discussing. Since she was only a couple of weeks on the job, her perspective was limited. She would essentially be a figurehead for the meeting to give the appearance of some semblance of order. It was not easy losing the top staff person indefinitely, and he had already received a few calls from board members inquiring as to how they were going to function without Donna. She had been a mainstay of the office, having survived the longest of all other staff associates over the years. She knew the history of the place better than any other existing employee. Yet here was her assistant criticizing her work. It raised Madison's hackles, but he filed his thoughts away for the time being and tried to focus on the task at hand.

The board meeting went fairly well. They covered the items on the agenda, and he dodged a bullet when discussing Donna's condition by not providing any specifics. It helped that he did not know many details to begin with. But he and Murphy had decided that it would be best to portray Donna's absence as a temporary situation, to enable Consortium business to proceed in the short term with as little disruption as possible.

Overall, Harding handled herself professionally. He decided to set up a meeting between just the two of them to spend more time going through procedures and goals.

"How about this Thursday or Friday night? My wife's taking the kids out of town to visit their uncle, so I won't be cutting into family time."

"I've got a meeting Thursday and I wanted to be at the program we're running on mainstreaming Friday night." She shook her head and sighed deeply. "This is going to be a tough week. I've got so many things to do, so much to learn."

Madison smiled. "Don't worry about it, you'll do fine. Just take it as it comes, and call me if you have any questions." He glanced back at his DayTracker. "Why don't we give you a little breathing room and take it a couple of weeks out, say the twenty-first?"

She tossed her hair back off her face. "Works for me."

He jotted down the meeting in his pocket calendar and said good-bye. He was already feeling better about her. New staffing situations rarely went smoothly, and invariably a few obstacles would surface that required attention. The key was quickly identifying the problems and taking steps to address them. Madison felt that in scheduling their meeting, they were already working toward ironing out any wrinkles in the fabric of their relationship. In addition, he found himself looking forward to finding out what Harding had identified in Donna's work that was lacking. Maybe she had indeed found something that could be improved upon. After all, Donna wasn't perfect. According to Murph, Harding had the basic skills; it was just a matter of tapping her potential.

Perhaps he was right.

It was seven o'clock on Thursday morning. The sun was out and rippling waves of heat could already be seen rising from the asphalt. It would hit a hundred today for sure, possibly even 105. Madison loaded the car with a couple of suitcases and he, Leeza, and the kids set off for the airport.

"You have your phone with you?"

"Yes, Phil. You've asked me that twice already."

"I know. I just want to make sure that you didn't forget it. You should carry it with you at all times—"

"In case of an emergency, I know. I've got it."

"Batteries charged?"

"Don't worry about us, okay? It's only Los Angeles."

"That's why I'm worried."

"Very funny."

They arrived at the airport and the skycap checked in the baggage. Madison handed him a few dollars and kissed everyone good-bye. As he reentered the freeway, he mentally reviewed his tasks for the day. He was scheduled to see patients beginning at nine, then do rounds at the hospital at four. He would stay extra late tonight, as he did not need to be home for any particular reason other than to feed Scalpel.

He arrived home a little after 9 P.M. and fed the dog, who showered him with licks. He changed into a pair of hospital scrubs for the rest of the evening and popped a couple of leftovers that were stored in Tupperware containers into the microwave for dinner.

As he sat down at the kitchen table to eat, Scalpel at his side watching his plate, the doorbell chimed its scale of music. He sighed, took a breath, and summoned his remaining energy to lumber down the long hallway toward the front entryway. He looked through the peephole. Brittany Harding was standing on his porch.

"Brittany," he said. "You said you couldn't meet tonight—"

"I know, I'm not here on CCMR business." She was holding her stomach and bending forward slightly. "I'm in a lot of pain. I went to that QuickCare doc-in-the-box in Fair Oaks, but the doctor was busy and they had me see the nurse. She didn't seem to care much." She stooped farther forward and took a step to catch her balance.

"Here, here, come in," he said, helping her into the entryway. "Lie down on the couch." He guided her across the room and she lay down on her back. Her satiny hair glistened against the deep blue and gold paisley pattern of the crushed velvet sofa.

The dog came over and sniffed, curious as to what was going on and who this visitor was. "Scalpel, get away," Madison said. "Go lay down." The dog complied, settling himself down across the room, in a strategic position to view the situation.

"Bend your legs. That should ease the pain a little." He stuffed a couple of small pillows under her knees. "Is that better?"

Harding shook her head no. She started to open her belt but had difficulty with the buckle. Madison was able to unlatch it.

"Where exactly does it hurt?" he asked, kneeling down in front of the couch.

"Here," she said, taking his left hand. She placed it over the region of her belly button and then moved it down across the lower abdomen. "The whole area." He felt uncomfortable allowing his hand to slide down so low on her stomach. He was a physician, but he was unaccustomed to performing lower abdominal examinations—especially on his couch, with his wife 400 miles away, no one else at home, and no nurse in the room.

Her eyes, an intense brown and gold, caught the light from the overhead spotlights and sparkled. They had a brilliance he'd never seen before. Despite the pain she was in, her face had a pristine look to it.

"Gastrointestinal disorders aren't my specialty," he said after gently palpating the area she had indicated.

"It just hurts so much. Can't you do anything for it? Ease the cramping, maybe?"

"When did it start?"

"Early this evening, around six, after dinner."

"What did you eat?"

"I had some Mexican food."

"Ever have this type of pain before?"

"A few times, but nothing this severe."

He felt around her abdomen again for a moment. "Relax your stomach muscles." He groped around a bit more. "No rebound tenderness," he said. "No pain over McBurney's point, no organomegaly, no palpable aneurysms—"

"What does all that mean?"

"Again, this is not my specialty. But I don't see anything major."

"Something's not right. The pain's so sharp at times."

"Have you been constipated, or have you had any diarrhea lately?"

"Constipation. Why?"

"You could have irritable bowel syndrome. It's quite common in females of your age group. And you've had some unusual stress lately, with the new tasks at work you've been handling."

"Is it serious?"

Madison laughed. "Irritable bowel syndrome? No, not at all. But it can be painful, and very annoying. You have to watch what you eat. Make sure you eat a lot of fiber and stay away from sweets. Increase your fruits, potatoes, cereals, grains."

"That's it?"

"Well, you should have a thorough workup tomorrow. Who's your primary physician?"

She belched. "Excuse me," she said, covering her mouth. "Dr. Vincente."

"I don't know him very well, but I hear he's a good man. Make sure you see him tomorrow."

"Okay, I will."

"Is it easing a bit?" He could tell by her face that the sharp pains had subsided.

"Yeah, it's much better. I think I can sit up now." She arose, slowly, grabbing his arm and steadying herself. "Just a little dizzy."

"Probably from lying down. You have low blood pressure?"

She nodded. "Mind if I use your phone to make a couple of calls? People must be wondering where I am," she said.

They walked into the kitchen and he pointed to the phone on the wall. While she made her calls, Madison let Scalpel into the backyard and then went into his den.

A moment later, she appeared in the hallway. "Well, no one's home. Answering machine both times. Just shows you that when you're missing, no one'll even notice."

Madison smiled and showed her to the door. "Do you really feel well enough to drive?"

"Yeah, I'm fine now. I'll be okay. Thanks for letting me barge in on you like that, I just didn't know where else to go."

He opened the door; it was quiet outside. The gardenias were blooming and their scent permeated the entryway. "How'd you find out where I lived?"

"Oh, I got it off the computer at the CCMR. The mailing list."

He nodded. "Good night," he said as he closed the door.

He stood there thinking for a moment. The only address the CCMR had on their computer system was his post office box. In fact, no one had his street address except for his close friends—he was very cautious about his privacy.

So where had she gotten it from?

CHAPTER
11

THE NEXT TWO weeks passed without event. Leeza and the kids returned from Los Angeles, and although Madison did free up some time in his schedule, something always seemed to interfere at the last moment. Any additional time he did have with them was admittedly not enough to make up for all his other absences. He tried to compensate by buying the kids a new computer game, but he knew deep down that what they really wanted was more attention from their father, something that couldn't be bought in a store.

A few days after Harding's appearance on his doorstep, Madison called her to make sure she had gone to her physician for evaluation of the abdominal pain. She told him that Dr. Vincente had examined her and reached the same conclusion as he had: irritable bowel syndrome. She changed her diet, and the pain and constipation subsided considerably.

Now, a week later, his call to her was strictly business. "We need to schedule a Monte Carlo Night committee meeting," Madison said, grabbing a moment to phone her between patients.

"I tried to ask Randy Yates what day he wanted the meeting to be and he just about flew off the handle."

"Why?"

"I don't know. I told him that we couldn't meet on the day he wanted because of a planning committee meeting and he just started giving me a hard time. He was very abusive. It wasn't pleasant."

Madison grabbed a piece of paper and made a note. "What do you mean by abusive?"

"Using language a woman shouldn't have to hear, that's what I mean."

"I don't know Randy very well," he said. "Give me his number, and I'll look into it."

"Joan, one of the secretaries, said he once cursed at her too, really made her feel awful. I don't think he likes women. Talks down to them all the time."

After writing down the number, he tossed his pen onto his desk. "I'll call him. Don't worry about it. How are we doing with that seminar, 'Job Placement for Adults with Mental Retardation'?"

"I haven't been able to get to it, but I have it on my 'To Do' list."

"It's only four weeks off—"

"I know. I said I'll get to it. It's next on my list."

Madison rubbed his temples. "Okay, I'll let you handle it. I've got a patient waiting. Are we on for Wednesday night's meeting?"

"I've got it down," she said.

"Why don't we meet at the Fifth Street Café, around six. We can eat and talk at the same time."

Madison hung up and hurried into the treatment room to consult with Mrs. Monhold about her low back pain and aching hip. He recommended physical therapy and a course of nonsteroidal antiinflammatories. She expressed concern about her pain, was provided with a prescription for Motrin, and agreed to attend her therapy appointments.

He saw a few more patients, read a series of x-rays and MRI scans, and then saw Mr. Skaggs, who had fractured his ankle. At six o'clock, he fell back into his soft leather office chair and looked at his desk. It was piled high with files to be reviewed, x-rays to be read, and reports to be signed. His voice mail had one message. It was Randy Yates.

He returned the call and was surprised to learn that Randy was a gastroenterologist. They chatted about practice, hospitals, and patients, stereotyping and laughing a lot.

"Randy, the reason why I called was to ask you about Brittany Harding. I spoke with her this afternoon and she told me about your conversation with her yesterday. Do you remember it?"

"Yeah, we talked about setting a meeting date."

"She said there were some problems."

"With what?"

"She said you gave her a hard time when you couldn't get the date you wanted. That you were . . . well, that you were somewhat abusive toward her."

"I was *what?*"

"Abusive. Used 'language a woman shouldn't have to hear.' "

"You've got to be kidding. All I did was ask her what other date we could schedule it for. We were both totally civil toward each other. She said I was *abusive?*"

"Yeah, those were her words."

"Why would I do something like that?"

It was a question for which Madison had no answer—and after having just spoken with Randy Yates, a peer who was well mannered and soft-spoken—he was that much more perplexed. Still, he thought, a person's behavior may be unpredictable when they are confronted with different situations and scenarios.

They talked briefly about the Monte Carlo Night planning schedule and hung up. Although it was late, he hoped to catch Harding before she left the office. He wanted some answers.

Her tone upon answering the phone smacked of anger.

"Sorry to bother you," Madison said.

"I've had a rough day."

"How so?"

"I just got off the phone with a member who was downright rude. All I did was mix up an appointment, and he went off on me about how incompetent women are, how his donation pays my salary, and if he has any say over things, there won't be any women employed by the Consortium in the near future."

"Who was this?" Madison asked. He pulled a legal pad from

his drawer to document the time and content of their conversation.

"Ed Dolius."

"Ed Dolius said that?"

"After a minute of listening to him slam women, I just hung up on him. I'll be damned if I'm going to sit back and take—"

"Are you sure you're talking about Ed Dolius? I've never known him to say anything derogatory about anyone," he said, writing as quickly as he could. "Also, I have to tell you that I just spoke with Randy Yates. He doesn't remember being abusive toward you at all. Are you sure you didn't misinterpret the situation?"

"Yes, I'm sure. I guess he's got memory problems as well as a disgusting personality."

Madison put his pen down. "Brittany, I've been friends with Eddie Dolius for nearly ten years, and I've always found him to be a good man. He's also had some pretty serious financial difficulties, and he hasn't been able to make a donation to the Consortium for the past couple of years."

"So what are you saying?"

"Just that I don't know why he'd bring up his donation when he hasn't made one. He's pretty embarrassed by the fact that he hasn't been able to afford it, and doesn't like to talk about it."

Harding was silent.

"It also doesn't make sense that he'd say anything negative about women. For one thing, he was a staunch supporter of ERA back in the seventies. And for another, I happen to know that he *likes* women."

"Well, what do you want me to say? That was then, this is now." She paused for a moment. "Do you not want me to tell you when things like this happen?"

"I want to know everything," he said. "I need to know everything." *Including what the hell is going on with you,* he thought.

"Then don't complain when I tell you things you don't want to hear or believe."

Madison shifted uncomfortably in his seat. He decided to

take a different approach. "Brittany, do you think that maybe there's a possibility that you're . . . misinterpreting what these people are saying?"

"None whatsoever."

"I'm just asking if there's a possibility."

"You're not hearing me. I said no. I'm not stupid, Phil—or are you saying that because I'm female I've got a problem with communication?"

"I'm not saying anything like that."

"Do you have any more antagonizing questions to ask me?"

"I'm not trying to antagonize you. I just want to figure out what's going on."

"I told you what's going on."

Madison sighed, rubbed at the wrinkles in his forehead. "Brittany, I think you should keep in mind that if Donna's going to be out much longer, we're going to have to assemble a search committee. I'll need to know if you're going to be applying for the position."

"I didn't realize that you were going to open the job up to outside applicants."

"You should assume it will be."

"Are you trying to tell me something?"

Madison sighed. "Look, I don't want to argue with you. Let's both make an effort to be less on edge with the people we deal with—including each other." If they needed to work together, even if only for a short time until the situation with Donna could be stabilized, he wanted to make sure they ended their conversation on a positive note.

"Fine," she said.

He confirmed their meeting at Fifth Street Café for Wednesday night and hung up. She could use a couple of days to cool off. He took one look at the files on his desk, removed his glasses, and rubbed his eyes. Deciding it could all wait until tomorrow, he called Leeza to let her know he was leaving the office and would be home in fifteen minutes.

CHAPTER
12

THE FIFTH STREET CAFÉ was a small yet atmospheric storefront restaurant located in the heart of downtown. Small tables were crammed in against one another—"a cozy setting" was the way one *Sacramento Bee* food critic described the layout. The menu was displayed in green fluorescent writing on a lighted board above the bar for everyone to see. For those nearsighted customers who had forgotten their glasses, a one-sheet typewritten menu was supplied.

Madison arrived ten minutes late, having been detained by a patient with a frozen shoulder. The hostess pointed him in the direction of Harding, who was sitting at a table near the window. She was wearing a tight burgundy knit shirt that conformed to her body. Her hair was brushed back and fell against her shoulders.

"Sorry I'm late," he said.

She motioned for him to sit down in the chair to her right. "It's okay, I was late too. I've got this pain in my right ear. It feels like I have something stuck in it." She plucked at it with her fingers. "It really hurts," she said, grimacing.

"Here, let me take a look," he said, leaning over toward her.

"Got stuck on the phone with this retarded kid's parent and he talked my ear off," she was saying as he examined it.

"First of all," he said, "it's *a child with mental retardation,* not 'retarded kid.' Second, I don't see anything in your ear."

"There's got to be something there," she said. "Take another look." She moved closer; he inched forward toward her ear. She tilted her head back and giggled. "That tickles," she said.

"Hmm. I still don't see anything."

"Oh well, hopefully it'll just go away. It's probably from spending too much time on the phone."

"So what did this parent want?"

"Oh, nothing. I handled it. Some people have all the nerve, though. I'll tell you."

He sensed more problems and although he was afraid to hear what had happened, he knew he had to ask. "What kind of nerve?"

The waiter came by to begin his recitation of specials for Madison, who then looked at the menu above the bar and squinted.

"Do you need a few more moments?" the man asked.

Madison glanced at Harding, who shook her head. "No, we're ready," he said. He gave the waiter their order, then unfolded the napkin and placed it on his lap. "So what kind of nerve?" he asked again.

"Very demanding. Wanted this and that for his daughter. I told him we couldn't help him, that we had a limited budget and the money only went so far."

Madison was hesitant to pry further. "How did he take it?"

"Not very well. He was persistent, so I finally had to tell him that if he didn't like what we had to offer, he could go somewhere else."

"You didn't really say that, did you?" he asked, instantly regretting his confrontational tone. "Why didn't you just say that you'd do what you could to help him, and if we couldn't get him everything he needed, you'd find out what other agencies he could contact?"

"I just didn't want to take his garbage anymore."

"Brittany, we talked about this Monday night—"

"Phil, I'm sorry, but you don't know what it's like dealing with these people."

"I deal with the public every day. People in pain, people who've had all sorts of terrible injuries. They're not always the most outwardly pleasant individuals to talk with at first. But you warm them up, pull them out of their doldrums."

"If I got paid as much as you do, I'd be more patient too." She stared at him smugly, apparently feeling that she had both justified her position and put him in his place.

Madison clenched his jaw, fighting back an angry response; it would only create a scene. He instead fell silent, hoping to communicate his disapproval in a more indirect manner.

She pulled out a compact mirror and checked her makeup. It appeared to Madison to be an attempt to ignore him, a power play, to show him that he had not rattled her. She pursed her lips, snapped the mirror closed, and faced him. "I really *have* made an attempt to be more pleasant with these people, you know."

He sat there looking at her, a bit perturbed. Was this her attempt at being civil, at making up? "Good. It's important to remember that we're servants of our membership," he said.

"I understand."

"You didn't answer my question the other day about whether or not you were going to submit an application for your position." He sat back and waited for her reaction.

"Yes I was," she said. "Unless you think it would be fruitless."

He gave an ambiguous shrug of his shoulders. He didn't want to lie to her. "Why don't we cover our planned agenda," he said.

As he began to list the issues they would need to cover, she picked up a piece of bread and tore it into pieces.

Several days later, John Stevens, Sacramento General Hospital's chief of staff, had just left his office and was on his way to lunch when he noticed Madison leaving the elevator. "Phil!"

"John, old boy," Madison said, heading over toward Stevens. "How goes administration?"

"The usual headaches. Lots of bullshit. I wish I were back in private practice, to tell you the truth."

"C'mon, it's me, John. Tell the truth. You love the power, you thrive on it."

They both laughed. Madison knew that John Stevens hated people with power. But unforeseen medical problems—a tremor that made it impossible for him to continue performing surgery—left him with few options. Since he was well liked and a hell of a good physician, the hospital offered him an executive position—at Madison's urging. He took it, and despite the fact that he hated paperwork and politics, he had actually thrived in his new career.

"Before I forget," Stevens said, "I've got a question about the Consortium."

Stevens had sat on the CCMR board last year as a favor to Madison, since Madison needed his friend's sound organizational skills and planning abilities. He had served his year obligation, but declined another term due to other commitments and a position on another organization's board with which he had worked for fifteen years.

"Sure," Madison said. "Go ahead. What do you want to know?"

"Well, I heard there's a lot of stuff going on—some problems, and I thought you should know about it."

"Problems?"

"With that interim admin officer. What's her name?"

"Brittany Harding." Madison suddenly felt the rudiments of a headache forming. "What've you heard?"

"That you and Harding had words the other night."

"Where the hell did you hear that?"

"I spoke with Kathryn Heath. She spoke with Chuck Nallin."

"Chuck Nallin?"

"He supposedly ran into Harding at a gas station and she started talking his ear off."

"I didn't realize Chuck knew her that well."

"That was the strange thing about it. He'd only spoken to her once before, a couple of weeks ago."

Madison said nothing. He stood there, staring straight ahead down the hall, trying to reason it out. Nurses and orderlies passed by and occasionally weaved around them. *What the hell is she doing?*

" . . . what's going on, Phil?" Stevens was saying.

"Huh?"

"What's the deal?"

"I wish I knew, John. When I figure it out, I'll let you know."

CHAPTER
13

"AND THAT," Madison said, staring out the window at the gray December afternoon, "was the beginning of my nightmare."

Ryan Chandler pushed himself up from the sofa. "Oh, man. I can't sit like that for such long periods," he said as he crouched down to stretch his low back.

Madison nodded. "See where my head is? I should never have let you sit on the sofa to begin with. They're the worst things for bad backs—"

The electronic ring of the phone interrupted him. Madison crossed the room to answer it while Chandler checked his watch, which was still set for New York time. They had been talking for nearly two hours. He twisted his torso first to the left, then to the right. It was good that the phone rang. He needed the break to clear his head. Although he usually adjusted his watch to the proper time zone while on the plane, it never seemed to help: the time change was disorienting no matter what the digital display read.

"It's for you, Ryan," Madison said. "Jeffrey wants to talk to you."

"Chandler," he said, taking the phone. " . . . What did they find? . . . Okay. I'd like to drop by and examine the evidence myself. And the bodies . . . I know, but it would still be wise for someone from our side to look it all over . . . who's in charge there now?" Chandler turned to Madison. "Jeffrey's checking on a name for me." He picked up his near empty can of Coke. "Man, it seems like Harding was really out there."

Madison combed his hair back with his fingers. "You've got

no idea. I haven't even gotten to the good stuff yet. If you think she's got problems based on what I've told you so far—"

Chandler held up a hand. "Yeah, Jeffrey, I'm here . . . Lou Palucci? . . . No, that's great. Lou and I go way back . . . Let me make a few calls and see what I can do . . . I'll let you know." He hung up the phone, dialed information and asked for the number for the Division of Law Enforcement. He then called Lou Palucci, the director of the Bureau of Forensic Services.

Palucci explained that they would have to do a security background check on him, as the rules restricting access to the areas where evidence is stored and evaluated had become more stringent in the past few years. Chandler knew that he would pass it without difficulty, and told him he would meet him in half an hour.

"They have some results back on the car," he told Madison. "I'm going to head over and see what they found."

Madison nodded and called his office to inform his receptionist he would be in by noon. With his practice a ghost of what it once was, he could now afford such luxuries. The patients who did come in invariably asked him about his arrest. It made for a very uncomfortable doctor/patient relationship, but he always politely brushed the questions aside and tried to satisfy their curiosity with a direct denial of the charges and a promise to come through all of this without difficulty.

He wished that Jeffrey Hellman could make him the same promise.

Chandler arrived at the Division of Law Enforcement exactly thirty minutes later. Located on Broadway near downtown Sacramento, the large, recently constructed two-story red brick structure that housed several agencies and employed 2,500 people was quite imposing. He drove into the large parking lot behind the building off 50th Street and proceeded to the security gate at the back entrance. He completed an information card on himself, and had Lou Palucci paged.

He looked around the entryway while he waited; a large

circular security desk was surrounded by a vast expanse of bulletproof glass; behind the Department of Justice guard were large black-and-white monitors that projected images of the parking lot, corridors, and strategic points of sensitive areas of the state crime lab.

Palucci was a man in his late forties, with graying temples and about thirty pounds of excess fat hanging over his belt. His dress shirt was pulled tight like the skin across a drum, the buttons fighting to contain the large belly.

"I still have my department ID if that helps," Chandler said as he shook Palucci's hand.

"Not a problem. I've already had you cleared."

"That was fast."

"It's easy when there's nothing to turn up."

"It didn't show my arrest for armed robbery last year?"

"You haven't lost your sense of humor, Chandler."

"So how've you been?"

"Real good," Palucci said. "Can't complain. Nobody'd listen anyway."

"Not to you, that's for sure."

"Probably right."

"Congratulations on your promotion. When did you move into the director's position?"

"Oh, been about three years now."

"Looks like it suits you well."

Palucci patted his stomach, taking a risk that the vibration would not force the buttons beyond their limits. "Well, the bad part is that I sit on my ass all day. That, plus Jan's cooking, and I had no chance. Crept up on me."

Jan was a good cook, no doubt about that—but Chandler wondered how gaining thirty pounds and buying a new wardrobe could "creep up" on you. He smiled and took the red badge that the guard handed him as Palucci signed him in.

"Nice digs," Chandler said as they walked past a couple of rooms with tan Formica table tops, Bunsen burners, Petri dishes, flasks, large computerized gas chromatographs, and comparison microscopes.

"We moved in about four and a half years ago. All this

equipment was written into the budget five years ago when the state's coffers were full and the economy was exploding. Now we're struggling to keep our current levels of funding. We're severely understaffed. Only two percent of the physical evidence the identification officers collect actually makes it into the crime lab. That's a pretty sorry statistic, huh?"

"Two percent? It's not a whole lot better in New York City. We're big, no doubt about that, but not necessarily better. Our lab's so specialized and departmentalized that last month when our toilets were out of order I had to get special permission from the Ballistics Unit just to use their john."

"New facilities notwithstanding," Palucci said, "being smaller is nice in some ways, frustrating in others. I wish we had the manpower you guys have."

"We've got the manpower, but we're so behind in processing the physical evidence that the DA sometimes has to go to trial before the tests and reports are completed. The prosecutors hate us because of the delays, the defense hates us because we usually turn up evidence that fries their client, and the judges hate us because we clog up the court system with continuances. Can't win."

They arrived at the trace evidence lab. Spread across the table top were several photos of the hood and fender of Madison's Mercedes. Close-ups of detail on the grille, showing clothing fibers and blood, and "perspective shots," which showed a broader range of location and relationships of one item to another, were cataloged and neatly arranged across the table.

Kurt Gray was pecking away on the computer near the photos. "Kurt, this is Ryan Chandler. He's a forensic investigator with the NYPD. He used to be a cop with Sacramento PD."

Gray pried his attention away from the monitor and swiveled his chair around to look at Chandler. A few pimples that decorated his forehead became noticeable as he brushed the hair off his face with his right hand. Moderately deep crow's feet emanated from the corners of each of his eyes.

"Glad to meet you, Kurt," Chandler said as he shook his hand.

"Chandler's working with the defense on the Madison double murder case."

Gray withdrew his hand. "Oh."

"I just want to know what's going on. I'm not going to bust your chops. I happen to know that Madison's innocent, and it's my job to find things that can help him prove it."

"Chandler's okay, Kurt. You don't have to worry about him. I've known him a long time, and he's been cleared. It's okay to answer his questions."

"Sure, boss." He looked back at his computer and talked toward the screen. "So what do you want to know, Mr. Chandler?"

"I've got a meeting to attend," Palucci said to Chandler, backing away. "I'll only be a half hour. If you need to leave, Kurt'll be your escort."

"Thanks, Lou."

"No problem."

Chandler looked back to Gray. "You can drop the mister," he said. "My friends call me Chandler."

"I'm not your friend," Gray said. "What is it you want to know?"

"Have you completed an analysis of the clothing fibers?"

The criminalist kept working at his computer. "Yes."

Chandler waited for further information, but after a few seconds it was obvious that none was being offered. "What did your analysis show?"

"The fibers that we pulled off Madison's car were an exact match to those in the clothing that the victims were wearing. An exact match," he said. "And there's a report in the file that says the blood spatter under the chassis of your client's Mercedes is consistent with the blood type that was found in the tire marks near the male victim. I guess your boy was in a hurry."

Chandler could tell that Gray had already concluded that Madison was guilty based upon the physical evidence. "My *boy* is one of the most well-respected orthopedic surgeons in all of northern California. My *boy* also happens to be innocent."

Gray did not reply. He was looking at the screen and punching a few buttons.

"What else do you have?"

"The interior of the car was dusted for fingerprints. Madison's prints were the only ones found."

"It was his car. And the driver could've been wearing gloves."

"Right." He had still not taken his eyes off the screen.

"Have you finished your report?"

"Look, this wasn't my case originally. Saperstein, the other criminalist, has some problem with an ulcer or something and is in the hospital. The boss threw the file on my desk and told me I needed to get it out ASAP. So that's what I'm trying to do. If you'd leave me alone for a few minutes . . . "

Chandler frowned. "Fine. I'll wait for Lou to get out of his meeting."

"Then have a seat over there," Gray said, nodding at a chair next to a desk in the corner of the room. "I can't let you out of my sight." He looked away from his computer screen for the first time and smiled. "Regulations."

"No problem," Chandler said, walking across the lab and sitting down on the chair. He picked up a newspaper as Gray turned his attention back to the computer and his report. The headline at the bottom of the front page of the *Sacramento Herald* was bold: "Police Commended for Quick Arrest in Doc Murders." He read on. "Confirmed sources indicate that evidence continues to mount against Sacramento orthopedic surgeon Phillip Madison in the hit-and-run double murder of one week ago. The source stated that an announcement was expected within the next couple of days that could likely seal the coffin of the prominent orthopedist even before his trial begins . . . "

Chandler threw the paper down. He hated this "confirmed sources" garbage. If people had something to say, they should put their names to it. If they were not prepared to put their names to it, they should not say anything, he thought. Many a lie had been couched behind the veil of a "confirmed sources" quote. Sacramento was much better off when the *Bee* was the only paper in town. When the *Herald* burst on the scene, it brought shoot-from-the-hip journalism to California's capital.

Chandler rubbed the small of his low back. *There has to be something that can clear Phil. But what?*

Twenty minutes later, Palucci returned just as Gray was completing his report. Chandler took Palucci aside, out of earshot of anyone in the lab, and asked if he could see the file.

"You can ask questions, but I can't let you see it. I'm already sticking my neck out in letting you come in here."

"Just let me take a quick look. I'm only out here for a few days, so anything that can help me be more productive during that time is important."

Palucci sighed and looked at Chandler's pleading eyes. "You sure this guy is clean?"

Chandler nodded. "Absolutely. You know who he is?"

"No, and I don't care to know. We just do our jobs the best we can, no matter who—"

"Hey, you're talking to me, Lou, not some idiot bureaucrat. Don't bullshit me."

Palucci picked the file up off the desk. "Why don't we grab a bite in the cafeteria," he said, leading the way out of the room.

Chandler bought lunch, a couple of cellophane-wrapped tuna sandwiches and Cokes. "Godawful food here," Palucci grumbled as he chewed the first bite of his sandwich. "That's why I bring something from home or go out."

Chandler did not hear a word he had said; he was scanning the various forensic reports, growing more dismayed as the evidence against Madison mounted. He felt the knots tightening down in his intestines. The war had begun, and it was beginning to look like the worst enemy would be the physical evidence against his client.

"Chandler, eat your sandwich," Palucci was saying.

"Huh?"

"Eat."

"This food's garbage."

"You haven't heard a word I've said, have you?"

"No. Sorry." He mumbled something to himself, then said, "This isn't going to be easy."

"I haven't seen the file," Palucci said. "But the forensics don't usually lie."

"In this case they have." He shuffled the papers in the file. "Get the police report yet?"

"If it's not in there, it hasn't come in yet. Either that, or it's sitting in the bin waiting to be filed."

Chandler looked up from the file and glared at his friend.

"No, I'm not gonna go hunting through the secretary's desk for it."

A moment later, Chandler closed the case folder. "Thanks for the sneak preview."

"I don't know what you're talking about."

They smiled and shook hands as Chandler rose from his seat, then threw his sandwich in the trash on the way out. He had no stomach for eating.

CHAPTER
14

CHANDLER SPENT the last hour of the afternoon reviewing his notes, then unpacking his clothing and shoveling it into the dresser in Madison's guest room. He called Denise, talked to Noah, and apologized for not being there for his first soccer game. He was supposed to be coaching the team, a responsibility he had to bow out of at the last minute due to his unexpected trip to California. Denise was still being tolerant of his need to be away, but Chandler knew there was a limit to her level of understanding. He figured he had another three, maybe four days before she began voicing her disapproval.

Denise told him that Hennessy, his boss, had called inquiring as to when he could expect his star forensic investigator to return. He had a murder case to report on, and he did not condone the taking of unauthorized vacations in the middle of a case workup. He, too, had a tolerance point for this type of behavior, star expert or not.

Chandler sat down at the teak desk in the large, meticulously decorated room and jotted down some supplemental thoughts on what he had seen in the forensic reports. The room was so well appointed, with elegant bedspread, plush carpeting, and lacy drapes, that he felt like he was staying at a two-hundred-dollar-a-night bed-and-breakfast inn.

As Chandler finished making his notes, Madison came home. He had been at the hospital late, consulting on a case as a favor to a friend.

"Hey doc," Chandler said as he descended the stairs from the third floor. "We've got a lot to talk about."

"Good. I just got a call from Jeffrey. He wants to meet us for dinner. He's anxious to hear what you found out today."

They drove over to the Bohemian Quarter, a provincial French restaurant tucked into the hills of old Fair Oaks, fifteen minutes from the house. The dimly illuminated candlelit interior was a perfect backdrop for the sobering, crow-eating discussion they were about to have regarding the evidence. The fireplace behind their table roared and occasionally crackled as the logs burned vigorously.

"How does it look?" Hellman was asking as the menus were handed to them by the hostess.

"How does it look? Let me put it this way. It looks like the good doctor is a cold-blooded drunken hit-and-run killer. Does that paint a clear enough picture for you?"

"Shit," Hellman said, reaching for his glass of water. "What have they got?"

"They have a left ear print on the Mercedes's windshield that matches the left ear of the female victim. They have no fingerprints in the car other than Phil's. An empty six-pack of beer in the backseat. The blood spatter on the underside of the car matches the male victim's blood type, and the tire mark found on the victim's coat matches the tread on Phil's car. There were clothing fibers on the grille, and guess what? They matched those on the victim's coat. Other fibers matched the ones on the wiper blade."

"I'm quickly losing my appetite," Madison said, closing his menu.

"The good news is that your blood alcohol level was zero."

"All I had was a glass of wine with dinner."

"Yeah, but because of the beer cans they found in your car," Hellman said, "they were probably thinking you'd consumed a lot more alcohol, like the entire six-pack. A solid positive reading and the fat lady would've been singing."

"But because it was zero," Madison said, "it hurts their case."

Chandler was shaking his head. "Not really. It doesn't hurt them but it doesn't help them, either. It takes about an hour for one drink to clear your system. But if you'd drunk six cans of beer over a period of time, the alcohol would've been completely out of your system in about four to five hours."

"And I was arrested, what, about five hours after those people were run down."

"Exactly," Hellman said. "Even if they claim you drank the entire six-pack, they'd have absolutely no evidence to support it. After five hours, the reading would've been zero. So blood alcohol levels won't have any bearing on your case one way or the other. I doubt they'll even bring it up."

"Great," Madison said. "Then all we have to worry about is the mountain of other incriminating evidence."

"Well, we're not giving up," Chandler said. "There are some things that have piqued my interest."

"Oh?" Hellman asked as the waiter came over. The man was dressed in a tuxedo and was all smiles. No one at the table wore a face of cheer, and being the seasoned waiter that he was, he appeared to sense the tension and adopted a more serious, professional appearance. He introduced himself by name and recited the various specials for the evening.

A moment later, they placed their orders. The waiter collected their menus and announced he would bring the salads shortly. Madison turned to Chandler. "You said there were a few things that piqued your interest."

"Your fingerprints aren't on any of the beer cans. And the prints on the steering wheel are smudged."

"Meaning that the driver was wearing gloves," Hellman said.

"What else?" Madison asked.

"Well, all the physical evidence proves is that the car was definitely at the crime scene. It doesn't prove that you were driving it. Am I right?" He was looking at Hellman.

"Yeah, it's all circumstantial. There's no direct link. In fact, I wouldn't be worried, except for the fact that Phil doesn't have an alibi, and there's no evidence pointing to any other suspect. Phil's easy prey."

"Jeffrey, Ryan's trying to make me feel good. Can I at least have a few minutes' peace before you knock him down?"

"Let's change our focus for the moment," Chandler said, trying to smooth things over. "Who else could have done this? I mean, it's not like some punk ran down a couple of people and fled the scene. This person broke into your garage, stole your car, drove it into the worst neighborhood in town, and then returned the car to your garage. He left a six-pack of empty beer cans in the backseat, and wore gloves. Now, this is not the work of a common criminal or car-theft punk. This was a calculated plot designed to frame you, Phil. We need to start approaching this from a different perspective." He had their attention; Madison was nodding his head in agreement. "Okay?" Chandler said, trying to get approval from Hellman.

Hellman nodded, eyebrows straining skyward, as if to say *I've got nothing better to offer.*

"All right. Was there anyone who hated you enough to construct an elaborate crime, kill two people, and then pin it on you?"

"Didn't you tell him?" Hellman asked, looking at Madison.

"I was telling him. Your phone call interrupted us."

Hellman shook his head. "I forgot that you take forever to tell a story."

"I didn't want to leave anything out. I thought Ryan should have all the details."

"Okay, fine," he said, leaning back as the waiter served the salads. He poured a glass of Gamay for Hellman, placed a Sprite in front of Chandler, and left.

"I take it that you mean Brittany Harding. The witch with a capital *B,*" Chandler said with a smile.

"The one and only."

Chandler tilted his head and crinkled his brow. "I doubt it."

"Maybe you should finish telling him the story, Phil," Hellman said. "Then he'll understand."

"So much for fine dining," Madison said.

Madison picked up the story where he had left off: Harding had gone beyond reasonable and professional conduct in telling Chuck Nallin about the disagreement Madison had had with her at the Fifth Street Café. "It wasn't as if it was an innocent conversation between friends," Madison told Chandler. "She made a deliberate attempt to strike up a conversation with someone she barely knew, just to spread word of discord between us."

A couple of weeks passed after the incident at the gas station. Madison asked John Stevens to keep his ears open and to let him know if any other Harding rumors came his way. Stevens sympathized with Madison and graciously agreed to keep him informed.

Madison's relationship with Harding was strained, at best. He attempted to minimize contact with her as much as possible, but it was time again to touch base regarding the up-and-coming board meeting. As he was about to call her late in the afternoon after a full day of patients, he retrieved a call on his voice mail from Michael Murphy. The message lacked its usual verve. Although there were more pressing calls regarding patients and the total hip replacement scheduled for tomorrow, Madison called Murphy first.

Murphy began by relating a conversation he had had with a prospective client, a twenty-two-year-old mother of a four-year-old who had mental retardation. "She called to complain," Murphy was saying, "because she was enraged by a comment Brittany had made during the intake interview."

"What'd she say?"

"Brittany asked the mother what kind of drugs she'd taken during her pregnancy that caused her son to become mentally retarded."

Madison leaned forward in his chair. "Tell me she didn't really say that—"

"This poor mother was in tears, Phil, she was a broken woman. She'd been harboring enough guilt about having given birth to a child with Klinefelter's . . . but to be subjected to such a question by the very organization that she came to for help . . . " His voice trailed off. Madison knew better than most that Klinefelter's syndrome was a genetic disorder that had nothing to do with drug abuse during pregnancy.

"She's a time bomb waiting to explode, Murph."

"I was beside myself, Phil. She represents the organization.

The public doesn't perceive her as just an employee. They look at her and see us."

Madison sighed and rubbed his forehead. "How'd we get ourselves into this situation?" It was something he had asked himself a couple of weeks ago. "We should get together and discuss all this. I'm sorry I haven't called you sooner, but I've been swamped. A few things have happened recently that you should know about."

"Good idea, 'cause I just got a call from Donna's husband. She's not gonna be returning. They found an inoperable brain tumor."

"Oh, Jesus. Did he say what kind it was?"

"Yeah, but I can't remember. After I heard 'inoperable,' I kind of spaced out the rest of what he was saying."

"I guess it all fits, especially the abrupt change in personality and erratic behavior." He shook his head. "She's only forty-nine, her husband must be devastated. I should give them a call, express my condolences—"

"Just let it go, Phil. He said she's deteriorated pretty rapidly. I let him know how sorry we all are." Murphy sighed. "We need to talk. When are you available?"

"When are you going to be in town?"

"When do you want me to be?"

"Tomorrow night, around seven. My office."

"Phil, we were going to spend tomorrow night together. We haven't had a night alone in three weeks," Leeza was saying with the phone propped on her shoulder as she cleaned up the chopped onions. Her eyes were tearing and she was sniffling. Madison did not know about the onions.

"Honey, I'm sorry. I know we had plans. I was looking forward to spending time together. But I don't know what to do about this. Murph and I have to meet and chart a course. He's just going to have to fire her before we have a replacement. I promise, once we figure out a plan of action, we'll be rid of her and her psychoses and then you and I can get back to normal."

"I don't want normal. Normal is I don't see you. The kids don't see you."

"It was better, wasn't it? After we talked and I rearranged my office schedule—"

"Yes," she said between sniffles, wiping her eyes. The onion was on her fingertips and only caused her eyes to tear more. "It was better. Not great, but better."

"Well, that's a start. I'll make it up to you, I promise. It's just been so damned stressful dealing with this nut. She's got problems, Lee, and she needs help."

"That's not your responsibility."

"No. I'm just interested in getting the Consortium back on track. Then things should ease. We'll make reservations at that bed-and-breakfast we went to in Monterey, okay? Just the two of us, walking on the beach at night . . . "

"I got a call today from Blair."

Madison's assistant had walked in and handed him another two messages. He scanned them quickly.

"Phil, are you listening to me?"

"Blair. Your conversation with Blair."

"Phil, you're impossible."

"I'm sorry. I've got a lot of things on my mind. I've got six calls to return before I leave."

"Blair said she heard a rumor that you and Brittany Harding were an item."

"An item?" he asked. "What kind of item?"

"Having an affair."

"Goddammit!" he said, crumpling papers that were beneath his right hand. "This Blair, she's your hairdresser, isn't she?"

"Phil, I know I'm being ridiculous, but just tell me it's not true and I'll let it go."

"Honey," he said, trying to compose himself, "it's not true."

"I didn't think so," she said. "The first thing I did was laugh. I thought, when would he have the time?"

Madison sensed a definite lightening of her tone after his denial. "Leeza, honey, there's nothing going on. Never has and never will be in a million years. You're the only woman in my life."

"It means a lot to hear you say that. I mean, I know that I am. It's just that it caught me totally off guard. I thought it was a joke until I realized she was serious. Rumors like this spread quickly, people look at you funny. They think it's true. And when you deny it, they think, *What's she gonna say?"*

Madison was nodding, clenching his jaw. "Where did Blair hear this?"

"She was talking to Serena yesterday."

"Serena. How'd she get involved?"

"Serena's cousin's niece is enrolled in the program at CCMR."

"Serena's cousin's niece . . . how would a rumor like that get started?"

"Supposedly slipped out during a conversation she was having with Brittany Harding."

"Slipped out," Madison said. "Now do you see why Murph and I need to meet tomorrow night?"

"Let's just get her out of our life, Phil."

"I'm working on it, honey. I promise you I'll find some way of ending this nightmare."

"I love you, Phil."

"Love you too."

He hung up the phone and buried his face in his hands. She seemed to handle it well and accept his denial without resistance. But as he was to find out, dealing with Leeza was the easy part.

CHAPTER
15

HIS MEETING with Murphy was short and to the point. "Mr. Positive" was anything but, having heard one story after another of Harding's systematic destruction of the Consortium from within. Madison's recent experiences were just icing on an already glazed cake. It was no longer safe to have her around, controlling the inner workings of the office, Murphy was saying.

"She's got to be let go now."

Madison just sat there and nodded his approval. He could see how Murphy used to be, before he discovered positive mental attitude therapy. It was easy to lapse back into reality and good old pessimism when the stresses of life interceded.

"Am I wrong, Phil, am I wrong?"

"No, Murph. I agree with you, it's got to be done. My only question is how we're going to keep things running without a staff person in charge, directing and running the program until we get someone hired."

"I can be up here most of the time for a couple of weeks. We'll just have to get someone hired within that time."

"When are you going to break the news?"

"I need to speak with our attorney, but everything should be in order. I'll probably talk with her on Saturday morning."

"Do I need to be there?"

"No, I can handle it. There's no sense involving you in this mess. Do you have any reservations about—"

"None whatsoever."

"Then it's a done deal. Don't worry, we'll find someone to take over. Go home and spend some time with Leeza. And give her my regards."

They shook hands and Madison left, feeling as if the monkey had been lifted from his back. In this case, King Kong—aka Brittany Harding.

CHAPTER
16

IT HAD BEEN A grueling day in surgery: a total hip replacement that lasted six hours and an ankle pinning that was supposed to be completed in thirty minutes, but took three times that due to complications with the Achilles tendon. Madison showered, changed into his street clothes, then checked his voice mail before leaving the hospital. A message from John Stevens caught his attention. On the slight possibility that Stevens was still there poring over a budget or reading a report, he took the elevator up to the third floor.

Madison was about to knock on the door when it opened. Stevens stood there staring at Madison, his sports jacket draped over his left forearm.

"On your way out?" Madison asked.

"Yeah, you?"

"I just got your message, thought I'd catch you."

"You in the garage?"

Madison nodded.

"Good, so am I; why don't we walk and talk."

"Your message said it had to do with Brittany."

"You wanted me to keep my ears open," he said, as Madison nodded. "Well, word is that you misappropriated some funds. Bought a boat with them or something, and that's why the Consortium is having financial trouble. You don't own a boat, do you, Phil?"

Madison shook his head. "Embezzlement?"

"That's what she's saying."

"We're talking about Brittany?"

Stevens nodded, as if to say, *Did you really need to ask?*

Madison smiled out of one corner of his mouth and shook his head.

"Is that funny?"

"What's funny, John, is that she really believes this bullshit."

Stevens looked at him as if he didn't understand.

"Yesterday I heard that she was spreading a rumor that she and I were having an affair."

"Should I ask—"

"No, you shouldn't. We're not having an affair, John. This woman has a very active imagination."

"Lost touch with reality, if you ask me. Delusional."

"Yeah, well, just between the two of us, Friday's her last day. This nightmare will be out of my life for good."

"Do you really think it's that easy?"

"What do you mean?" Madison asked, his smile fading from his face.

"Someone like this doesn't merely just stop spreading rumors because she's fired. Mark my words. This is going to get worse once she loses her job. Then it gets vindictive. Personal. And there's absolutely nothing you can do about it."

"Oh, come on. What makes you think—"

"I lived through it. Ten years ago. We had a staff person with Concerned Environmentalists who was pissed off at her firing. A little different circumstance, but basically what happened was that she started spreading rumors all over the community. Nasty stuff, mostly aimed at the president at the time. I was just a VP, so I didn't catch much of her wrath. But it was pretty ugly at times. And there was nothing that he could do about it."

"What happened?"

"Eventually, his term as president was up, and someone else stepped in. That slowed the assault. But every now and then he hears some weird rumor. He finally stopped asking where the rumor originated."

"Well, I'm going to think positively. This'll be the last I hear from Brittany Harding."

"Borrowing a page from Mike Murphy's manual?"

"No, it's the way it's going to be."

"Mark my words, Phil. This isn't over. It won't ever be over."

Madison stood in front of his Mercedes in the brightly lit parking garage. Stevens lifted a tremulous hand, patted him on the back, and walked off toward his car.

It won't ever be over. Madison kept replaying it in his head. Stevens was wrong. He had to be. If there was one thing Madison was sure of, it was that he could not spend an indefinite amount of time dealing with all sorts of rumors and false accusations. He knew what the result would be: an ulcer . . . a nervous breakdown, and a big fat divorce.

CHAPTER
17

THE WAITER BROUGHT the check and placed it by Hellman's elbow. Hellman picked up the vinyl case and opened it.

"In New York, he who picks up the check pays it," Chandler said.

"I never heard that."

"When was the last time you were in New York?"

"Ten years ago."

Chandler flashed a crafty smile. "A lot's changed in the past ten years."

As Hellman pulled out his credit card, Madison pointed to the check. "He'll just add it to my bill, that much you can count on," he said, eliciting a smile from Hellman.

"So," Chandler said, "I'm beginning to understand why you think that this Harding chick was responsible for framing you."

Hellman held up a hand. "Oh, you haven't heard the best part yet."

"It gets better?"

"Or worse, depending upon how you look at it," Hellman said.

"Tell me more."

Madison sighed. "Well, I thought that Stevens was nuts. I thought I'd really be able to put the episode behind me. Actually, I was able to, it's just that she wasn't."

They paid the check, parted company with Hellman, and the story continued in the car on the way home . . .

* * * *

Madison had been pruning back the rose bushes in his expansive front yard. He had a gardener who manicured the grounds, but the roses were the one thing he insisted on doing himself. It gave him a few minutes out in the fresh air every so often, alone with his thoughts. It was a beautiful day, 70 degrees and a quiet, clear blue sky. Leeza was in the house; the kids had slept at their cousin's and had not as yet returned.

This morning, Murphy had taken care of placing the last nail in the coffin of one Brittany Harding, put out to pasture with all of her delusional visions and phantasmal rumors. Madison took a deep breath of fresh air. "Free," he said to himself as he exhaled.

Fifty yards away, out on the street, he could see the twirling spirals of a football being hurled back and forth. His neighbor, Matt Jeffries, was playing ball with his son Scott, the starting quarterback for Rio Americano High.

A car pulled up at the curb and the horn started honking, brutally piercing the solitude of the moment. Through the slits in the trees and the stone wall beyond, Madison could see Matt talking to someone. A woman. Brittany Harding.

She drove her car up the circular drive and stopped hard in front of Madison. Slammed the door. "You goddamned fucking son of a bitch!"

"Brittany, what are you doing here—"

"You liar!" she shouted. "You'll get yours!"

"Liar? What are you talking about?" he said, taking a step toward her, the pruning shears still in his right hand.

"You said that if I slept with you I wouldn't lose my job! All I'd have to do is sleep with you!"

She was yelling at the top of her pretty little lungs, flinging her purse at Madison and knocking the shears from his hand. He ducked and dodged another roundhouse swing, threw up his hands, and leaned backward. As she swung again, he grabbed her from behind, strands of her strawberry-scented hair flying into his mouth as she squirmed and struggled to wrestle free of his grasp.

"I don't know what you think you're doing, Brittany," he said, forcing air into his lungs as he kept her torso pressed tightly against his body. "You need psychiatric help. Serious help . . . " he managed to blurt.

She swung free, out of his grasp. "You pig! I'm going to the police—tell them what you did to me!" she yelled. "You're gonna pay for this!"

She jumped back into her car and screeched off along the circular driveway, leaving displaced gravel and a pile of dust behind her. Madison stood there, the trimming shears lying on the grass ten feet away, his mouth open, watching the car drive off. Matt Jeffries and his son were standing at the entrance to the driveway, staring at Madison.

And Leeza was up at the third story window, crying.

CHAPTER
18

LEEZA WAS IN TEARS for two hours before Madison could get her to calm down. He gave her a capsule of Valium he kept in the medicine cabinet for those times when he needed to sleep following a particularly stressful day. He had been taking quite a few lately.

As she calmed down, he again assured her that nothing had happened between Harding and himself. But Leeza kept coming back to what Serena had told her: that he had had an affair with her. Now, after what she had witnessed, she was not sure what—or whom—to believe.

"Honey, I swear to you. I never laid a hand on her. I have never, ever even thought of getting involved with her."

"Oh, come on, Phil. She's gorgeous. You can't tell me that you've never had fantasies about her."

"Lee, she's attractive. So are a lot of women in Sacramento. What does that mean?"

"Yeah, but you don't go out to dinner with those other women."

He did not like what he was hearing. She was adding up all the little tidbits of circumstantial occurrences, throwing them into the broth with the rumors she'd heard, and cooking them into a hearty serving of deceit. Pausing for a deep breath, he realized that she, too, had been feeling the stress of recent weeks.

"Lee, you're just going to have to believe me. Nothing happened." He looked at her and let his eyes penetrate hers. "She may be physically attractive, but she's crazy—a nut job.

Nothing could be more ugly than the type of behavior she's been exhibiting."

She dropped her chin to her chest and nodded.

He knew that she needed some time to herself to unwind; he told her that he would take care of the boys for the afternoon, freeing her to take a ride over to the mall where she could spend a few hours shopping for clothes. He spent the rest of the day with the kids—a rare day with just Dad—playing in the yard with them. Scalpel chased balls while he and the boys played basketball.

He, too, tried to forget the incident with Harding. He called Hellman and relayed the sequence of events. His friend told him he was on his way out with his brother for the weekend, but he promised to call him back Monday morning unless he returned home early enough on Sunday night. "Don't worry about it, Phil. I know exactly what needs to be done," he said.

Leeza came home with a new dress and a couple of pantsuits from Nordstrom. Her spirits were better, but she was still touchy. He could tell that she had been crying during the day. There was a package from Victoria's Secret, but he did not dare ask what was inside.

CHAPTER
19

THE WEEKEND passed without further incident, with one exception. Madison ran into Matt Jeffries late Sunday afternoon while wheeling the recycling bins and garbage can out to the curb. His neighbor was polite, but wanted to know what had happened yesterday with "that looker." Madison, in turn, was curious as to what she had said to him before storming his driveway.

"Something about you being a pervert," Jeffries said. "I don't know, Phil, she was raving mad. To be honest, with Scott standing right there, I didn't want to provoke her. She seemed a bit off."

Jeffries was a psychologist, and although Madison didn't know him professionally, he was impressed that he'd pegged her that quickly.

Madison's face flushed deep red. "Honestly, Matt, I don't know how much you saw or heard, but I haven't got a clue as to what she was talking about."

"I didn't think you would."

Although Jeffries had made his opinion of Harding known, Madison couldn't help but notice something on his neighbor's face that indicated a shred of lingering doubt. He knew what he must have been thinking: she might be "a bit off," but that doesn't mean that what she was ranting about didn't really happen . . .

Madison made the long walk back to the house, hoping that Hellman would return to town in time to talk with him tonight. He wondered what course of action his friend had in mind.

Monday morning was overcast and unusually humid. As Leeza helped Elliott get ready for school, Jonah sat in front of the tube watching *Sesame Street* in the playroom on the second floor. Madison was knotting his tie when he heard a knock at the door. Leeza, thinking it was their car pool, allowed Elliott to answer the door. She was in the kitchen when she heard him shout to her. "Mommy, there's a policeman at the door! And a girl, too."

"A policeman," Leeza said as she wiped off her wet hands and walked toward the entryway. "Can I help you?" she asked.

"Mrs. Madison?" asked the man in the suit, holding up a badge.

"Yes."

"Detective Coleman, Sacramento Police Department. This is Detective Valentine," he said, nodding toward his female partner. "Is your husband at home? We have a few questions to ask him."

"Elliott, run upstairs and get your father. Hurry," she said, giving him a slight push on the buttocks.

"What's this about?"

"We'd rather discuss it with your husband. No offense, ma'am."

"Offense taken," she said, turning and walking back toward the kitchen.

Madison came trudging down the stairs, Elliott following closely behind, almost hiding behind his father's legs.

"Can I help you?"

"Are you Phillip Madison?"

"Yeah, what can I do for you?"

"We'd like to ask you some questions about Brittany Harding."

He shot a glance at Leeza across the hallway, then looked over at Elliott, who was staring with fascination at the gun that was planted in the male detective's holster inside his suit jacket.

"I have to get to the office, can this wait—"

"It'll only take a few moments, sir."

He sighed, reasoning that he was just as curious to find out what this was about as they were to ask him the questions. "Come in here," he said, leading them into his den. As they walked into the richly appointed room complete with floor-to-ceiling mahogany bookcases and a large matching desk, Leeza came over. He motioned with a nod of his head for her to look after Elliott.

They took seats opposite the large desk. "Mr. Madison," began the man, "I'm Detective Paul Coleman and this is Detective Kimberly Valentine."

"It's *Doctor,*" he corrected, "and I'm glad to meet you."

"We have a complaint sworn by Brittany Harding. Do you know her?"

"Just what kind of complaint are we talking about?"

"Do you know her?"

"Yes."

"Where were you on the night of September eleventh?"

"Why?"

"We'll ask the questions, sir," Coleman said.

"Not without my attorney present."

Valentine glanced over at Coleman, an *I told you so* look on her face.

"Fine," Coleman said. "Call him. We'll see you at the station in a couple of hours," he said as he handed Madison his card. They stood up and left, leaving him sitting behind his desk, staring at the card, pondering what wonderful surprises were in store for him now.

CHAPTER
20

WHEN HE WALKED into his office through the back door to the orthopedic clinic twenty minutes later, he saw the red light blinking on his phone. He picked it up and retrieved his voice mail messages. Hellman had called, apologizing that he had not returned home earlier last night. He had hit three hours of traffic and did not arrive until midnight. "I won't be back in the office until maybe ten or eleven, but if you need to reach me, I'll probably be at home."

As Madison moved a hand toward the phone pad to dial, his intercom buzzed. "Doctor, we have Jan Harvey, Bill McNally, and Loril Kennedy waiting. They're in rooms and ready to go."

He sighed. "Thanks, Monica. I need to make a quick call," he said, glancing over at the clock on his wall. Seeing that he was already running behind, he buzzed her back. "Who's first?"

"Jan, in Room One."

He walked out of his office and grabbed Jan Harvey's file that was in the receptacle on the exam room door. In general, he himself hated to wait, so he made it a policy not to do it to his patients. After all, he reasoned, their time was valuable too.

The call to Hellman would have to wait. Besides, Madison had already left him a message from his car phone fifteen minutes ago on the way in to the office. Cursing the fact that Hellman was probably still asleep, he forced a smile and opened the exam room door. "How are we doing today, Jan?"

* * * *

The flow of patients was a welcome stimulant for him. It took his mind off his collateral personal problems, and it invigorated his spirits. Contact with his patients was one of the more rewarding parts of practice for him.

At noon, he tried Hellman. "He's just walking out the door, doctor," said the nasal receptionist.

"Well, catch him, please. This is important."

He heard a click and he was placed on hold. He was not sure if she had hung up on him because she did not like his tone, or if she was actually retrieving Hellman before he was out of reach.

"Phil," came the voice at the other end of the phone. "I got in late—"

"Yeah, I know. Listen, Jeffrey, I've got a problem, and not much time to explain. What are you doing now?"

"I was on my way out to get a bite."

"Meet me at Spinelli's?"

"Sure, but I have to be back at one-thirty to prepare—"

"I'll see you in ten," he said, and hung up. He threw his lab coat on the chair behind him and buzzed Monica to tell her he was leaving.

"I was able to get the Pincer surgery rescheduled for tomorrow morning," she said.

"Fine," he said. "I'm going to lunch. I'll be back around one-thirty."

The Pincer surgery. He had Brittany Harding and the police breathing down his neck for some godforsaken reason and he had to worry about major surgery in twenty hours. He rubbed hard at his temples to ease the developing headache. If only the human body had an emotional on-off switch somewhere, one that the great anatomists and physiologists of the world had long overlooked.

Madison filled Hellman in on the visit by the detectives and then backtracked and told him of Harding's appearance at his home on Saturday morning.

"Sounds like it was quite a scene, Phil," Hellman was saying in between chews on his veal parmigiana.

"I thought attorneys avoided understatement."

"She said, 'What you did to me . . .'?" Hellman asked, confirming the wording. He received an affirmative nod from Madison. "Do you have any idea what she's talking about?"

"I assume she means firing her, but why would she threaten going to the police for that?" Madison asked, playing with, but not eating, the large, three-cheese ravioli on his plate. His head then shot up straight. "Wait a minute. She said something about me forcing her to sleep with her so she could keep her job."

"Okayyy," Hellman said, nodding his head, "now things are starting to make sense."

"What do you mean?"

"Sexual harassment."

"What sexual harassment? I didn't sleep with her."

"Doesn't matter. Can you think of anything else, like maybe you told her sexually suggestive jokes or hinted at special employment considerations that could be made if she did something for you . . . "

"Jeffrey! What's wrong with you? You know me better—"

Hellman was waving his hands in front of Madison, glancing side to side with his eyes to see if any of the other diners were looking. "Calm down, Phil. I was just asking a question. The police are no doubt going to ask you that question as well. If you explode like that—"

"I won't explode. I was just . . . " he paused, searching for the right word, "insulted that you would even ask me that. You, of all people."

"*Me* of all people is your attorney. Asking you questions like that is my job. Now, let's get back on track. So you made no innuendoes, no remarks that could be taken the wrong way—"

"No. Nothing. In fact, when we went to dinner a couple of weeks ago, I even told her that she should put in an application for the position."

"Dinner? You went to dinner with her?"

"Yeah, but—"

"Where?"

"Fifth Street Café."

"Fucking great. The Fifth Street Café? Could you have picked a more trendy, romantic place?"

"Oh, come on, Jeffrey."

"Phil, I'm just trying to point out—"

"Don't point out. Just look at the facts. We had a meeting to discuss the programming for the up-and-coming seminar. That was it. We started talking about her caustic attitude toward people, and we got into a minor disagreement. I told her that she should consider the fact that the position was going to be opened up to other applicants. I wanted her to realize that she was going to have to fight for her job, to shape up or get out."

"Was anyone else at this meeting with you?"

"No."

"Hmm," was all Hellman said, falling silent, chewing on his veal.

"Look, nothing happened. She didn't keep the job, did she?"

"That's why she's so pissed. She'll say you reneged on your deal."

"What are we looking at here?"

"I'll know more once we meet with the detectives. Obviously they don't have enough evidence yet to charge you. We'll go meet with them and see what they have to say. Just keep your mouth shut. Answer the questions they ask with as few words as possible. No details. In other words, don't volunteer any information they don't directly ask you."

"Like a deposition or court trial."

"Exactly," he said, chewing. "And if they ask a question that I don't want you to answer, I'll stop you."

"Okay."

"Okay?"

"Yeah, I guess so."

They chewed on their food some more. Both sat in silence. Madison pulled out his DayTracker wallet and thumbed through the pages.

"What's the matter?"

"September eleventh was a Thursday, the day Leeza and

the kids went to L.A. I bet that was the night when Brittany dropped by my house complaining of abdominal pain."

"She did what?"

"She came by and said that she had gone to the QuickCare clinic for treatment of abdominal pain, but the nurse practitioner saw her and blew her off. She was having a lot of cramping. I took a quick look at her, and told her that I thought it was just irritable bowel syndrome."

Hellman put his fork down. "Can you define what you mean by taking 'a quick look at her'?"

"A cursory abdominal exam. To rule out appendicitis, hepatitis, aneurysm—"

"How long did this exam take?"

"A minute, maybe. It was nothing, really."

"And that was it?"

"I told her to follow up with her doc in the morning. She was feeling better, relieved that it wasn't anything major, and she left."

Hellman took a drink of water. Swallowed, deep in thought. "No one saw her there? I mean, no one dropped by, no UPS deliveries, nothing like that?"

"No."

"Well, it's not in your appointment book, and it's probably not in hers, because she dropped by unexpectedly, right?"

"It wasn't a meeting or anything."

"Okay." He paused. "Who was the doctor she was going to see the next day?"

"It was . . . John Vincente. Family practitioner."

"Know him?"

"No, but I know of him."

Hellman pulled out his cellular phone and called information, jotted down Dr. Vincente's office number, and input it. Sat and listened. "Yes, hi, this is Elmore Elkins, a claims adjuster for California Prudent Health Insurance. I have a claim form here submitted by a Brittany Harding, with a date of service of September twelfth. But when I try to input it into the system, I see that she was off our plan on that date.

I'd like to pay this bill, but can you tell me if Miss Harding was in your office on that date?" He looked up at Madison, who was stifling a smile. "She wasn't? Hmm, when was the last time she was at your facility? . . . May fifteenth for her annual Pap? . . . Okay, great, then this must be a mistake. Thanks for your help." He flipped the phone shut and looked at Madison.

"Do people do that to my office staff too?"

"It's easier to get info from medical offices than people think."

"So much for the Privacy of Information Act."

"She never went in to see Dr. Vincente after you saw her, so there's nothing documented in his records about her having been examined by you."

"Yeah, so?"

"So I don't think you should bring it up."

Madison made a face, as if to say "I don't know."

"Look, Phil, nothing happened, am I right?"

"Right."

"So why arouse suspicion by putting yourself in a vulnerable position? Your wife and kids are away, here's a beautiful woman who you admit came over to your house in the evening, you play a little cutesy game of doctor and then you make sexual overtures. Do you see what they can make it look like?"

"So I shouldn't say that she was even there."

"I'm not telling you to lie. I'm just saying don't bring it up."

"No one saw her come by. There's no way they could even prove she was there."

"Then stop worrying. Besides, if anything comes up, you could just say that you forgot about it, you didn't have anything written in your calendar, and you see so many patients and have so many meetings, that you can't even remember what happened yesterday, let alone six weeks ago. Then, just tell them the truth." He looked hard at Madison. "Okay?"

Madison hesitated. "I guess."

"Phil," he said, putting his fork down. "You have nothing to worry about. We'll take care of this. You did nothing wrong. We'll make it go away."

Madison sighed. "While you're at it, make *her* go away too."

"Miracles have been known to happen, Phil."

CHAPTER
2 1

IT WAS NEARLY six o'clock that evening when they entered
the interview room with Detectives Coleman and Valentine.
It was dimly lit, a few bare bulbs hanging from the ceiling.
The medium-sized room was just large enough to hold a rectangular table, which measured about six feet by four feet.
Madison and Hellman were sitting with their backs to the
wall. Coleman, entering and introducing himself to Hellman, told them that Detective Valentine would be joining
them shortly.

"So are you going to charge my client?" Hellman asked,
getting right to the point.

"We're currently in the investigative phases. Nobody's been
charged with anything. This is strictly an interview."

"Because you don't have anything on my client. This is
just a fishing expedition."

"I wouldn't be so quick to make assumptions."

"What are you investigating?" Hellman asked.

"A crime, counselor. I'm not at liberty to discuss the complaint any further at this time."

"And why's that?"

"The substance of the complaint should have no bearing
on the truth, and all we want this evening is the truth." He
threw a forced, contrived smile at Hellman.

"If you want our cooperation, which we're prepared to
give, then you'll have to tell me what the complaint is
against my client. Otherwise, I can't advise him properly on
this matter."

"I really don't think the substance of the complaint is relevant."

"You're not an attorney," Hellman said. "As Dr. Madison's counsel, I most definitely feel that it is relevant."

"Would you prefer that we charge the good doctor right now? Then you'll have all the information you want. Of course, his reputation might be a bit tarnished."

"Charge him with what?"

Coleman looked at him, as if to say, *Nice try, counselor.*

"Fine. Give me a moment with my client," Hellman said, showing Coleman the door with his eyes.

The detective nodded, then walked out; his shadow could be seen through the stippled glass in the door.

Madison wiped away a few droplets of sweat from his forehead. "What's all this posturing about?"

Hellman leaned close to Madison's ear in case they were being observed. "They don't want to tell us anything about what they're investigating, what the complaint is against you. I want to know, so I can know how much leeway to give you when you're answering questions. It could be significant later."

"And if they won't reveal the complaint?"

Hellman sighed and cocked his head to one side. "Then, we have a choice. We can walk out—there's nothing keeping us here—and hope that they don't arrest you and charge you. My guess is that if they had enough evidence, they would've already arrested you. However, since you're innocent, it may not hurt to give them some info to refute the complaint and see if it goes away. They'll get a feel for you as a person, and conclude that you probably didn't do what the complaint says you did. That could be very important." He paused, allowed Madison to assimilate all this. "On the other hand, they can arrest you even though they really don't have enough to keep you more than a few hours. They'll hope to gain something from your fear of being locked up. It can be quite an effective motivator. Think of what being arrested would do to you. It could be severely damaging to your reputation. Even if they don't have enough evidence and have to let you go, you'll look guilty as hell, having hired a sharp, high-priced lawyer who confused the issues and got you off."

Madison was shaking his head. "Too much to risk. I'll talk to them."

"Okay. But first let me see what I can do. Be prepared to follow my lead and walk out. Assuming they don't arrest you, we can always walk back in."

Madison gave a reluctant nod; Hellman walked over to the door and knocked on it; Coleman came back in.

"Well?" he asked, sitting down.

"We want to know what the complaint is, or we're leaving. You can charge him if you want. I think it's easier to just tell us what the gist of the complaint is and you'll have our full cooperation."

Coleman sat there, his closed mouth making contortions while he thought.

Suddenly, Hellman took Madison's arm and rose from his seat. "Let's go, Phil. We're leaving."

Coleman remained seated. "Hold it," he said, raising a hand. "If I told you that there's a complaint of sexual misconduct, would that satisfy your curiosity?" He looked at Hellman, who began to sit back down. "It'll have to," the detective said, "because that's all I'm going to say."

"Is there or isn't there a complaint of sexual misconduct?" Hellman asked.

Coleman shrugged. "I said all I'm gonna say."

The door swung open and in stepped Detective Valentine, her ID clipped on the collar of her maroon blouse.

"Gentlemen," she said, addressing her audience.

"Jeffrey Hellman," he said, rising again and extending his hand out toward Valentine across the table.

"Mr. Hellman."

Madison and Valentine exchanged nods.

No doubt assuming that the little bit of information he had given Hellman was enough to secure his cooperation, Coleman initiated the interview. "We have some questions about the night of September eleventh of this year."

"What about it?" Madison asked.

"Where were you?"

"I don't recall specifically."

"Do you keep a calendar?"

He reached into his inside suit coat pocket, pulled out his DayTracker, and opened it up. Hellman took it from him and began to thumb through it, reading the pertinent entries surrounding the date in question. Satisfied, he flipped back to September eleventh and returned it to Madison. "Okay."

"I had a surgery at nine A.M., did rounds at one, went to lunch and met with the chief radiologist, Bill Slavens, to consult with him on a few MRIs. Then I went home and ate dinner."

"Did you see Brittany Harding that night?"

He looked again at his DayTracker. "I don't have anything written in my calendar . . . " He flipped through a couple of pages. "We had a meeting a few days later."

"What's the nature of your relationship with Miss Harding?"

"She was filling in for the administrative officer of the Consortium for Citizens with Mental Retardation. I'm the president of the board of directors. We had periodic meetings and phone conversations with each other."

"Is the presidency a paid position?"

"That's irrelevant," Hellman said before Madison could answer.

"Is there any reason why your client shouldn't answer?"

Hellman thought for a brief moment, turned to Madison, nodded.

"No, it's strictly volunteer. I don't get paid."

"Have you ever had any other kind of relationship with Miss Harding than the one you just described?"

Valentine was sitting off to the side, not saying a word, no doubt observing Madison and his responses.

"Like what?"

"Romantic."

"No."

"No dates, dinners, movies, rendezvous in hotels—"

"My client said he had no other types of relationships."

"Does that mean no to all of the above?"

"Correct. That's a no, with a capital N. But I have had dinner with her."

"Oh?"

"It was a meeting. We discussed an upcoming seminar for the Consortium, if I recall."

"And what date was that?"

He looked in his book. "Let's see," he said, thumbing through a couple of pages. "Here it is, October first. Fifth Street Café."

Hellman flinched slightly. He had made it clear not to volunteer any information unless asked.

"Fifth Street Café, that's a pretty hip establishment for just *a meeting.*" This from Kimberly Valentine, whose voice seemed to come out of nowhere.

"They have good food. It's got a nice atmosphere," Madison said. "It's one of my favorite places to eat downtown."

Valentine nodded, and disappeared again into the background.

Coleman directed the focus back to him. "Were you, as president of the Consortium, in the position to dictate who was hired and who was fired?"

"I had input, but Michael Murphy, the regional executive officer, does the hiring and firing."

"Let's get back to the night of September eleventh. After you got home and ate dinner, what did you do?"

"I don't remember. Probably watched television."

"You're married, aren't you, doctor?"

Hellman pulled him over toward him, whispered into his ear. Madison did not react.

"Yes."

"Was your wife at home on the night of September eleventh?"

He glanced down at his calendar. "No. She and my children were visiting a relative out of town."

"Hmm," remarked Coleman. "Did anyone—"

"Look, detectives, with all due respect, I think we're done here. We want to cooperate, but it's getting late; it's enough for one night, and Dr. Madison has surgery scheduled for early tomorrow morning."

"Can I see your pocket calendar, doctor?"

Madison glanced at Hellman, who took the DayTracker and looked at it again. Flipped a couple of pages, read the entries. "You can look at September eleventh and October first," he said, handing him the wallet opened to the correct page.

Coleman scanned the pages. "Okay," he said, closing the wallet and returning it to Madison. He looked over at Valentine, who gave him a nod. "Thanks for your time."

CHAPTER
22

BRITTANY HARDING was pacing back and forth in front of her coffee table, smoking a Marlboro. "What do you mean you don't have enough evidence?"

Detective Coleman stepped to his right in an attempt to avoid the lingering cloud of smoke. "I mean we don't have enough to charge the man with anything. We talked with him and he seemed pretty credible. It didn't look like he had anything to hide. I even saw his pocket calendar. There was nothing in there mentioning you on September eleventh."

"Rape is a very serious charge, Miss Harding," Valentine said. "We usually like to make it stick when we arrest someone. It's painful enough for you to have to relive the experience, to go through it in public during the trial. We want to make sure we have enough to put the guy away. Right now, we don't. It's hard enough even when we have all the evidence we need."

"Unless there's some piece of evidence, someone who saw you there at his house that night," Coleman said, "we don't even have any proof that you were there, let alone raped. The clothes you were wearing would be a good start, if you haven't washed them. They'd still have his semen on them."

Harding took a puff on her cigarette. "I threw them out. They got torn when he ripped them off me. I could've had them repaired, but to be honest with you, just seeing them reminded me of what he did to me." She took another drag. "But I've got the belt I was wearing that night. He touched it while unbuckling it. You can see if his fingerprints are on it."

"You haven't worn it since September eleventh?" Valentine asked.

Harding shook her head. "It only goes with two outfits—the one I threw out, and a pantsuit I haven't worn since then."

"Okay, we'll take it," Coleman said, "but we need something to prove that you were in his house that night. We might then be able to link the fingerprints on the belt, if there are any, to the fact that you were in his home."

"It's a reach," Valentine said, "but you never know. It may give us enough to rattle him, at least get him to admit that the two of you were together that night and that something happened."

Harding blew a puff of smoke toward the ceiling and watched it rise. "How about a couple of phone calls?"

"Phone calls?"

"Yeah. I made a couple of calls while I was there, before he attacked me. One was to my mother, and one to my sister. I'll give you the numbers. Check his phone bill."

"Okay, now we're cooking," Valentine said. She pulled out her pad and made a note of the numbers. "We'll be in touch in a few days."

"Don't forget the belt," she said, the trail of smoke following her like a snake as she disappeared into her bedroom.

CHAPTER
23

ELEVEN DAYS PASSED without event. Neither Madison nor Hellman had heard anything from the detectives. Hellman assured him that no news was good news—if they had enough to charge him, they would have already done so. Still, Madison's concentration was off; he had difficulty focusing on the patients while they were talking to him during their examinations. His mind kept coming back to the Harding matter, and what it could mean to him and his family should they arrest him and charge him with sexual misconduct. He reasoned that about the only charge that could be more damaging to a physician would be rape. Being innocent had nothing to do with it: given the nature of the difficulties in obtaining definitive evidence in sexual misconduct cases—unless there were witnesses, generally it was one person's word against another's—the charge would stick in the collective mind of the public for years to come.

If he was found not guilty, they would say it was because of a lack of evidence, her word against his; if he was found guilty, not only would he be a victim of a sick mind, but it would no doubt destroy his family. What's more, no matter how it turned out, it would haunt him for the rest of his medical career, hanging over his head like a lead umbrella.

The red light on his phone was flashing when he returned to his office. He had been seeing patients steadily and this was the first moment he had had to himself. He hit a couple of buttons and listened to the message. It was Jeffrey, urging him to call as soon as possible.

The receptionist with the nasal voice put him right through.

"Phil, I got a call from those detectives this morning."

His heart skipped a beat. "I thought no news was good news."

"They want to get together tonight. Something about new evidence."

"New evidence?" he asked, suddenly aware of the moisture forming across his forehead. "What the hell kind of evidence could they have?"

"I was going to ask you," Hellman said.

"There has to be something about that evening . . . " Madison said. "Maybe someone saw her or her car leaving."

There was a brief moment of silence. "Look," Hellman said, "let's assume they have something we didn't think of. It can't be too damning, because if it was ironclad, they would've just come over and arrested you."

"Gee, that's comforting."

"We'll go over later and play it by ear. If the situation seems right, go ahead and tell them that she was there and you examined her, but forgot about it, and you didn't think it was on September eleventh, but it could've been. Just make it convincing."

"I knew it, Jeffrey. It's always best to tell the truth. Then you can't get caught in lies. You don't have to worry what you've told to whom."

"I never said you shouldn't tell them the truth. I just said you shouldn't volunteer the information."

"Whatever."

"I'll meet you in the lobby of the station at six-thirty. Can you make it?"

He looked down at his calendar and schedule for the day. "Yeah, I can cancel my fund-raising committee meeting tonight."

"Don't worry, okay?"

"Worry? What have I got to be worried about?"

"Phil—"

"I'll see you later, Jeffrey," he said, hanging up without waiting for a response.

*   *   *   *

Hellman sat in the lobby, waiting for Madison to show. He looked around, his eyes taking in the decor and clamor of the police station. But his mind was a million miles away. He was thinking about the times when he and Madison were young teenagers, playing one-on-one basketball at the high school playground. Madison's height advantage was sometimes too difficult to overcome. But Hellman always proved a worthy opponent, practicing hard and focusing on playing intelligently so as to minimize his friend's physical advantages. Their competitions were fierce, evidenced by the fact that nothing deterred them—not rain, cold, or darkness.

". . . Jeffrey," Madison was saying.

Hellman shook his head. "I was daydreaming. We were playing ball at Burkett playground."

"I was winning, right?" Madison said. "I always won."

Hellman smiled as they walked down the hall to meet the detectives. "We're on the same team now. A hell of a combination. Unbeatable."

They ascended the stairs and were led to the same interview room, where they sat down opposite Coleman and Valentine. "Okay, Dr. Madison, let's talk about that night again. September eleventh of this year. Do you remember our last conversation?" Coleman asked, consulting his notepad. "You said that you had nothing in your calendar about meeting Brittany Harding that night."

"You saw my calendar."

"Yes, we did."

"Maybe, instead of interviewing me again, you should be speaking with some of the people who've witnessed this lady's bizarre behavior. She's a nut."

"Is that your medical opinion of Miss Harding?"

"Detective, let's not play cat and mouse," Hellman said. "Can we just get down to the nuts and bolts? You said you had new evidence."

"We do."

Detective Valentine pulled a couple of papers from the folder that was sitting on the metal table in front of her. She handed one of them to Madison, who tilted it so that Hellman could see.

"Is that a copy of your phone bill, doctor?" she asked.

"Yes, it appears to be. My wife pays the bills, I never see them."

"Is that your telephone number at the top?"

"Yes."

Valentine handed him another page. "Do you recognize the two phone numbers that are highlighted in yellow?"

He looked at them and then instantly remembered. Harding had made two calls from his house before she left that night. How convenient. No, *how clever.*

Valentine leaned forward. "Doctor?"

"What?" Madison asked, not looking up. "No, I don't recognize those numbers." Hellman was beginning to sweat.

"You'll notice those calls were made on September eleventh, at ten-fifteen and ten-sixteen P.M."

No response from Madison. He was still staring at the paper.

"Those numbers," Valentine continued, "are local toll calls to the phone numbers of Sue Harding, Miss Harding's mother, and Nancy Bonham, her sister."

"Hmm," Madison mused, as if the news was intensely interesting.

"Detective," Hellman said, "if I could have a moment with my client."

"Wait a minute," Madison said. "She made a couple of calls one night when she came over to my house complaining of abdominal pain."

"So she *was* at your home that night," Valentine said.

"Well, if she made these calls on the eleventh, I guess the night she came over was the eleventh. She wasn't a patient. I didn't keep treatment notes of her visit."

"Apparently, it *was* September eleventh, Dr. Madison." She paused. "Wasn't it?" she said, locking on his gaze.

"It would appear so."

"So Harding's story is taking on some truth," she said to Coleman.

"What are you talking about? What possible reason would

I have for making advances to Brittany Harding? I have a wife, two kids, I'm happily married—"

Coleman leaned forward toward Madison. "She's a looker. Twenty-five, long legs, big tits. You had something she wanted . . . her job. And you saw an opportunity. You told her that if she wanted to keep her job, she'd have to grease your pole."

Madison winced at the street talk of the detective. "You've got it all wrong."

"Then what happened that night?" Valentine asked.

Madison looked over at Hellman, who nodded for him to tell the story.

"She came over complaining of abdominal pain. She had been to some local QuickCare facility where a nurse told her it was nothing to worry about. She said she kept having sharp pains and didn't know what to do, so she came by my house on the way home."

Valentine leaned back in her chair. "Is that it?"

"Well, I gave her a brief abdominal exam, which was essentially negative, and diagnosed her with irritable bowel syndrome."

"Anything else happen?"

"She started to feel better and left."

"Describe an abdominal exam, the way you did it on Miss Harding that night," Valentine said.

"The patient's knees were flexed to relax the stomach muscles, and I placed my hand over her abdomen. I felt for rigidity, masses, and effusion. I made sure there were no aneurysms, and then I palpated the organs and checked for rebound tenderness."

"How far down on the stomach did you go?"

"I examined the entire abdomen. From just under the rib cage down to the upper groin area."

"You didn't go any lower than the 'upper groin area'?" Valentine asked.

"No."

"And what happened after the exam?"

"Like I said, she just left."

"And the phone calls?"

"Oh. I think she made them just before she left, so no one would worry about her not having been home all evening. I let my dog into the yard and then went into my den."

"What about sexual advances?"

"What about them?"

"I'm asking if you made any. You know, 'Gee, you look very pretty tonight. I like your dress, how about going to bed with me—'"

"All right, that's enough," Hellman said.

"I'll answer that, Jeffrey."

"You don't have to, Phil."

"It's okay," he said, turning to Valentine. "Detective, I swear to you. I examined her abdomen, I diagnosed her condition, urged her to get subsequent care from her personal physician if her symptoms returned, and that was it. No innuendoes, no overtures, *undertures,* comments, inappropriate behavior . . . nothing."

"Do you usually examine patients' abdomens at your home?"

Madison clenched his teeth but remained composed. "No, I don't. I made an exception because it was someone I knew and she was in a great deal of pain. I'll never make that mistake again, I assure you."

Valentine sighed. "So that's it? You were the perfect gentleman, just trying to help out a friend in need? I don't buy it."

"You know, you're so focused on me. But what about her? Why don't you ask her how she knew where I lived? She said she pulled it off the Consortium computer. But they only have my P.O. box."

"We're focused on you because you're the one under investigation. How she knew where you lived is irrelevant. Maybe you gave her your home address and forgot."

"No, I wouldn't do that. But I'll tell you how she knew. She must've followed me home one night. She's stalking me—"

"Leave the paranoia at home, Doc."

"Is that all you have?" Hellman asked.

"No. We've got one other item to discuss," she said, motioning for Coleman to hand her the belt from the bag on the floor.

"Ever seen this belt?" she asked, showing it to Madison. It was tagged with an identification sticker.

"Not that I can recall."

"It was the belt Harding was wearing the night she was at your house."

"Yeah, so?" Hellman said.

"So it's got your fingerprints on it."

"I examined her abdomen, and she was in a lot of pain. I helped her unbuckle it."

"Yeah, but—"

"Look," Hellman said firmly, "my client has answered your questions and explained everything he possibly could. Now, are you going to formally charge him?"

"Not yet." Valentine said this staring deeply into Madison's eyes. He stared back, a game of cat and mouse.

"Fine," Hellman said, arising and taking Madison by the arm, breaking the stare. "Then we thank you for a most stimulating evening, detectives."

They walked toward Madison's Mercedes in silence. "Well, what do you think?" he asked Hellman as he unlocked the door.

"I think we're okay, but I don't like it. Too many implications. They could make a case of it. It would be dismissed, but not before your name was plastered all over the newspapers. I'm not going to deceive you. It would wreak havoc with your practice."

"Tell me about it. It's all I've been thinking about."

"My gut feeling is that they're contemplating more than just sexual misconduct. They're thinking rape."

"Rape?!"

"Yeah, but it would be a huge reach. It's been how long since the alleged incident? To have the most credibility, the woman has to report it and get to a doctor within twenty-four hours to be examined."

"But they said sexual misconduct."

"An understatement," he said. "Cops lie during inter- views. They do what it takes to get the information they're after."

"Then it doesn't matter what they charge me with. Even if we get it dismissed, I know what people will think."

"Let's just take one day at a time. So far so good. You're out here and they're in there, right?"

"Yeah, right." Madison had a difficult time feeling relief, any relief at all.

Leeza was walking down the stairs as he came through the back door. "Hi," he said, trying to appear upbeat.

"You had a call from Ed Dolius," she said as she kissed him. "He wanted to know why the meeting was canceled."

"Oh," he said, removing his coat and hanging it in the closet. He had not called Leeza from the office to tell her about the change in plans and the scheduled interview with the detectives.

"Where were you all this time if the meeting was canceled? I tried you at the office." A hint of curiosity in her voice. The rumor of the affair was no doubt in the back of her mind.

"I had an interview with Jeffrey and the detectives at the station," he said, sifting through his pile of mail. "They wanted to ask me some more questions."

"Why didn't you call me?"

"I didn't want to worry you. Besides, I figured that since I was supposed to be at the meeting, you weren't expecting me to be home."

"How'd the interview go?"

"I'm here, aren't I?" he said, forcing a smile and borrowing a line from Hellman.

"That's not saying much."

"That's because not much happened." He pushed his mail into a stack and faced Leeza. "They asked me some more questions and I gave them some more answers. It's all a load of crap, and they know it. Jeffrey tried to push them into just letting the whole thing go."

"And?"

"We'll see. Jeffrey thought they'd asked enough questions, so he told them the interview was over and we left." He loosened his tie. "What's there to eat?"

"Hungry?"

"Starving."

"Go change your clothes and I'll heat something up," she said. "Be quiet. The boys just went to sleep. They had a hard time going down tonight for some reason."

That'll make three of us, he thought.

CHAPTER
24

THE WEEKEND CAME and went. Madison had a sour face on, and his kids sensed that it was better to give him some time alone. This made him more frustrated, as he actually had the time to spend with them. Problem was, he couldn't seem to relax enough to enjoy their company.

Monday used to represent a fresh start to the week; today, it meant he had to climb out of his funk and return to work. He could not remember the last time he did not want to get to the office and start seeing patients. It was good that he did not have any surgeries scheduled for today.

Hellman had just returned from a deposition at eleven o'clock when his secretary informed him that there was an attorney holding on line two for him. It had to do with Brittany Harding.

"Hmm," he grunted as he walked into his office. Picked up the phone, buzzed the secretary. "What's his name?"

"Movis Ehrhardt."

"*Movis?*"

"Movis, like Moe in the three stooges," his secretary remarked, laughing as she hung up the phone.

"Movis . . ." he repeated to himself, trying it out. Hit the line button. "Hello, this is Jeffrey Hellman."

"Mr. Hellman, my name's Movis Ehrhardt, and I'm representing Brittany Harding in a civil matter pertaining to your client, Phillip Madison."

A civil matter, that's what this is about. "And . . ."

"And we have some issues that need to be addressed."

"Such as," Hellman asked, trying to gather as much information while saying as little as possible.

"Such as the evidence against your client in the rape of Miss Harding."

"What rape?"

"Oh, come on, counselor. Have the police not interviewed your client?"

I was right. They were thinking rape. "Go on."

"I would think that such an allegation, if made public, could be . . . somewhat problematic for your client. He's a surgeon, isn't he?"

Hellman gritted his teeth. "Where is this leading, Moovis?" he said, purposely mispronouncing his name.

"It's Moe-vis," he said, phonetically enunciating it. "And what I'm getting at, is that I'd think it would be embarrassing if the good doctor was charged with rape. You know, bad publicity and all the stuff that goes with it."

Hellman was silent. He was too busy fuming and simultaneously trying to calm himself. He knew all too well where this was headed.

"So," Movis was saying, "I could help you. Make sure your client never gets charged."

"And how's that? This is a police investigation."

"Well, let's just say that my client might not be willing to cooperate. Wouldn't make a very good witness. Bad memory and all that."

"I see," he said, pausing. "But my client's innocent."

"I'm sure that's what he's told you."

"It happens to be the truth."

"Truth, schmooth. You and I both know that that truth doesn't amount to diddly. It's all about appearances and salesmanship. My client makes a very convincing victim." He paused. "Considering all the factors involved, how does my offer sound to you?"

"I didn't realize there was an offer on the table. I must've missed it."

"We want fifty grand."

"Fifty grand," repeated Hellman. "I can be kind of dense sometimes. At least, that's what my wife used to say," he said with a chortle. "Are you telling me that if my client pays you fifty grand, your client will withdraw her complaint and be struck with sudden amnesia?"

"I don't think you're so dense. How does it sound?"

"It sounds like extortion, a shakedown."

"Whoa, counselor, fancy terms there. I just thought it was a reasonable offer. Helps your guy by making all this go away real fast. Helps my client, too. She doesn't want to have to sit through a trial and relive all the horrors of that night."

"Spare me the bullshit, Moovis, this entire thing was a setup. And it pads your pocket with, what, fifteen grand, all for a ten-minute phone call."

"Don't worry about what it does for me, Mr. Hellman," he said, his tone changing abruptly. "Worry about what'll happen to the good doctor when the cops come to arrest him at his office."

"He's still out on the street, seeing patients and performing surgery, *Moovis.*"

"Well, we'll see about that. There's some more evidence you obviously don't know about."

"I know all about the phone calls and the belt."

"I'm not talking about that. Those are old news."

Hellman sat up straight in his chair. "What evidence are you talking about?"

"Why don't you discuss the offer with your client, Mr. Hellman. Fifty thousand."

"You're a goddamned fucking sleazebag, Moovis."

"That's hardly a way to talk to a guy who's trying to help your client. Obviously *you're* not doing such a hot job."

"Go to hell."

"Talk to your client. The offer disappears in twenty-four hours."

Hellman slammed the phone down. *What other evidence could there be?*

He dialed Madison. "Get him out of the room," Hellman

was saying, the anger evident in his voice. "The patient will wait, Monica."

Two minutes later, Madison picked up the extension. "What's going—"

"You were honest with me, right?" Hellman asked.

"About what?"

"About the goddamned rape thing. You didn't touch her?"

"No, I didn't touch her. I told you everything. What the hell is going—"

"I just got a call from an attorney who's representing Harding in a civil matter. The complaint the police were investigating is a *criminal* matter. When there's a civil suit, it's against you personally, for damages. Monetary damages. Remember the Michael Jackson child abuse suit years ago, where they demanded money from him in exchange for dropping the charges?"

"Didn't he pay them a few million?"

"Harding's attorney wants fifty thousand. You pay it, she withdraws the complaint."

"Fifty thousand dollars?! *I didn't rape her.* It's all a lie, Jeffrey." He looked up and noticed the door to his office was open—and the nearest patient room was only ten feet down the hall. He stood up and, stretching across his desk, flung the door shut.

"Lie or not, if they charge you . . ."

"Yeah, I know." He sighed, sat back in his chair. "What did you tell him?"

"I told him he was a goddamned fucking sleazebag."

"I can't believe this is legal."

"It's not. It's unethical to the level of criminality. It's extortion, is what it is. But I didn't want to completely alienate him, in case we decided to take his offer. And I certainly don't want to blow this up to the point that the media gets hold of it—because then it doesn't matter what we pay the crook."

"Christ. What the hell am I going to tell Leeza?" he asked.

"Ah-ah-ah. Speaking as your friend, I don't know if I would tell her. Even though we know you're innocent, she may not understand. She's already sensitive to Harding and the affair bullshit. It'll look to her like you were guilty, and paid her off to shut her up."

"Jeffrey, how did I get into this mess . . ." he said, his voice uneven, as tears began to well up in his eyes. "Why is this happening to me?"

"Phil, Phillip. Stop it. Don't do this to yourself. You didn't do anything wrong. There are sick people in this world. You just happen to have crossed the path of someone who had the ability and circumstances to make your life miserable."

"What do you think I should do?"

"I think you should take the evening and think about it. I have until tomorrow afternoon to get back to him."

"I don't want to do it, Jeffrey."

"I know you don't. But I want to do what's in your best interest. Let's not think with our emotions, okay? Take a few breaths, compose yourself, and get back to work. I'll talk to you tomorrow."

Madison made it home early that evening, just as the kids were finishing dinner. He played a game of Hungry, Hungry Hippos, and rolled on the floor with the children while Scalpel barked and licked him, fighting for attention. He capped the evening by lulling them to sleep with a story about dragons. Leeza was reading and vegging on the family room couch, having been relieved of her nightly duties for the first time in weeks. She was enjoying every minute of it.

Madison looked at her several times during the evening while they were watching the tube, and almost asked her her opinion about what he should do. He never really consulted her on monetary matters. He ran that aspect of their lives, just as she paid the bills when they came in. He deposited the money in the bank, and if she needed more, she would tell him and he would have the money transferred into their account. She would never notice the missing fifty thousand dollars.

Each time he thought of bringing up the topic, he heard Hellman's voice in the back of his mind: *It'll look to her like you're guilty. She may not understand.* While that might in fact be the case, he just did not feel right about keeping it from her. Maybe she would feel better about it and would understand if she were consulted about it from the beginning.

As they were sitting there and Madison was about to broach the subject, Leeza received a call from her sister, who was living in Texas. She had not spoken to her in months, and that was that for the evening. Nearly two hours later, she came to bed. Madison was fast asleep, exhaustion winning out over stress. He had not gotten a decent night's sleep in days.

The next morning, low, gray clouds hung from the sky. It had unexpectedly drizzled a bit, dampening the *Sacramento Herald* that had been lying on the step when Madison opened the door.

He thumbed through the paper, skimming the front page and catching some current events before turning to the sports and business pages. Suddenly, his eyes settled on a column by Carrie Anson. The headline struck him like a brick across the forehead:

WHEN YOUR DOCTOR IS ACCUSED OF RAPE

He swallowed hard; felt a bit lightheaded. He began to read: "Rape is a disease in our society, one which occurs not only in dark, back streets and alleys, but now seems to pervade even the safest of places: our doctor's office . . ." He felt a rumbling deep inside his gut. ". . . When a woman places trust in her doctor, a prominent member of the medical community who has received numerous state and national awards, we must wonder just how safe we are when that door closes and clicks shut . . ." He started to skim, and caught key phrases: ". . . heading up a popular local nonprofit agency . . . had made overtures to her in public and now this tragic event. How could this happen in our community . . ."

Leeza walked into the kitchen to make the kids breakfast. She would want the newspaper when he was done with it. "Anything interesting?" she asked absentmindedly as she poured the pancake mix into the bowl.

"Hmm? Oh, nothing. The usual." Remembering he had

wanted to reup his subscription to the *Bee* and cancel the *Herald,* he closed the paper, buried the front page under the Metro and Living sections, and gave her a kiss.

"Leaving so soon?"

"I have a few reports to get to before surgery this morning."

"Have any idea what time you'll be home tonight?"

"I'll shoot for six, right after rounds, okay?"

"Sounds good," she said, pouring a couple of dabs of batter onto the skillet.

He left and drove off. Dialed Hellman from his portable phone. Caught him in his car on the way to the office.

"Have you seen the *Herald?*"

"That's what you called about?" Hellman asked.

"I take it you haven't read it."

"It's sitting on the seat here next to me," he said as he exited the freeway.

"Pull over and read Carrie Anson's column. Page two. Call me right back."

Thirty seconds later, Madison's phone rang. He reached over and hit a button. "Yeah."

"Jesus."

"Pay them the money, Jeffrey."

"Phil, I can go after them for this article. This is libelous."

"Jeffrey, I've had enough. Even if you get them to print a retraction, they didn't mention any names. What are they gonna say, the doctor we didn't mention didn't really do it? Are they going to say they made it up? No. Will they say we're sorry we wrote the story, that there have been no formal charges filed against anyone? It'll look like someone threatened them with a lawsuit, which is exactly what you'd be doing."

"Phil—"

"Pay them the money, Jeffrey. Get her out of my life."

"I'll see if I can get the figure down a bit. I'll get her to sign a release, and something stating that she'll refrain from filing any further complaints against you—"

"Whatever. You deal with the legal garbage—just get it done. I'll get the money together and have a cashier's check in your office by two o'clock."

*   *   *   *

The law offices of Hellman, MacKenzie & McKnight were ornately decorated, and dated back to a time when it was a sole practitioner's office . . . before Hellman expanded into the adjacent suite and took on two partners. The atmosphere was lavish: forest greens and burgundies, with rich golds woven in between. The walls were papered with a velvet-textured paisley; the chairs were hand-embroidered needlepoint, and the desks were cherrywood.

Hannah Hellman had been partners with Leeza Madison in a small but successful interior decorating company when she and Jeffrey decided to get married. After the firm expanded into the new office space, the Hellmans spent many an evening poring through decorator books, playing with color chips, and matching everything down to the floor tile used behind the reception desk. Hannah had insisted that Jeffrey have input on all the selections. Together, they gave the standard office space life, a personality, an atmosphere.

When Hannah Hellman died of ovarian cancer three years ago, she left behind a few snapshots, five minutes of videotape a friend had once recorded at a party, and the memories of decorating the law office. Since they had only begun to redecorate their house, the office decor was the only substantive daily reminder of her personality, of the evenings spent collaborating on a theme that would become her living legacy. Although the firm's partners had more than once brought up the logical idea of moving into larger quarters in the Welles Tower across the street, he had put them off each time. He could not abandon Hannah. There was something special about feeling her presence every morning of every day.

He strode into the office, nodded to Theresa, and picked up his messages. He pondered the phone call to Movis Ehrhardt . . . one call Hellman did not want to make; but, his best friend had felt that this was the most prudent way of putting the matter to rest. And, given the circumstances, he did not have any better solutions to offer.

He called Movis and began the tedious process of negotiating, trying his best to stoop down to the charlatan's level so they could be on common ground. They finally agreed on forty thousand dollars, a sum that was better than fifty thousand, but which was still exorbitant, and still extortion—no matter how you sliced it.

The deal all but done, Hellman wanted one last dig. "That newspaper column was a cheap shot."

"Hold on, counselor. I had nothing to do with that. I don't even know if my client did, either."

"And I'm just supposed to believe that because you're an honest guy."

"You should be talking to the paper and the columnist, not me."

"I'd rather talk to you, because I already know where the story came from."

"Well, let's just say, for fun, that suppose my client had a friend who was a columnist and she had innocently mentioned her ordeal to that person. If that person chose to write about it, well, that's the way it goes. But timing *is* everything."

"You son of a bitch."

"You've got quite a vocabulary, counselor. Between your comments of yesterday and today, I'd be inclined to think that I was a pretty horrid individual."

"Socrates said it was wise to know oneself." He felt a bit better, but it still had not changed the facts of the situation.

Hellman laid out the conditions of the agreement, which prevented Harding from being the source of any further newspaper articles, from disclosing their agreement, and from having any contact with Madison or his family. In all, he had listed fifteen different terms. Ehrhardt did not object to any of the provisions—for a cool thirteen grand, his take on the forty thousand, he was not going to do anything that jeopardized his fee. His client did not care either; she got what she wanted: revenge, and money—and not necessarily in that order.

They faxed each other back and forth, and in three hours, the contract was signed.

The check was delivered.

And the dirty deed was done.

CHAPTER
25

LIFE WAS MOST definitely sweeter for the Madison family. They were a little lighter in the bank account, but whoever said that money could not buy happiness did not know the dilemma that Phillip Madison had been facing in recent weeks. He came out of his shell and started to settle into a routine of normalcy, enjoying a sense of safety he had not known in almost two months.

Leeza had periodically attempted to ask him about the complaint, and why it had been withdrawn. Each time there was either a convenient interruption or Madison managed to fob her off with a general comment about the lack of merit of Harding's accusations. When she finally pressed him on the details, he responded by telling her that since there was no proof of anything, the police had nothing left to pursue. It was a logical conclusion, and it seemed to satisfy her.

They barely had much time to enjoy their renewed stability, as Madison had to attend a seminar in San Diego on November 14 on advances in total hip replacement prosthetics. It was a $1,200 continuing education seminar that he had paid for six months ago. He invited Leeza to come along with him, but she was unable to arrange for a baby-sitter for the weekend. He promised to make it up to her. In fact, he told her to plan a mini vacation to New Orleans, where they had gone a few years ago and had the time of their lives. She booked it the minute he left for the airport on Friday afternoon.

That evening, Madison returned to his hotel room and

threw his seminar binder on the bed. He was exhausted, having listened to eight hours of boring recitation. Thank goodness it at least included slides and videotape, to break up the monotony. He stretched and started to change into something more comfortable for dinner with his old medical school buddy, Barney. He had not seen Barney since the last seminar in San Diego, and he missed his company. Still, he dreaded the question Barney never failed to ask: *So, Phil, what's new in your life?*

As he unbuttoned his shirt, he noticed that the message light on his room phone was flashing. "Probably Leeza," he said as he dialed the front desk.

"Yes, Dr. Madison, we do have a message here for you, from your wife," the attendant said.

"Yeah, what is it?"

The attendant paused. "Well, sir, perhaps you should come down and read it for yourself."

"Look, I'm in a little hurry to get to dinner. Just read it to me."

"It may be personal—"

"That's okay. Just read the message," Madison said, not making any effort to mask his impatience.

"It came in at ten-fifteen this morning."

"Yeah, and . . . "

"It says"—he paused—"'You goddamned lying bastard. I'm moving out. Don't bother calling.'"

"What?"

"I'm sorry, sir. I didn't want to read it—"

"Please have someone bring it up to my room immediately." He hung up the phone, dialed Leeza. It was six o'clock; the message came in eight hours ago, meaning that she could be long gone by now. *But why?* He sat there, the inane, monotonous ring coming every other second. No answer. Machine. *Leave message? Yes.* "Lee, honey, it's me. I got a very strange message at the front desk just now, and I don't know if it's some kind of sick joke or not, but please call me at the hotel when you get home. The number here is 619-555-2400. I love you."

He hung up the phone. Sat down and rubbed his temples. *What the hell is this all about?*

A knock at the door broke his daydream. The bellman handed him the message; Madison slipped a ten into his palm, never bothering to look at the man, and shut the door. He studied the slip of paper, as if staring at it would suddenly cause new information to appear.

He dialed Leeza again. No answer. Another message. He called Southwest Airlines and booked a seat on their last flight out to Sacramento, which left in one hour. He called a cab, gathered his clothes, called Barney, and told him he had to leave to deal with a family emergency. Then he phoned Hellman and asked him to pick him up at the airport. *Shit,* he thought, *what now?*

The flight home was agony. What if the message was a hoax—he would be coming home and missing the rest of his seminar for nothing. That would be a Brittany Harding tactic. But other than his office staff, no one knew of the seminar, let alone the hotel where he was staying. It was not likely a hoax.

Hellman was waiting outside in his Lexus; Madison tossed his bags into the trunk. He explained all that he knew and showed him the crumpled message he had received from the bellman. Hellman did not know what to make of it either. "Maybe she found out about the settlement, and you weren't home to explain it," he said.

"Jeffrey, if that's it, I'm going to wring your neck. Again, I should have told the truth and didn't, and now it's come back to haunt me—"

"Hold it, hold it," he said, waving a hand out in front of the dashboard. "You're jumping to conclusions. Let's just wait till we get there."

Leeza's van was not in the garage. He opened his front door and everything appeared to be dark. Scalpel came running into the entryway and licked him on the face. Madison walked into the den, looking for a clue of some sort, something to explain what the hell was going on. Leeza usually left notes for him on the desk.

Hellman threw on some lights in the hallway and walked into the kitchen to look around for a message of some sort.

Madison looked down and saw an 8 by 10 photo on his desk. He picked it up. "Jeffrey," he called, his voice weak and unsteady. "Jeffrey!" he tried again, attempting to muster more force through his choked throat. He turned the picture over and saw a copy of the settlement check Hellman had sent to Harding's attorney. "Oh, my God," was all he could mumble.

"What? What's the matter?" Hellman asked, walking into the room. He saw the ashen color of Madison's face and sat down next to him. Then his eyes found the copy of the check. "Why do you have—" he started to ask as Madison flipped the picture over in front of it. It was a photo that appeared to depict his client kissing Brittany Harding. "Oh, shit. Fucking shit."

They sat in silence for a moment, both staring at the picture. "Phil, what *is* this? What are we looking at?"

He cleared his throat. "This was taken at the Fifth Street Café. She said she'd been on the phone a lot that day and had some kind of sharp pain in her ear. She wanted me to take a look at it, but when I couldn't see anything, she moved closer. Somebody must have snapped the picture at that moment. The whole damned thing was orchestrated."

"Why was she laughing?" Hellman asked, still looking at the picture.

"She said it tickled." He let loose a stifled grunt. "I wasn't even touching her."

"But it looks like—"

"I know what it looks like!" he shouted. "Apparently, so did Leeza." He continued to stare at the picture. "She's left me, Jeffrey. She's taken the kids and left me." He said it matter-of-factly, like no amount of explaining in the world could reverse it. A done deal. Set in stone. Fact.

"Shit, Phil. I'm sorry." He shifted in his seat. "How the hell did she get this? Where . . ." he said, as his voice trailed off. He saw the manila envelope on the desk. "Don't touch anything. Put the picture down," he said.

"Why—"

"Just do it. I'm going to have it dusted for prints. I bet I know exactly who sent this."

"Harding."

"Had to be," Hellman said. "Who else would have a copy of the check?"

Madison did not answer.

"Or, it could've been Movis Ehrhardt."

"Who?"

"Harding's attorney," Hellman said, rubbing his forehead. "Right before we settled, he said that there was more evidence, but the detectives never said they had anything other than the belt and the phone bill. After you assured me that nothing else had happened, I thought he was bluffing." There was quiet again in the room. "She never gave the police this picture. My guess is that she was going to turn it over to them if we didn't pay her off."

"But—but didn't we have an agreement, a contract?" Madison asked.

"In a perfect world, yes, we did have a contract. But she's a sick individual, Phil." He sighed. "I'll get on Movis's ass Monday morning. File a claim with the bar . . ."

Madison wasn't listening. New Orleans had popped into his mind. New Orleans and Leeza, and how nice their trip might have been.

CHAPTER
26

"YOU'RE A goddamned fucking sleazebag, you son of a bitch!" Hellman yelled into the phone.

"Ah, Mr. Hellman," guessed Movis Ehrhardt.

"You double-crossing extortionist!"

"Just let me know when you're done."

"Done?" Hellman asked. "I'm just getting started."

"How about telling me what this is all about?"

"Let's start with the destruction of a family, you unethical—"

"Whoa, counselor, what the hell are you talking about?"

"Either you or your client sent Madison's wife a picture that makes it look like he was kissing Harding in a restaurant."

"Of course, it's your position that that's not what he was doing."

"She was complaining of ear pain. He was taking a look at it for her."

"And you think that this picture was sent to Madison's wife by me?"

"You or your client. And given my past dealings with you, it wouldn't surprise—"

"Why do you think I had anything to do with it?"

"The picture was accompanied by a copy of the settlement check I sent to you."

There was no response at the other end. The usually vociferous, answer-for-everything Movis Ehrhardt fell silent.

Finally, Hellman broke the interlude. "Well?"

"I need to look into this."

"You sound like you already know what happened."

"Well, I shouldn't be telling you this, but before my client left here, she asked me for a copy of the check. I thought she just wanted it for her records." There was silence again. "If she did this, I'm very sorry. Regardless of what you may think of me, I'm really sorry about this."

"I'm having the picture dusted for prints. If those prints come back a match for you or your client, that money better be returned in certified funds within twenty-four hours of my call—or I'm going to find a way of tying you into this scheme and have you disbarred. I'll make it my hobby."

"I didn't have anything—"

"We'll talk tomorrow," Hellman said just before he slammed the phone down.

CHAPTER
27

IT WAS one o'clock in the morning and Ryan Chandler was yawning, fighting to keep awake. "You've been talking for hours, Phil, but you don't even look tired."

"Dredging all this up has stirred some very unpleasant thoughts. And I miss Leeza and the kids. It's been three weeks since they left. I can't tell you what this has done to me, Ryan."

"I can understand. It would tear me apart if Denise and Noah suddenly left me. But I guess I can't fully grasp what you're going through."

"Let's just say that I hope you never have the experience."

They both smiled. Chandler yawned again; he was half slumped in his chair, and his low back ached. "I think it's time for me to hit the sack, or I'll be useless in the morning."

"We're almost through," Madison said.

They said good night and Chandler was asleep five minutes later, not even bothering to take his clothes off. Madison lay awake the rest of the night.

The morning brought welcome sunshine; it was supposed to be 60 degrees today, a refreshing respite from the rain and 45-degree weather that had been feeding Madison's depression.

When he walked into the kitchen, Chandler was sipping coffee and scanning the morning paper. Madison said hello and then launched into the rest of the story, as if he had been a VCR placed on "pause" for the evening. Chandler figuratively hit "play" by acknowledging his presence.

"I awoke the next morning and found a fax in my machine from Leeza," Madison continued. "She was staying at her sister's in the Bay Area—I recognized the number at the top of the fax." He found the handwritten letter, which was stuffed into a cubby next to the kitchen phone, and handed it to Chandler, who began to scan it:

. . . Please don't call around looking for me. The boys and I are safe. I need some time to sort all this out. I can't tell you how much you've hurt me. I feel like I don't know you anymore. You never lied to me before, and this was such an important thing. I don't know what hurts me more, the fact that you lied to me or your infidelity. Maybe you thought you were protecting me from getting hurt. But how can I forgive the fact that you slept with this woman? Did you really feel the need to go elsewhere? I always felt secure with you. I thought that that was one of the safest things in my life. The money was nice, sure, but nothing can replace your soul, your heart. This has taught me that people can say anything they want, but it's their actions that really count. Talk is worthless if the actions don't back it up.

I feel betrayed.

I need time to think things out, decide what to do. Maybe it's best that we just part now and go our separate ways, before the kids get too much older. I'll contact you soon.

Leeza

After Chandler finished, he handed the fax back to Madison.

"I felt the same way about our relationship as she did, Ryan. Trust isn't something you can buy, for any amount of money. It's earned. And once it's lost, it's real hard to get it back."

"There's no doubt she was very hurt by what she thought was going on, Phil. But things have a way of working themselves out. Let things calm down a bit. She'll come around."

Madison was staring at the letter. "She was a part of me, Ryan. I don't know how to describe it. She gave me balance, made me see things in ways I was too busy to see. It's like Harding destroyed a part of me when she made Leeza walk out that door."

"Stop talking about your marriage in the past tense. She'll be back, Phil. I know it."

After a long moment of silence, Madison folded Leeza's letter, shoved it back into the bin next to the telephone, and continued the story.

After reading the fax, Madison felt like running into the middle of the street and screaming as loud as he could. But he had patients to see, and a facade that was in need of some repair. He walked outside into the cool, still air, took a few deep breaths, and left for the office.

The day was routine, which was good: he needed that. No important decisions, no critical diagnoses, no unusual test results to interpret. Tomorrow three surgeries were scheduled. He had another fourteen hours to get his head into shape before taking the scalpel in hand.

Madison sat down at his desk and signed a few reports without even bothering to proof them. When his phone buzzed, he glanced at his watch. He had been sitting there, lost in a thoughtless daze, for nearly twenty minutes.

"Jeffrey Hellman on line two," Monica said.

He looked down at the phone, noticing the blinking red light. He had not even listened to his messages. "Have him hold for a moment," he said, while he checked his voice mail, hoping there was a call from Leeza. Nothing. Just a call from Jeffrey, urging him to call him for "some—finally—good news."

He disconnected the voice mail and picked up line two. "Hi."

"I would've thought you'd have called me by now, with that message I left."

"I just got it. I've been a little preoccupied, I guess."

"Could you use some good news?"

"Sure. Hit me with it," he said in a monotone that reflected his emotional fog.

"I have a forty-thousand-dollar check in my hand. Certified funds, signed by Movis Ehrhardt."

"I don't understand."

"Movis the Airhead and I had a conversation yesterday about the picture. I'll bet that both his and Harding's prints were all over it. By sending it, she broke the terms of our agreement. I threatened to sue both of them for damages, pain and suffering, extortion, assault, and whatever else rolled off my tongue at the moment. Threatened him with a complaint to the bar and told him I'd make it my goal in life to create enough trouble for him that his professional existence would be a living hell. I convinced him that it wouldn't be worth the thirteen grand he made off it. He cut us a check this afternoon."

"That's great," Madison said flatly.

"Yeah, I can tell. What's going on in that head of yours?"

"I've just got a lot on my plate right now. I'm thinking about Leeza, my marriage, my kids. I'm not handling it very well. I didn't think it would get this bad."

"Maybe you should see a shrink."

"I'll put myself on some Elavil. Got some around here somewhere . . ."

"Be careful with that stuff, Phil."

"Oh, thanks, *Doctor* Hellman."

"That has a nice ring to it," Hellman said, trying to bring some humor to the conversation. "Maybe I should've listened to you, Phil. Gone to medical school, become a surgeon. We could've been in the same class. Pity that instructor."

The attempt at levity was futile. "I've gotta go," Madison said. "I have to pick up some food at the market tonight. There's nothing in the house."

"You want me to come over later?"

"Nah, I'm not really in the mood for company."

"If you need to talk, give me a call. I'll be home."

The neighborhood Food & More market was a bright, upscale full-service facility, complete with child-care-while-you-shop, a Bank of America branch, espresso bar, sushi counter, and Chinese take-out. He had wandered through the frozen foods section, stocking his basket with ready-made dinners—on which he would subsist for the next who knew how many days until Leeza would allow him to explain the check and picture.

As he headed down the aisle toward the checkout line, his basket collided with one that belonged to another shopper. He looked up to apologize and upon seeing Brittany Harding's face, froze up instantly. "What the hell are you doing here?" he managed to blurt. This was not the neighborhood he expected to find her in.

Her face contorted in anger as she opened her mouth and let loose a barrage of expletives at a volume that made the nearby checker down the aisle turn his head.

". . . you bastard! You and your attorney think you're so smart, huh? Rape never goes away. You'll have to live with that, just like I will. What nerve you have thinking you can violate a woman's body and get away with it. You cost me my job, you pervert!"

Between anger and the embarrassment of being called a rapist in the neighborhood market, Madison broke out into a sweat and his heart began to pound. Hiding his face, he looked down and noticed a six-pack of beer in her cart. Instantly, Hellman's admonition about appearing confident popped into his head. He looked up, directly into Harding's enlarged pupils. "Why don't you go home and drown yourself in that beer? Drown out the pitiful life you lead. Look at yourself! What drugs are you on now, anyway?"

Her expression changed from anger to surprise; she clearly did not expect him to strike back at her so aggressively.

"You're delusional," he shouted. "Leave me and my family alone!" He was as taken aback by his tone as Harding appeared to be. Seldom-tapped feelings of anger were speaking, not Phil Madison, surgeon and philanthropist.

She took a deep breath; her chest was heaving. He wheeled around her cart, away from her, down the aisle toward the checkout register.

"You bastard! You'll pay! I'll get you for this!" she was yelling after him.

He hurried to get away from her as quickly as possible.

Away from the war, the embarrassment, the confrontation. Out of the market.

"Go home to your retarded brother!" he could hear her shout in the distance.

Poor Ricky. How did he get dragged into this? Madison took a couple of deep breaths to compose himself; glanced up to see where he was. The checker was looking at him, a young man of perhaps twenty years of age. He appeared tentative, unsure if he should say anything. "Hey, you okay?" he finally asked.

Madison looked up at the checker, a bit disoriented. He turned and glanced around behind him. People were staring at him down the aisle from where he had just come. Harding was standing with them, no doubt filling their ears with detailed lies of the nonexistent rape her scheming, deceitful mind had dreamed up.

"Twenty-one forty-two," the man said, pointing to the green LED readout on the register.

Madison fumbled for his checkbook.

"Cash only," he said, craning his neck up to the sign above his head. "You're in the express lane. Fifteen items—"

"Yeah, okay," Madison said, still somewhat shaken, opening his wallet and pulling out a couple of twenty-dollar bills.

"What's her deal?" the checker asked.

"Huh? Oh, she's got some emotional problems."

The checker nodded while making change. He handed Madison the receipt. "Take it easy."

"I'll get you for this, you son of a bitch!" He heard her shouting again, behind him somewhere, like a nightmare that returns after you manage to fall back asleep. She was on line behind him now, three people back. "Who've you raped lately?" she asked. "You'll pay for this, you son of a bitch!"

Madison managed to keep his head as he walked on out into the cold evening air of the parking lot, leaving her screaming behind him. *Some emotional problems,* he repeated to himself. *Understatement of the year.*

And Jeffrey thinks I *need a shrink.*

CHAPTER
28

CHANDLER FINISHED his third cup of coffee and looked up at Madison, who had stopped talking. He was just staring at the table, the lack of sleep apparent on his face.

"Phil?"

Madison sat for another moment, seemingly mesmerized by the pattern of the wood grain on the butcher block table.

"Phil? You okay?" Chandler asked.

"Huh?" He looked up. "Yeah, I'm fine." He forced a smile. "That's it. That's the story. They came to my house a few days later and arrested me."

"And here we are."

"Here we are."

"Did you ever speak to Leeza?"

He laughed bitterly. "A couple of days later she called to let me know she and the boys were okay. I told her what had happened, about the bogus evidence they had, and the settlement Jeffrey negotiated, and why we agreed to it. And of course I told her about the picture. She listened to what I had to say, but she didn't really give much of a response. Said she'd have to think things over, let it all sink in. She wasn't sure who to believe, if she should believe anyone at all. There was no trust, no common ground. It was very awkward."

"When was that?"

"I don't know, a couple weeks ago."

"Have you spoken to her since then?"

"Yeah. I went by to see the kids. Took them to the park. Jonah wanted to know why they had to stay at his aunt's house and why they couldn't see me. It was terrible, Ryan." He paused, staring at the table again. "I call them every other day. Lee doesn't say much to me. When I was arrested, she drove out to help me with bail. We talked a little. She was still upset that I'd never told her that Harding was even at the house that night. She wanted to know why I didn't tell her—she was really fixated on that. After all, if I couldn't trust her, who could I trust? And then the kicker: if I lied about Harding being in the house, how could she know for sure that I didn't lie about raping her?"

Madison shook his head, then continued. "I told her that I didn't lie about the rape, and I told her that I didn't kill those two people." He laughed mockingly. "Said she believed me about the murders, because she knows I'm not a murderer. She wanted to be here for me, but she didn't want to come back because of a crisis. Bottom line was that she needed to resolve the other situation in her mind before we could move on and be together again."

Both men were silent for a moment. Then, Madison nodded at the vase on the table. "Leeza used to buy fresh flowers every week. While she's been gone, the flowers died. Just like everything else in my life. Me, my marriage. My family. My career."

"Phil, come on. Enough of this negative talk." Chandler tried to meet Madison's downcast eyes. "Hey, are you there?"

Madison's voice was low, almost as if he was talking to himself. "It's so unlike her. I really didn't expect her to react like this."

Chandler sighed and decided to make an attempt to disperse the black cloud that had descended over their conversation. "Okay, we need a plan of attack. First, I want to make a list of all the people who have something to offer us in support of the assertion that it was Harding who was driving the car. That will include people who can attest to the public threats she made against you, the fabricated stories, the people who witnessed the erratic behavior—"

"For what?"

"Because we're going to build a case against her, to show

that it was her who committed the crime, not you. Didn't you ever watch *Perry Mason?*"

"I guess I was too busy studying."

Chandler laughed, realizing that that statement was probably all too true.

"Isn't Jeffrey going to be doing this?"

"Phil, you brought me here to help you. I don't intend to just sit around on my ass examining physical evidence. For that matter, it'll be a few days before we'll even know if I'll be allowed access to it. In the meantime, I want to make the most of my time—and my skills. Besides, it gives me a chance to spend a few days with my first love—investigation."

They made up a list of people for him to visit, a list Chandler was sure would grow as he spoke with those people Madison had identified. He was determined to clear Madison, and the best place to start was with the person who in all probability committed the crime. His plan was simple: dig up a ton of evidence, build a strong and compelling enough case, and the jury would have to acquit on reasonable doubt.

But Chandler knew that simple plans often run into complications.

CHAPTER
29

PROSECUTOR TIMOTHY DENTON was sitting at his desk with a small halogen light on. Files were piled high around him, almost haphazardly, even though he always professed to anyone who commented on its disarray that he knew where everything was. A half-filled cup of black coffee sat on his desk, left over from this morning.

Detective Bill Jennings walked in without acknowledgment and sat down heavily on the thinly padded chair in front of Denton's desk. "I'm fucking bushed," he said, popping open a can of Coke and throwing his boots up on top of Denton's desk. He moved a couple of files over with his heel so he had a spot to rest his feet comfortably.

"How goes the investigation, Detective?"

"Why so formal?" Jennings asked. "You never call me 'Detective' unless there's someone else in the room."

Closing the law book he had been reading, Denton looked up at Jennings for the first time. "This is a big case, Bill. I've got to devote all of my time to it. If we screw this up, I'll be hearing about it from now until the next election. So . . . if you have something of substance to say, please, regale me with it; otherwise, get your boots off my desk and your ass out of my office."

Jennings, not one to mince words, took a swig of Coke. "I hear that Ryan Chandler is investigating this case for the defense."

"Yeah, so, who the hell is Ryan Chandler?"

"Let's just say that he's no friend of mine."

"And what possible relevance does this Chandler guy have to this case?"

"'Relevance' . . . goddamn lawyer talk. Why's everything gotta have relevance? Can't it ever just be personal?" He paused, noticing that Denton was not following him. "It's relevant because I hate the guy's fucking guts." He pulled his boots off the desk, leaned forward, put his Coke down.

"Fifteen years ago Ryan Chandler left the Sacramento PD and became an investigator for the DA. They had a suspect in custody in a serial murder case when, all of a sudden, there's a killing that's kind of similar in Stockton, where I was working at the time. The Stockton case was assigned to me. Chandler suggested that we work together on it, because he thought it was the same killer. Said he was going to get pressure to drop the case against the guy they'd already charged. I didn't agree. The MO was so different that I thought there's no way this could be the same guy. Chandler said the MO had changed only because the killer was adapting to what he'd learned in the prior murders. He thought the guy was getting better at what he did and because of that the MO looked different. I thought Chandler was full of shit and I fought his efforts to merge the cases. He argued hard and loud, and pissed me off in the process. I was going through my divorce at the time and didn't need any more bullshit in my life. I told him to fuck off."

Denton, who had only been half listening, realized that Jennings was going to finish his story whether he was paying attention or not. He leaned back in his chair and clasped his hands behind his neck.

"Chandler persisted, and kept working up his case that way. Leaked it to the papers. Reporters from the Bay, reporters from Stockton, Sacramento . . . they started asking questions, dogging me all over the fucking place. *Do we have a serial killer in Stockton? Is it safe to go out? Is it true that you're refusing to cooperate with Sacramento authorities in their investigation? How many more people have to die before you take this seriously and cooperate with them?* Shit like that. The heat was on. But I wouldn't back down. Didn't give Chandler shit. I blocked every inquiry he tried to make. Tied everything up in red tape," he said with a slight smile.

He rooted out a cigarette from his sport coat pocket and lit it. Denton was about to object, but realized that getting into an argument over smoking in his office would only prolong the time Jennings would be interrupting his evening.

"Finally," puffed Jennings, "Chandler got the FBI involved and convinced them that the cases were related. They drew up a profile, and the soup got thicker. They agreed with his theory about the different MOs." He took another puff. "Everything was all fucked up. Too many cooks, you know?" He blew a mouthful into the air above him and watched it hang in the air for a couple of seconds.

"Five days later another victim went down in Stockton. Two days after that, one in Old Sacramento. The killer's signature matched the one downtown a couple of weeks earlier, and was pretty damn close to the ones down in Stockton. With the help of the profile, Chandler and a dick friend of his in Homicide nailed the guy a couple of days later and got a confession on all the murders."

He paused, bowed his head. Blew the smoke down onto his boots. "I fucked up, Tim. Looked real bad. Drew a reprimand from the captain and everything. Chewed my ass real hard. Had I cooperated with Chandler from the start those last two people might not have gotten killed. One was a woman with two little kids. Took me years to get over the guilt."

Denton realized that Jennings was near the end of his story. He sat forward to say something, but Jennings interrupted him.

"Hearing Chandler's name brought back the memories. The nightmares." He took a long drag. "*That's* the fucking relevance."

"Well, we're all adults, aren't we, Bill? That was then, this is now. This is your chance to make up for your past mistakes," Denton said.

Jennings was brooding, silent.

"It if helps, I've known Jeffrey Hellman for years. He and I started out in the Barrister's Club together twenty years ago.

We worked together a lot, planning social functions and lining up speakers. Later, we served as officers in the Bar Association." Denton stopped, as if reflecting on years past. "He went through some pretty rough times a couple of years ago when his wife died of cancer, but he's okay. A real good attorney . . . very sharp. I've never known him to do anything underhanded or unethical. I have a lot of respect for him."

"That doesn't mean that the clients he represents are innocent," Jennings said.

"Of course not. But I have more confidence in something Jeffrey tells me than something someone else tells me." Jennings shrugged as Denton continued: "Just keep a clear head and run things by the book. Get me the strongest case you possibly can."

"Madison is fucking guilty, Tim."

Denton's face hardened. "Then let's nail his ass."

CHAPTER
30

CHANDLER FINISHED interviewing ten people: five board members, Michael Murphy, Ed Dolius, and three clients—all in four days' time. He had nearly filled his notepad with solid evidence of Harding's erratic behavior. There were still two weeks before the preliminary hearing.

Chandler had spoken with Denise nightly since arriving in California; after the third day, she began asking when he was going to return home. Noah missed him, and they had agreed to start trying for a second child four months ago. But there always seemed to be a reason why he could not be home; or Denise had to study for a law school exam; or he came down with the flu. His pledge of "next month, I promise" was in jeopardy. This month, everything had gone according to schedule, except for one thing: as the crucial day approached, Chandler was 2,500 miles away.

"I'll try to get as much as possible done over the next day or so and catch a flight back."

"I'm on break from school," Denise said, "so I'm relaxed and I don't have to get to bed so early. Don't screw this up, Ryan. If you're not home in two days, forget it," she said, making her request as clear as AT&T's fiber optics technology would permit.

He wrapped up as much as he could over the course of the next twenty-four hours, bid farewell to Madison and Hellman, and vowed to return as quickly as possible. He hoped to have access to either the physical evidence or Gray's report by then so he could begin his own analysis.

On the six-hour flight home, Chandler made use of his time by organizing and rewriting all of his data into a cohesive plan. He had all the circumstantial evidence he needed against Harding and a relatively good case, with one exception. He could not place her in Madison's car on the night of the murders. In fact, he couldn't place anyone in the car. But even absent direct evidence linking Madison to the act of driving the vehicle, the circumstantial evidence against him was damning: it was his car, no one else's fingerprints were found, the Mercedes had not been reported stolen, there was no sign of forced entry, and he had no alibi.

On the other hand, the homeless person who thought he saw a male driving the car could be impeached without too much effort. In court, a few confusing pictures flashed in front of him and he'd have to admit the driver could easily have been a female with her hair pulled up, wearing a baseball hat. The weakness of his testimony would be laid bare in front of the jury.

Witness aside, he needed to find some way of placing Harding in that car or Madison would be facing a very depressing, uphill battle. *There's got to be something I'm overlooking. I can't stand by and let a good man go down for a violent crime he didn't commit.* With this thought, he closed his eyes to rest.

The next voice he heard was that of the pilot announcing they would be landing at John F. Kennedy International in ten minutes. He straightened his seatback, stretched his neck, and rubbed his eyes. His mouth was dry. Looking out the window, he saw the familiar lights of the Rockaways flickering beneath him. He was home.

Denise and Noah greeted him at the gate. When Noah saw his father deplane, he ran through the crowd of bodies and into his arms. Chandler threw him up into the air as the boy laughed devilishly. He gave his son a big hug and a kiss on the cheek, then handed him a box containing a poseable action figure he had bought on the way to the airport in Sacramento.

"Cool, Dad!" Noah shouted as he struggled to open the box.

Chandler gave Denise a hug with Noah in his arms as they trudged down the aging and outdated 1960s-style terminal toward the baggage concourse to retrieve his lone suitcase.

"I missed you guys," he said.

"I missed you too, Daddy," Noah said, twisting the Action Ranger's arms into a battle pose. "Are you going away again?"

Denise shot a glance at Chandler.

"Well, Daddy's home for a while, but then I'll need to go back to California again."

Denise's smile reversed into a frown.

"Denise, this is a very tough case. Phil is innocent, but he's been framed, and it doesn't look good. I think I know who did it, but I just have to prove it."

"So, to get your attention, I have to get accused of murder and hire you to get me off?"

"By then you'll be an attorney. First get one of your buddies to defend you, then hire me to get you off," Chandler said with a smile.

"This isn't a joke, Ryan."

He sighed, the smile melting from his face. "No . . . no, it's not. I realize it's hard on you, but I don't really have a choice. I can't let Phil go down on this." He looked over at Denise as they arrived at the baggage concourse.

"There's one thing I never told you about—how I got around to coming out of my funk. Maybe it'll help to put things in perspective." They had stopped at the baggage claim area and were waiting for the conveyor belt to start. "One night, a few months after I had to accept a disability retirement from the department, Phil found me on a street corner in downtown Sacramento, a block from the station house. I was blitzed, yelling crazy things at anyone who passed. I was so drunk I didn't even recognize him. He was afraid someone would call the police on me for drunk and disorderly conduct and the press would get all over it. He knew the department would try to distance itself from me to minimize its embarrassment, saying I was retired and no longer a member of the force.

So he put me in the back of his car and drove me to his house, where I stayed for the next two weeks. He hired someone, at his expense, to look after me twenty-four hours a day to make sure I didn't hurt myself or touch any booze. Then he got me an appointment with a shrink he knew."

Chandler retrieved his luggage from the baggage claim conveyor belt, taking care not to strain his back, and they headed off toward the short-term lot across the street.

"So," Denise said, "that's how you started getting therapy."

Chandler nodded. "That's why when this guy calls and tells me he's in trouble, I have to do whatever I can to help him. He saved my life, Denise. I was heading in a bad direction. I would've done it with a gun. God knows I'd thought about it enough in those days right before he found me."

He put his suitcase in the back of their minivan and gave Denise a kiss. "Hopefully I'll have this thing wrapped up in a few more days."

She kissed him back. "I missed you."

"I missed you too. And if you're ever accused of murder," he said with a smile, "you wouldn't have to hire me. I'd work for free."

Fatigued from boredom and stiff from incessant sitting, Chandler started the shower, hoping it would allow him to unwind before going to bed. While he waited for the water to reach a tepid temperature, he walked over to Denise and hugged her tightly, drawing her body close and enveloping it. He gave her a long kiss. She smiled and ran her fingers through his thick light brown hair.

She marveled at how some couples could be away from each other for days at a time when one of them had a job that required frequent trips out of town. Her mind flashed on her life before Chandler, when she worked as a software engineer at a large mainframe company, all-job-and-no-play, the ultimate career woman. No time for men or family. It seemed like a lifetime ago, she told him.

"And when you graduate from law school, you'll enter the rat race again."

"We'll see. It all depends on what I do with the degree. That's why I want to get pregnant now, try to time it so I'm all done by the time I graduate and pass the bar."

Chandler gave her another kiss, told her to hold the thought, and walked into the roomy stall that was decked out with glass-block walls, a tile seat, and massager shower head. Savoring the wet heat against his taut back muscles for a couple of minutes, he then turned around and stood facing the nozzle as the water rained down on his scalp. He leaned against the wall and flexed his tired neck. The warmth was soothing, comforting.

As he adjusted the spray to a beating pulse, he felt a gentle brush against his buttocks, five fingers cupped around each side . . . squeezing lightly at first, then more aggressively. Relaxing into Denise's hold, he felt her breasts press into his back. He turned around and pulled her close.

She placed her arms around his neck, the hot water drumming against his lower back and buttocks. He kissed her, his tongue moving in and out of her warm mouth, exploring and groping and rolling around her tongue, teasing it.

Denise gently pulled on Chandler's neck and moved him around so he was sitting on the tile seat in the corner of the stall. They moved rhythmically, matching the pulsing beat of the water, until both felt the building grasp and sudden release.

As they toweled off, she fell silent.

"What's on your mind?" Chandler asked.

She shook her head, bringing her thoughts back to the present. "Wondering what we just created." Denise wrapped her hair in a towel, turban style, and slipped on her white silk robe. She lay down on the bed, on top of the down comforter, and put her legs up and over a pillow. "I bet it's a girl," she said.

"How can you be so sure it even worked?"

"I know. I can tell."

Chandler pursed his lips and nodded. "Okay, assuming you have some special power to know this, a girl would be fine with me," he said. "But I'd be happy with another boy too."

Denise smiled and told him that if it were up to him, he would have nine boys, enough to field an entire baseball team. He laughed, realizing that she was right.

"But even if we had a girl," he said while towel-drying his hair, "I'd teach her how to play ball, too."

She adjusted the pillow beneath her neck. "Just as long as you let me dress her up, do her hair, take her shopping for clothes . . ."

"Sounds like you're talking about playing with your favorite doll."

"Absolutely." Denise reminded him that he was lucky to have made it home at the right time, or they might well have had to wait another month—a situation that had already caused them enough anxiety.

"It's all water under the bridge now."

"Or sperm in the canal," she said with a laugh.

CHAPTER
31

ONCE MADISON returned from dropping Chandler off at the airport, he received a call from Hellman. He had some bad news, real bad news, and was debating whether or not he should break it to him over the phone.

"Why don't we meet for lunch?" Hellman asked.

"I'm not much in the mood for socializing, Jeffrey."

"This isn't a social lunch."

"Then I'm not in a mood to talk business."

"This is kind of important, Phil."

"If there's something you need to tell me, just say it straight out."

Hellman sighed. Brief pause. "It really would be better if we talked face-to-face."

"Just tell me," Madison insisted. "I'm not in the mood." Another pause. "Okay, let me guess. More bad news."

"Sorry to be the bearer . . ." Hellman started to say, his voice tailing off.

"But . . ."

"But the prosecution has refiled the complaint."

"What the hell does that mean?"

"It means that the charges against you have been modified. For the worse."

"Why'd they modify them?"

"I don't know for sure, but there are rumblings. Like the prosecutor, Denton, is trying to take advantage of a high-profile case to move up the ladder. I've known him for years, and I wouldn't rule it out."

"My luck. I have to get a bloodthirsty prosecutor driven by greed."

"Politics. Driven by politics."

"Same thing." He sighed. "You lawyers—"

"Phil, listen to me. They're bringing more serious charges against you. The first set of charges outlined during the arraignment were those filed by the investigating detectives. The prosecutor has revised them upward."

"What, four to twelve years isn't enough?" He laughed. "What are they asking for now, my firstborn?"

"Phil—"

"No, seriously. How many years of my life do they want, fifteen?"

"Denton has refiled for one count of vehicular manslaughter—which you knew about—and one count of second degree murder. With malice."

"Which means what?"

"Under these circumstances, murder carries a sentence of fifteen years *to life.*"

Madison fell silent. He found the chair behind him and eased into it slowly, trying to absorb all this.

"Now you know why I wanted to do this face-to-face," Hellman said.

Madison cleared his throat. "What did you mean by 'under these circumstances'?"

"Malice means that you acted out of abandonment with a malignant heart."

"What the hell is a malignant heart?"

"It's an antiquated term. But apparently, the medical examiner determined that the second victim, the woman, died of internal hemorrhage. They're claiming that had you stopped after hitting her, being a physician you could have provided emergency medical care that could have kept her alive—and at the very least, you could've called 9-1-1 from your mobile phone and had emergency care there within five minutes. There's a good chance she would've lived."

"You're talking like I did it."

"Oh, come on, Phil. I was speaking figuratively. I know you didn't do it."

Madison sighed, ran his fingers through his hair. "So what does all this mean?"

"It means that we go before the judge again and Denton gets to file the modified charges against you. It's a new arraignment, same as the one before. We'll be in and out in ten minutes."

"Another ten minutes of humiliation."

"It also means that we're now fighting for more than preserving your reputation as a fine surgeon. We're now fighting for your life."

The new arraignment was set for nine in the morning at the Municipal Court building, at the same department in which the original arraignment was held. Judge Barter drew the call again, and sat high on his bench, looking somewhat bored. Hellman disliked Barter, but made every attempt to mask his feelings. Hellman was known for his polite manners: no matter what a judge would say to him or his client, he was always respectful. Firm, but respectful. It was behavior of this sort that earned Hellman some brownie points when the score was close—and criticism from opposing counsel who knew exactly what Hellman was doing, but who were not nearly as adept at pulling it off. When Hellman did it, it sounded genuine; when others did it, it was transparent and contrived, and the judge usually admonished them for it in open court.

"Your Honor," Prosecutor Denton said, "as you know, we have refiled the complaint against the defendant."

"Proceed," Barter said.

Denton arose and tugged on the bottom of his suit coat. "We have determined that circumstances exist which constitute abandonment with a malignant heart, section 830.2 A and B of the Penal Code. There are also grounds for two counts of leaving the scene of an accident."

Barter removed his glasses. "Mr. Hellman, has your client been made aware of this refiling?"

"Yes, sir."

"Does he understand the implications, counselor?"

"Yes, Your Honor, I've explained the situation to him. He's well aware of the possibilities."

The judge looked down at Madison for a moment, then nodded. "Very well."

Denton arose again, tugged on his suit. "Your Honor, the people request that bail be reconsidered in light of the new charges, and be upgraded to one million dollars."

"Again with the million dollars," Madison said under his breath.

Barter glared at him, then turned to Hellman. "Counselor, your response?"

"Your Honor, as I mentioned at the arraignment, Dr. Madison poses no flight risk. He's married with two children, and not likely to skip town on them. Further, he's a respected member of the community and would like nothing more than to clear his name and continue with the practice of medicine. In fact, he has several difficult surgeries scheduled. He wouldn't abandon his patients."

"Your Honor," blurted Denton before Barter could rule, "the people believe that Dr. Madison does indeed pose a flight risk. More so than before, in fact. His wife and children have left him and moved to an undisclosed location. And his practice has been falling steadily—"

"You son of a bitch!" Madison yelled at Denton.

"Your Honor?" Denton shouted, looking back and forth between Barter and Madison.

"Enough is enough," Madison said, his face red, his eyes boring into Denton's. "I don't have to take that—"

"Dr. Madison," Barter said, "I'm not going to tell you again. If you so much as utter a word when not spoken to, I will have you removed from this court. And you should count your blessings that this is not the beginning of your trial wherein I'm the presiding judge."

Hellman kicked him hard in the shoe with his foot. Madison looked up at the judge.

"I will not have these types of disrespectful outbursts in my courtroom. Am I being clear?"

Madison nodded, took a deep breath. "Yes sir. I'm sorry, sir."

"Good. Now, on the matter of bail, I believe that the sum of five hundred thousand dollars previously established is and was sufficient. Any objections, Mr. Hellman?"

"None, Your Honor," Hellman said.

"Mr. Denton?" Barter said. Denton shook his head and the judge appeared satisfied. "Very well." He banged his gavel and tossed the file aside.

Hellman gathered his papers together, then turned to Madison. "Phil—"

"I know, I need to learn to keep my mouth shut."

"I had stronger words, but that's the idea."

"I'm sorry. This whole thing has had its effect on me. Sometimes I can't even believe my own behavior."

"Well, hopefully this 'thing' will go away. Until then, don't help Denton bury you. He's taking notes on you, studying you. That comment about Leeza leaving you had nothing to do with the amount of bail he wanted—he was testing your reaction, to see how you'd handle pressure as a witness should I decide to put you on the stand."

"It's all a game to him, isn't it?"

"I don't think he considers it a game, Phil. But if you want to use that analogy, then just remember this: he's playing to win."

The preliminary hearing was scheduled for five days following the arraignment. When the bailiff called Madison's case, Judge Barter had been sitting behind his bench for three hours and was anxious to break for lunch. Hoping to dispose of the hearing with relative speed, he turned to Timothy Denton and nodded. "Mr. Prosecutor, I assume you have a few witnesses."

"Yes, Your Honor," Denton said. "We call Detective William Jennings."

The doors in back of the courtroom were opened and Jennings appeared. Dressed in his usual wrinkled off-the-rack gray sport coat, he ascended the two steps to the witness

stand and took a seat. After being sworn in, he faced the prosecutor.

"Detective, were you the investigating officer in this case?"

He nodded. "Myself, and Detective Angela Moreno. I was
primary."

"When you arrived on San Domingo Street, what was your
impression?"

"The crime scene had been secured by Officer Sanford and
looked to be in excellent condition. There were two dead bodies, apparently the victims of a hit-and-run accident. After evaluation of the physical evidence by a criminalist, and after
speaking with an eyewitness, it was my impression that a crime
had indeed been committed."

"How many homicides have you investigated?"

"I'm a homicide detective," he said. "Hundreds."

"Do these include hit-and-runs?"

"Yes."

"Thank you, detective," Denton said as he walked back to
his table. "That's all I have."

Hellman arose. "Detective, did you personally examine
the physical evidence yourself?"

"No, I did not."

"Do you have any witnesses that positively identified Dr.
Madison as the driver of the vehicle?"

"No, we do not."

"Did you get a description of the driver of the vehicle from
any witnesses?"

"Yes, we did."

"And what was that description?"

"That of a clean-shaven white male who was wearing a
baseball cap."

"Were there any distinguishing marks on the driver's face,
according to your witness?"

"No."

"What color hair did the witness specify?"

"He didn't specify a hair color."

"Did you ask him what hair color the driver had?"

"Yes I did."

"And what did the witness say?"

Jennings's eyes narrowed slightly as if he didn't like the question. Hellman stood in front of the witness box, waiting for an answer.

"He didn't know."

"So the witness did not see the driver's hair, then."

"No." Hint of frustration in his voice.

"Hmm." Hellman turned and paced a few steps, then spun around to face Jennings, ten feet away. He placed a hand on his chin, as if he were genuinely trying to figure this out while he stood there. Although there was no jury present, Hellman could not help himself, always the showman. "Were there any markings or facial features that led the witness to conclude that it was a male and not a female that was driving?"

"Not to my knowledge."

"Did your witness estimate how tall the driver was, or how much he might have weighed?"

"No. He didn't see him get out of the car."

"What time of day did this incident occur?"

"Approximately eleven-thirty P.M."

"And is there any special lighting other than normal streetlights, detective?"

"No."

Hellman nodded. "So aside from a clean-shaven white individual, your suspect could be male or female, with blond, brown, or gray hair. She could've been a five-foot-tall secretary or a six-foot-six football player. Is that right, detective?"

Jennings glared at Hellman.

"Detective, please answer my question."

"Yes."

"So, would it be fair to say that your witness really did not get a good look at the driver?"

Jennings was clenching his jaw. "Yeah, I guess that would be fair to say."

"You *guess,* or *it is* fair to say?" Hellman pressed.

"It is."

"Thank you, detective. Nothing further."

"Redirect, Your Honor." This from Denton, who was standing.

"Mr. Denton," Barter said.

"Detective, what evidence do you have that led you to suspect and later arrest Phillip Madison?"

"We had two witnesses identify the vehicle as a Mercedes, and we got a partial plate that we ran through DMV and came up with Phillip Madison's car. We obtained a search warrant and proceeded to his residence, where the car was parked in his garage. There was damage to the front end, clothing fibers on the grille and windshield wiper, and blood spatter on the underside of the fender area. Dr. Madison was the legally registered owner of the vehicle. There was no one else at home of driving age, he had not lent the car to anyone, and there was no report of the car having been stolen. And he had no alibi for the reported time of the murders."

"Thank you, detective." Denton turned on his heels and headed back to his seat, flashing a slight smirk at Hellman, who absorbed it like a gentleman.

"Your Honor," Hellman said, "the defense moves for immediate dismissal of the charges due to insufficient evidence."

Barter frowned. "Denied, counsel. The state has sustained their burden."

Madison leaned toward Hellman's ear. "If you ask me, I think all the burden's on me."

The thirty-minute preliminary hearing resulted in the filing of an Information, which meant that the judge felt there was probable cause to believe that the defendant had committed the crime.

"It's nothing to be overly concerned about, Phil. All the prosecution needed to show was probable cause that a crime had been committed, and that most likely you're the one who committed it. It was a slam dunk as far as Denton was concerned. This went exactly as I'd expected it would."

Madison shrugged. "You're the expert. Hell, given the evidence, I probably would've reached the same conclusion."

He drove home and found a couple of messages on his machine. There was one message from the gardener, informing Madison that he was overdue on last month's bill. Another message from a salesperson hawking vinyl siding. The last message was from Catherine Parker. She left only her name and number.

Madison sat down in his leather easy chair, took the cordless phone in hand, and smiled. Catherine Parker. It had been years since he had heard that name—and for good reason. To say that nothing good ever came out of his relationship with her was not entirely fair . . . but it was also not far from the truth. He dialed the number, more out of curiosity than anything else. Redheaded Catherine Parker.

"Energy Data Systems," said the voice at the other end of the phone.

"Catherine Parker please," Madison said.

A few seconds passed. "This is Catherine," he heard, the same sultry and seductive undertones permeating her voice.

"Catherine, Phil Madison."

"Well, well, well. Phil Madison. You obviously got my message."

"What prompted you to call, after all these years?"

"I've been following your story in the paper. It's quite an ordeal, huh."

An ordeal? "Yeah, it's been tough. But, needless to say, I'm innocent, and my attorney and I are working hard to prove it. Jeffrey—Jeffrey Hellman's my attorney."

"How is Jeffrey?"

"Jeffrey is . . . Jeffrey. Fine. He's doing fine."

"Are you free for dinner sometime this week?"

He was taken aback by how forward she was. But that was Catherine. "When?"

"How about tomorrow."

"Tomorrow? Sure, I guess that'd be okay." There was nothing more pressing that he needed to do. And he always did have a difficult time turning her down.

"Great. I'm looking forward to it," she said, her sultry voice stimulating memories of fifteen years ago . . . a time with fewer complications, fewer restrictions, more passion.

They set the time and place. He would meet her in Vallejo, forty-five minutes away. The drive would do him good; give him time to think about happier times. *Why shouldn't I go? I could use some female company.*

Then again, when it came to Catherine, he could rationalize anything.

CHAPTER
3 2

THE MINUTE Madison laid eyes on Catherine, he instantly felt fifteen years younger. They spent the first part of dinner laughing, hard at times, at some of the things they did when he was just finishing up his residency at the University of California, San Francisco and she was in her second year as an associate at an up-and-coming law firm in the city.

"Where have those years gone?" she asked him.

"Gone, Catherine, they're gone," he said with regret in his voice, noticing that her left ring finger was bare.

"How are things with your wife?" she asked. "The paper reported that she left you."

"You read that? In the newspaper?"

She nodded. "The *Vallejo Times*. A page three story."

The irritation was evident on his face.

"You know the press," she said. "They don't leave any stone unturned."

"Yeah, I guess my personal life is now public domain. Get accused of a crime and lose everything dear to you. Even your privacy. I stopped reading the paper weeks ago."

"I'm sorry."

"Yeah, well, Leeza and I are separated. I don't know if it's temporary or permanent, but I do know one thing—it's hell."

"Such an ordeal."

There's that word again. Ordeal. Fuck the ordeal shit. It's hell. I said HELL. "Why don't we talk about something else. How about your life? Fill me in."

"Well," Catherine said, "you remember Tom?"

Madison's face hardened. He remembered Tom. It had taken Madison months to get over the bitterness before he was able to feel any pain . . . the hollow pain of a lost love.

"Tom was good for me at the time, Phil."

"He stole you right from under my nose. Waved big bucks and jewelry in your face, and off you went. You left me in a heartbeat. You'll excuse me if I didn't think he was so good."

"He wasn't good for *you,* that's for sure. For *me,* well, that's another story."

Madison smiled. "Maybe I'm being too hard on him. He was good for me. If it weren't for him, you and I would've gotten married."

"Oh, and that would have been bad?"

"That's not what I meant. If he hadn't intervened, I wouldn't have met Leeza."

"I guess the jury's still out on that one, huh?"

He gave her a stinging look.

"I'm sorry. I didn't mean that." She sighed. "Guess I've got some leftover bitterness too."

"Ah, it's all right," he said, waving a hand. "We did have a good thing, though. I thought with all my heart that we were going to be together for all eternity."

"So did I. Until Tom came along. That changed everything." The waitress came over to fill her glass with more iced tea. "You weren't very accessible. That was part of the problem. I know you want to think it was the money, but that was only part of it. A big part of it," she said, smiling, "but it wasn't the whole story."

"I was finishing up my residency, Catherine, what was I supposed to do?"

"I don't want to argue about it now. I'm just saying that I hardly saw you, and we were tight financially. When a prince dressed in an Armani suit comes along and flashes the good life in your face, you jump at it. It was like falling in love all over again. I got taken in."

"More like taken."

"Well, that's actually truer than not."

"Why? What happened?"

She gave a mock laugh. "Too much of a good thing. Tom continued to play the market. Did real well at it, too. But I kept telling him we should stop trading and just leave the stocks alone for the long term, or at least put some of the money into something safer, like a house." She combed her hair back with her fingers, out of her eyes. "But he didn't listen. He made a few bad decisions and lost it all. And I mean all. Even the money I had put away in a CD from the bonus I'd gotten for making partner. It was like he'd become a gambler, betting on the stock market. The more he lost, the riskier the stocks were that he picked, hoping to catch up by hitting it big."

"I'm sorry," he said.

"I was married to Tom for three years. It ended in disaster. We wound up suing each other, and the attorneys ended up with more than either of us." She took a swig of wine. "It got so messy that I had to take time off the job. That kind of broke my partnership agreement, so they bought me out. I lost everything. Had to start over, with my own office. That failed, and now I'm in-house counsel for Energy Data Systems. It's never quite been the same. I haven't enjoyed law ever since. Kind of resent it, actually."

"That's sad. You used to love it." *Now I'm doing it. Sad? Where the hell did that come from?*

"Well, it's been lonely." She smiled at him, the toothy smile that used to grab him by the testicles and hold him, mesmerized. The years had been good to her. The red hair was redder than he remembered. It fell about her shoulders and shimmered in the overhead spotlights of the private table she had reserved for them. He had to unglue his eyes from her hair. *What was she saying?*

". . . the paper said you're very prominent in your field."

He shrugged. "It's hard to talk about yourself."

"It said that you're the top orthopedic surgeon in northern California." She tilted her head slightly, well-manicured red-painted nails fingering the rim of her wineglass.

He smiled, consciously aware of what her fingers were doing. His accomplishments had always turned her on. He had forgotten about that. She played; he watched. He had to break the spell. "Want to see pictures of my boys?"

"Sure," she said, dropping her hand from the glass.

He pulled out his wallet and flipped through the photos of Leeza, coming to rest on the pictures of Elliott and Jonah. She looked them over.

"They're gorgeous," she finally said.

He had forgotten how much she had wanted to have children.

"I guess I should've adopted a child."

"It's not too late."

"I suppose. But I'd prefer to have my own. It's kind of hard when you don't have any prospects. Takes two."

He caught her looking at him. "I've got enough problems right now, Catherine, without fathering your child."

"You could supply the sperm. I could draw something up that would remove all responsibility for you."

"Is that what this is all about?"

"All about?"

"This dinner."

"No. I was genuinely interested in seeing you. I just thought that while we were on the topic . . ."

"Well, it just wouldn't work out."

"I understand," she said, taking a bite of her veal.

He changed the subject, asking her about old friends with whom she was still in contact. They finished their meal and left the restaurant. He walked her to her car, their breath fogging the cold winter air.

"Why don't you come back to the house?"

He looked into her warm hazel eyes and felt the allure of her invitation.

"I'll make some coffee and we'll have some dessert, relive old times."

"Catherine . . . reliving old times with you means ending up in the kitchen, all right. On top of the table."

"And what's wrong with that? It used to be fun."

"I'm married. A couple of months ago, I was happily married. If I'm to hold out any hope of salvaging it, the last thing

that would help would be sleeping around with an old girlfriend. Think what the papers would say about *that.*"

"You always were the most honorable man I've ever
known, Phil."

"Tell it to the jury."

She gave him a kiss on the cheek. "I'd be glad to, if I
thought it would help."

He opened her door for her. She sat down, sinking into the
bucket seat of the well-maintained 1986 280ZX, apparently
one of the few possessions left over from her law partner
days.

"We had a good thing once. If things don't work out with
Leeza, there *is* a future here for you, Phil. Remember that."

"That's the nicest thing anyone has said to me in
months."

He closed her door, gave her a wave, and trudged back to
his car, hands thrust into his jacket pockets. It was indeed
cold out, but his heart had just been thoroughly warmed.

CHAPTER
33

"DO YOU REMEMBER Catherine Parker?" Madison asked while Hellman was trying to read his message slips. The mention of the name from the past stopped his gaze in mid-sentence.

"Do I remember Catherine Parker? That's like asking me if I like a tender filet mignon."

"She was something, huh?" Madison said.

"She represented all the things our mothers told us to watch out for. She also represented the wildest times of our lives."

"Brings back memories."

"Yeah, of competing with each other on virtually everything. Women, grades, basketball . . ." Hellman was staring up at the ceiling at nothing in particular, his feet on the desk, the messages he was so intently studying a moment ago stacked to the left of his feet.

"And I won the woman," Madison said, needling Hellman.

"Temporarily," he said. "Until somebody with more money came along."

"There was more to her than that," he said, placing his own feet up on Hellman's desk. "She had her faults, but she had a good heart."

"What made you suddenly think of her?"

"I had dinner with her last night."

"You did what?" Hellman asked, yanking his feet off the desk and sitting straight up.

"I had dinner with her."

"Your wife's left you and you think the way to coax her

back is by having dinner with an old flame who you almost married? An old flame who was hotter than—"

"Jeffrey, nothing happened."

"Phil, what am I gonna do with you? You're well-meaning but you seem to be looking for ways to bury yourself."

"Look, I don't regret meeting with her. She made me feel good about myself for the first time in a long time. Is that so bad?"

"She wants to get in your pants. She wants to crawl inside your chest and capture your heart again. Fifteen years ago she made the mistake of her life and now she sees an opening. She's swooping down for the kill."

"You're reading it all wrong."

"Am I?" Hellman asked.

"Yes."

"And what do you base that on?"

Madison paused. "Because you just are."

"Oh, okay, the old 'I-just-know-it's-true-but-I-really-don't-have-any-proof' defense."

"Must you always look at things from a legal perspective?"

"I can't help it. I live and breathe the law." He sighed. "Let me guess . . . she's divorced from that rich guy. What was his name? Todd?"

"Tom. Yes, they're divorced."

"Gee, that's a surprise."

There was silence for a moment. "She wanted to use my sperm to impregnate her."

"You're kidding, right? No, you're serious. With Catherine, I'd believe just about anything."

"I turned her down, don't worry," Madison said.

"I'm not the one who has to worry."

"Jeffrey, what does it matter? I had dinner with an old friend. She made a proposition and I turned her down. So what?"

"So I know how much your family means to you and right now you don't need stirred-up memories of Catherine the vamp floating around in your sea of hormones."

"Just because you lost out on her doesn't mean—"

"Oh, come on, Phil. I put that behind me many years ago. I got over her and moved on with my life."

"And you're saying I didn't?"

"No, I believe you did. Sort of. You more or less placed your feelings in suspended animation. She's reawakened them."

"I don't need this bullshit right now."

"Right now is exactly when you need it."

Madison shook his head, stood up, and walked toward Hellman's eighteenth-floor window that looked out over downtown Sacramento. "But I didn't do anything. We just had dinner. Proposition aside, she seemed very genuine."

"She may have been genuine. She may've just been trying to be a friend at a time when you need one. But how many years has it been since you've spoken to her? Is that the mark of a true friend?"

Madison did not say anything.

"I know you better than anyone else in this world. At least as well as Leeza knows you—but at the moment, her view's been influenced by external forces. You're only human . . . and if you have this trump card—Catherine the vamp—in your back pocket, then subconsciously you may not try as hard to get Leeza back." More silence. "Putting your emotions aside for the moment, if you can honestly tell me that that's not a possibility, then I'll leave you alone."

"Okay, it's possible."

"Don't talk to her again. Focus on getting Leeza back. Appreciate her, Phil. I don't have that luxury. I lost Hannah. Don't let that happen to you."

Madison turned and faced Hellman. "I told Catherine I still held out hope of getting Leeza back, and I spent the rest of the night alone."

"Well, that's a good first step. What else are you going to do?"

"Try to get Leeza to come home."

Hellman nodded. "Are you okay on this?"

"Yeah, I'm okay," Madison said.

"Good. I've got to return all these messages," Hellman said, picking up his stack of slips. "I'll call you later."

Madison left Hellman's office. Alone in the elevator, he pulled out his wallet and looked at a picture of Leeza and the kids he had taken at Marine World before his life began to fall apart. A vivid reminder of what he had waiting for him, of what he had to lose. He rested his head against the elevator wall and took a deep breath. "Please come home," he whispered.

CHAPTER
34

IT WAS RAINY, 10:30 at night with a steady wind swirling around and rapping against the side of his house. Madison had spoken with Chandler a couple of hours ago. He was going to be returning to Sacramento in five days.

Madison had built a fire and was sitting in front of it, reminiscing about the first time he and Leeza had lit the fireplace after the house had been built. There were no kids and they had the evening to themselves. George Winston's gentle piano solos tinkled from the CD player. As they sipped Chardonnay and kissed, he remembered feeling the drawing heat of the fire warming the skin on his neck. They made love right there, on the carpet in front of the fireplace, Leeza's moans drowning out the crackles and pops of the burning pine cones.

As he lay there now, sipping Chardonnay and reliving that night with Leeza, he marveled at how easy life had been. Not a worry in the world. A bright future lay ahead of them, two beautiful children merely one detail in the grand plan of plans.

A knock at the door broke his daydream; he shook his head and shuffled his thoughts back to reality. As he started toward the door, he thought his prayers had been answered: *Leeza.*

His heart beating faster than he could walk, he opened the door and saw, dripping wet in the rain, Catherine. *Catherine the vamp.* He could hear Jeffrey's voice loud and clear in his head. It must have shown on his face.

He stood there, the door open; she stood there, dripping wet.

"I thought you'd be glad to see me," she said.

"I . . . didn't expect you to be at the door."

"Were you expecting someone else?" she asked.

He hesitated, looked down at his torn jeans and old flannel shirt. "No."

She shivered. "Can I come in? It's freezing out here."

"Oh. Sure," he said, wishing he could instead tell her to get back in her car and leave, to stay the hell away from him.

Catherine walked into the marble entryway and hung her coat on a decorative rack against the wall. "I had a good time last night," she said. "I don't get up this way that often, but I was in town for a deposition that was supposed to last a couple of hours. It went six. I grabbed some fast food and then thought I'd drop by on my way out of town to say hi."

"How did you get my home address?"

She smiled. Pearly white teeth. "Is that important?"

"Well, as a matter of fact, it is. I don't give it out."

"Let's just say I have a friend at the DMV who owes me. Big."

"That's illegal."

"This person isn't concerned with legalities. He's more interested in a date." She smiled again, but he diverted his gaze away from her face. She was dressed in a suit. Form-fitting, yet professional. She was probably telling the truth. But he didn't want to see her. Not now. Not with the fire burning in the living room, the alcohol infecting his thoughts.

She ventured toward the fireplace, stopped in front of it, and placed her hands out to warm them. Madison walked over next to her and faced the fire. He stood there, watching the flames dance, feeling guilty having her in his house. In Leeza's house.

"Look, Catherine," he started to say, just before she planted a hard, passionate kiss on his lips. He leaned back, but she pushed farther forward into him; they fell backward into the large, plush loveseat that sat perpendicular to the fireplace. She was on top of him, kissing him. He wasn't resisting as hard as he should have, allowing her tongue to penetrate his mouth, while her hand slid down between his legs. Felt the zipper open. Pressure against his—

"Catherine," he mumbled, her mouth bobbing up and down as he tried to speak.

She lifted her head up; he moved his shoulders a bit to gain some room. "I just can't do this. It's not that I don't find you attractive," he said, feeling passion starting to build again at the mere focus of his attention on her hair. Her scent. *That scent.* "Quite the opposite. I want to rip your clothes off—"

"Then do it. Don't—"

"No—" he managed to say before she planted another passionate kiss on his lips. The wine. Her soft lips. He let them linger on his for a moment. Shook his head, trying to free his mouth to speak. "I can't. I'm married. I'm—"

"Hoping that Leeza will come home."

He nodded. She sighed, hung her head. Climbed off him, straightened her suit, brushed back her hair with her hands.

"She could walk through that door any minute."

"I know that that's what you'd like to believe."

"It's what I have to believe. Or I wouldn't be able to face each day."

"I understand," she said, folding her arms on her chest and walking over to the fire. "I don't like it, but I understand."

He arose from the couch, zipped his pants. "If this were another time . . ." he started to say, and stopped. "I'm sorry."

She lightly stroked his cheek with the back of her hand and walked over toward the entryway. Picking her coat off the rack, she walked out of the house, the rapid clickety-clack of her spiked heels against the marble floor echoing in his mind, matching the rhythm of his heartbeat.

CHAPTER
35

EXCEPT FOR THE HUM of the refrigerator, all was quiet in the kitchen of Leeza's sister's house. The kids had gone to the zoo with their aunt, leaving Leeza alone for some time to think. She sat, staring at a piece of paper with a phone number scribbled across it. Three times she had picked up the phone to call, more out of curiosity than anger. A couple of days ago, when she retrieved the messages off her phone machine at home, she was unnerved by one from Catherine Parker, a woman out of Phil's past whom he had not spoken to in nearly fifteen years. For a long time, it was a name and only a name, until she caught a glimpse of some pictures that Jeffrey had placed in an old shoebox.

Aside from the pictures, she vaguely remembered the stories that Jeffrey and Phil used to tell when talking of what fierce competitors they had been in their school days. And from what she could recall, Catherine was considered the ultimate prize. But neither of them had brought her up in at least a decade, at least as far as she knew.

Now here was a message on her answering machine. Why had she called? What did she want? She couldn't possibly know that she had left Phil. Unless he had called her first. No, this was not that kind of message. This was *a-person-from-the-past-trying-to-reestablish-contact* type of message. With *a hi-remember-me* flavor.

Leeza picked up the phone for the fourth time. Punched in the numbers. Felt nauseated, dirty. She spoke to the Energy Data Systems receptionist and was placed on hold.

A moment later, someone picked up the line. "This is Catherine."

"Yes, hello, this is Leeza Madison, and you left a message on my answering machine."

"A message . . . oh, that," Catherine said, playing it out just a bit. "It's already been returned."

"It was. Oh," Leeza said, unsure of what to say next. "By my husband?"

"Is Phillip Madison your husband?"

"Yes."

"That's who returned the call."

"Do I know you?" Leeza asked, playing dumb, trying to prolong the conversation.

"We've never met. I'm . . . an old friend of Phil's. I hadn't spoken to him in years and I was going to be in Sacramento, so I thought he and I could get together."

Get together, she replayed in her head. *She got together with Phil.* "Oh. Well, as long as Phil returned your call . . ." She was beginning to feel awkward, realizing that she never should have called. It was a mistake. There was nothing to gain here. "I'm sorry to have bothered you."

"Leeza, wait. Don't hang up." She paused for a second, then said, "I think you're a very lucky woman."

Leeza did not reply.

"I don't mean to meddle in your personal business," Catherine said, "but I feel that I have to tell you something. Woman to woman."

Oh, here it comes. Her heart sank; she felt weak. *She slept with him. That bast—*

"Your husband's very loyal to you. He loves you a great deal."

"What do you mean? How do you—"

"I had dinner with him a couple of nights ago. I'd read in the paper that you'd left him. The press catches everything." She paused; there was no response from Leeza. "Anyway, I don't know if you're aware, but Phil and I almost got married fifteen years ago. I left him for another man who turned out to be a shadow of the man Phil was—I mean, is. I have to admit that I wanted him back. And I tried my best—I put everything out on the table. But he wasn't there for the taking, Leeza. Turned me down. I pushed, he retreated. Said that you were too important to him."

Leeza was still silent. Another deafening second passed.

"Leeza, are you still there?"

She had not thought of all the things that could be happening to Phil while she was gone. He'd had dinner with an old girlfriend and she hadn't even known. Had she been too quick to rush to judgment?

"Leeza?"

She cleared her throat. "Yes. Yes, I'm still here. Sorry. This has just caught me a little off guard."

"Nothing happened between us. He wouldn't allow it—not that I didn't give it the old college try . . ."

"Why are you telling me all this?"

"That's a fair question, I guess." She paused. "I don't know what happened between the two of you, but if it was so terrible that you could never be comfortable with him again, then end your relationship with him. Make it clear and let him get on with his life. Part of my motive is selfishness: if you make your separation official, it enables me to move in. Sorry to be so blunt, but I've had a miserable fifteen years. I made a bad decision and although I've tried to live with it and move on, I now see an opportunity to make right what's been so wrong."

"And that's it?"

"Well, I care a great deal for Phil. He's a special person. He'd do anything for those he loves. I don't want to see him hurting so much. If my telling you this brings you two back together, then so be it. I hurt him very much a long time ago. This would be my way of making up for it."

"I don't know what to say, Catherine. I appreciate your candor."

"Consider your situation very carefully, Leeza. Because I'll be in the background waiting."

Leeza thanked her, hung up. She felt uneasy at the thought that this woman had made a pass at Phil—and he'd had dinner with her! What was he thinking? Anger mixed with guilt as her emotions swung back and forth like a pendulum.

What a strange, unnerving conversation.

CHAPTER
36

CHANDLER ARRIVED on the 8 P.M. flight, exhausted. Denise had worn him out while he was in town, making sure to cover the days when she was ovulating. Noah, glad to see his father, had him running around on the weekends through parks, bowling alleys, and toy stores. Chandler even had the courage to return to work, weathering a bluster of Hennessy's threats and obscenities. Hennessy became particularly hot when he first told him he was going back to California for a few days to finish his work on the Madison case.

"You've only been back two weeks and you expect me to let you go again? You're not God, you know! You're replaceable!"

"Then replace me," Chandler said, turning and heading for the door. "This goes beyond employment, chief. I owe this man big. I'll be back in a few days, I promise."

"Don't you walk out of here, Chandler!" Hennessy shouted as the door closed.

Chandler hurried off down the hallway before Hennessy came after him hurling pointed objects.

Five days later, Madison picked Chandler up at Sacramento International and briefly filled him in on the episode with Catherine. He told Chandler he didn't think it had any great significance to his case, but he wanted to make sure he knew everything that had transpired.

Chandler was livid when he heard that the district attorney had refiled the charges. He knew instantly that it was a political move, a fact that Hellman and Madison had already gathered. But whatever the motivation, it did not matter. The charges were there and had to be dealt with.

Chandler thought Madison could use some positive news, so he told him that he had gathered some interesting material on Harding before leaving for New York.

"You spoke to everyone on the list I gave you?"

"And more. I knew the people on the list you gave me would lead me to others. I may have struck pay dirt on one of them. He sounded particularly interesting, but I couldn't meet him before I flew out. I called him yesterday and made an appointment for tomorrow. I feel real good about this one."

"What have you got?"

"I'll let you know all the details once I meet with him. I don't want to get your hopes up."

They arrived home at nearly nine o'clock. Madison pulled the car in front of the house to unload Chandler's suitcase. As he placed his key in the door, it swung open.

"Surprise!" Elliott shouted.

"Daddy, Daddy!" Jonah said as they both huddled around him.

"What are you guys doing here?" Madison asked, a broad smile spreading across his face.

"Decided we're stronger as a family if we're all together," Leeza said, walking into the hallway behind them. "Ryan," she said. "It's been awhile."

Chandler stepped around the boys and gave Leeza a hug. "Welcome home."

"Look what I made," Elliott said. It was a multicolored drawing of something that looked like monsters perched on a hill. It was, the boy explained, a crude rendition of everyone in the family standing on the front lawn.

"I've missed you guys so much," Madison said, squeezing the boys and giving Leeza a kiss on the cheek.

"I'll just get this stuff up to the guest room," Chandler said tactfully, giving them a chance to spend some much-needed time together.

* * * *

Madison sat on the edge of his four-poster bed, watching Leeza unpack a few things. "I missed you so much, hon," he told her.

She stopped unpacking and walked over to sit down next to him. She ran her fingers through his hair and looked into his eyes. "I missed you too," was all she said. He sensed she wanted to say more, but he realized it was probably too soon.

He took her hand and kissed it, then drew her close and hugged her. She pulled up on his shirt, exposing his skin, then ran her fingers across his back. She let her hands slide around to the front of his pants, where she unbuckled the belt and pulled the zipper down. She kissed him once on the lips, and then knelt at the foot of the bed. He lay back, forgetting for the moment what the future held . . . the uphill battle for his life.

As they lay in bed, Leeza cuddled up to him under the warm and fluffy down comforter. She must have felt the tension in his body, because she suddenly lifted her head and studied his face.

"What's the matter?" he asked.

"Something's bothering you," she said. "I can tell."

"It felt good to forget about things for a while," he said. "But the problem is, it's like a vacation. Once it's over, all of your problems are still there."

She placed her head on his chest. "We'll get through this, I promise."

"The last few days I've found myself obsessing about prison. There was this story Jeffrey told me awhile back. A dentist was convicted of raping and killing a patient while she was under anesthesia. They threw him in a maximum security prison, and the other inmates used his rectum as if it were a hole in a dam that needed continuous plugging." He looked down at her. "The guards didn't do anything to stop it. His lawyer tried to get him transferred twice, but it fell on deaf ears.

"A couple of years later," he continued, "DNA testing found its way into the courts. They tested the dried semen they'd found on the woman—and it didn't match. They realized they'd made a mistake, that it probably had happened just like the dentist had claimed: someone came into his office, knocked him out, and raped that patient. He was innocent. They tried to get the evidence admitted so that he could be released from prison. But the day that the judge had ruled the new evidence admissible, they found his body in the corner of the showers. He'd been beaten so badly that his face was barely recognizable. His skull had been crushed."

He looked down at Leeza's face as it rested on his chest, rising and falling with his respiration. She lay still. "I forgot about that story until I read about a similar case a few days ago."

She began to rub his stomach. "You can't think about those things, honey. You're innocent, and you have to believe in yourself, that justice will prevail and they'll dismiss these charges. Or that the jury will see right through their case and find you not guilty."

He sighed heavily. "It's a scary thought. Leaving your fate up to twelve people who don't know you. Would you trust your life to twelve people you never met if it weren't in the context of a trial?" He paused, but not long enough for Leeza to answer. "Of course not. Who in their right mind would even consider doing such a thing?"

"As flawed as our legal system is at times, at least it gives you a chance to prove your innocence. To stand up and present evidence in support of yourself."

He lay there, taking in what she was saying, but not responding. As stimulated as he was only a few moments ago while making love, his body was now numb.

"Right now," she said, stroking his face, "you've put your fate in the hands of two people you trust, who know you very well. Jeffrey and Ryan will pull you out of this mess somehow. I have faith in them."

CHAPTER
3 7

CHANDLER WAS UP at six, planning his day. His first appointment was at eight o'clock, with Mark Stanton of Stanton Management Consultants, Inc. Brittany Harding had been an employee of Stanton's two years ago, and he had told Chandler that he would be willing to discuss his former employee provided it was kept confidential. Chandler met him in the large, plush downtown office that overlooked the snaking Sacramento River.

Stanton was a tall man at six foot five, with chiseled facial features and jet black hair. The kind of good looks that exude confidence and success. He greeted Chandler with a smile and a firm handshake. Plaques of accomplishments and achievements lined one of the walls adjacent to his large maple desk.

Chandler slipped into one of the plush leather chairs and displayed all forms of his law enforcement identification, past and present, for Mark Stanton to review. He scanned each one of them and handed them back to Chandler. "It all appears to be in order," he said. "What can I do for you?"

"As I told you the other day, I'm looking for information regarding Brittany Harding."

"You said something about Miss Harding being involved in a crime your friend's been accused of."

"That's right."

"Well, it wouldn't surprise me," Stanton said, leaning back in his large chair. "That woman was nothing but trouble for me from the day I hired her."

"How so?"

"Look, can we cut to the heart of the matter? I have an appointment in fifteen minutes," he said, checking his gold watch, "and I believe I know what information you're after."

Chandler raised his eyebrows. He didn't think it would be this easy. "Let's hear it."

"Two months after Harding was hired, I was having some difficulty collecting from a rather large account of mine. At the time, this account was sixty percent of my income, so it was wreaking havoc with the bottom line. I started taking measures to protect my company's solvency, which involved pay cuts, doing away with overtime for a couple of account managers, and the elimination of one of my support staff positions—the one Harding happened to hold. The day before I was going to terminate her, she informed me that it would be a mistake if I let her go. I took it to mean that she thought she was a valuable employee, and that laying her off would be a loss to the company. I didn't see it as a threat. I explained to her that it wasn't really my choice, that I needed to make some difficult decisions." He raised an eyebrow. "The next morning, I had papers on my desk naming me in a lawsuit that had been filed, accusing me of sexual harassment. She claimed that I called her into my office and told her that if she wanted to keep her job, she'd have to perform certain . . . activities that went beyond her job description. I then supposedly began to fondle her breasts. She said that she refused my advances, and as a result, was fired."

"Let me guess that it didn't end there," Chandler said, pulling his pad out to take notes.

"No, it didn't." Stanton leaned forward in his seat, rested his forearms on his desk. "Not by a long shot. I got a call from her attorney, who was considering a civil suit against me. Wanted fifty thousand dollars to make it all go away."

"And you paid it?" Chandler asked.

"Wouldn't you have? Here I was, fighting to keep my company afloat . . . the last thing I needed was a groundless civil suit that would've smeared my name across the papers. She'd once told me a friend of hers was a reporter with the *Herald*, who I'm sure would've jumped at a juicy story for the front page of the business section: *Imposing, dominant male president and CEO fondled the breasts of his attractive staff person while she cowered in his shadow, fearful for her life . . . "* He waved a hand through the air. "I had too much to lose and nothing to gain by fighting it. It would've been a massive smear campaign. Even if I was found not guilty, would you hire a management consultant who himself was charged with sexual harassment?" He shook his head, as if he were reliving the distasteful choice that had to be made at the time. "There were no viable options. I had to pay her the money."

"Do you remember the name of her attorney?" Chandler asked, hoping he could solidify the pattern of behavior that appeared to be forming.

"Movis Ehrhardt. Can't forget a name like that."

Chandler smiled.

Stanton waited for Chandler's next question, which did not materialize. He looked down at his watch. "Have I been of assistance, Mr. Chandler?"

"Definitely. Mind if I give you a buzz if I think of anything else?" Chandler asked.

"Sure, just as long as you keep our conversations confidential."

"Would you be willing to testify as to what you told me today?"

He folded his hands and gazed down at the desk in front of him. "I need to discuss that with my attorney," he said, "but my inclination is *no*. I'm sorry, but the very reason for spending the money was to put this incident behind me, and to keep this garbage out of the papers."

"Please talk to your attorney. You've been there, you know what Brittany Harding's capable of. Your testimony could make a huge difference for my client." He stood and they shook hands.

"I'll be in touch," Stanton said.

CHAPTER
38

FOLLOWING HIS CONVERSATION with Leeza, Madison felt that he should make the most of his time together with his family. With so few patients to be seen, on a virtual vacation that could turn out to be permanent, he involved himself in every aspect of the children's activities. Each time he would catch a phrase that Elliott would come up with, or observe the look of excitement in Jonah's eyes with the discovery of something new, the horrifying thought that he might not get to see them grow up invaded his emotions and brought an instant choking sensation to his chest. *Fifteen to life,* he kept hearing in his head. The stakes were high . . . higher than he had prepared himself for: two to six was bad enough. But *life?* A gulp of air would help relieve the pressure in his chest, but it would be only a temporary fix.

However, when Chandler informed him of the information he had obtained from Stanton this morning, all of their spirits appeared to be buoyed. As they sat around the table preparing to eat their Subway sandwiches, Chandler explained to them how this could fit into the trial and Hellman's planned defense of "someone else did it." More importantly, they knew who that someone else was. The more they dug, Chandler was saying, the greater the likelihood that they would find something of use.

Having been given the day off from his factory job due to scheduled maintenance on the equipment, Ricky was invited over to the Madisons' for lunch. "Thanks for calling him," Madison told Leeza.

"I just figured with all that's been going on, you haven't seen him in weeks."

"I feel awful. I shouldn't have let that happen. My parents said he was angry with me for neglecting him."

"You had a lot of stuff on your plate, Phil. I explained that to him yesterday when I called. At least he's here with us now. Look at him," she said, motioning to Ricky running around the backyard with Scalpel and the boys. "He's having a ball."

Ricky's thick-tongued speech was difficult to interpret at times. He often became frustrated when he could not adequately communicate, and due to his difficulty expressing his true feelings, he would yell, throw something against the wall, or cry, depending on how frustrated he became at the time.

After Leeza called everyone to the kitchen table, they unwrapped their sandwiches. Ricky took a swig of his soda, leaving a film of brown foam on his face. He wiped it away with his shirt sleeve. "Want th'ome?" he said, offering his drink to Chandler.

Elliott jumped out of his seat. "No, Uncle Ricky! Mom says you're not supposed to share your drink. It's got germs, right, Mom?"

"That's right, Elliott." Leeza turned to Ricky. "That was nice of you to offer, but I'll get Ryan a can of his own." As she brought a plate of pickles and Chandler's soda over to the table, she asked, "Do you think we'll have enough evidence to get Phil off?"

Chandler popped open his Coke. "All we need is enough to create reasonable doubt. As long as there's a hint of doubt in the jury's minds, they're not supposed to convict him."

"What are our chances?" Leeza asked.

"That's really a question best answered by Jeffrey. But I think we're on a roll." He picked up his sandwich and held it a couple of inches from his mouth, preparing to take a bite. "I just wish I had stronger evidence linking Harding to the crime. If I could only place her in the car somehow." He took a huge bite of his pastrami hero.

"But there weren't any fingerprints in the car except Phil's, right?" Leeza asked.

Chandler nodded while his jaw swayed to and fro, trying to negotiate the enormous bite he had placed in his mouth.

Leeza brought a few more napkins over to the table. "So if her fingerprints weren't there, how else do we place her in the car?"

"Finding something belonging to her would certainly help," Madison said.

"How about strands of hair," Leeza asked. "Did they find any of her hair in the car?"

"Mm-mm," Chandler managed, shaking his head "no."

"Then what else would be there if she was driving the car?" she asked. "An article of clothing—"

Chandler's eyes became round and large, as if he were choking. He held up an index finger and gestured while he struggled to rapidly chew his food and swallow. He munched animatedly, while Leeza looked at Madison, who was staring at Chandler.

"What?" Madison asked. "You have an idea?"

He nodded affirmatively and swallowed hard. He walked over to the phone on the wall, punched in a few numbers.

"Ryan, what have you got?" Leeza asked. Chandler was focused on his call. "What's he got?" she asked Madison, who shrugged.

"Yeah, can you connect me to Kurt Gray in Trace Evidence?" Chandler asked into the phone, looking over to the Madisons and covering the mouthpiece. "The cans. There might be—hello, Kurt? This is Ryan Chandler . . . Yeah, Lou's friend, the Madison case. Listen, those beer cans that were found in the backseat of the Mercedes—have they been examined for saliva?" Chandler smiled and looked over to Madison. "Yeah, saliva. I'll bet you find some. Where have the cans been stored? . . . Excellent . . . Well, you're going to find that the DNA in that saliva will not match the DNA of the suspected driver of that vehicle . . . No, I told you, the driver was not Phillip Madison."

Chandler stood there listening to Gray speak when suddenly the enthusiasm drained from his face. "Jennings? Bill Jennings is on this case?" Chandler squared his shoulders and refocused himself. "Well, regardless of Jennings's opinions, I'd appreciate it if you'd run the tests."

Shaking his head out of frustration, he placed a hand on his hip. "Fine, check with Lou. Can you put me through to him?" Chandler tapped his foot on the floor and waited. "Yeah, Lou, it's Chandler. I stumbled onto something that may clear my client. I just ran it by Gray, but he was less than enthusiastic about it . . . Yeah, would you?"

Chandler nodded a couple of times. "Fine, get it cleared through the DA. I don't have to tell you what's at stake . . . Thanks, man. I'll call you in a few days."

As he hung up the phone, Leeza spoke. "Saliva? How is that going to—"

"DNA," Chandler said. "It's contained in all our bodily fluids—blood, semen, and *saliva*. And everyone's DNA is different, like a fingerprint. If we can identify the DNA in the saliva on the beer cans, it'll tell us the genetic makeup of that individual—the one who was driving the car and drinking the beer."

"If we're assuming the cans belonged to Harding, why weren't her fingerprints on them?" Leeza asked.

"There were a few sets of smudged prints, but nothing we could use to make an identification."

"Do you think there's enough saliva to run the tests?" Madison asked.

"First we have to see if there's any on the cans. If she drank the beer, for sure there'll be enough. If she didn't drink it, and just poured it out in the sink, we're shit out of luck. But if she took a couple of swigs while emptying it into the sink . . ."

"Then we've got her?" Leeza asked.

Chandler nodded. "I believe so. We'll have to wait and see." He started to pace the kitchen.

"But why would she take a swig of beer while emptying it?" Leeza asked.

"Maybe she likes beer, so she took a few swigs and emptied the rest down the drain. Hell, maybe she drank all of it."

"But she wouldn't drink the beer," Leeza said. "That'd be taking an awfully big chance."

Chandler was shaking his head. "To her, she wasn't taking any chances at all. The average person doesn't know about saliva and DNA testing—heck, before the O. J. Simpson trial, the average person didn't even know what DNA was. And I can guarantee you that most people still don't know that it's found in saliva."

"Would the saliva still be intact after this much time?" Madison asked.

"Sure. In fact, behind blood and semen, saliva is the best medium to get DNA from. And DNA's very stable. Aside from fingerprints, it's at least as reliable, if not more so, than conventional forensic tests. For one thing, it's a more stable molecule than the proteins and enzymes that we've used in forensics for years. The problems with DNA come when you have a very small sample to work with, or if the evidence is mishandled. Left in direct sunlight in front of a window, for example. Even then, the glass from the window filters out most of the harmful UV. If it's been stored at room temperature, it should be fine. Plus, saliva generally provides a big sample, so given normal conditions, there should be close to zero chance of contamination. From what Gray told me, the beer cans were stored appropriately. You have an excellent and well-respected lab here in Sacramento."

Everyone sat there for a moment, trying to put it all in perspective. Ricky looked at everyone, wondering why they had all fallen silent. "What'th D—DA?"

"D-N-A," Madison said. "It's part of what makes your skin, your bones, your face. It's sort of like a code that Mom and Dad gave us."

He nodded, perhaps understanding some of it, enough to satisfy his curiosity. Then, "Ith that what made me retarded?"

Madison glanced at Leeza, gave her a look like *how did I step into that one?* "Well, yes, Ricky, that's what caused the Down's syndrome."

"But," Leeza said, "because everyone's DNA is different, it makes each of us special. You're special, just like Phil and Ryan and I are special."

"You're the one who gave me the idea of checking for the DNA," Chandler said. "You may've saved your brother's life."

Ricky smiled.

"How long till we get those results from the lab?" Madison asked Chandler.

"Given the time frame, they're probably going to do it by PCR method, which takes about three weeks."

Leeza leaned forward. "Three *weeks?*"

Chandler nodded. "Could be less. But the other method can take three *months*. Matching DNA is a painstaking process." He sat there staring at his plate. "You know, there is one other thing we could check. If she did take a drink, she would've left a lip print."

"A what?" Madison asked.

"A lip print. The pattern of the skin on our lips is different, in much the same way fingerprints are individual. It's not a well-known or often-used forensic, but in certain situations it could be very revealing." He picked up the phone again, dialed Palucci, and asked him to dust the can for the lip print as well.

"You know," Madison said after Chandler had hung up, "when I saw her in the market, she had a six-pack in her cart."

"Why didn't you mention that before?" Chandler asked. "That's a very important detail to leave out."

"I didn't remember it until just now. Otherwise I would've told you."

"Do you remember the brand?"

"The cans were gold and black, with some white on them, I think," he said, looking up at the ceiling as he tried to recall their appearance.

"Millstone Draft?"

"Yeah, that's it."

Leeza looked at Chandler. "Why is that so important?"

"Because if we can find someone else who saw that brand of beer in her cart, and at least one of the beer cans has her lip print on it as well as saliva that contains her DNA, then we've got a very strong case for them having accused the wrong person."

Chandler gave Madison's shoulder a squeeze. "It looks like the good guys are starting to make a comeback."

*   *   *   *

Chandler met with Hellman later in the afternoon and informed him of what he had set in motion. Hellman was as enthusiastic as Chandler. His mind was miles ahead on the legal details, mentally preparing the pretrial motions as they spoke.

Chandler also told him that Bill Jennings was on the case and that they'd had problems in the past.

Hellman looked up from his desk. "What kind of problems?"

Chandler recounted the history of the case in Sacramento and its effect on their relationship. "He took it very badly. He behaved like an asshole and then wasn't enough of a man to admit it after the fact. We ran into each other one day when I was downtown, seeing Phil, actually, for an exam—and he said that he'd heard about what had happened to my back. Called me a cripple and said that I deserved it for making his life miserable. Can you believe it?"

"You think he's still got it out for you?"

"Who the hell knows. I haven't seen or spoken to him in years. If he's the same way he used to be, I'd say it's likely he's still carrying a grudge."

Hellman sighed, arose, and stared out the eighteenth-story window of his office. Off to his right were the buildings of Old Sacramento, erected when California was hosting the Gold Rush and forming the beginnings of organized state government. Although he was looking directly at the buildings, he was not seeing them. He was mulling over what Chandler had just told him.

Finally, Hellman turned around to face his investigator. "I don't think it'll have an impact on the case. So far, he hasn't done anything inappropriate, and I'd kind of think that if he has an ounce of common sense, he'd be reluctant to risk compounding his past blunders with a brand new screw-up in this case."

Chandler nodded. "I'll keep an ear and eye open for anything out of the ordinary. The last thing I want to do is make Phil's situation worse because of my involvement. Just the opposite."

"I understand that. I'd tell you to get the fuck out of town if I thought this posed a real threat."

With that, they chose to focus on all the positives that had occurred during the day, and what lay ahead: the arraignment in Superior Court.

At the crime lab, Madison was escorted to a tiny room where a phlebotomist waited with her paraphernalia spread out on a table. She explained that she would be taking only a small sample for purposes of performing a DNA analysis. Madison nodded, knowing full well why he was there. The DNA in his blood was going to be matched against the DNA in the saliva he hoped they would find on the beer cans.

The technician snapped the rubber tourniquet around Madison's right arm, patted the vein a few times with her latex-gloved index finger, and began the draw. Madison watched the blood pump into the tube . . . and along with it, his future and fate.

CHAPTER
39

THE SACRAMENTO Superior Courthouse was a city block long and a city block wide. Its 1980s modern cement-textured facade stood out against all the trees and cars that lined the streets. People flowed into and out of the building. Well-dressed attorneys in blue and dark gray suits, white shirts, and red ties toted their leather attachés while chatting animatedly about everything from plea bargains to Sunday's football scores.

Judge Cecil Tyson was assigned to preside over the arraignment in Department 17, third floor. The hallways were wide and well lit, with flat, padded black benches opposite the entrance to each courtroom. Double wood doors with small blacked-out rectangular windows provided an effective barrier against those people who sat in the corridor and waited for their turn in the witness chair. On the wall, next to each set of doors, was a cork board with typed papers listing the schedule of cases for the day.

Inside, the courtroom was relatively large, the size of a small auditorium. Walnut-stained wood dominated the decor, lining the walls from floor to ceiling, and covering the desks, judges' bench, and handrails in the imposing and impressively appointed room. Spotlights, recessed into the towering ceiling, flooded the room with slightly less than adequate light. There were no windows. The spectators were treated to padded movie theater–style seats, creating a deceivingly relaxed atmosphere.

Crowding the first two rows were representatives of the press, sketch pads and pencils at the ready, notepads and pocket tape recorders on their laps. Off to the left and in the last two rows of the galley were representatives of Kindness for the Homeless, a nonprofit organization whose members had the reputation for making their opinions known in a loud and intimidating manner when anything political or controversial occurred involving their cause. The NAACP had sent a couple of representatives as well, to set the table for documenting yet another case of racially motivated violence against African-Americans.

Madison and Hellman sat at the defendant's table to the left of the room. The bailiff's desk was off to the right. The judge's bench, towering above everything else and positioned like a crown jewel set against the back wall, was ten feet across. There was no doubt that this was the hub of all that spun from this courtroom.

"Remember, when he asks you to enter your plea," Hellman said, whispering into Madison's ear, "look him in the eye and speak in a loud, confident voice. Tell him the truth. Let him know that you're not guilty and that they have the wrong man."

The Honorable Cecil Tyson ascended the steps to his bench and sat down. Tyson was a thin, frail man of seventy-three years, who looked ten years older. But the counsel who made the common error of thinking that old Judge Tyson was a pushover had something coming—and it was not pleasant. It was best to be congenial and respectful, perhaps more so than usual, due to his sensitivity over his age. Fresh, slick attorneys who did not yet know the court and its judges made the mistake of trying to be too aggressive, feeling they could push him a bit, put one over on him, or pursue a line of questioning that was already ruled inappropriate. Tyson was still sharp and quite cantankerous. He did not like to be taken advantage of.

His Honor opened up a file and pulled a document from it. He placed his reading glasses on the tip of his broad, pockmarked nose. "I have here Information number 12762, which resulted from the preliminary hearing," he said, waving the document in the air. The Information, the Superior Court's version of the charging document that was presented during Madison's arraignment in Municipal Court three weeks ago, was filed by the district attorney and outlined the charges against the defendant. Further, in filing the Information, the Municipal Court judge had indicated that he had found that sufficient evidence existed to establish probable cause that the defendant had committed the crime.

"Dr. Madison," Tyson said, "this document has been served to your attorney. Have you had a chance to review it?"

"Yes sir."

"Very well. You're charged with one count of vehicular manslaughter, resulting in the death of Otis Silvers; and one count of second-degree murder with an abandoned and malignant heart, resulting in the death of Imogene Pringle."

Hellman cleared his throat. "Your Honor, defense waives formal reading."

Tyson nodded, removed his glasses, and set the paper aside. He looked down at Madison. "Dr. Madison, do you understand the charges against you?"

"Yes."

"Do you understand that if convicted you could be sentenced to fifteen years to life in prison?"

He stared Tyson right in the eyes and cleared his throat, prepared to speak with authority in his voice. There was none. A weak "Yes, Your Honor" escaped.

"Then how do you plead, sir?"

He cleared his throat again. Forcing air straight up from his lungs to the back of his throat, he squared his shoulders and said, "Not guilty."

The judge's slight frown clearly indicated that he was unimpressed: to him, Madison's response was undoubtedly expected and routine. Hellman placed a hand on Madison's shoulder and gave it a slight squeeze. The reporters in the first couple of rows scribbled furiously on their notepads.

"Very well," Tyson said as he replaced his reading glasses. "Dr. Madison, your trial is set for Monday, February fifteenth. All pretrial motions and matters should be filed by . . . January twenty-first, and disposed of by February first." He looked down at the two attorneys. "Is there anything unusual that I should suspect or prepare for?"

Denton stood. "Your Honor, the People request that the trial date be calendared for no earlier than March fifth. We need adequate time to prepare all the evidence, complete our tests, and appropriately conclude our investigation."

"Your Honor," Hellman said, trying to muster all the sugar he could in his voice, "my client has a right to a speedy trial. His practice is a shambles while he stands accused of a very heinous crime. He is innocent, and delaying the declaration of his innocence is damaging to his reputation."

The judge raised his eyebrows. "Mr. Denton."

"Your Honor, the criminalist assigned to this case who collected the physical evidence is out ill with ulcerative colitis. Someone else has been assigned to the case and is completing the workup, but it's possible that not all the tests were run that will be needed to complete our case for the People."

"This is all very interesting, Mr. Denton." Tyson leaned forward in his seat. "In my opinion, you have adequate time to make your case against Dr. Madison. I don't feel that it's necessary to detain the doctor any longer than necessary. Since he's innocent until proven guilty, I will give him the benefit of the doubt on this one. The trial will begin February fifteenth. Have your house in order by that time."

"Yes, Your Honor."

He looked over at his clerk and nodded. She opened the large book and thumbed through it. "Judge Calvino is available."

"Very well. Judge Calvino will preside." He rapped his gavel, and the people at the tables in front of him dispersed. Denton tossed Hellman a dirty look, as if he had just banished him to overtime hell for at least the next four weeks. He was now going to have to put his nose to the grindstone in order to be properly prepared.

Hellman, on the other hand, was stunned, still standing and facing Tyson, who was busy shuffling paperwork. Drawing Judge Calvino was a blow to Madison. Although he had known it was a possibility, the chances of drawing Calvino were slim.

Calvino had taken the bench in 1974, and had himself gone through a personal tragedy several years ago when his wife was struck by a drunk driver while crossing a street at dusk. The defense had argued that with the sun preparing to set, even a completely sober driver could not have seen or avoided his wife. The jury took two days to decide in favor of the defendant.

Calvino was furious, failing to comprehend how the jury could overlook the fact that the driver had three glasses of beer half an hour before he began his joyride. He was not the same judge afterward, three times being reprimanded for giving inappropriate instructions to the jury on murder trials. Following his wife's death, he seemed to wage a personal vendetta against all defendants—in his courtroom, they were guilty unless proven innocent—and there was no place for reasonable doubt. He admitted as much during a rare argument Hellman had with him in his chambers after his remarks to the jury resulted in a quick conviction—one that Hellman appealed and later won.

Calvino's most recent time on the bench had been less turbulent. Circulating rumors had him undergoing counseling, which helped him deal with his wife's death—something he had never accepted nor come to grips with. During the past several months, in demeanor he was more like the judge he had been before the incident: temperamental, sometimes even petulant—yet overall, relatively evenhanded.

But the past bothered Hellman, as he was keenly aware of the fact that Madison's case contained similarities to the one involving Vivian Calvino's death. He could not help but feel that this was a bad omen, but one which he was not going to share with Madison. Madison's contempt for the judicial system was a topic they had debated for years, and this certainly would not help matters. In fact, Calvino's case had been debated by them once at a barbecue, when Madison vehemently argued that the judge should have been relieved of his duties since he was no longer an impartial purveyor of justice . . . a view shared by many more qualified experts at the time. Fortunately, Hellman never told him the judge's name—he would have a fit if he learned that this was the same man who was just assigned to preside over his case.

Hellman sighed and shook his head as he gathered his papers together. *Bad omen? Curse would be more accurate.*

CHAPTER

40

WHEN MADISON ARRIVED at his office, there was a crowd gathered in front of the main entrance. Since it was raining and he did not want to roll down his window, it was difficult for him to see what was happening.

He parked, grabbed his umbrella, and walked over toward the entrance to the one-story building. As he approached, he heard someone shout "There he is!" and he saw twenty or thirty heads turn in his direction. He was quickly surrounded by the mass of people as he attempted to make his way through to the front of the building.

"Murderer!" he heard a man shout near his ear.

They tossed him about as he struggled to reach the entrance.

"You don't deserve to live!" shouted another.

"Let me through," Madison said. He took another step and tripped, falling against the glass of the front entrance.

He stood up, sliding against the wet door, trying to muster enough traction with his feet to push against it and escape the mob. As it finally swung open, he literally fell inside—his umbrella lost somewhere in the crowd, and his hair soaked by the rain.

Bonnie, his receptionist, came running over to him. "Are you okay?"

"I'm fine. Kind of a rude greeting, though," he said, trying to make light of it. He straightened his tie and ran his fingers through his hair in an attempt to make it presentable. He turned and looked outside at the horde of protesters as they shouted at him. In the back of the crowd, he could have sworn that he saw . . . Brittany Harding. He looked again, but the crowd was moving, and he lost sight of her.

". . . I tried reaching you on your car phone," Bonnie was saying, "but couldn't get through. They've been here for the past twenty minutes shouting all sorts of things. A couple of your morning patients turned around and left. They wouldn't let them in."

"So that's their game, huh? Who are those people?" he asked as he walked into his office and hung up his raincoat.

"There are a couple of NAACP signs out there. But from what I could see, most of them are with the Homeless Advocate Society."

Madison was nodding as they walked behind the large, pearl-colored Formica reception desk. "The people I'm accused of killing worked for that organization."

He sat down at his desk, where files were piled higher than his line of sight. He sighed, pushed them aside against a stack of partially read journals, and picked up the phone to call Hellman. He got through immediately.

Hellman answered in a flurry, speaking quickly. "I'm about to go into a deposition, so we've gotta make it fast."

Madison related what was going on outside his office.

"Yeah, and why do I want to know this?" Hellman asked.

"Because they're blocking my entrance and won't allow my patients in to see me. And because they damn near assaulted me as I tried to get into the building. I think I even saw Harding in the crowd."

"Have you called the police?"

"No, you're my first call. I didn't know what to do."

"Well, people have a right to protest, so you can't move them based on the fact that they're there. But they don't have a right to use physical violence or force on anyone. I'll make a call and get that taken care of."

"What about Harding? What the hell was she doing there?"

"I don't know, Phil, but she has a right to be there, too. You need to thicken your hide. Don't let all this extraneous stuff get to you. In a few weeks, we'll have you cleared and you can get on with your life."

"And until then?"

"When the going gets tough . . ."

"Oh, sage advice, Jeffrey."

"Let me make that call and get those people dispersed."

By the time Madison had returned a few calls, the police had come and informed the crowd that if they wanted to protest, they had the right—but they could not obstruct business, accost people, or prevent them from entering or exiting the building. The shouting continued for another hour, but the pouring rain helped to discourage them from maintaining their onslaught.

A few of the morning's patients were rescheduled for the afternoon; Madison's referrals had dropped off dramatically since the murder charges were brought, so any additional loss of patients was eating away at an already crumbling dam. Problem was, each time he plugged a hole, another two seemed to pop open. Unfortunately, as he was soon to find out, there were more weak spots lurking beneath the surface.

And the dam was about to burst.

CHAPTER
41

WHEN MADISON returned to his office following lunch, he noticed a message on his voice mail: it was John Stevens at the hospital. He had something very important to discuss and could not do it over the phone. He needed him to come down to the hospital—tonight, if possible. He'd wait there for him if necessary.

Madison phoned Stevens and informed his secretary that the earliest he could be there would be seven; then he called Leeza to apologize. Since he had been home often lately, the time away from the house this evening did not seem to loom as significantly as it had in the past.

Stevens's office was the only one of the entire administrative suite that was still aglow by the time Madison walked in at 7:15 P.M. Stevens was sitting at his desk, his room lit by a single desk lamp that cast a warm, orange hue. Judging by the look on his friend's face, however, there was nothing cozy or comfortable on his mind.

"Phil, please sit down," he said, motioning Madison to the seat in front of his desk. Usually, when Madison had come to speak with Stevens in his office, he would direct him to the sofa against the far wall, where they would sit next to each other while chatting. This meeting had a very formal air to it. This was all business.

"So what's on your mind, John? I can tell that something's bugging you."

Stevens nodded, then sighed. He placed his tremulous right hand on the desk, covered it with his left. "Phil, you know that in the past, I hated administrators because of what their focus was: money. The bottom line. Income and expenses. Risks and exposure." He paused on this last sentence, then looked up at Madison. "Risks and exposure are what the board is most concerned with at the moment. With increased risk comes greater exposure, and with greater exposure comes increased risk."

"You're talking in circles, John. What the hell are you saying?"

Stevens wiggled a bit uncomfortably in his seat. "I'm talking about increased risk of lawsuits. Of risking this hospital's excellent reputation. Of risking the loss of research grants which are vital to the operation of this institution."

"Why are we discussing this? What could I possibly do to help you with the risks the hospital faces?"

Stevens scratched the back of his head. "Phil, there's been talk." He looked up at Madison. "Talk of a loss of research funds if we don't relieve you of your privileges."

Madison swallowed hard. "My privileges? What on earth are you talking about?"

"You're going to make me spell it out, huh?"

Madison sat there, staring at him.

Stevens heaved a big sigh. "You've become too great a risk to the hospital, Phil. The board doesn't want you to be associated with us right now. They're concerned that your presence here will result in our loss of funds—grants that we can't afford to lose."

Madison stood up. "This is absolutely ridiculous!"

"Phil, please sit down."

"No, I won't sit down. I demand a better answer than that. How dare you? We've worked together how many years? How can you do this to me?"

Stevens remained in his seat. "Phil, it's not my doing. I think you know that. I fought them on this. I fought them hard. They wanted you off the list. Gone, good-bye, never to return. Regardless of how your trial turns out."

"Guilty no matter what, huh?" Madison said, beginning to pace.

"I was able to push something through. They didn't like it, but I was able to push hard enough to get it through."

"Guilty. I can't believe they would do this to me . . ." he said, his voice trailing off.

"I was able to get them to suspend your privileges *temporarily.*"

"Oh, gee, thanks, pal, what a deal. Suspended privileges. How long is 'temporarily'?"

"Indefinitely."

"Indefinitely," he said. "That's utter bullshit, John, and you know it."

"I'm sorry, Phil. I did the best I could."

"John, when this hospital was on the brink of financial ruin, who stepped in and got us the grants to keep our research staff intact? Who was the one who was able to bring our reputation up a notch by performing the first knee replacement surgery in California? Who was the one who got the investor group together when we needed to take the hospital public so we could raise the five hundred million cash to purchase all that new equipment down in the OR suites?" He stood and leaned across the desk, two feet from Stevens's face. "*I was.* I was the one who saved this hospital several times over. And this is how they repay me? I get falsely accused of a crime and they want to give me the boot out of here?"

"Phil, it's not just a crime you're accused of, it's *murder.* Double murder."

"I know what it is! I live it, I breathe it, I can't get away from it." He sat back down and looked up at the ceiling. "You think I'm guilty, John?"

"What I think is unimportant, Phil. It's what the big boys think that matters."

"Answer my question."

"Absolutely not. You're innocent without question."

"I had to ask. I need to know where I stand with you." He paused, shook his head. "There were protesters outside my office today. They wouldn't let any patients in. They assaulted me as I tried to go in through the front doors."

"I know. That was the last straw for the guys upstairs. They heard about it from a patient of yours who couldn't get in to see you this morning, so she came over here for a refill of her meds.

She told the receptionist about her ordeal, and the receptionist told Nancy Block, the RN who had the hots for you—the one you told in no uncertain terms that you'd never have an affair—she told Scott Smilton, the cardiologist who sits on the board. Then, by about noon, we had our own group of protesters outside the hospital. Only about twenty of them, but they sure made a lot of noise. Stood under the overhang and shouted for two hours until they lost their voices. That was all it took to convene the board for a special session. By three o'clock we were meeting. Twenty minutes later it was all over. And I spoke for fifteen of those twenty minutes, trying to change their minds."

"John, this just isn't fair."

"Fair? Hold it a minute, Phil. Let's look at this purely from a business perspective."

Madison made a face.

"No, hear me out," Stevens said, holding up a trembling hand. "Those protesters out there are bad for business. They left for today, but they'll be back tomorrow, and the day after that, and the day after that. I know for a fact that we'll lose the grants if you stay on. I really can't blame the board for their decision. What else could they do? Should they risk all the good that this hospital does for thousands of people just so that we don't hurt your feelings? Surely you can see that wouldn't be a defensible position."

Madison sighed. "Who's going to perform the surgeries I have scheduled? I've got a posterior strut fusion and a three-level fracture of the axis to repair—"

"Your surgeries were assigned to Jim Plankston."

"Plankston! These aren't simple surgeries, John."

Stevens threw up his hands. "What do you want me to say? I did my best."

"Plankston. Well, they could have done worse, I guess. It could've been Cadwell[1]."

"He's assisting."

"Why didn't they at least assign Fred Oliver—"

"It wasn't my decision."

Madison sat down on the couch and sank in. "This is what they'd rather have over me?"

Stevens looked down at his desk, avoiding eye contact.

Madison stood up, turned and faced the couch. "We've had a lot of good chats on this sofa, haven't we, John?"

Stevens arose and moved next to Madison, in front of the couch. "And we'll have a lot more. Look, maybe this is the best thing anyway. Take the time off. Get your house in order. It's probably best if you don't operate under these conditions anyway. Clear your head, spend time with your family, get your legal matters out of the way, and then we'll get you reinstated. I promise. I'll make it happen."

Madison forced a thin smile. "One day this will make for one big joke. We'll laugh about it, right?"

"You said it," Stevens said, patting him on the back. "Let me know if there's anything I can do to help."

As the door closed behind him, Stevens sighed deeply. He had been dreading the conversation and it had been just as bad as he feared it would be. He would never forget that when he was diagnosed with the tremor, it was Madison who fought hard and lobbied the board members to offer him the position in administration.

But business was business, and that was a long time ago. This was the present, and it was now his responsibility to look out for the hospital's best interests. While the hospital was protected from death, injury, and/or disability to their star orthopedic surgeon, the one thing they did not have insurance protection for was criminal behavior. The fiscal impact was going to be severe—and he could not allow the problem to compound by keeping Madison, an accused murderer, on staff.

Still, as he sat on the couch, he realized that this was the lowest he'd had to stoop since becoming an administrator. He walked back over to his desk and took a swig of his Diet Coke. He had to get the bad taste of betrayal out of his mouth.

Outside, Madison walked down the hall into the bright light. He squinted as a tear came to his eye and ran down his cheek. He was filled with sadness as he looked around, not knowing if he would ever be reinstated to the hospital he helped build into a revered, state-of-the-art teaching institution. As he punched the elevator button, he suddenly became aware of the pounding pain threatening to explode from his temples.

He never thought it would get to this.

CHAPTER

4 2

LEEZA WAS STRUGGLING to button Elliott's coat, but the boy wouldn't stay still. While he zoomed his plastic spaceship through the air fighting off the evil empire, Leeza managed to get the top button fastened. But as she moved down to the next one, the phone rang.

It was Hellman calling from his car, relieved that he'd caught her before she left to drop the kids off at day care.

"I've got something I have to discuss with Phil," he said.

She told him Madison was in the garage, building a toy box for Jonah. "He's been in there for three hours, since six-thirty this morning, pounding away, taking out his aggressions with a hammer. I guess it's good therapy for him."

"Not for a surgeon," Hellman said. "He's not supposed to be doing those things. His hands are—"

"Jeffrey, he doesn't care. And right now, I can't say that I blame him. The hospital revoked his privileges."

"Which hospital? Sac General? The one he pulled from the trenches ten years ago?"

She blurted a laugh filled with disbelief. "Is that a kick in the ass or what?"

"Well, I guess I won't tell him why I called."

"Why *did* you call?" she asked, wedging the phone between her ear and shoulder so she could button the rest of Elliott's coat.

"You haven't seen the *Herald* this morning?"

"No," she said as Chandler came down the stairs. "Let me guess, more bad stuff."

"It ain't good."

"Phil asked me to switch us back to the *Bee*, but I haven't gotten around to it yet." She patted her son on the buttock and moved the phone away from her mouth. "Ryan, would you get the paper out front?"

"I haven't read the whole article yet," Hellman said, "but it covers the protests yesterday, makes some snide remarks about Phil's still seeing patients and that all he cares about is the money. I just wanted to smooth things over for him."

"You're a good friend, Jeffrey. He could use the cheering up," she said as she and Chandler opened the paper.

"Let me talk to him."

She walked over to the intercom and buzzed the garage. "Pick up, honey. Jeffrey's on his car phone."

"I don't feel like talking."

The sound of a hammer pounding a nail reverberated through the intercom.

"Just pick up. He needs to talk to you."

Madison picked up the wood, tossed the hammer aside, and grabbed the phone off the wall. "Yeah."

"Phil, I'm sorry," Hellman said. "We'll get through this, buddy, I promise you."

"Yeah, I know. It's easy for you to say. It's my life that's falling apart."

"You forget that we're about to blow the lid off the prosecution's case—"

"We better, because I can't take much more of this. What the hell am I going to do, Jeffrey? If I'm not a surgeon . . ." He trailed off, ignoring the larger picture, which included a lifetime of incarceration. "It's all I've ever wanted to do."

"Phil, this is nonsense talk. First of all, you'll get past all this bullshit. We'll repair the damage once this thing fades into the dust."

"I don't know if it'll ever go away. I'm only now beginning to realize that."

"Don't make any earth-shattering decisions just yet. Give yourself some time and perspective. *Then* you can assess the situation. Not now."

"I can't ignore what's been happening. Look at how they're treating me. My name—my reputation—was once worth gold. Now, no one wants me around. I mean, who would've ever thought that Sac General would abandon me? After all we've been through together, after all I'd done for them, I figured they'd be the ones in my corner. Sticking by me through thick and thin. But nothing counts for anything, I guess." He tossed the piece of wood to the ground. "The past is the past, and money is money, and business is business. And an accused murderer is bad for business."

"Are you done? Because now that you've got that out of your system, you need to listen to me. Put your emotions aside for the moment. I know you better than I know myself. When you get backed into a corner your emotional side takes over. Rein it in. Contain it so that you can get on with your life. I need you strong right now, not falling apart. Got it?"

"You're trying to handle me, Jeffrey."

"Damn right. Get your act together. I'll call you later."

"Ryan, did Phil happen to give you the spare keys to his car?" Leeza asked as she rummaged through the drawers in the kitchen.

Chandler was pushing his arm though the sleeve of his black leather jacket. "No, I'm using the rental. Why?"

"They're not here. They're usually hanging on this hook by the phone."

"You need a ride somewhere? I can take you."

"No, no, I'm fine, I've got my van. I was just wondering where the keys were."

"I'll see you a little later," Chandler said. "I've got some people I have to catch up with today."

As he walked out the door, the phone rang. Leeza tucked it against her shoulder as she continued to search through the drawer. "Oh, hi Denise, this is Leeza, Phil's wife. Let me see if I can catch him—he just left. Hang on a second."

She ran to the door and called Chandler in from the car. She handed him the phone and walked over to the far end of the kitchen, where she was watching over the turkey that was cooking in the oven.

"Just tell me what's wrong, honey," Chandler said.

"I found something, Ryan. I don't know what it is, but I'm afraid."

"Denise, what are you talking about? What did you find?"

"A lump."

"A lump? Where?"

"In my breast, Ryan. I found a lump in my breast."

Chandler was silent for a moment. "Have you ever felt it before? How big is it?"

"It wasn't there before. It's maybe the size of a large pea. I had Joanne come over and feel it, and she thinks I should go in and get it biopsied."

"Whoa, wait a minute. Call Jason and make an appointment. Let him examine it and then we'll figure out what needs to be done. Don't be talking about a biopsy."

"But Joanne's a nurse."

"At a nursing home, Denise." He sighed. "We should have a doctor look at it."

"I want you to come home, Ryan. I need you here."

Chandler's mouth was frozen, half open. "I'll be home in a few days. There's just—"

"I want you to come home now."

He sat down on the last step of the staircase and chewed on his lip for a moment. "Look . . . I've only got a few loose ends to tie up. As soon as I do that, I'm out of here."

"Ryan, you don't understand . . ." she said. "Breast cancer is a leading cause of death in women. My grandmother had it, and it runs in families. I don't want them to cut off my breast, but I don't want to die."

"Honey, listen to me. Nobody said anything about cancer. Nobody said anything about you dying. And nobody said anything about cutting off your breast. Go in and have Jason examine it. I trust him. Once he takes a look, we'll go from there. But I promise you that no matter what happens, no matter what it is, we'll get through it."

"That's why I need you here. I'm not handling this well. I feel so far away from you."

"You're under a lot of stress—worrying about your mid-term grades, having to do double duty taking care of Noah while I'm gone, and now this . . . it's got you all tied up in knots."

"I'm glad I have your permission to be stressed out. A lot of good that does me."

Chandler paused, rubbed his forehead. "Okay . . . okay. Call Jason's office and make an appointment. Then call me and let me know when it is. I'll see what I can do."

"That doesn't sound like you're on the next flight home."

"Denise, I'm at a critical point in trying to prove that Phil's innocent of murder. If I fail, he could go to prison for life. He was there eight years ago when I needed him. I can't just walk out on him."

"What if Jason tells me that it doesn't look good and I need a biopsy? I don't know if I can handle that alone."

He arose from the step. "All right. Make the appointment. I'll call you later and we'll take it from there."

"Take it from there?"

"You know, we'll talk about it. Let's deal with first things first."

"There's nothing to talk about, Ryan. You've told me all I need to know. Phillip Madison is more important to you than I am."

"You're the most important thing in the world to me, Denise. You and Noah. You should know that."

"Saying it is one thing. Showing it is another."

"Denise, if I knew for sure this was serious I'd be home on the next flight. But right now, we don't know that it's anything more than, what's it called, a fatty nodule?"

"I'll call you with the appointment information."

A second later, the line went dead. Chandler slumped back down onto the step.

"Ryan," Leeza said, approaching him. "I wasn't eavesdropping, but I got the gist of your conversation." She sat down next to him. "Mind if I give you some advice?"

"Please . . ." Chandler said, motioning for her to continue. "God knows I screwed up royally handling it my way."

"Women deal with these types of things differently than men do. Men tend to see things analytically, logically. They want to find ways of solving problems—to them, finding the solution is the most important thing."

Chandler nodded. "Shouldn't it be?"

Leeza smiled. "Depends. As women, we tend to look at things more emotionally. When we tell you about a problem or an insecurity we have, we're not looking for solutions. We're looking for support."

"I can see where support's helpful, but all the support in the world isn't going to solve your problems."

"True, but it validates our feelings, and sometimes that's more important." She looked at him to make sure he was grasping what she was saying. "For example, instead of saying 'I'm sure everything will be fine,' you could say 'I know you're scared, this is a very frightening thing to deal with. I'll be there for you, don't worry.'"

Chandler stared off at the wall for a moment. "I did kind of the opposite, didn't I?"

"She probably felt as if you were dismissing her fears as just hysterical ranting."

"But that wasn't my intention."

"Don't tell me, tell her."

Trying to put Denise out of his mind for a few moments proved difficult for Chandler. He stopped in at Food & More, the market where Madison and Harding had their public argument, to see if he could locate the checkout employee who was working the night the altercation occurred. Madison had been able to give him only a loose description of the young man, but he hoped that it would be enough. With the store manager off, he was able to assemble only a partial list of employees fitting the checker's description. To determine which ones on his list had worked the night in question, he would have to wait until the manager returned. Chandler said he would stop by tomorrow.

He walked over to a public phone on the corner and called the crime lab in New York. He made the mistake of asking Valerie, Hennessy's assistant, how the office was holding up. Not so well, she responded, and proceeded to tell him about the leaky roof and the tainted evidence that resulted from the water damage. "The division head blamed maintenance, which blamed scheduling and supply. But no matter whose fault it was, the evidence was ruined, and they're gonna have to let Bobby Lee Walker go free. You can imagine what's going on here," she said. "It's a real political mess for the mayor, letting a murderer go free, Ryan, I'm telling you. Made him look bad. He was real pissed off and said on the six o'clock news that heads were gonna roll. Heat's coming down from everywhere."

"So let me guess," Chandler said. "Hennessy's on the warpath."

"The director came down on him this morning. So now the captain's walking around saying 'I'll wring Chandler's neck when he gets back.' That's a direct quote, Ryan. But I kind of spared you all the cursing."

"How did I get involved in this? I'm not even there."

"He was babbling up a storm, but he said something about if you were here, the evidence already would've been evaluated and logged, reported on, and secured in the storage room, long before the roof leak."

"Let me talk to him, Valerie."

"Are you crazy? He hasn't gotten over it yet. Maybe you should wait until things die down a bit."

"I'm a big guy, Valerie. I can take it."

A moment later, Hennessy picked up the line and launched into a continuous sea of expletives; Chandler held the phone away from his ear until he detected Hennessy's need to take a breath.

"I'm going to be coming home in a few days," he managed to get in.

"You cocksucking asshole! Do you understand what I'm telling you? I want you back here now!"

"Fine, then beam me over. Otherwise, you'll have to wait till I arrive on the flight that I have scheduled for Tuesday night."

"Chandler, you're in deep shit. I'll own your ass when you get here."

"Sorry, chief, my wife's already laid claim to that part of my anatomy." Chandler held the phone away from his ear until Hennessy was done shouting.

"Chief," Chandler said, trying to get a word in so that he could end the conversation. "Chief, I've got to go."

"It's captain!"

"If you want me to be on that plane, I need to get off the phone. I have leads to follow up on before I leave."

Hennessy made some comment about Chandler caring more about his case out West than he did about those that he was being paid to work on by the City of New York. Chandler agreed, not listening to what Hennessy was saying, and hung up. It was then that he realized that Valerie was right, he never should have bothered. Then again, this confrontation with Hennessy was no different than any other conversation they'd had over the years.

CHAPTER
43

MAURICE MATHER was a relative newcomer to television news reporting, with only three years of on-the-job training to his credit. But eagerness was molded into his tanned face and he was aggressive. He had learned from his mentor while serving as a copy editor that a good reporter does not always take "no" for an answer: he does what's necessary to obtain the story he's after.

A precondition for this interview with hospital administrator John Stevens, however, was that it would have to be held off-camera. While this obviously did not present a problem for a newspaper reporter, it strained the patience of their television counterparts, who relied on the visual aspect of their presentation as much as the verbal information they conveyed.

"This is Tom Ingle, a copy editor and trainee at the station," Mather said, introducing his assistant, a curly-haired twenty-five-year-old. Ingle and Stevens nodded at each other.

"So what do you want to know?" Stevens asked.

"I want to know why Phil Madison was kicked out of your hospital."

"Dr. Madison was not kicked out. His privileges were temporarily suspended."

"Why?"

"It was an upper-level management decision."

"Does it have anything to do with the rape charges against him?"

"Rape charges?" Stevens sat forward in his chair. "What are you talking about?"

"The rape charges," he said again, as if repeating it would stimulate Stevens's memory. "Say two or three months ago. The charges he tried to sweep under the rug by paying off the woman who brought the complaint."

Stevens was silent for a moment, staring off at the wall behind the reporters.

"Dr. Stevens," Mather said. "Does it or does it not have to do with those rape charges?"

He cleared his throat. "I have no comment, other than to say that this is an unrelated matter."

"Then this is solely a means of distancing the hospital from a murderer, severing a relationship before it becomes more damaging than the association already is."

Stevens crinkled his face and squirmed a bit. Ingle was scribbling notes on a pad. "Phillip Madison is not a murderer."

"Assuming you're correct, let me rephrase the question. The action the hospital board has taken is intended to distance the hospital from an *accused* murderer, severing a relationship before it becomes even more damaging than it's already been. Isn't that right, Dr. Stevens?"

Stevens's head bobbed back and forth, left and right. "Essentially."

More scribbling. "Do you feel that Madison is capable of committing murder?"

"I can't speak for the actions of another," Stevens said cautiously, playing the role of administrator and bureaucrat. "But I can tell you that Dr. Madison is one of the finest human beings you'll ever meet; I've never known him to hurt a fly. He's also responsible for building this hospital into what it is—a valued teaching institution with state-of-the-art equipment and an expert staff of distinguished surgeons. He's dedicated his life to saving people, not killing them."

"Would you say that one's actions in the past are an indication of what their actions will be in the future?" asked Ingle, the rookie, trying hard to contribute.

"As I said, no one can guarantee the actions of another. To do so would be like trying to predict the stock market. It's just not possible to do with any degree of accuracy."

"What about the hospital's exposure on Madison's arrest?"

"What about it? We had nothing to do with the murders."

"Could it be said that the hours you force surgeons to work, the stress these doctors are under, results in a high degree of alcoholism, of driving while under the influence?"

"Do you really think I'm going to answer such an absurd allegation?"

"Statistics don't lie, Dr. Stevens. The rate of alcoholism, and even drug abuse amongst surgeons is quite high compared to the general—"

"If you're going to persist in this line of questioning, Mr. Mather, then this interview is over."

"Fine. I'll move on." He looked down at his pad.

"A question if I may, Maurice." This from Ingle. Mather waved him on.

"Dr. Stevens, you acted as if you didn't know of the rape charges against Dr. Madison."

"I have no comment on that."

"I'll take that as a no."

"You can take it just as I answered the question."

"Then you didn't know of the payoff he made to the woman to keep her quiet."

"I'll have to answer that question the same way as I answered your last question." Ingle scribbled some notes.

"How long have you known Madison?" Mather asked.

"About thirteen years. We started out at the hospital together."

"Would you consider him your friend?"

"Yes, I would."

"And would you say that you would go out of your way to protect your friend?"

"Mr. Mather . . . yes, I would go out of my way to assist a friend in need. But that does not mean I'd go so far as to do anything that would impair my job as a hospital administrator, nor would I do anything that would jeopardize this hospital in any manner. Now, I believe this interview is over. Gentlemen," he said, as he stood from behind his desk and walked over to the door.

After they exited his office, Mather began walking at a fast clip. "We'll have Andy get some footage of the hospital interior, and a few seconds of Stevens's door as we try to open it, and then have it close hard on the camera. It dramatizes the way we were shut out from filming the interview."

"But he was pretty cooperative, he just didn't want to go on-camera."

"That," Mather said with a grin that could sour milk, "will turn out to be a mistake."

The mobile van sat parked out in front of the hospital with its huge antenna telescoping into the sky fifteen feet. The beta camera was mounted on a tripod just to the left and in front of the hospital's main entrance. A small television monitor sat below the tripod on the floor, as they set up for a live remote shot for the noon newscast. Ingle was helping Andy, the cameraman, set up the shot while Maurice Mather stood with his lapel microphone in place, his handwritten notes on a small pad in front of him.

"We're a minute thirty out," Andy said as he pressed the headset radio against his ear.

Mather looked into the camera and practiced a few lines from his pad. "How did we sound?" he asked into the mike, listening through his earpiece to the director back at the station. "Testing, one-two-three," he said.

"They're not getting us," Andy said. "Your mike's dead."

"Do we have another?"

"I'll let you know." Andy trotted over to the van and rummaged through a box of electronic equipment and jumbled wires.

"Thirty seconds out," called Mather, trying not to show visible signs of sweat—perspiration did not look good on camera. Ingle was standing next to the tripod, sweating profusely, watching as Andy rummaged through the box, counting out the remaining seconds.

"Got one, but it's a handheld job," he said as he fumbled to plug the microphone into his camera. He handed it to Mather and jumped back behind the tripod to check its position. "Counting," Andy said, holding up five fingers. "Five-four-three-two-one."

As Andy hit "two" in the count, a broad smile spread across Mather's plastic face and he brought the mike up to his mouth. "Thanks, Patrick. We're here at Sacramento General Hospital, the very hospital where Dr. Phillip Madison was on staff at the time of the grisly hit-and-run murders. The hospital administrator, Dr. John Stevens, refused to allow our cameras in, but he did permit us to interview him." Mather watched the monitor as the tape that Andy had shot an hour earlier was rolling at the station, reviewing the prior events in the story, showing the hospital footage, and setting the stage for the remainder of Mather's report. Mather squinted into the lens of the camera, adjusted his hair in the reflection, looked down at his pad to review his notes. Glanced at the monitor. Caught his cue.

"And Patrick, Dr. Stevens said that Madison's privileges were suspended due to an upper-level management decision. A decision designed to protect the hospital from further embarrassment by disassociating itself from the accused murderer before the relationship created irreparable damage." Mather glanced down at his pad. "Dr. Stevens declined to go into details about the payoff that Madison made to a woman who accused him of rape a couple of months ago. But he did say that the hospital's current decision to suspend his privileges was a separate issue from the rape. Now, interestingly, when I asked Dr. Stevens, who's a longtime personal friend of Madison, if he thought his star surgeon was capable of committing murder, his response was that no one can predict the actions of another. Not the strongest statement of support, Patrick," Mather said with a slight smile. "In fact, he likened trying to predict Phillip Madison's behavior to playing the stock market—apparently, he's unpredictable and it's impossible to know how he'd react in any given situation with any degree of accuracy."

The monitor showed a split screen, with Mather on one side, and news anchor Patrick Baud on the other. "Maurice," the anchor said, "it seems quite interesting that the hospital would not take any disciplinary action against Madison for suspicion of rape, but they did suspend him for suspicion of murder."

Mather smiled; it was the exact question he had recommended that Baud ask him. "Yes, Patrick. It seems that the hospital does not consider rape a reason to discipline its doctors—but that's a subject of an investigative report. Perhaps we should leave that story to *Hard Edition*," he said, giving a toothy smile for the camera. "This is Maurice Mather reporting for KMRA news."

Mather kept smiling until Andy gave him the cue that they were off the air. As Andy began breaking down the equipment, Ingle walked over toward Mather.

"Well, there it is, Tom. Your first live remote. Interesting, huh?"

"Yeah," was all Ingle could manage.

"Any questions?"

Ingle looked down at his shoes and hesitated. "Well, you kind of left out some important information."

"How so?" Mather asked.

"Well, Stevens also said that Madison was one of the finest human beings he'd known, and that he'd never even hurt a fly," he said, consulting his notes.

Mather smiled and began to walk back toward the van. Another news truck pulled up in front; its telescoping antenna began to unwind like a giant corkscrew ascending toward the heavens.

Ingle followed at Mather's heels. "Didn't Stevens also say that he didn't know about the rape, and that's probably why no action was taken against Madison at the time? It had nothing to do with the hospital looking the other way, which is how you made it sound."

Mather stopped walking and turned to face Ingle. "I believe he said 'no comment' when I asked him about the rape."

"Maurice, he only said that after you pressed him on it. It

seemed to me like he didn't know what you were talking about. And if the hospital didn't know about it, then what you said—"

"Tom, do you know for sure that the hospital *didn't* know about it?"

"Well, I—"

"Do you really think that a doctor like Phillip Madison could be accused of rape, and the hospital wouldn't be aware of it? Come off it, Tom." Mather turned away and started back toward the van.

"Well, I'm just saying that we don't know whether they knew of it or not."

"We certainly don't know for sure that they *didn't* know, do we?"

Ingle hesitated. "No . . ."

"That's right, so we didn't say anything that was factually wrong."

"But isn't omitting information just as much of a lie as giving false information?"

Mather turned hard and faced Ingle. "Tom, do you remember that ratings chart I showed you before we left the newsroom? KONE was beating the pants off us. We need to boost our ratings, or we stand to lose some big money. And if we continue to lose more money, then cuts are going to be made—especially with a new GM taking over next month. I don't intend to lose my job or take a pay cut, do you?" He climbed into the van as Andy finished packing up the equipment. "News sells, Tom, if you know how to present it. I'm just trying to be more aggressive, that's all," Mather said, holding both his hands out in front of him, palms up.

Ingle climbed in, shut the door, and watched the competing news cameraman prepare to set up his live remote shot while the reporter entered the hospital. As he wondered what angle that reporter would choose to take, the KMRA van pulled away and headed back to the newsroom.

CHAPTER
44

CHANDLER AND MADISON were sitting around the conference table watching Hellman pace the room. The law library at Hellman, MacKenzie & McKnight was appointed like the rest of the office. Decorated by his wife, it had the flair and professional appeal of the most expensively decorated law libraries of the wealthiest firms in the state. Books lined two of the longest walls, with three large picture windows occupying the other wall of the room.

Hellman made another pass in front of Madison. "It had to have been Movis Ehrhardt. That asshole must've leaked word of the payoff to the press. I'll bet he was so pissed off at having to return the money that this was the only way he could get back at us."

"Sit down, Jeffrey. You're making me nervous," Madison said.

"I can't sit down. I'm all worked up. I think better when I'm pacing."

Chandler sat up straight in his chair. "I say we forget about Movis Ehrhardt, the press, the protesters, and concentrate on what we're all here to do: get Phil off, have the case thrown out, and build a case against the real murderer." He looked at Madison and Hellman for their buy-in to this seemingly obvious suggestion.

"You're right," Hellman said. "Getting pissed off at everyone isn't doing us any good. Let's get the case against Phil dismissed, and then we'll deal with damage control."

"Isn't there something we can be doing while we're waiting for the DNA results?" Madison asked.

"I'm continuing with my interviews," Chandler said. "In fact, I have a real good one coming up: Brittany Harding."

"How'd you arrange that one?"

"I told her I was investigating your case, and that I heard about the rape on the news. I said I didn't want to work for you if you'd done something like that. Since you denied it, I wanted to hear her side of the story, about what she'd been through. Being that she's psychotic, I knew she'd welcome the chance to get her digs in, and I'm giving her that opportunity. We set up a lunch appointment for tomorrow."

Hellman and Madison looked at each other. "Now you know why I asked you to hire Ryan Chandler," Madison said.

Upon leaving the firm's law library, Chandler was intercepted by the receptionist. "This call just came in from Dr. Madison's wife. She said I should give it to you immediately."

Chandler took the message slip, and after barely taking the time to read all the words, body-slammed the front door on the way out of the office, headed for the elevator.

"What's going on?" Hellman asked, who had just reached the reception desk.

"Mrs. Madison called and said that some guy from the lab told her the lip print analysis was ready."

Hellman reached over and gave Madison's shoulder a squeeze. "It's okay to breathe, Phil," he said. "We'll know the results soon enough."

Blowing past the thirty-five-mile-per-hour speed limit signs at near fifty, Chandler made it to the Department of Justice in under ten minutes—just as Gray was preparing to leave for a late lunch.

"They are likely not Madison's," Gray said as he brushed a lock of stringy hair off his face.

"What kind of probability match would you give it?" Chandler asked.

"Well, it was only a partial," he said, offering him an

enlarged copy of the lip print. "I'd give it a seventy percent probability that we're dealing with someone else."

"Seventy percent," Chandler said, looking at the swirling lines of the print. "Seventy percent . . . not enough to get them to drop the charges. This helps, but we're gonna need the DNA in order to get him off."

Gray shrugged and glanced at his watch. "Look, you got what you wanted. Mind if I go to lunch now?" He pushed past Chandler and headed out of the lab.

Chandler yelled a thank-you through the rapidly closing door, and then left with his escort. While the results bolstered the argument for Madison's innocence, they did not go far enough. For the prosecution to drop its case, he would need to produce clear and convincing evidence that his friend and client was free of all guilt . . . and that someone else was responsible. And although he was gaining momentum, he was still far from being able to do that.

In the late afternoon, a collect call for Detective Jennings came through to the station from a person who lived in Del Morro Heights. An hour later, Jennings and Detective Moreno swung by to meet with Clarence Hollowes, the homeless man who had witnessed the hit-and-run.

"I was walking by this Giants store over by the mall," Hollowes said, chewing on a piece of gum supplied by Moreno. "And I saw this hat there, a black job with a white design." He paused, eyeing the female detective. "Got anything else to eat?"

Moreno pulled a few singles from her pocket. "Buy yourself a sandwich, Clarence."

"But first tell us about this hat," Jennings said. "What kind of design was on it?"

"Take me by the store, and I'll show you."

The mall, a fifteen-minute drive from Hollowes's neighborhood, was teeming with shoppers. They pulled up in front of the San Francisco Giants store and Moreno took their witness inside.

"That's it, right there. That's the hat."

"Chicago White Sox?"

"That's the hat I seen."

Moreno pulled it from the rack and turned to Clarence. "Are you a Giants fan?"

"No ma'am. Dodger blue, through and through."

Moreno grabbed a Dodgers hat and brought them both to the register. As they walked out of the store, Clarence fingered the bill of the cap and carefully shaped it before placing it on his head.

Moreno shoved a few dollars into his palm. "Use that money for dinner."

"Yes, ma'am," he said, throwing his right hand up to the bill of his new hat.

She smiled. "C'mon, we'll drive you back to the neighborhood."

Denton, at the courthouse on an unrelated case, ran into Hellman in the hallway and informed him of the new information pertaining to the White Sox logo.

"Brittany Harding is from Chicago," Hellman said.

Denton waved a hand in the air as if he were trying to make Hellman's words disappear. "We have our man," he said. "And unfortunately for you, it's your client. White Sox fan or not."

When Chandler arrived home, he found a message from Denise scrawled out on a piece of paper that was left on his desk by Leeza. She wrote under it, "Remember—validate her feelings."

The message indicated that Denise's doctor's appointment was three days away. Before calling her, Chandler called United Airlines and booked a flight, a red-eye leaving in twenty-four hours, arriving in New York the morning of her appointment.

He dialed Denise, who answered with a monotone, "Hello, Ryan. You didn't need to call me, I left a message."

"I did need to call, to say I'm sorry." He paused, but she didn't respond. "I wasn't thinking clearly. You must be scared, with your family history and all. I booked a flight that leaves tomorrow night."

"I am frightened, Ryan. Of what it could mean. And what if I'm pregnant . . ." Her voice trailed off.

He could tell she was on the verge of tears, and probably had been since he had last spoken to her a few hours ago. He rubbed his temples, took a deep breath.

"Then we'll face it together," he said. He felt terrible; he had never seen her like this before. In all the years he had known her, she had never appeared so vulnerable. Perhaps it was because she was married now, with a young child . . . the mothering instinct overpowering everything else of significance.

"I love you, Denise. Whatever comes our way, we'll deal with it together. As for this lump, I understand it's a terrible thing to have to deal with, no matter what it turns out to be. But I'm telling you everything's going to turn out okay, I just know it." He was not sure what gave him the authority to make that assertion, and he knew it might not be what she wanted to hear. But right now, it was all he could do to hold things together—if not for her, then for himself.

CHAPTER
45

BRITTANY HARDING was more attractive than Chandler had envisioned. She was taller than he had thought—about five foot eleven, he figured. The blackmail picture he had seen of her had not done her justice.

Her perfume was light but distinct, her makeup minimal yet strategically applied to emphasize her striking features.

She had suggested Sing Palace, an upscale Chinese restaurant located downtown. Since Chandler was paying, he reasoned that she chose a place that she would not normally go to on her own when she was picking up the tab.

The hostess showed him to the table where his guest was already sitting and waiting.

"Miss Harding," Chandler said, extending his hand as he sat down.

"Please, call me Brittany," she said with a big toothy smile, extending a limp hand in response.

"Brittany." Chandler smiled back, his eyes inadvertently locking on the sheer, form-fitting outfit she was wearing.

The waitress came over and handed them two menus, quickly reciting the specials they were showcasing for today's lunch crowd. Most of the patrons were business executives having power lunches, negotiating deals, networking, finalizing contracts, or drumming up new business.

"You aren't a Sacramento native, I take it," Chandler said, trying to start their relationship off on a light note.

"My mother's Japanese, my father's American. I grew up in Chicago, can't you tell?"

Chandler flashed a coy smile. "Well, I did detect a little Midwestern dialect. What brought you out here?"

"Long story. Let's just say I'd moved in with this guy when I was twenty, around the time when my father's job transferred him to Sacramento. My parents and little sister moved and I stayed behind. My situation went from bad to worse, and I followed them out here. That was about four years ago."

They chatted for another minute, then picked a couple of dishes off the menu and placed their order with the waitress.

"So you said on the phone you wanted to talk to me about Phillip Madison."

"A long time ago I learned there are two sides to every story. Between the rape and the murder, I'm trying to unravel exactly what happened."

"Well, about the murder, I don't know how I can help you. Not that I want to. I'd actually take great pleasure in seeing Phillip Madison behind bars."

Chandler nodded. Wished he had that comment on tape. "Well, I thought we'd chat a bit. Maybe you can be of help, maybe not. After all, you did work with him."

"We didn't exactly have a good relationship, you know. I'm sure he's told you."

"No, I got your name from someone else at the Consortium. Dr. Madison didn't review the entire list of people I'm interviewing." Actually, the truth.

"Well, I'm sure he could give you a mouthful."

"Why's that?"

"He raped me and then denied it. I had evidence of it, too. He was so guilty that he had his attorney call my attorney and offer to pay me off. To keep quiet."

"I didn't know that," Chandler said. He crinkled his eyes and forehead as if he were having second thoughts about his client. "Tell me what happened."

"Oh, he's got a fancy lawyer. Tried to make it tough on me. Said he'd bring out things in my past, make my life hell. He promised me that testifying in court would be an experience I'd regret the rest of my life. He'd make it feel as if I was on trial instead of his client."

Chandler reasoned that it was probably Movis Ehrhardt, not Hellman, who had told her that that would be one possible approach of the defense—no doubt what Ehrhardt would do if he were in Hellman's shoes. "So you decided on an out-of-court settlement," Chandler said.

Harding nodded, a slight tear appearing in the corner of her eye. "I didn't have a choice."

"That's exactly what I would've done if I were in your shoes."

She looked up and met his eyes. "Really?"

"Sure." He wanted to gain her confidence and then move on to more important and pertinent matters. "Tell me, did you ever know Phil Madison to drink?"

"He drank like a fish whenever we'd go out for dinner."

"What would he drink?"

"Beer. Why's that important?"

"It may not be. I'm just gathering information." He knew that Madison did not drink beer—he was a wine person. For Chandler, it was yet another reason why the planting of the six-pack in the car meant that whoever had framed him didn't know him very well. Although drinking preferences did not have significant evidentiary value in court, Chandler considered the information helpful.

"He ever drink and drive while you were with him?"

She pulled out a cigarette. "A few times." Fumbled with it between her fingertips.

"Doesn't California have a law about smoking in restaurants?"

"Holding it helps me relax," she said, placing the cigarette in her mouth.

Their soup came, followed by the main course; Chandler continued to pepper the meal with more questions about Madison.

"So how'd you hear about the hit-and-run?"

"It was all over the papers," she said. "His arrest was like a dream come true. The bastard is finally getting what he deserves."

"So you think he did it?"

She laughed as he poured her some tea. "Who doesn't? I mean, his fingerprints were the only ones in the car, his empty beer cans were in the backseat, their blood was all over his car, and he didn't have an alibi."

"Just because someone doesn't have an alibi doesn't automatically make him guilty."

She pulled another cigarette from her purse. The other had been lost somewhere on the table amongst the plates. "No, but it leaves the door wide open."

He was leading the conversation where he wanted it. "It was eleven-thirty at night. There aren't many people who have alibis for that time of night. I bet you don't have one for that night."

"That's true, I don't. But that's not the only bit of evidence they have on him." She looked down at the cigarette. "At least according to the papers."

Chandler nodded. No alibi; just what he wanted to hear. He really wished he had a tape recorder. What's more, he wished it would have been admissible in court if he did have one—but he knew better.

"If you'll excuse me, I'm going to step outside for a moment to take a few drags. I'll just be a couple of minutes."

"Sure, go ahead." Take all the time you want, he thought, shaking his head; this woman had more fabrications than an upholstery manufacturer.

As she arose from her seat, the busboy came over and began to clear the table. Chandler caught sight of the other cigarette, grabbed it by the end, and placed it in a plastic Ziploc bag he pulled from his jacket pocket.

Chandler sat and waited for Harding to return. He paid the bill and stood up to stretch his back, which had begun to ache. Ten minutes after Harding had left for "a few drags," he walked outside to see what was keeping her. He wanted to ask her a few more questions and then get her cigarette over to the lab for analysis. He waited outside the restaurant, tapping his foot as the seconds passed. Finally, realizing she was not going to return, he left.

After arriving at the lab fifteen minutes later, he was escorted to the tool impression lab, where Gray was focusing a microscope.

Holding up the Ziploc bag, Chandler said, "I need a favor."

Gray stood there, looking poker-faced at Chandler, as if he were speaking a foreign language. Chandler read his mind: *I don't owe you any favors.*

"This cigarette has saliva on it, as well as a lip print. I need to know if it matches the DNA and the lip print on the cans of beer."

Gray shook his head and made a face. Turned and walked away.

"Hey, this is important, I think I've got something here."

Gray turned hard and faced Chandler, who was following close behind. They were closer than comfort would usually allow. "Look, this is not your private lab. Maybe that's the way you operate in New York. Pulling strings to get private evidence analyzed in a state lab. Well, it won't fly here. I should report you to the lab chief and let the attorney general look into how you operate."

Chandler could feel his face turning red, a deep shade of crimson.

"And your pal Lou is on vacation for two weeks," Gray continued. "Left yesterday evening. Good luck trying to locate him." Gray's face was slightly radiant. "But, the DA did give the okay to test the saliva on the cans for DNA."

"That hasn't been started yet?"

"Hey, look, I do what I'm told. Except when *you* tell me to do something."

"Now wait a minute," Chandler said, trying to contain his anger. "I'm here for only one reason: to get to the bottom of this crime. My client is innocent. He didn't do it. So in my short time here, I have to find out who did. Isn't that what we're all after? Finding the real guilty person and punishing him?"

Gray did not answer. Instead, he turned to walk away. Chandler grabbed his arm and gently pulled him back. "Let go of me," Gray said calmly.

When Chandler released his grip, Gray brushed his hair back and returned to the stool in front of his microscope.

"Look, how hard will it be to run the lip print for me?" Chandler asked, his tone softer. "Tell you what. If the lip print doesn't produce a reasonable and probable match with the beer can, then I give up, okay? You won't see me again." He paused to let this sink in. "But if there is a reasonable match, you'll run those DNA samples." If he refused, Chandler could still take the cigarette back with him to New York and run the test himself—but it would add a few variables that he wished to avoid: a different lab, accusations of bias, and the danger of contaminating the sample during the trip.

And even then, once he had his DNA results, trying to get a copy of the beer can's DNA pattern from Gray would be like asking your worst enemy for a loan. It just was not going to happen. He would have to have Hellman handle it through the court. Time-consuming. Messy.

Gray stood there, appearing to chew on the offer for a moment. Chandler knew what he was thinking: it was an attractive offer in that it would rid him of Chandler's presence—which was threatening to become as annoying as his dandruff itch. He would not have to face Palucci's wrath when he returned, nor would he have to deal with all the paperwork and questions from the chief if he did report Chandler.

Gray took the plastic bag without saying so much as a word and headed out of the room.

"Do we have a deal?" Chandler yelled after him.

"Yeah," Gray shouted back as he turned the corner and walked into the hallway.

CHAPTER

46

THE SUN HAD SET half an hour ago and the wind had whipped up a bit, bringing a cool chill to the air. It was 45 and headed down to the low 30s.

When Chandler arrived at the Madison home, Hellman was getting out of his car with a small bouquet of flowers. They walked up the front steps together and chatted for a moment before Leeza answered the door.

"Jeffrey, these are beautiful," she said, taking the flowers from him and bringing them up to her nose. "Thank you."

"My pleasure," Hellman said.

"So what was the purpose of the motion you filed?" Chandler asked as he walked into the living room.

"The whole idea was to keep this thing from degenerating into a three-ring circus. I wanted the cameras out of the courtroom during the entire proceedings."

"And?" Madison asked, entering the room. He leaned over and planted a kiss on the back of Leeza's neck as she placed the cut flowers in a vase.

"And the judge agreed and granted the motion. You should've seen Denton's face."

"Must've been ten shades of red," Chandler said. "I'm sure he wasn't happy about giving up the spotlight."

Hellman smiled and nodded. "It's still an important case for him, he just loses some of the fanfare that goes along with it. Anyway, I was thinking that maybe we could do an interview with that reporter from KMRA and give the media some things to chomp on, divert their focus away from Phil."

"It seems like everyone assumes I'm guilty before I even go to trial. I can't even go to the zoo with my family without being harassed by nuts who've seen the news painting me as a dreg of society."

Chandler rubbed his forehead, contorted his face. "A TV interview."

"I know you didn't want to think about peripheral matters," Hellman said, "but a strategic, exclusive interview could neutralize the negative PR and actually work to our benefit."

"Isn't this precisely what you argued against in front of the judge today?" Madison asked.

"This is different. First of all, it gives us a chance to have equal time after that bogus report Mather did on his interview with John Stevens. We do this one spot and that's it. Then we stay away from the media. But I really think it could have a positive effect."

"How do you figure?" Madison asked.

"We tell the press we believe we've found the real killer and are in the process of building enough evidence that will not only exonerate you, but will point to someone else. And of course once we have all the evidence in order, we'll cooperate fully with the police and turn it all over to them."

"The police," Chandler said, "are going to be pissed as hell. You're showing them up. They accused the wrong guy, so *you* are going to show them the right way to conduct an investigation. You're such a damned good attorney that you're not only going to get the charges against your client dismissed, but you're also going to hand them the real killer. After all, they're just a bunch of screw-ups." He raised his eyebrows and shook his head. "Don't expect them to be your buddies."

Madison spoke first. "Why don't we give Denton what we have now and see if they'll cooperate with us?"

"By cooperate you mean drop the charges," Chandler said.

Hellman shook his head. "Forget it. They're already deeply committed to your prosecution. Doing a one-eighty at this point would invite criticism from everyone and their uncle. They'd end up with egg all over their faces." He shook his head, as if he were convincing himself of something. "In fact,

I spoke with Denton yesterday. Their witness, that homeless guy, remembers that the driver was wearing a Chicago White Sox baseball hat—"

"Harding grew up in Chicago," Madison said.

"I know. I pointed that out to him. He wanted no part of it. He said, quote, 'we have our *man.*'"

"I don't think we have enough of anything to give them now anyway," Chandler said. "Let's wait until we get the DNA results back. Then we'll hopefully have more than enough to make this thing go away."

"It used to be that you wouldn't tell the prosecution anything about what you expected to bring out during trial . . . the thinking being that if you gave them key evidence that you had, it would give them time to properly investigate it and possibly find a way of refuting it. But if you spring it on them in the middle of the trial, they may not be able to get it investigated in time. If they don't know what's coming, they can't prepare for it. It was a big tactical advantage. Some defense counselors would never give anything to the prosecution; others would feed the prosecution bad info to make them waste time on a wild goose chase. Problem with that method is that once you got a rep for doing that, they'd never again believe anything you told them—and then when you really needed them to look into something legit, they'd tell you to go to hell."

"So then maybe we shouldn't tell them anything," Leeza said.

"Can't do that. As of about ten years ago, Prop 115 made it so that the prosecution got reciprocal discovery. That means," Hellman explained, noticing her twisted face of confusion, "that if the defense gets hold of something pertinent to the case, they have to turn it over to the prosecution. The reverse is also true—if they come across something that might be of assistance to us, they have to give it to us."

"And if you withhold something," Chandler said, "the judge could exclude that witness, or fact, or document, from the trial."

"So it all boils down to the fact that we probably don't

have a choice. According to the laws of discovery, if we have something, we have to turn it over, regardless of the tactical advantage we may be losing."

"But we can fudge a little on *when* we have to give it to them," Hellman said. "Right now, we're not required to turn anything over to them because I don't think we have anything concrete enough. We can do this interview or we can wait and see what happens. Things may lighten up on their own."

"Wait and see. Wait, wait, and then wait some more," Madison said, getting up from the table. "That's all I've been doing."

"Phil, say the word and I'll set up that interview with KMRA."

Madison looked at Chandler, who shrugged. "It's your decision, Phil."

"Let's do the interview," Leeza said. "It's time we took the offensive."

"Fine," Madison said. "Set it up. Let's divert their attention, get them the hell off my back."

CHAPTER
47

THE MORNING SKY was bleak, black thunderhead clouds engorged with moisture once again threatening to unleash yet another storm. Chandler called Denise but there was no answer. He left a message, told her that he loved her, and that he would see her soon.

He reviewed his notes, planned out his day, and phoned a friend of his father's in New York: John Donnelly. A retired private investigator, Johnny was a seventy-six-year-old former cop who had gotten caught in a corruption ring back in 1969 at the height of his career with the NYPD.

"I knew you'd be up," Chandler said.

"Junior, that you?"

"Yeah, who else?"

"Your father'd like to talk with you, Junior."

"First, tell me how you're doing."

"I still put my shoes on in the morning and go for my walk. As long as I can put my shoes on, I'm doing okay."

"How's Keara?"

"She's doing fine, Junior, just fine. Thanks for asking." Keara, Johnny's younger sister, had contracted cancer, and had no medical insurance to cover all the hospital bills and medication while supporting her two children. Her husband had left her one night in a drunken fit—and had never returned. Johnny, a cop with meager pay, gave her what he could to help out—but when that was depleted he went on the take—narcotics dealers were paying him to look the other way on his beat. The payoffs subsidized his sister's care, and the cancer went into remission—but at the cost of his career. As he was about to ask for a transfer to a different beat to covertly end his arrangement with the dealers, a druggie he had once busted found out about his having gone on the take, and turned him in. A classic case of irony.

But Johnny, ethics violations and embarrassment aside, had saved his sister's life, and as a result, had few regrets. He resigned as part of a deal that was arranged in lieu of a long, drawn-out investigation and trial that would have been embarrassing for the department. He ran a successful private investigation practice for twenty years, and remained friends with Chandler's father, who was one of the judges sitting on the bench at the time of Johnny's arrest.

"So what can I do for you, Junior?"

"I need to find this witness, a checkout clerk who recently moved back east. Guy's name is Ronald Norling," he said, consulting his notepad. I got his name from the manager at the supermarket where he used to work."

"I take it you don't have no address on this fella."

"I have a PO Box in Rhode Island and a social security number. Should be enough."

Johnny took down the information on Ronald Norling and agreed to assist Chandler in locating him.

"It's real important to this case I'm working out here," Chandler told him.

"Okay, Junior, I've got it," Johnny said. He was one of only two people who still called him Junior. But Chandler didn't take offense, since Johnny reminded him of his father.

"We'll get together sometime soon, okay, Johnny?"

"Maybe your dad'll join us, what do you think of that, huh, Junior? Grab some supper over at O'Malley's."

"I don't know, Johnny. I don't know."

"He misses you. He'd like to see his grandson, his daughter-in-law. It's time already, four years now."

"We'll see, Johnny. I'll think about it." He thanked him and hung up. Chandler doubted his father really wanted to see him. He figured it was in fact Johnny who felt that the two of them should make amends, and this was his way of bringing them together. But his father's inability to accept the fact that Chandler's back injury genuinely prevented him from being a cop created a friction he felt would never go away. For his own part, he was proud of his work as a forensic scientist. He enjoyed it, and just as with his career as a cop, he excelled in it.

He shook his head and tried to put his father out of his mind—he did not need another complicating factor in his life at the moment. He called the Department of Justice's state crime lab to see if the print results were completed on Harding's cigarette. He was hoping that Kurt Gray had actually run the comparison and was not just giving him lip service at the time to wiggle out of an uncomfortable situation.

Chandler tapped his foot while waiting on hold.

Finally, the receptionist returned to the line. "He's busy," she said.

"What does 'busy' mean?" Chandler asked.

"It means that he can't take your call right now."

Chandler clenched his jaw. "When *can* he take my call?"

"Just a minute," she said with a sigh.

A moment later, she was back on the line. "He said he'll call you."

Chandler bit his lip. Damn ambiguous answers. He took a deep breath. Keep it calm. "Does that mean today? Sometime this week?"

"Look sir, he can't speak to you right now. I'll leave him a message and he'll call you back."

Chandler left his number, and explained that he would be there for only a few more minutes. He would have to call back—hence the reason for his asking when Gray would be available. She told him to try again in an hour. Chandler was unsure if that was her way of putting him off, a useless guess, or if it really was when Gray could take the call. Either way, it seemed as if the criminalist was avoiding him. Not what he needed now. Time was precious.

He made his scheduled appointment at the KMRA studio, where Hellman's Lexus was parked out front. He entered and explained to the receptionist why he was there. She buzzed

Maurice Mather, received authorization, and handed him a visitor's pass. An escort was summoned to the lobby to take him into the studio.

There were three chairs positioned around a small round coffee table. Behind the set was an expansive blue backdrop as well as two white pillars that were fashioned to match those on the state capitol building's facade. This was where *Politically Speaking* was filmed every Sunday morning.

As Chandler walked into the studio, he saw Ingle, the intern, standing nearby, jotting down a few notes. Mather was standing off to the side with Hellman, who was touching his index finger into his opposing open hand, as if he were going point by point. ". . . Dr. Madison will not be participating. He will not be answering any questions, and he will not be directly addressed, even though he will be standing off-camera. Are we clear on this?"

"Clear."

"My purpose in insisting that this be taped rather than shot live is so that I can view it when you're finished editing it. If I'm not satisfied, and there's no acceptable way to edit it, we pull it and nothing gets shown. Are we clear on *that?*"

"Clear," Mather repeated.

"This outlines our agreement," Hellman said, handing him a one-page document. "Initial at the bottom that you received it."

Mather scribbled his initials and handed it back to Hellman, who provided him with a copy.

Hellman moved over toward Chandler, off to the side and out of earshot of Mather and the camera crew. "Anything new?"

Chandler sighed. "The lab guy won't take my call. Says I'm supposed to call back later. Rotting piece of— "

"Easy," Hellman said, motioning with both hands and keeping an eye on Mather over Chandler's shoulder.

"I'm gonna call him back in an hour. I just want to make sure he ran the lip print comparison."

"Fine," Hellman said, "we'll worry about it later. About this interview. We keep it short, to the point, and we don't divulge any specifics. We only tell them enough to whet their curiosity. But we can't say anything that's not factual and we can't make claims we can't substantiate."

"C'mon, Jeffrey. That doesn't leave us a whole lot of leeway."

"No, you're missing the point. We can discuss the new evidence we have, without saying what it is specifically, and we can discuss its significance without outlining exactly how it's going to have an impact on the case."

Chandler appeared uneasy. "We're not magicians. This is gonna be difficult."

"You don't have any experience as a politician."

"I've dedicated my life to catching criminals, not acting like them."

Hellman smiled. "That remark could be considered blasphemy being that we're so close to the state capitol building."

Mather was approaching from behind. "We'll be ready to shoot in two minutes, gentlemen."

Hellman nodded and turned back to Chandler. "Comb your hair, will you? There's a mirror over there on the wall behind the cameraman."

Chandler obliged, realizing that appearing professional and confident would play an important role in achieving their goal. He straightened his tie and took a few deep breaths to wipe the lines of stress from his face.

Mather and Ingle were waiting for Chandler and Hellman to take their seats. Mather sat to the right of Hellman and Chandler, who sat beside each other. Large spotlights shone down upon them, bathing the small area in bright white light. Ingle stood off-camera, to the far left of Chandler, near Madison and a large television monitor.

The director held up three fingers and counted down, then lowered his hand. Mather began speaking, introducing the viewers to the setting, and stating the purpose of their interview.

"Mr. Hellman," Mather said, "I believe it's safe to say that you feel your client is not guilty."

"He isn't just 'not guilty,' he's innocent."

"I didn't realize there was a difference," Mather said, a broad smile creasing his face.

Hellman maintained a serious, almost clinical expression. "'Not guilty,' in my opinion, carries a negative connotation. Simply stated, Dr. Madison is completely innocent of this crime and is being wrongly charged. In fact, we are in the process of amassing evidence which demonstrates that he was framed."

"Framed?" Mather asked. He straightened in his seat.

"That's what we're working on right now. Ryan Chandler is our investigator," Hellman said, nodding toward his associate.

"Are the police working with you on this?" Mather asked, turning toward Chandler.

"The police are not involved in our investigation at this time."

"And why is that?"

Chandler leaned forward a bit. "We're still putting together all the details. We felt it would be better that we have all our cards in order first. We don't want them to think we're making a baseless accusation. Then we wouldn't have their confidence, or even their cooperation, when we complete our work and have more solid objective evidence to turn over to them."

"Are you saying that the police were delinquent in their investigation of this case?"

Hellman glanced over at Chandler. Being that Chandler was "one of them," it was preferable that he address such an issue.

"Not at all," Chandler said. "The police, I'm sure, have been as diligent in their investigation as is required. They brought in a suspect, and they did it within a reasonable period of time following the murders."

"What would you consider to be a reasonable period of time?"

"Three, four days. Longer than that, and your chances of catching the suspect decline significantly. Evidence is destroyed, suspects and witnesses disappear, people forget what they saw."

"Do you think the police feel they have the right man?"

"I'm sure they feel confident in the evidence they've amassed, and I have to admit that it does point to Phillip Madison. However, Dr. Madison was not the driver of that vehicle. He's been falsely accused."

"Understanding that you've been hired by the defense, Mr. Chandler, what gives you the objectivity to make such a statement?"

"Seven years with the Sacramento Police Department; two years as a special investigator with the Sacramento County District Attorney. I'm currently a forensic investigator with the New York Police Department. I've seen the evidence, and I'm in the process of awaiting results on tests that I strongly believe will show that Dr. Madison was not the driver of that vehicle."

"These tests you mentioned. Are these tests on physical evidence that you're conducting?"

"Yes," Chandler said.

"If Dr. Madison was not driving, do you have any theories on who was?"

Hellman stepped in. "Yes, we do."

"Who then?"

"We're not prepared to say just yet."

"And why is that?"

"For the very reason that Mr. Chandler said what he said a few moments ago. We're not going to release the name until we've gotten our house in order and we've spoken with the police and district attorney."

"Mr. Hellman, some would say that this is just a ploy on the part of a clever defense attorney to create reasonable doubt for his client. You produce another possible suspect, and then the jury is confused and can't return a verdict beyond a reasonable doubt. You've done that several times in the past—"

"I'm not here to discuss my past cases," Hellman said. He paused for a moment, then continued. "This is not a defense ploy. I believe not only that Dr. Madison is innocent, but I also believe that once we have all our tests completed, this case will not be going to trial, so there'll be no jury to 'confuse,' as you put it. The prosecutor, Mr. Denton, will drop the charges."

"You're that sure of your evidence."

"I'm that sure."

"How can the People be sure that your test results will be accurate?"

Hellman looked over at Chandler.

Chandler leaned forward. "The facility running the tests is reputable, I assure you." He suddenly realized he had not told Hellman where he'd taken the samples. "And the DA would of course be free to conduct his own tests."

"This brings me to another topic I wanted to touch on. What's the story behind those rape charges?"

"First of all, there never have been any rape charges. Second of all, rape has nothing to do with this case—"

"But it goes to Dr. Madison's credibility, doesn't it, Mr. Hellman?"

"Dr. Madison has never been charged with anything except the charges he is currently facing," he said.

"But he *was* the subject of a rape case."

Chandler realized that Hellman was cornered. However, the trump card was their ability to edit out anything they did not find acceptable.

Hellman shifted a bit in his seat. "There was an investigation the police conducted involving a complaint on the part of a woman, but the police later closed the case and she withdrew her complaint. There was no truth to any of it."

"Was the woman paid off, Mr. Hellman?"

"I believe you've heard the saying 'crime doesn't pay,'" Hellman said, "and since the complaint was filled with lies, I'll let you draw your own conclusions."

The reporter leaned forward. "By that do you mean that this woman did not receive a payoff to keep quiet and drop the charges?"

"She did not benefit one red cent," Hellman said.

Chandler looked over at Hellman and saw a thin trail of perspiration rolling down the side of his face. If a copy of the Harding contract Hellman had drawn up had made it into Mather's hands, it would be an uncomfortable revelation—regardless of whether or not it was later edited out of the final cut. The existence of the document would still make it onto the eleven o'clock news. And if Mather had a copy of it, others in the press could get their hands on it as well—and then the task of preserving and restoring Madison's reputation would require something bordering on divine intervention.

The rest of the interview consisted of a few mundane questions about facts already known by the press; Mather requested more depth and information where none existed. Although this appeared to frustrate the reporter, it allowed Hellman to conclude the interview without incident.

Afterward, Chandler, Madison, and Hellman accompanied Mather into an edit bay, a small six-by-six room with large digitized Betamax video machines. They watched as the seven-minute interview was edited down to three, and concluded that the final product served their purpose. They looked confident and cool, and did not give away any valuable information; however, it provided enough for Mather to bill it as an exclusive interview with new information on "The Madison Murders."

As they began to walk out of the studio, Chandler headed over to the bank of pay phones near the lobby to call Kurt Gray while Hellman detoured to the restroom. It had been a little over an hour since he had last called, and this was when Gray was supposedly going to be able to talk.

"Yeah, I remember when you called last," came the less-than-enthusiastic reply from the receptionist. "Hold please," she said.

He tapped his fingers on the side of the pay phone and turned to Madison. "This guy better not be playing games—"

"Mr. Gray says he'll have to talk to you tomorrow," the receptionist said.

"Tomorrow?" Chandler took a breath. "Please tell him I need to talk to him now."

"Hold please."

He ran his fingers through his hair. *Tomorrow. That lying son-of—*

She came back on. "I'm sorry."

"Well, you tell Mr. Gray that I spoke with Lou Palucci today up at his cabin in Tahoe, and he told me that if Gray didn't cooperate, he'd come back early from his vacation and set him straight personally. Tell him that!"

"If you know where the guy was, why don't you just have him call?" Madison asked.

Chandler cupped the phone and motioned for him to be quiet.

The next voice he heard was Kurt Gray's. "I got a match on the lip prints. Now, will you leave me alone?"

Hellman was walking over from the restroom; Madison informed him that Chandler was on the phone with the lab.

"How much of a match?"

"Ninety-five percent."

"I like that better than seventy."

"I can't tell you how pleased I am that you're happy with the results. Can I go now? I'm busy."

"The DNA. Are you running the DNA on that cigarette?"

"I've already started it, and I'll have an answer in three weeks, about the same time that the other tests on the beer can DNA are ready. I'm giving the receptionist specific instructions not to put any more of your calls through." Without further comment, he hung up.

"Yes!" Chandler said. He looked at Hellman and Madison, who were standing around him. He motioned them outside, into the parking lot, out of the earshot of the news people in the immediate vicinity.

"The lip print off Harding's cigarette is a ninety-five per-cent match to the lip print taken off the can of beer that was found in the back of the car."

Hellman's face was spread into a broad smile.

"What does that mean?" Madison asked.

"It means, Phil," Hellman said, "that we're one step closer to getting this case dismissed."

CHAPTER
48

THE INTERVIEW WAS aired as part of a four-minute segment on the noon news. It caught the attention of the rest of the media, and Hellman suddenly had a list of calls to be returned to reporters from the *Herald,* the *Bee,* the other four television news stations, and a few out-of-town papers. There was also a call from Judge Calvino: Hellman was to report to his chambers in an hour.

When Hellman arrived, Denton was sitting on the stiff leather couch adjacent to the wall of law books, a magazine opened across his lap. Calvino's mood was etched in the deep furrows of his brow. It was evident that he and Denton had not been conversing.

Calvino was in no mood for a discussion. His orders were clear: no more trying this case in the media. Denton attempted to argue, no doubt about to say that he had not contacted nor spoken to the press. But Calvino did not give him the opportunity to speak.

"The next person who gives an interview, leaks information to the press, or comes within five feet of a reporter will be held in contempt. I'm doing it as much for the ability to empanel an impartial jury as to preserve Phillip Madison's reputation should he be found not guilty."

Hellman knew that Calvino could not give a damn about Madison, but he figured the judge was at least trying to give his decision an air of impartiality and fairness.

"The fewer juicy tidbits the media can get their hands on," Calvino said, "the less publicity there'll be. And the less publicity, the greater the chance that everyone will forget the case shortly after its resolution. There are a few emotionally invested groups interested in this case, and the last thing I want is another O. J. Simpson fiasco."

Hellman and Denton nodded and thanked the judge, then left his chambers like dogs that had been properly disciplined. They walked down the hall toward the elevator bank, silent at first.

"Sorry," Hellman said.

Denton waved him off. "Shit, I would've done the same thing. You saw an opportunity for your client."

"Mather pissed me off with that bullshit report from Sacramento General. I felt I had to get some positive press to neutralize it."

"I can take some heat from Calvino. It's not a big deal."

"Look, Tim . . ." started Hellman, unsure if he should go any further. "I have a thought on who may be the real murderer. You interested?"

Denton stifled a laugh, and then realized that Hellman was serious. He pushed the down button again. "Damn elevators."

"I'm not kidding. And I'm not just saying this as a defense ploy. I've known my client for thirty years. I really believe that Phil Madison is innocent. I know he is."

"Jeffrey, need I tell you how many times I've heard that from defense counsel?"

"Tim, you and I also go back a long time. We've had our fights over the years, some tough cases. But I've always been aboveboard with you. How many times have I told you I don't like your wardrobe?" he asked, smiling. This drew a smirk from Denton. "Point is, I've always considered you a straight shooter, and you know I am too."

"So what do you want me to do, drop the charges? It isn't going to happen, Jeffrey, even if I do believe you—which I don't."

"All I ask is that you look at things with an open mind. Don't sell my client down the river. Don't use him as a political stepping-stone—"

"Stop right there, Jeffrey," he said, his face getting red. Wrong button to push. "I don't have to listen to this. Political stepping-stone," he repeated. "Who the fuck do you think you are? Suggesting that I would prosecute someone just because they're high-profile, all for my personal gain?"

Hellman stared him down.

The elevator came, and they entered together. "Just tell me that if I turn something over to you and it makes sense, that you'll give it unbiased consideration. Because when I get everything together, I'm confident that you'll have enough to at least reopen your investigation and dig until this other lead proves either sweet or sour."

Denton, who did not say a word, just stared at the control panel, still apparently seething at the suggestion of impropriety.

"Tim, one of the basic tenets of our criminal justice system is to protect the rights of an innocent man to the extent that if there's any reasonable doubt that he committed a crime, he's supposed to be set free. It's better to let a guilty man go free than to put an innocent man in prison." He paused, knowing that Denton was well aware of the legal rhetoric. "All I'm asking for is an open mind. Will you at least do that?"

Hellman detected a barely perceptible nod. He gave an affectionate nudge to Denton's shoulder as the doors opened. "Sorry I hurt your feelings," Hellman said. He walked out and down the hall toward the parking lot, hoping the seed he'd planted would take root just enough to pry open Denton's notoriously closed mind.

CHAPTER
49

SHORTLY AFTER LUNCH, Chandler drove to Mark Stanton's office for a follow-up interview. First on his list of questions was how he'd handled Harding's sexual harassment payoff a couple of years ago. It was a matter that could be handled over the phone, but Chandler's method of doing business was always face-to-face whenever possible, and it appeared that that was the way Stanton preferred it as well.

There were two people dressed in business attire sitting in the lobby of Stanton's plush suite, patiently awaiting appointments with him. Chandler walked in and announced his arrival to the secretary, an attractive thirty-year-old with a headset attached to her face. She nodded to him, asked him to have a seat, and alerted Stanton that Chandler had arrived.

A moment later, she led him to Stanton's office, despite his comment that he already knew the way. Stanton was on the phone and motioned to Chandler to have a seat. He punched a couple of keys on his computer. "I'm faxing it right now. Yeah, give me a call back as soon as you've had a chance to review it."

"Sorry," he said, hanging up the phone and turning to Chandler. "Client from Russia. An American company attempting to open a branch and expand their company. They already have one in Europe . . . but you didn't come here to discuss my business."

"Thanks for seeing me. The case for my client is coming together nicely, but the icing on the cake would be your testimony. We need it to establish a motive."

"Well, I did speak with my attorney, as I told you I would.

He recommended against getting involved. He said I paid a lot of money to put the incident behind me, and that's precisely what I should do. Said I shouldn't stick my nose in any more sexual harassment suits. Especially as a witness."

"Oh, this isn't sexual harassment, Mr. Stanton. It's murder."

Stanton sat forward in his seat. "Murder? How does Brittany Harding fit into a murder case?"

"We have evidence and reason to believe that she killed two people and is trying to frame my client for it. If convicted, he could be facing life imprisonment." He looked at Stanton's face: his brows were furrowed and his mouth agape. Chandler was getting through. "She'd falsely accused him of raping her a few months back, and then demanded a payment of fifty thousand dollars. Like you, he decided it was better to pay than suffer the publicity it would generate. But that wasn't enough for her. She sent a copy of the check to his wife, violating the agreement she'd made with him, and his attorney forced her attorney—Movis Ehrhardt—to return the money. Harding was furious, and framed him with this murder. The evidence against my client is all circumstantial, but it may just be enough to convince a jury. Your testimony as to her prior conduct and behavior will establish a pattern and fit well with what we have on her so far."

Stanton shifted in his seat. "Murder," he said. His telephone intercom buzzed. "Mr. Stanton, Judy Myers on line four."

"Take a message and tell her I'll call her back in ten minutes."

"You also have Ms. Bieles and Mr. Canvir waiting."

"Okay, Amanda," he said, a slight edge to his voice. "Then tell Judy I'll call her back in an hour."

He arose from behind his desk, walked over to one of the paintings on his wall. As he removed it, a safe was visible; he began spinning the tumbler, placing his body between the wheel and Chandler's line of sight. Chandler looked away obligingly. Stanton fumbled around in the safe and pulled out a videocassette, handed it to Chandler.

"What's this?"

"It's my meeting with Harding, when I gave her the check.

I got her to talk about the payoff, asking her why she was doing this to me. She admitted it was all for the money. She said I could afford it, and aside from being out the money, no harm would come to me. Watch it. It's all there. Pretty damning, if you ask me."

Chandler was struck speechless by his good luck. "Why'd you tape it?" he finally managed.

"Just in case she tried to extort more from me in the future. You know, a bimonthly occurrence, like drawing a paycheck."

"Why didn't your attorney handle the transaction?"

"He said I should do it. He had some private investigator come in and set up a tiny camera, right there," he said, nodding to a large, seven-foot-tall leafy plant. "He was watching the whole thing go down on a monitor in another room down the hall. Handled it all by remote control."

Chandler nodded. He liked this attorney, whoever he was. Knew how to play ball.

"Take it, make a copy of it. Just don't lose it. I should've made a copy of it a long time ago, but never got around to it."

Chandler was reluctant to take responsibility for it, but he was too curious to see what was on it to turn it down. "I'll get it back to you right away," he said. "About testifying . . ."

"The tape should be sufficient."

Not wanting to walk out the door without the videocassette, Chandler decided to back off the issue. If need be, Hellman could subpoena Stanton to testify. Not the best way to treat a witness you needed for your case, but an option nonetheless. At this point, the judge still had to rule on the admissibility of the evidence. If he threw it all out as being unduly prejudicial, Stanton's story would never make it to the courtroom.

He stood, dwarfed by Stanton's six-foot-five frame, and they shook hands.

Upon returning to Hellman's office, Chandler informed him of the Stanton video. Although there was a client waiting, they took the tape into the conference room and watched it.

The date was displayed in the lower-right corner of the screen. It was recorded a little more than two years ago. The camera angle was adequate, showing Harding without question; same auburn hair, slightly different cut. Stanton maneuvered himself behind her for a moment while he was removing something from the credenza behind her chair—a checkbook. He looked straight into the camera. Good so far. He sat down behind his desk and opened the check register to a clean page while they chatted about how this was capital he needed to keep the company afloat.

"You'll find a way to keep it running," she said. "You've eliminated my salary."

"Why are you doing this to me?" he asked, taking his pen off the check, as if the completion of the transaction were contingent upon her response.

"Because I deserve more than to be fired."

"Laid off, Brittany, laid off. There's a difference. I didn't have a choice. You weren't singled out—I've eliminated all nonessential personnel."

She sat straight up, her jaw tight and her eyes narrow. "I'm nonessential, huh?"

"That's not what I meant—"

"Oh, yes it is."

"Technically, I'm the only essential person in this company. Without me, there is no company. The same can't be said about you. It was not meant as a reflection on you or your abilities."

"Well, you won't miss the fifty grand. It's only money. You'll get over it."

"But sexual harassment. Jesus, couldn't you have thought of something else?"

"It perks people's ears up. It got your attention."

"But it's flat-out lying. It's extortion."

"You do what you need to do to keep surviving, I do what I need to do. If you want to call it extortion, fine." She crossed her legs and threw her head back, using a finger to help sweep the hair off her face. "If it makes you feel better, think of it as a business transaction. I'm launching a new career." Her eyes sparkled in the light that was peering through the blinds behind Stanton's desk.

Stanton began to write again. He swirled his pen, scrawling what appeared to be his signature. He was obviously satisfied with what he had gotten on tape. "How much of this does your attorney get?"

"Too much," she said. "But I don't suppose you would have agreed to it had he not been involved." Stanton did not say anything. "Then again, it would have been your word against mine in court. I say you fondled me, you say you didn't. Who do you think the jury would've believed?" She smiled. "Then again, by the time it got to a jury, you'd be out of business. Much cleaner this way for you . . . but obviously, you already know that or you wouldn't be writing this check."

"A lie, that's what this check is. Fifty thousand lies."

"It cashes and spends the same way."

He ripped the check off his register and threw it on the desk in front of him. "I can honestly say I regret the day I hired you, Brittany. One of the worst business decisions of my career."

"It certainly paid off for me." She smiled, rose from her chair, and walked out the door. Stanton turned to the camera, his face a crumpled picture of anger. Then the screen turned to white and gray snow.

Hellman flipped off the tape. "Damn good work, Chandler. Damn good."

"Think the judge will let it in?"

"Don't know. But I can tell you this. If your cigarette DNA comes up positive for Harding, this tape will help persuade him to issue a search warrant for a blood sample and a few strands of Harding's hair."

Chandler nodded. "We need to make a copy of this, get it back to Stanton."

"I'll have someone run it over to my copy service company. They can duplicate it for us."

"I thought they only did documents and x-rays."

"And videocassettes," Hellman said as he stood up and ejected the tape from the VCR.

"Have them make an extra copy for Stanton. That's his only copy, so be careful with it." He arose from his chair. "I've got some personal things to deal with, so I'm heading back to New York in a few hours. I think I've got everything squared away."

"We'll keep in touch. I'll let you know what's going on," Hellman said. "We probably won't need you out here until we get the DNA stuff sorted out."

"If I turn anything else up before I leave, I'll call you."

Hellman extended his hand. "You've been a jewel, Chandler. Thanks."

"I've been called a lot of things over the years, but I don't remember anybody ever calling me a jewel," he said, sharing a smile with Hellman.

Chandler had been resting, attempting to grab a short nap before leaving for the airport. However, he was unable to fall asleep: thoughts of Denise consumed him. It was the first time it had actually hit him: what if the lump really was cancer? It would change their lives forever. To begin with, deciding which treatment she should receive would be a difficult decision. Medical science offered more than one approach, but it was unclear which was best on a long-term basis—and there were no guarantees. The wrong decision could be deadly. You did not get a second chance to catch the disease in its early stages, which is a must for a successful cure regardless of the treatment method selected.

Finally, at some point he settled into a light sleep. Shortly after awakening, he splashed his face with some cold water and checked in with Denise. She was feeling more at ease, having had a couple of days to put everything into perspective. "I realized it's ridiculous to decide on my fate before I've had an exam and an appropriate workup," she told him.

"I agree with you a hundred percent. We shouldn't worry about something that's not yet a problem." He told her he had been thinking of her, and that they would be together soon. After hanging up, he realized that their thoughts had taken them in opposite directions: she had been able to put her mind at ease, while he had succeeded in putting his in knots. But he was glad that she was now approaching it optimistically.

Chandler packed his clothes and scanned his list of follow-ups. As he wrote down a few thoughts on his pad, a sudden wave of exhaustion struck him. He launched into a sustained yawn and tossed his notes onto the bed. Although the clock on the wall read 8:30 P.M., it was 11:30 New York time. With a six-hour red-eye flight only an hour and a half away, he accepted the fact that he would be fighting fatigue for the next few days.

He stood up to stretch and invigorate his tired limbs, then grabbed the phone and called Johnny Donnelly to inquire about his success in locating the checkout clerk.

"Old Ronald's proving a bit hard to find, even for a snoop like me, Junior."

"What have you got?" he asked, stifling another yawn.

"Checked DMV. Nothing. He ain't applied for a license. Probably just using his California license. Checked the post office, no one seen him come by his box. Mailed him a note to call me, told him there was a reward. Didn't say how much. I'll give him a five spot if he presses me on it. You'll owe me five, Junior."

Chandler laughed. "What about parents, anyone else by his name in town or the surrounding areas?"

"No one. If he's got family, they got a different last name. Could sure use a picture of the guy though."

"Wish I had one, but I don't. What about the unemployment agency, state disability, local hospitals?"

"That's on the plate for tomorrow. You know me, Junior. I'm up till four in the morning, but nobody else seems to like that schedule."

Chandler told him he would call tomorrow when he returned to New York; he gathered up his suitcase and wheeled it onto the staircase elevator.

Madison watched the copy of the Stanton tape with Leeza that evening once the boys had been put to bed and Chandler had departed for the airport. As the video ended, Leeza pressed rewind on the remote.

"This is just what the doctor ordered," she said.

Madison nodded, the pun lost on him. "It'll probably be inadmissible in court, and the bogus evidence against me will still be hanging over my head. Not to mention all the legal hurdles we need to overcome and the fact that my practice is a shambles. But in spite of all that . . . I feel good."

"You needed the emotional lift," she said, resting in his arms and running her fingers through his hair.

"What matters to me most, Lee, is that we're together. Not just physically, but emotionally. It's hard to believe it took such an incredible run of events to show me what we've been missing the past few years."

"Better that you realized it now, rather than years down the line. It's not too late to make changes."

Madison sighed. "Whether or not it's too late remains to be seen."

CHAPTER
50

MANHATTAN WAS one of those places that, with rare exception, was considerably less attractive following a snowstorm. Unlike the Sierras or Andes Mountains, where the snow accentuated the natural beauty of the surroundings, snow in Manhattan quickly turned to gray and black slush, with some yellow sprinkled in here and there from a dog whose bladder needed relief.

On most of the busiest sidestreets, mounds of snow lay piled against the curb, the result of a snowplow's pass earlier that morning. Those people whose cars were parked at the curb would find an unanticipated wall of hard-packed snow holding their vehicles prisoner. The sight of angry business-men and -women in suits heaving the frozen white stuff away from their cars with folding shovels at the end of a long workday was not an unusual one in certain parts of the city. Those who were fortunate to be able to commute by subway, bus, or cab had a definite advantage at this time of year.

As the cars swished by on the densely trafficked avenues, a light rain fell. In the past, whenever the temperature fell into the teens, thin sheets of ice coated the sidewalks—and caused an unusually high number of people to report to emergency rooms or chiropractic offices with slip-and-fall injuries.

This morning, Denise had taken Noah to day care. She and Chandler made plans to meet for brunch at ten o'clock to give him time to check in at the office and deal with the imminent tongue-lashing he was likely to receive from Hennessy.

"I hate driving in the city," Chandler said to the Iranian

man who was weaving in and out of traffic with the reckless abandon of a seasoned New York City cabbie. "It's like a war fought without guns. People use their cars to take out their aggression."

The taxi driver, periodically launching into a barrage of vile language aimed at certain vehicles he cut off en route to his destination, curtailed the expletives long enough to agree with his passenger. "But I consider myself a soldier, a soldier who wins most of his battles. That is why I get you where you want to go on time," he said, pulling up at the Police Academy building on East 20th Street.

After he paid the man and exited the cab, Chandler ascended the slush-covered steps of the square, gray-brick building that had been built in the 1970s. He paused at the doorway and filled his lungs with cold air. It felt good to be home again, on his own turf.

He opened the door and walked in across the slate entryway, glancing over at the glass-enclosed academy gymnasium. He flashed on his days in training, when he was young and eager to graduate and become a beat cop. That was before he decided to move to California, to put distance between himself and his father. He shook his head at the irony that left him showing up on his father's doorstep nearly ten years later, disabled and without a job.

He took the elevator to the eighth floor, and waved at Nick in the evidence lab, who called for him to come answer a question. Shouting that he would be back in a little while, he proceeded down the hall and stopped outside the door of his boss. "Capt. James Hennessy" was lettered in black on the dimpled glass. He grabbed the dented brass knob, twisted it, and braced for the worst.

Hennessy was seated behind his fifty-year-old wooden desk, which was mounded with papers. A dim fluorescent fixture hung from the ceiling. A half-eaten sandwich in crumpled tinfoil lay on the desk next to an open bottle of Yoo-Hoo chocolate drink. A steady stream of hot air blew up from the grating in front of the window on the far wall, where files were piled into not-so-neat stacks.

Hennessy, a man just shy of five feet and in excess of 175 pounds, looked up and saw Chandler as he walked through the door. "Chandler, you fuckin' asshole. You just waltz in here and expect to pick up where you left off, huh? Is that what you expect? Leave me to answer for your whereabouts with Gianelli while you're out enjoying the California sun? You dick-faced cock. Nick's been working double tours trying to get your work done. Do you care? Nah, you ain't got the goddamned balls enough to care. All you care about is yourself." As he stood there, he was only a foot taller than Chandler, who was sitting in the metal chair that was perched in front of Hennessy's desk.

"Are you finished?" Chandler asked.

"Yeah, I'm finished."

"It's good to see you too."

"Don't give me that bull-fucking shit. You're not glad to see me. I'm gonna ride your ass till you retire."

"I'm taking an early lunch today. Ten o'clock. I should be back by eleven-thirty. Wife has a doctor's appointment. I'll stay until seven to help Nick out with whatever it is that he needs help with. Starting tomorrow, I'll come in two hours early every morning until I'm up to speed on things. And I'll find something on that Bobby Lee Walker case to bail you out of your jam. That sound okay to you?"

Hennessy made a noise that was a cross between a grumble and a growl, but Chandler took it as a yes. "How is it that you do this to me, Chandler? Everyone else here hates my guts. They're scared of me. You, you don't seem to care what the fuck I say."

Chandler smiled and arose from the chair, towering over Hennessy. "I know that underneath that gruff exterior is a caring man."

"Bullshit."

"Don't shatter my illusion," Chandler said, opening the door. "I'll be with Nick," he called as the door closed behind him.

Hennessy flung a year-old *People* magazine at the door. "Asshole."

*   *   *   *

The office of Dr. Jason Bloom was newly remodeled: sleek halogen spotlights were recessed into the taupe-colored ceiling, while a white Corian reception desk with several computers mounted into ergonomic work stations blended well with upholstered chairs that matched the wallpaper of the reception room.

Chandler let out a slight whistle. "I guess Jason finished his remodel. Remind me to let him pick up the check next time we go out to dinner."

As they took a seat, a smile broke out across his face. "Remember when you first started seeing Jason? All your friends thought it was so weird for us to be friends with your gynecologist."

"We were friends first, and then when what's his name—Levins—had that heart attack, I needed a new OB. We thought I was pregnant, remember?"

Chandler nodded.

"And from what I recall," Denise said, "it wasn't just my friends who thought it was weird, you did too."

"I did?"

"You don't remember? In the beginning, it was real hard for you to get used to the fact that one of your college buddies, who you drank beer with and went to Jets games with, was going to be examining my private parts."

"Yeah, but after the first few times, I got used to it."

"Denise?" A nurse was standing at the doorway holding a chart. "Come on back with me."

The examination went well. Dr. Bloom kept the conversation light but professional while he poked and prodded her breast. He felt it methodically and carefully, and then had her lean forward and move her arms into various positions. "It feels okay . . . the lump is mobile, it's small, there's no discharge from the nipple, and the skin isn't dimpled." He reached for a prescription pad from City Radiological Imaging. "I'm convinced it's nothing, honestly. I'd tell you guys if it wasn't. But for peace of mind, I'm going to send you for a mammogram. It'll be good to establish a baseline for the future anyway." He signed the slip and handed it to Chandler. "And while we're at it, we'll get a blood draw and run a pregnancy test. Maybe we'll have some more good news."

"Denise wants a girl."

Bloom smiled. "Girls and their daddies are a special thing, Chandler."

"That's what everyone tells me. But I wouldn't complain if we had another boy."

"Knowing you," Bloom said, "you'd probably throw a party." He leaned over and gave Denise a peck on the cheek. "Keep him in line. I'll see you guys on Saturday."

After the nurse performed the blood draw, they left his office. "This is good, Denise," Chandler said, taking her hand as they walked to the elevator.

She nodded weakly. "I'll feel better once I get the results back from the mammogram."

City Radiological Imaging was located in the same building as Jason Bloom's office. Upon completion of the x-rays, which took less than ten minutes to perform, Chandler hailed a taxi for each of them.

As the cabs pulled over to the curb, he gave Denise a kiss on the cheek. "I've got to get some things squared away at the lab, and then I'll be home. I've pushed Hennessy about as far as I can." He took her in his arms and squeezed tightly. "I'm glad the news was good. And I'm glad I was here to go through it with you."

Denise stroked his face with her fingertips. "Me too."

When Denise arrived home, there was a message from Jason Bloom on her machine. According to a preliminary reading from the radiologist, the lump appeared to be a benign fibroid mass—which coincided with his exam findings. "So don't worry, Denise," the message said. "We'll follow up in six months and do a comparison. Meantime, I'll call you with the assay from the lab on the pregnancy test as soon as I have it."

Later that evening, after she relayed the results of the mammogram to Chandler, he smirked.

"I know that look," she said.

"What look?"

"That look that says 'see, I told you.' You always think you know it all."

He held up a hand. "First of all, that's not true. No one knows it all. I just know more than most people." He grunted as the pillow from the couch flew across the room and struck him square in the face. Before Chandler knew it, he was flat on his back. Noah was bouncing on his stomach, Denise was tickling him, and the dog was licking his face.

"It's good to be home."

After dinner, Chandler checked in with Johnny Donnelly again to see if Ronald Norling had been located. Johnny confessed that he'd had no luck with the hospitals, unemployment office, or junior colleges.

"I checked the utility companies to see if he'd applied for electricity, heat, or phone service. Again, there was nothing. I was beginning to think the PO box was just a dead end, when sly old Ronald called me asking about his reward. I told him to hold his gombunies, that he'd get it as soon as we got to talk to him. The youngster's a slimeball, Junior. Not sure how good a witness he's gonna make."

"All we need to do is have him tell the truth as to what he saw and heard. You get a number on him?"

"Is the pope Catholic? What kind of an investigator do you think I am?"

Chandler took the number, thanked him, and promised to get together with him soon.

"I assume we'll invite your pop along too, right, Junior? Consider it my fee for finding this Ronald fella for you."

Chandler was too tired to argue. "Sure, Johnny."

As he hung up the phone, he thought that perhaps it was time to make amends with his father. But that was an issue he would have to deal with some other time.

The five-dollar "witness fee" that Johnny thought would carry weight became a fifty-dollar advance, paid by Chandler. He had travel expenses to cover, he explained. Once Chandler peeled off the five ten-dollar bills and placed them in his witness's hand, Ronald Norling's memory became instantly more acute. It was obviously not the first time he had played this game. Chandler wondered about Ronald's background: where he came from, what trouble he'd been in, whether or not he had a record . . . things that would become credibility issues were he to testify. But that was all information he could glean from the computer at the precinct.

Right now, he had to find out exactly what Ronald saw that night in the supermarket, and how well he remembered it. He had brought a picture of Harding along, as well as a picture of Denise and Denise's sister, Shari Moore. Before committing Hellman to a witness, he wanted to be absolutely sure that this cocky twenty-year-old could at least identify the suspect from a photo.

"As I explained to you on the phone, I need information regarding an incident that occurred while you were employed at Food & More."

"Yeah, right."

Chandler pulled a small microcassette recorder from his pocket.

"Whoa, what's that?" Ronald asked.

"A tape recorder. We'll tape what we talk about. It's for my boss, to prove that I was here and did what he's paying me to do. This way, he can also listen to what you said so you don't have to go through all of it again. You okay with this?"

"Yeah," Ronald said with a shrug. "But if I don't like what we say, I want the tape."

Chandler nodded. "I can live with that." He switched on the recorder. "This is Ryan Chandler and I'm in Rhode Island at the rest stop along Interstate Ninety-five, near Hope Valley. I'm interviewing Ronald Norling, a former clerk for Food & More in Sacramento, California. This is being recorded on Saturday, January 9, at nine-fifteen in the morning." He looked up at Ronald. "Ronald, you understand that we're taping this, right?"

"Yeah."

"And so far all we've discussed is the need to record this, and the fact that we're going to talk about an incident you may have witnessed while employed at Food & More, is that correct?"

"Yeah, that's right."

"Okay. Do you remember a shouting match that occurred in the market between a gentleman and a woman in late November?"

"The market's in a real nice neighborhood, so we didn't get much problems. But late November . . . yeah, I remember some crazy lady. She was screaming at this guy. She was real nasty, like out of her mind. Just screaming at him. I felt bad for him."

"I have pictures of three women here," he said, handing him the photos. "Do you see the woman from the store in any of them?"

"Yeah, that's her," Ronald said, popping gum between his teeth. "A real piece. I won't forget that face. Or that body," he said with a smile that rose slightly from the corners of his mouth.

"Ronald, can you turn that picture over, the one of the lady you said was in the store? And read me the name that's written on the back."

"Brittany Harding."

"Now turn the other pictures over and read me the names."

"Denise Chandler . . . and Shari Moore."

"Do you remember what the lady in the picture—Miss Harding—said when she was screaming in the market?"

"Yeah, something about getting even. Like 'You'll pay for this. I'll make you pay for this.' She said he raped her or something. But you look at this guy, and you think he's not the kind of guy who goes out and rapes someone."

Chandler nodded. Somehow he knew that Ronald would know a rapist if he saw one. "You remember anything about what she bought that night?" The second most important question . . . and Chandler needed a home run on this one.

Ronald stood there and thought for a moment. "Not really. Just some food. There weren't too many things. It was a cash-only fifteen-item limit line. Oh, she had beer. A six-pack. What the hell kind was it . . ." he said, gazing off at the freeway. "Millstone. It was Millstone. I thought like, what's a lady like this drinking a dark beer like that? I even asked her about it. You know, just to calm her down. Take the edge off. She was pretty wound up." He laughed. "She nearly took my head off. Told me to mind my own fucking business. Said she has a right to drink anything she wants. She's got a real mouth on her, for a lady I mean."

"What did you say to that?"

He laughed. "I didn't argue with her. I just wanted her off my line. She gave me the creeps. She's like the kind of person you worry about pulling a gun out of her purse and blowing your head off."

Chandler thanked him and turned off the recorder. He told Ronald that he might need to ask him some more questions, took down his address, and gave him his card. Ronald studied the card, seemingly intrigued by the title of forensic investigator.

"Maybe you can come by my lab one day when you're in town. I'll show you around, what we do."

"Hey, that'd be cool. You'd do that?"

"Sure. Just call me so I know you're coming. I'll need to get clearance." Chandler suspected that there weren't too many people in Ronald's life who took an interest in him simply for Ronald's sake.

They shook hands and Chandler left. He phoned Jeffrey Hellman once he returned to the city and gave him the good news. He made a copy of the microcassette tape and sent it to him via Federal Express.

CHAPTER
51

THE REMAINDER of the three weeks passed quickly for Chandler. He became engulfed in his cases again, working with Nick on the flood-tainted evidence to see if there was some way he could salvage the state's case against Bobby Lee Walker. He went back to the crime scene, the victim's apartment, and was able to secure an intact latent print from the underside of the coffee table near where the victim was found. With this sole piece of evidence, the prosecutor was going to go to the grand jury to try to secure an indictment. There was motive, and all they had to do was place the suspect at the murder scene.

The indictment came down, and again Chandler's back was patted for his fine work. Hennessy growled and grumbled at Chandler's luck, at the same time privately marveling at his natural talent for finding a way to fix whatever went awry.

Denise's pregnancy test was positive, elating both of them as they began discussing the changes a new child would bring to their lives. But despite the numerous diversions, as the days passed, Madison's case returned to the forefront of Chandler's thoughts. Although he had marked the date on his calendar as a reminder to call about the DNA test results, his internal clock was ticking away, poised to notify him like an alarm chronograph set to beep at a predetermined time.

It had been nearly two weeks since the Madisons had seen Hellman when Leeza called to invite him over for dinner. He arrived early, with a bouquet of flowers in one hand and a medium-sized box in the other. "I know how much you love chocolate. I saw this cake in the market when I was picking out the flowers and couldn't resist."

Leeza took the flowers and planted a kiss on his cheek. "Maybe we'll skip dinner and go right to the dessert," she said, forcing a smile.

"No word yet," Hellman said, reading Leeza's taut face. "But we should be hearing soon."

"My stomach has more knots than a roomful of men wearing ties. I don't know how much more of this I can take."

Hellman removed his suit coat and tossed it over the back of the couch. "You need help with anything?"

"No, we're fine. Go sit down."

Hellman took a seat at the dining room table. Madison walked into the room and gave Hellman a pat on the back. "Any news yet?"

"Nothing," Hellman said.

"So how is all this going to work, with the DNA?" Leeza asked.

"If they don't match Phil's DNA to the DNA on the beer cans, the prosecution would have no choice but to reopen its investigation and essentially look for another suspect—something they don't want to do because it'd make them look inept. But if that's the way it goes down, I'll force them into it." Hellman lifted a tray of chicken and placed a breast on his plate beside the yam and string beans. "If Harding's DNA matches the DNA in the saliva on the beer cans, you'll be able to rest even easier—because then I'd be able to accuse Harding with absolute certainty: I'd know the winner of the horse race before the starting gun was fired. The case would likely be dropped against Phil."

"If the beer can DNA doesn't match mine, will they immediately dismiss the charges against me?"

"No. Denton won't dismiss against you until he's reopened his investigation and charged a new suspect with the crime. He'll probably try to dig up some more evidence on you while they investigate Harding. Once he sees that tape and hears my theory as to what she's done, I think he'll listen. He'll probably go before a judge and request a search warrant based on motive and all the corroborating evidence we're going to give him. The warrant will enable the detectives to get a sample of hair and blood from Harding for DNA testing."

"Will the judge give him the warrant?" Leeza asked.

"We're getting a little ahead of ourselves, but I think there's a good chance he would. But nothing's guaranteed. It depends on how Denton presents it. Which I guess means it depends on how much Denton believes that she framed you. And then there's the variable of the judge. You don't know who you're getting, and if you're catching him or her on a good or bad day."

"For a system that's supposed to be objective," Leeza said, "there's sure a lot of subjectivity. I don't like all those 'ifs.'"

"I know, but we're real close," Hellman said. "I have to think things are going to go our way." He rubbed at the beard stubble on his face. "One thing we haven't covered yet, though. Denton's gonna ask me how Harding was able to steal your car without the alarm going off. Because if she set it off, for sure you would've heard it. Any ideas on how she did it?"

Madison shrugged. "Obviously she did it, so there has to be a way."

"I can accept that, but Denton won't."

"She must have had the key," Leeza said. "That night when she was here, she must've taken it."

Hellman looked at Madison. "What key?"

"Leeza couldn't find the spare key to my Mercedes. We kept it by the phone in the kitchen."

"And it's gone?"

Leeza nodded. "I even checked with Ryan. He hadn't seen it either."

"Okay," Hellman said. "Denton should accept that."

Their attention was suddenly diverted as Elliott and Jonah came downstairs with their Masters of the Galaxy swords and costumes on.

"C'mon, Dad. Let's play!"

Madison looked over at Leeza.

"Oh, go ahead. I'll keep your dinner warm."

He wiped his mouth with a napkin and then took off after the boys, chasing them through the living room and dining room, around chairs and underneath the table before finally catching them.

Leeza turned to Hellman. "It's time to put this matter to rest, Jeffrey."

Hellman looked at Madison wrestling with the boys on the floor, then nodded.

CHAPTER
52

IT WAS A Monday morning, two weeks and five days since
Kurt Gray had begun his testing on the samples. Trying to
keep focused, Chandler went to the lab and pretended to
work; Nick sensed what was bothering him—Chandler had
told him all about the case when he first returned to New
York—and he tried to take his partner's mind off it.

Although he was a couple days shy of three weeks, Chandler couldn't wait any longer. He glanced at his watch. Given
the time difference, it would be a few hours before the Sacramento lab would be open.

At eleven o'clock, Chandler walked over to his desk and
dialed Palucci.

"Lake Tahoe cabin, huh?"

"I needed him to run the test, Lou, and Gray was being a
total asshole."

"Why, because he wanted to go by the book? Things are
different out here, remember? You used to work here. All that
New York smog has clouded your judgment or something.
This could really get me in deep shit if it ever got out—"

"Lou, I'd love to shoot the breeze with you, but my
curiosity is getting the best of me. I haven't slept in three
nights."

"Your guy is clean. No match on the DNA. But that other
sample is another story. Whoever's DNA that was is a dead
ringer. Good match with the saliva on the beer cans."

Chandler sighed relief. "Lou, you've just helped bring the
wheels of injustice to a grinding halt."

"Yeah, well, it's not for publication. Just keep it between you, me, and the bedpost, will you?"

"Of course," Chandler said. "Take care of yourself, man."

"Yeah, you too."

"And tell Gray I said thank you."

"I think I'll leave him out of this, if you don't mind."

Chandler hung up and immediately dialed Hellman. Hennessy would have a fit if he saw the long-distance phone bill.

In a deposition.

Interrupt him.

Can't do that.

Interrupt him. He'll thank you later.

Hellman came to the phone. "You got it?"

"No match on Phil. Dead ringer on Harding."

Hellman let out a shrill war whoop that caused his entire staff and the visiting attorneys to turn their heads toward his office. "Shit, I forgot to close the door," he said, reaching with his foot to kick it closed.

"You okay?"

"I'm on cloud nine."

"Go back to your deposition."

"Deposition? It'll wait. I have to call Phil." They agreed to talk in a few days.

"Oh," Hellman said, "when is the lab report going to be ready on the DNA? I'll need to turn it over to Denton."

"Yeah, right."

"I'm serious. It's an issue of discovery, you know that."

"Jeffrey, there's not going to be any report. If they produced a report, all hell would break loose."

"What are you talking about?" Hellman felt for his chair and sat down. "Chandler, where did you have these tests run?"

"At the lab."

"What lab?"

"You know, the lab."

Hellman's mouth dropped open. "The state lab? Chandler, you know they're not supposed to run tests for us. We need to go through a private lab—"

"Look, we needed the results and we needed to have it done by a lab where the methods and techniques were the same. We had to be sure before we went public with our accusations. I had the connections. Bottom line, I got it done."

"But now I don't have a report to take to Denton."

"Doesn't matter, we've got enough. He'll buy the case on motive alone. Tell him to do a DNA test on her and he won't be disappointed."

"Chandler—"

"Jeffrey, we hold all the cards—we know the results of a test that officially hasn't been run yet. I told you I'd get the job done, and I came through. Now the case rests in your hands. Do your thing. Get the charges dropped."

Hellman told Chandler it wasn't that simple—and that a lot of things had to happen in order for Madison to walk away from this a free man. "I think you fucked up on this one, Chandler."

"Regardless of what I should have or shouldn't have done, bottom line is you've got what you need to get Phil off."

Upon hanging up and clearing his mind, he realized that Chandler was right—he had to focus on the task at hand. He had all the tools and evidence he needed: all he had to do was convince Denton to look at Harding as the prime suspect. Considering Denton's ego and political aspirations, he would need to make a compelling argument in order to convince him to abandon his high-profile suspect. But if he approached Denton properly, subtly giving him a choice between losing his high-profile case and prosecuting the wrong man, a prominent surgeon, Denton would opt to prevent either from occurring.

He dialed Madison and told him he had the results. He started to tell him a story about a case he once had handled in order to give the test results some perspective, but Madison would have nothing of it.

Leeza, who had picked up the cordless extension, was coming down the stairs. "Jeffrey, just give us the results!" she said.

She gave Madison a big hug as Hellman relayed the good

news. He was reminding them that they were not out of the woods yet, that they still had some hurdles to overcome, a speech that really would have been better expressed by the little anecdote he had tried to relate a moment ago. But neither of them was listening. "I'll call you later when I'm done with my deposition."

They made immediate plans for a baby-sitter—Madison's parents—and went to the Palace, a grandiose Chinese restaurant near the Hyatt that was outfitted with gold-accented stemware, gold wall ornaments, and gold utensils. Some considered it gaudy, but the food was unparalleled.

Madison was uncomfortable calling this a celebration. He felt he should try to temper his emotions until the charges were formally dropped. For now, they would just enjoy the good news and try to view it in relation to what their lives had been like of late.

Together they toasted forensic science, the lab technicians, and even the very existence of DNA and God's wisdom in creating it. They would wait to toast Chandler until the formal celebration: a party, they decided, at the house, with everyone there they could think of, if and when Harding was convicted.

CHAPTER
53

IN THE MORNING, Hellman scheduled a meeting with Denton, who immediately requested that the lab fax a copy of Gray's DNA report over to him. As they both read the conclusion indicating that Madison's DNA did not match that on the beer cans, Denton nodded. Hellman wished it said something about Harding's DNA and the cigarette, but at least the report ripped significant holes in the prosecution's case.

"You look disappointed," Hellman said.

"I spend two months investigating and preparing a case against a defendant, we're days away from trial, and then it turns out he may be innocent? You're damn fucking right I'm disappointed." He looked at Hellman, who took a breath to speak, but Denton held up a hand. "You're going to tell me that I should be glad that justice is being done, that we're not going to prosecute the wrong man."

"That's exactly what I'm about to tell you."

"Spare me."

"I strongly urge you to look at Brittany Harding. She's got motive and I've got plenty of evidence that you'll be interested in. If you take this information in good faith and investigate, you'll be able to corroborate everything I'm going to give you. Tim, I can practically hand you a case, complete with evidence, on a silver platter. I'll make you look good."

"I don't need you to make me look good."

"You know what I mean. We both know that for the next two or three weeks you're going to have a little egg on your face." He figured it was better not to sugarcoat it. "But I'm telling you: look into Harding and you'll have your suspect—with a very reasonable chance of conviction."

"Let's hear this so-called ironclad evidence," Denton said, loosening his blue tie and sitting down behind his desk. Although it was only nine in the morning, he looked exhausted . . . the lines in his face deeper, his complexion a bit pallid.

"I wouldn't use the term 'ironclad,' but it's damn good." Hellman recounted the rape complaint Harding had filed, showed him a copy of the contract he wrote that bore the signatures of Movis Ehrhardt and Brittany Harding, and a copy of the forty-thousand-dollar check. He also showed him the picture Harding had staged and explained how it had been taken. Told him the complaint was withdrawn and the money returned by Ehrhardt. Produced a copy of the returned funds' cashier's check. His presentation was building up steam when Denton interrupted him.

"What the hell does all this—"

"Motive, motive, and motive. Shut up and listen."

Hellman reached into his attaché case and pulled out a videotape. "You need to see this. Got a VCR around here?"

Hellman provided a brief introduction to Mark Stanton, and the information that Chandler had gleaned about his experience with Harding. As he briefed Denton on the background, a TV and VCR were wheeled into the office. Hellman slipped the cassette tape in and leaned back in his chair.

As the gray and white snow filled the screen at the end of the tape, Denton arose. "Compelling, I'll give you that."

"Compelling? That's it?"

"It goes to motive, and motive is still circumstantial."

"But it's the best case you have, circumstantial or not. Your case against my client was circumstantial and it was a damn shot weaker than what you have against Harding."

Denton ejected the tape and handed it back to Hellman. "I'd like a copy of that tape."

"Keep that one," Hellman said. "I already had a copy made for you."

Denton was shaking his head, apparently absorbed in a conversation with himself. "I'd have to litigate the collateral matters as well . . . not only would I have to prove that Harding was the driver of the car, but I'd also have to prove that she extorted Stanton and Madison, and that Madison had not, in fact, raped her. I've got three separate trials in one. Not to mention the fact that this videotape is possibly inadmissible," he said.

"But Mark Stanton probably would not be. He's in town and I could get him to testify." Slight stretch of the truth, but he would worry about that later. "And . . . this tape will help you establish motive, and get you a search warrant for a sample of Harding's DNA."

"You're assuming that Harding's DNA will match the DNA on the beer cans, which would then suggest she was driving the car."

"Exactly."

"Okay, but how'd she get Madison's car? Does he leave it unlocked at night?"

Hellman explained about the missing key, then sat back and studied the prosecutor's face.

Finally, Denton sighed and shook his head slightly. "Complicated. Too many places to trip up."

"Complicated, but not impossible. You've handled tougher cases with less than you've got here."

Denton rubbed his eyes. "Yeah, I guess I have."

"And I have one other piece of information that'll be of use," Hellman said.

Denton sat down again and leaned back in his swivel chair. "I'm listening."

"How about an eyewitness who saw Harding with a six-pack of the same brand of beer in her shopping cart a few days prior to the murders. And how about that same witness hearing Harding screaming at Madison, 'You'll pay for this, I'll get you for this!'? Would that make you feel better?"

"Do you have such a witness?"

"A supermarket checkout clerk at Food & More. He moved back east, but we can get him out here if needed."

Denton raised an eyebrow. "Now that's quite promising. But I'd have to interview the guy myself, get him on record."

"How about a tape of him identifying Harding and describing what he saw in the market?" Hellman asked, removing the microcassette from his attaché.

A smile fluttered across Denton's drawn face.

"Are you starting to feel better about your case?" Hellman asked.

"Maybe it won't be such a bad day after all."

Hellman shut his attaché and stood up. "Tomorrow I'd like to go to the media with the DNA info."

Denton sat up straight, as if he had just been awakened from a nightmare. "No, not the media. Not yet."

"Tim," Hellman said, softening his voice down to one of reason, "my client has gone through hell. He's just about lost his practice, he lost his privileges at the very hospital he saved from insolvency, and he almost lost his marriage. Shit, I don't even know if he could overcome all this to salvage his reputation." He leaned forward. "With those beer cans pointing to a different suspect, the case against my client is very weak. If you're going to continue pursuing him in light of this new evidence . . ." He tilted his head and let his voice drift off, allowing what he did not say to speak volumes: lawsuit. Big, expensive lawsuit.

Denton took the hint. "Fine, go to the media. Give them the DNA results and try to clear Madison's reputation. But don't go overboard. Just tell them that new evidence has come to light and it looks good for your client. I'm not dropping the charges yet. I need to be more comfortable with Harding than Madison as the murderer before I dismiss. In the meantime, assuming your client will agree to it, I'll move for a continuance."

"Get a search warrant and a DNA sample. Believe me, Tim, that'll satisfy your curiosity."

"You seem quite confident."

"I'm confident in my client's innocence and in the evidence I've given you on motive."

"Fine. But you make no mention of Harding as a suspect when you talk to the media. That's my party, if and when the time comes."

Hellman nodded. He had Denton thinking the way he wanted.

CHAPTER
5 4

IT WAS AFTER eight and everyone in his office had gone home hours ago. Hellman gathered his papers and was preparing to leave when he paused to gaze out the large picture window behind his desk. Eighteen floors below, flickering street lights mimicked the city's pulse. Off in the distance, the Tower Bridge was bathed in a splash of orange-yellow radiance from the large floodlamps mounted along the banks of the Sacramento River. Against the black sky, the span looked like a showcased painting in a museum.

The ring of the phone jogged his attention away from the nightscape. He briefly thought of letting the machine answer it, but he had never been able to do that. When he used to work in his father's shoe store as a teenager, if the phone rang, even if it was after hours, his dad answered it. "You never know when it's a new customer on the phone," his father would tell him.

It was Lou Palucci over at the Department of Justice crime lab. There was a major screwup, he was saying. He needed to talk with Chandler.

"Chandler's back in New York," Hellman said.

Palucci was talking fast, apologizing for something.

Hellman slowed him down. "Please, start from the beginning."

"We've got a problem. A major problem." Instantly, Hellman's mind flashed on the DNA: something happened to the beer cans with Harding's DNA. Things like that happened occasionally in evidence rooms. Items got lost, misplaced . . .

contaminated. There was nothing more threatening to the validity of DNA analysis than contamination. Although it was a very stable material, mishandle it in just the wrong manner and it was good for nothing.

". . . and I should've seen it coming," Palucci was saying, "but I've been swamped since getting back from vacation and I didn't have any control over it. I should never have allowed it from the start—"

"Did the DNA sample get contaminated?"

"Oh, no," Palucci said. "No, it's nothing like that. God, no. No, this is, well . . ."

"What then?" Hellman said, nearly yelling. Had he been in the same room with Palucci, he might have grabbed him by the shoulders and shook him.

"The criminalist on the case, Kurt Gray, had had words with Chandler, and I guess they kind of squared off. I didn't think it was important, but you know Chandler, he gets real involved in his cases, and . . ."

"And what?" prompted Hellman; he was wearing his wool overcoat and he was beginning to perspire.

"And I don't know how much you know about this, but he brought in this cigarette and asked Gray to run a DNA test on it. He convinced him it should be run on my authority, but I was out of town. I should've cut it off before the test was completed, but I let it go through. Chandler and I go back a ways, and—"

"Please, Mr. Palucci, I can't stand the suspense. What's the problem?"

"Gray mouthed off about the cigarette and how Chandler—"

Hellman began to sigh relief. *Is that all this was about?* "Mr. Palucci, I thank you for calling, but Chandler's no longer an active member of the police force. Therefore, whatever evidence he gets hold of, and how he does it, is of no legal consequence."

"You're missing the point. Gray isn't concerned with legal procedure and issues of admissibility. He's been saying Chandler pulled strings all over the place and used the state lab as his own private agency. When Gray told Bill Jennings—"

"He told Jennings?" Hellman sat down and slumped in his chair. A sudden blanket of perspiration broke out across his body, and it had nothing to do with his overcoat. Bill Jennings. Bill Jennings, the guy who had gotten into it with Chandler fifteen years ago, and who likely still carried a grudge.

Hellman's mind was racing, trying to assimilate the impact and consequences of what Palucci was telling him.

"Gray told me that Jennings said something about misuse of public funds. He was going to the chief of the lab, and if he doesn't get satisfaction, he'll go all the way to the attorney general and file a complaint with the Bureau of Investigation."

"Bureau of Investigation? What would he want with them?"

"My guess, Mr. Hellman, is that he's going to try and stir up as much trouble as he can."

Hellman pulled out a handkerchief and wiped the perspiration from his face. *Bureau of Investigation. What the hell kind of power would they have over Chandler? Civil rights violation? Public fraud? Violation of public trust? Are they going to try and nail me instead, being that I'm an officer of the court and—*

"Mr. Hellman?" Palucci was saying.

"Yeah, yeah, I'm here. I'm just . . . thinking." *Stressing out.*

"I thought maybe Chandler could call up Jennings and straighten him out, get him to calm down and—"

"Thanks, Mr. Palucci, I appreciate your concern. I'll handle it from this point. If anything else comes your way, please give me a call."

"You don't understand," Palucci said, his voice vibrating with anxiety. "My neck's in the sling on this one. If Jennings so much as mentions it to the chief, I'm out of a job. Terminated. Twenty years down the tubes. Internal Affairs will rip me apart."

"What makes you think Internal Affairs will get involved?"

"Once the chief knows about this, he has no choice but to report it to them."

Hellman sighed, rubbed his forehead. "Okay, I hear you. I'll get on it right away, talk with Chandler, see what I can do."

Hellman hung up the phone and sat there for a while.

Beads of perspiration crept down his forehead and onto his cheek, tickling him back to reality. He wiped his face again, reached for the phone, and called Chandler.

The next morning, Chandler was returning from a crime scene when he was flagged down by the desk sergeant: a Jeffrey Hellman had called, and his wife was on the line.

He reached across the large desk and took the phone. "Denise? Where are you?"

"At school."

"Everything okay?"

"Yeah, fine. I checked our machine during a break, and there was a message from Jeffrey Hellman. He said he tried reaching you last night, but we were out. The baby-sitter obviously forgot to give us the message."

"Did he say what it was about?"

"Just that it was very important. I've got the numbers if you want to call him."

Chandler jotted down the information and reached Hellman in his car on the way to court for an unrelated case. Their conversation was interrupted by occasional crackles.

"Shit," was all Chandler could manage at first. "What are the ramifications?"

"Well, if Jennings tells Denton, which is certain to happen, I really don't see any harm to you—what are they going to get you on, petty theft of a cigarette? There's just nothing there."

"So then what's the problem?"

"It seems that most of this falls on your friend, Lou Palucci. I've been running it over in my head, and it's probably going to go like this: if the chief of Forensic Services finds out about it, he's going to get Internal Affairs involved, and your friend Palucci will be out of a job. And if the chief doesn't report it to Internal Affairs, Jennings is going to go straight to the attorney general and he'll get the Bureau of Investigation to look into it. Either way, Palucci is history."

"I can't let that happen, Jeffrey. He was doing me a favor."

"And that's why Jennings is going to be all over this. But

there's more, and this would come from Denton. He could get you—and me—on obstruction of justice."

"Because we didn't turn over the Harding DNA results?"

"You got it. We technically should have alerted them to the results immediately. I did tell Denton that he should obtain a DNA sample on her, but I didn't tell him why. I didn't tell him that we'd already run the tests."

"You couldn't tell him."

"Yeah, thanks to you, I couldn't tell him." He paused. "If you'd only run it through a private lab—"

"Look, I don't want to go through all that again. It's counterproductive."

"It's messy, Chandler, it's just damned messy. If Jennings is out for blood, I'd say he's got a good case. His vampire teeth are polished and poised for action." They were interrupted by a crackle.

"Should we talk about this later, when you're back at your office?" Chandler asked, concerned about the security of the cellular signal.

"I'm on a digital phone. We're fine."

"What if Harding and her attorney find out about this? Could they file a federal suit against me for violating her civil rights?"

"Remember, Chandler, we're talking about a cigarette. A piece of consumable merchandise. Petty theft of a cigarette, for Christ's sake."

"No, we're talking about DNA. There's nothing much more private than your own genetic code."

"Did she see you take the cigarette?"

"I don't know if she did or didn't." Chandler thought for a moment and remembered that she did not return to the table after leaving to take a few drags. Was that the reason—did she see him bag the cigarette and slip it in his pocket? He shook his head. "I doubt she saw me take it. Unless she left it there purposely to set me up—"

"Now you're getting paranoid."

"Who the hell knows with her?" He took a deep breath and let it out. "Look, even if she didn't see me take it, it doesn't take a rocket scientist to figure out that she took out a cigarette during lunch with me, and then a couple of hours later there's a cigarette in the crime lab that I'm asking Gray to run a lip print and DNA analysis on."

"I just don't see a fourth amendment issue here."

"What about a civil suit? Could Harding and her attorney sue me for violating her civil rights?"

Hellman laughed. "I don't have to tell you that anybody can file a civil suit for anything. All it takes is a couple hundred bucks. It doesn't stand a chance of winning, but yeah, they could file one. And you'd be spending a lot more time in California away from your family than you'd like. Win or lose." He paused. "But I really think the biggest problem lies with your buddy Palucci and the obstruction of justice issue."

Chandler clenched his jaw. "What if I call Jennings myself and confront him?"

"No. That'll be worse."

"Fine. Then I have another idea," Chandler said. "Let me make a few calls and I'll get back to you."

"Tell me what you're going to do."

"I will, I've just gotta make some calls first."

"Chandler—" Hellman started to protest, but suddenly realized he was talking to a dead line.

Chandler's first call was to Lou Palucci.

"I heard," Chandler said. "Sorry, man. I had no idea that Gray would blabber it all over the damn place. I thought he was a professional."

"He's on the strange side, Chandler. Normally, he'd be okay," Palucci said, "but this is not the kind of thing that comes up regularly. Not to mention the fact that he's fairly green. But it's not like he was telling everyone about it. Apparently, he and Jennings got into a pissing match over you. Each had his own story to tell. And it just came out. At least, that's the version I got."

"Why don't you talk to Jennings. Tell him what kind of an impact this is going to have on the lab—and on *you*. Tell him it could cost you your job."

"I spent the entire night thinking about it. Can't you just see the headline? 'Director of State Crime Lab Involved in Scandal.' If he doesn't know what's going on in his own department, what kind of a director *is* he? And if it does get out that I did know, it'll be worse: I knowingly violated procedure, abused my position, allowed the usage of taxpayers' money for personal interests . . . it'll be filled with all sorts of juicy things for the media to grab hold of."

After a moment of silence, Chandler sighed. "Lou, listen to me. All you have to do is talk with Jennings. Now, before he gets to Denton, the chief, and the attorney general. Just make sure you impress upon him the fact that if he takes the lab down in an effort to take revenge on a fifteen-year-old dispute, he'll be blacklisted by the very lab he relies on to make his cases."

"I think I've got a better source of persuasion for Jennings."

"Who's that?"

"Someone who saved his ass a few years back. Jennings owes him."

Chandler gave him his number in New York and hung up. Ran his fingers through his hair and leaned his elbows on the marble-slabbed counter. "Shit."

CHAPTER
55

A DAY AFTER his discharge from the hospital and an hour after returning to work, criminalist Stuart Saperstein was dispatched to a crime scene. Three hours later, he settled down at his desk to log in all the evidence he had collected. Before he could finish, however, he was summoned to Lou Palucci's office.

He tossed the microcassette recorder onto his desk and trudged down the hall.

As he walked through the doorway, Palucci was hanging up the phone. "Stu," he said. "Close that door and grab a seat."

"You look like you haven't slept in days," Saperstein said, tilting his head back and peering at his boss through soiled glasses.

"See, that's why you're a criminalist. Very observant. You don't miss a damn thing." He sat down behind his desk. "I've got a situation here that I need your help with. Your buddy, Bill Jennings, is threatening to bring some serious heat down on me and the rest of the lab and you have to stop it cold. Before it gets anywhere."

Palucci spent the next five minutes providing the details of Chandler's involvement with the lab. Finally, Saperstein interrupted the explanation. "So," he said, removing his glasses and poking at the dust on the lens with a finger, "what you're saying is that this guy Chandler used the state lab for private gain, and Bill found out about it, and you're afraid he's going to raise a stink." Saperstein replaced the glasses on his face. "I don't get it. Why would Bill care?"

"There was an incident about fifteen years ago involving Jennings and Chandler. The two of them squared off, and Chandler turned out to be right. Big case, big blow-up. Jennings came out looking real bad."

"His chance to get even," Saperstein said.

Palucci nodded. "With us in the middle." He shook his head. "If this gets out to the chief . . ." Palucci started to say as he stood up. He waved a hand at the air. "I should've stopped it before it had a chance to go any further."

"You want me to see what I can do."

"You saved his career. He owes you."

Saperstein sighed, stood up and paced. "Jesus Christ, Lou, I've got ulcerative colitis. I just got out of the hospital. Couldn't you wait a few days before laying all this on my shoulders?"

"I'm sorry, wish I could have. But timing is everything. You can see what a potentially sensitive matter this is."

Saperstein nodded. "Yeah, yeah, yeah." He headed for the door. "I'll talk to him. Give him a dose of reason. It's all I can do."

When Hellman called his office for messages after court had adjourned, he was informed that Denton had called. Hellman's stomach tightened. "Did he say what he wanted?"

"No, just that it was extremely important."

Hellman picked up the phone; although it was after five, he knew Denton would be there. The prosecutor answered his own line.

"Jeffrey," Denton said with an air of indignation. "Is there anything you'd like to tell me before we talk?"

"Tim . . ." sighed Hellman.

"Don't give me 'Tim.'"

"What the hell do you want me to say? I've got an overzealous investigator who's accustomed to doing things . . . differently than we do them here. I just found out myself."

"You'll have to do better than that," Denton said. "He used to be an investigator with this office. He should've known better."

"I'm sorry, okay? Is that what you want? Yeah, he should've known better and he fucked up. But it doesn't change the facts. And the facts are that Madison's DNA does not match your sample. Someone else's does."

"Yeah, Harding's does. That's why you were so sure that if I got a sample of her DNA I'd be satisfied that your client is innocent and the charges should be dismissed."

Hellman did not say anything.

"This is the wrong way of going about it, Jeffrey. You should've disclosed the evidence you had. Remember the laws governing discovery?"

"Tim, what was I going to do? Chandler didn't tell me where he'd taken her DNA sample. I was going to turn it all over to you once I had the results, but when he told me where the tests had been run, we were in a bind. I couldn't tell you what I had because you'd want to see the report, and when I had no report, you would've asked why and then I would have had to tell you that it was done at the state crime lab, and for sure all hell would have broken loose."

"Oh," Denton said, "so this way is better. Don't tell me about the information you've uncovered; hide it from me. Kind of violate discovery, but not really, because you strongly hint that I should check out this other suspect. But what you don't tell me is why you're so convinced that she's the guilty party. You hand me this cock-and-bull story about motive and extortion—"

"It's not cock-and-bull. It's absolutely real. And it'll make your case."

"That's not the point. You should've told me what you had."

"When I heard what Chandler had done, I was hoping that no one would find out. I thought that Gray would keep his mouth shut, because if it got out, it would spell trouble for the entire lab, not to mention get his boss fired."

"Well, it did get out, didn't it?"

"Look, Tim, let's put this behind us. It's not doing us any good."

"Put this behind us? Tell that to Jennings. He has a history with Chandler—"

"Yeah, I know all about it. But if you're going to let Jennings stir up all sorts of shit all because of a disagreement fifteen years ago—"

"In case you hadn't realized, Jeffrey, Jennings is a big boy. He's not a marionette. I don't have control over what he says and does. If he wants to go blowing wind all over the goddamned station about what Chandler did, there's nothing I can do to stop him. If he wants to go to the lab chief, again there's nothing I can do to stop him."

"If he ever wants to step foot in that lab again, he'll keep his mouth shut."

"It's his decision."

"Why don't you let him know your position?"

"And get accused of trying to assist a cover-up?"

Hellman did not like the sound of that. It meant that Denton was going to take action on this himself, regardless of what Jennings said or did. "Don't tell me that you're going to get involved."

"Get involved?" Denton asked, his voice rising a couple of octaves. "Get involved? I'm already involved. The only question is what I should do about it. And really, there's not even a question. I have no choice."

"Well, before you do anything rash, think about your actions."

"What the hell do you think I've been doing all morning since Jennings told me? It places me in an ethical bind."

"You can deny that Jennings ever disclosed any of this to you."

"I can rationalize all sorts of things. But you're asking me to do you a favor that—"

"Whoa, hold it a second. I'm not asking for any favors whatsoever. It's your lab that's going to be raked through the coals in the media. The lab's never had a better manager than Lou Palucci. You know that as well as I do. But you have to ask yourself if one error in judgment is worth not only destroying a man's career but also causing a tremendous upheaval in the lab at a time when it's enjoying one of the most impeccable reputations in the entire country."

"Jeffrey—"

"Wait a minute, I'm not finished. If you don't care about the greater good, look at it selfishly. Every time you introduce a piece of evidence gathered at a crime scene, think about what every defense attorney who's worth his weight in gold will say about it. It came from a corrupt lab. Who knows what's tainted and what's not? Who's doing who favors? Who's been paid off? Hell, some congressman vying for votes could push for a full-scale investigation. Maybe a few other skeletons will fall out of the closet. Not just at the lab, but at the DA's office too. And then where will you be?"

"That's a distortion of the situation—"

"Oh, is it? It's an edge for the defense. I'd use it, I'm telling you right now. And I have a bunch of friends who I'm sure would use it."

There was a long silence. Hellman knew that sometimes saying nothing elicited more of a response from his adversary than continuing to argue.

"I'll give it some more thought. Talk to Jennings."

"I think that's a good idea, Tim. Let me know what happens."

Hellman hung up and walked out into the cold air with his head spinning. His mind was sifting through several emotions, the most primal of which were frustration and anger aimed at Chandler. He found his car and headed over to his health club for a dose of weights and a visit to the steam room. He needed to work off some stress before it tied him in a knot from which even Houdini would not be able to escape.

"I'm not asking you to overlook your duty as a homicide detective, Bill," Saperstein was saying. "I'm just telling you that you shouldn't let what happened fifteen years ago affect your good judgment now."

"And why not?" Jennings asked.

"Because you have to look at the big picture. What are you going to accomplish and who are you going to hurt along the way?"

"I can't look the other way for personal reasons."

"But you're obsessed with this because of personal reasons. You can't deny that. At least, if you're honest with yourself, you can't deny it."

Jennings sat there in Saperstein's cramped office, a six-by-eight cubbyhole with a desk shoved against the wall. There was barely enough room for Saperstein to squeeze past the desk en route to his chair.

"Bill, it's not worth it. I know about the incident that happened between you and Chandler fifteen years ago. It's time to let go of it. Don't let it destroy you all over again."

"What are you talking about?"

"If you go through with this accusation, it's going to cause a shake-up in the lab. We could be mired in scandal for months, if not years. Lou Palucci will come under fire from the chief, and then he'll be canned. Guaranteed. That won't go over well here. We're a tight family. We look out for each other. And I'm going to get the cold shoulder because you and I are friends; all of us are going to be looked at by outsiders with contempt. And it will tarnish our credibility for years to come. Every defense lawyer will harp on it: They're corrupt. Taking evidence in through the back door. Using taxpayers' money for personal favors for someone with connections. Preferential treatment. And then my favorite: Who knows what else they're doing over there? Manufacturing results? Slanting reports toward the prosecution? The list of accusations will be limited only by the defense attorney's imagination. There'll be reporters doing investigative exposés for tabloid TV, and internal investigations all over the department. Shit, remember what went down at the LA crime lab after the Simpson trial? Not to mention what's happened to the FBI lab in DC—and their rep was impeccable."

Saperstein paused, took a breath. Jennings was staring at the floor. "Lou has worked awfully hard to get us positive publicity. Anyone willing to listen to him gets an earful of all the good we do in this lab. He's been a one-man public relations firm for us—hell, his efforts have reached across the nation. If your selfish actions result in his demise, you'll be doing damage we may never recover from."

Jennings continued to stare at the floor. Saperstein was not sure he was listening.

"If that's not enough," he said, "look at it this way. Turning us in will only create a situation where none of us is going to look after your ass."

Jennings looked up at Saperstein with narrowed eyes. "Is that a threat? From you, Stu?"

"A statement of fact. Look at it objectively. Do you think anyone here would be willing to do favors for you? Do you think anyone would want to work on any of your cases? And God forbid you needed something done right away. No prosecutor would want to have you on his case. You'd become a liability to him."

"He's done it to me again," Jennings said with matter-of-fact levelness.

"Who? What are you talking about?"

"Chandler. Hasn't worked here in years, he's living on the other side of the country, and he still has more pull than me. Fucking little prick—"

"Bill," interrupted Saperstein. "He hasn't done anything to you. You're in the right here. Chandler acted inappropriately. You brought it to everyone's attention, and I guarantee you, it'll never happen again. You've accomplished what any good detective would hope to accomplish. If that's all you're after, you've done the right thing and served everyone well. If you're after revenge, then get the hell out of my office. I've got no sympathy for you."

Jennings stood up and nodded; turned, and slammed the door closed on his way out. Saperstein stood there, not sure if he had gotten through to him. But he knew he had at least given it his best shot.

CHAPTER
56

HELLMAN STOOD on the courthouse steps, black wool overcoat covering his dark gray double-breasted suit and red tie. The air was cold with a slight wind that ruffled through his black hair. Microphones were crowding his face.

". . . and the DNA that was found on the beer cans did not match Dr. Madison's," he said.

Questions were shouted from a couple of reporters simultaneously. Hellman picked the one he heard most clearly: something about what the district attorney is going to do now. "In my opinion, this evidence means that the DA and his investigator have to reopen their investigation."

Then: "Is the DA going to dismiss the charges against Dr. Madison?"

"I'm confident that within the next few weeks, the DA will drop the charges against my client."

"Why not right away?" another reporter asked.

"I can't answer for the district attorney. You'll have to ask Mr. Denton that."

"You said recently that you knew who the driver of the vehicle was. Who was it?"

"It's not my place to accuse or charge someone with a crime. That's the DA's job. Suffice it to say that I'm confident they'll make an arrest very shortly. Right now, my client is anxious to resume the practice of medicine so he can get back to helping people and serving the public as he has done in such a distinguished manner for the past eighteen years."

"How does your client feel right now?"

Hellman smiled. "How would you feel?"

Madison caught the interview on the evening news; it was carried on several channels, and was the lead story on two of them; essentially, their legal analysts all stressed the same point: that the charges were not yet officially dropped, but it looked good for Phillip Madison. Aside from issuing a statement that said they were reopening their investigation, the DA's office had no comment.

Jennings and his partner, Angela Moreno, arrived at Denton's office at a little past five. "Detective Moreno," Denton said, "I ordered sandwiches for us. They're waiting down at the desk sergeant's station. If you'd be so kind . . ." he moved his head in the direction of the door, motioning her out.

"Why don't we just call down and have the clerk—"

"I'd like to talk with Detective Jennings for a moment in private, detective," Denton said.

"That's not necessary, Tim."

Denton locked eyes with Jennings. "I think it is, Bill."

"I'll go get the sandwiches," Moreno said.

As the door closed, Denton walked over and stood face-to-face with Jennings. "I don't want to hear any more about the cigarette DNA, Bill."

"I've got nothing more to say on the subject," Jennings said. "I was assured that it wouldn't happen again, and I'm satisfied with that. I won't be reporting it to anyone."

"Well, I never heard you say anything about it," Denton said as he walked back behind his desk and took a seat.

Jennings opened the door to the office to signal Moreno that their conversation had concluded.

Denton pulled the case file in front of him and opened it. "We're here to draw up a search warrant for Brittany Harding. Have you reviewed the memo I sent you on what we've got so far?"

"Yeah," Jennings said. "Looks good."

Moreno appeared and took a seat next to Jennings; she dropped the bag containing the sandwiches on the desk.

"We're talking about the search warrant for Harding," Jennings said to Moreno before turning back to Denton. "Do you think that we'll need this warrant or do you think she'll voluntarily give us the blood and hair samples?"

"If she's guilty, why should she contribute to her own prosecution?" Moreno asked.

"But if she's not guilty, she may offer up the samples without making us go before a judge," Jennings said.

Denton was shaking his head. "Without a search warrant, if we ask and she refuses, she'll have time to hide or destroy any incriminating evidence."

"Such as a Chicago White Sox cap," Moreno said.

"Hellman tells me she's a nut. I say we go in with a warrant and not take any chances. In the long run, it'll be easier."

They all nodded their heads in agreement.

Denton grabbed his pen and began to jot notes. "We look for gloves, baseball hats, keys to Madison's car, beer cans, and any incriminating notes written by her. And we get a sample of her hair and a vial of her blood."

"And if she won't cooperate?" Moreno asked.

"Then haul her ass in for contempt of court. Or if she refuses to be pricked with a needle, we'll have her spit in a glass. Just remember that blood's easier for the lab to analyze." He rubbed the ridges on his forehead. "Anything we're forgetting?"

They sat and thought for a moment; the consensus being that there was nothing else, Denton thanked them and then started drawing up the warrant and affidavit.

Armed with his attaché case and a file folder full of papers that included his affidavit, Denton sat in Martin Elegante's chambers while the judge thumbed through his document. He chose Judge Elegante because he was unfamiliar with the case, and it would be easier to obtain a search warrant from him than from Judge Tyson, to whom he'd gone previously claiming that Madison was the guilty party. Now, faced with having to switch gears just prior to the start of the trial, Tyson would no doubt grill him and Jennings on why they had arrested the wrong man, making a shambles of a prominent physician's life and career in the process. Denton did not need to hear it.

Generally thought of as sharp, fair, and relatively easygoing, Elegante was a rotund African-American justice whose portly figure filled out his robes and made him appear formidable and intimidating.

The judge was sitting and rocking slowly in his large desk chair. It creaked rhythmically under his weight as he swayed back and forth. After quickly scanning through the affidavit, he tossed it onto the desk in front of him. "Mr. Denton," he announced in a loud, baritone voice. "Talk to me."

"Your Honor, I'm requesting a search warrant on a suspect in our investigation, Brittany Harding." He placed a hand on the warrant. "Through our investigation—"

"I'm confused. Didn't you arrest a doctor on these charges? A . . . Phillip Madison if my memory serves."

"Yes, Your Honor, we did. But DNA testing that was performed on a piece of crucial evidence indicated that Dr. Madison was not the driver of the vehicle."

"And you have reason to believe that Miss Harding was the driver?"

"Yes, sir."

Elegante leaned back in his chair amidst loud creaking. "Go ahead, Mr. Denton. Bend my ear. Let me hear your reasoning."

Denton would like to have told the judge about the cigarette DNA, but for obvious reasons, could not. "We have evidence that Miss Harding has attempted to frame Phillip Madison with this crime. She had motive as well as a prior history of extortion."

"Let me hear about the motive."

"A couple of months ago, Harding accused Madison of rape—a complaint which was later withdrawn on account of a payoff by Dr. Madison. Although the state's case was weak, with very little proof—she came forward five weeks after the alleged incident, so there was no physical evidence to support her claim—Madison felt that the cost of defending himself would be a wash against a payoff. Not to mention how damaging public disclosure of a rape accusation would be to a prominent surgeon."

The judge began tapping the desk with his pencil. "Please, Mr. Denton, get on with it."

"So he paid her off, but then Harding sent a copy of the agreement and a copy of the check to Madison's wife—which violated their agreement. Madison's attorney insisted that Harding return the money. Then, a few days prior to the hit-and-run, Harding and Madison ran into one another in a supermarket and she went off on him, calling him a rapist and threatening to get even and make him pay. A grocery checker witnessed the incident."

"This checker is available to testify as to what he saw?"

"That's my understanding, Your Honor."

Elegante nodded for him to continue.

"We don't have a witness who can place Harding in the car, but we do have beer cans that were found in the vehicle after the accident, and a DNA pattern was lifted off it. Those beer cans were the same brand that the checker will testify to having sold to Harding the night she had the altercation with Madison. We also have proof that two years ago, Harding extorted a prior employer, using a similar MO, for fifty thousand dollars."

"What kind of proof?"

"I have a videotape the victim made without Harding's knowledge."

"Do you have it with you?"

Denton nodded and opened his attaché case.

"Let's see it, counselor."

Denton pulled it out and handed it to Elegante, who pushed it into the VCR on the cabinet shelf to the left of his desk. The judge watched the tape intently; he did not divert his attention until the white snow filled the screen. "A real model citizen," Elegante boomed. He looked over at Denton and motioned for him to continue.

"It's the prosecution's belief, Your Honor, that Harding blamed Madison for the loss of her job. That, coupled with her failure to extort money from him on the rape charge, drove her to seek other forms of revenge—such as creating trouble for him with his wife by sending her a copy of the check and settlement agreement. But it was too easy and the effects too personal. She wanted something that would publicly humiliate him and destroy his reputation. And that's why she framed him with murder. Even if he was found not guilty, his career and his life would be destroyed." Denton paused to catch his breath and summarize. "I thus have reason to believe, Your Honor, that sufficient motive exists here . . . and that the DNA on the beer cans found in Madison's car will match that of Brittany Harding."

"Very well, Mr. Denton, I'll buy it. In my opinion, you've got reasonable grounds." Elegante was looking again at the document. "This appears to cover everything you related to me. Your warrant is granted," he said, scribbling his signature across the document. "Let's hope the second time's a charm."

Jennings and Moreno arrived at the home of Brittany Harding, a one-story house built nearly thirty years ago. They parked in her driveway behind a tan Honda Civic and trudged up the cement path, taking note of how well the grass and shrubbery were maintained. It was in stark contrast to the landscaping of many of the other homes in the neighborhood, where cars parked on the front lawn were not an unusual sight.

Harding answered the door dressed in jeans and an oversized sweatshirt.

"Miss Harding?" Jennings asked.

"Yes . . ."

"I'm Detective William Jennings and this is Detective Angela Moreno," he said, holding up his badge. He did not pause long enough for her to speak. "We have a search warrant for your premises. May we come in?"

Harding took the document and looked at it. "What's this about? I don't understand," she said, frantically scanning the paperwork and standing her ground, blocking the doorway.

"The warrant gives us the right to search your premises, Miss Harding. Can we come in?"

She did not move, her eyes still transfixed on the document.

Jennings cleared his voice. "You really don't have a choice in the matter, miss. Please step aside."

She looked at him with a furrowed brow.

Jennings stepped forward and squeezed past her as Moreno followed, politely asking her to stay out of their way while they carried out their orders.

"Do I need an attorney? Should I call my attorney?"

"I can't advise you on legal matters, miss, but if you have an attorney you're certainly within your rights to call him."

She ran into the kitchen and fumbled for Movis Ehrhardt's number. A moment later, Moreno could hear Harding talking to Ehrhardt, even though she was in the other room and was doing her best not to eavesdrop.

"That's all it says . . . I don't know . . . must have something to do with Madison." There was silence for a moment, then "But what the hell does this mean? What are they looking for?" Moreno heard the sound of pages turning and papers rustling. "Blood and hair samples, gloves, baseball caps . . ."

Moreno passed by the kitchen on her way into the bedroom.

Following another moment of silence, Harding's voice rose in anger. "I can't afford that! . . . A public defender? Are you serious?"

Jennings came down the hallway with an empty can of Millstone Premium Draft in a plastic bag, pulled from the garage recycling bin, and a Chicago White Sox hat hanging from a pencil; he placed the hat into an evidence bag with Moreno's assistance. He walked into the kitchen, past Harding, who had hung up the phone. Her face was a uniform shade of reddish pink, the kind of flush that arises from anger rather than from health and vigor.

Jennings opened the refrigerator and pulled another can of Millstone Premium from one of the shelves.

"What do you want with the beer . . . and my hat?"

"Miss Harding," Moreno said, "we're also going to need a sample of your hair and a vial of blood." Jennings and Moreno had decided before they left the station that it would be better if Moreno, a female, asked for the samples. A male asking to yank out some hair by the roots and stick her with a needle might be perceived as being insensitive.

"What do you need my blood for?"

"We're under court order, Miss Harding. We do what we're told to do. That's all I can tell you."

She stood there, stunned, and for perhaps the first time in her adult life, speechless. "This may sting for a few seconds," Moreno said. "May I?" she asked softly, with reassurance in her voice. Harding turned and faced Jennings, her back to Moreno, as the detective gently lifted the back of her suspect's hair and gathered approximately five strands together. Jennings saw tears forming in Harding's eyes—tears that had nothing to do with the pain of the quick, sharp tug at her hair.

Jennings nodded to the police phlebotomist who was waiting outside with the blood draw paraphernalia. The latex-gloved woman entered and took the syringe and vial out of a small pouch and placed it on the kitchen counter.

Harding looked down at the needle as the phlebotomist placed the rubber strip around her arm and tied a quick knot. A tear dropped from her cheek. "That goddamned son of a bitch. I'll get him for this," she said as the woman stabbed her vein with the needle.

CHAPTER
57

HELLMAN WAS RAISING a glass of champagne over dinner. Earlier in the day, he had met with Denton, who informed him that he was going to drop the charges against Madison and arrest and charge Brittany Harding with the murders.

"Congratulations," Hellman said. "To smooth sailing from this point forward."

Madison clinked his glass against Hellman's. "Thanks for giving me my life back. I guess time will tell what kind of effect this whole episode has had on my career."

"If Harding's trial goes well, and she's brought down in a convincing fashion, with some luck you may be able to resume some sort of normal practice."

"How do you convict someone unconvincingly?"

"Believe me, there are ways—the judge loses control of the courtroom, there are surprise juror issues like misconduct or conflicts of interest, the police or crime lab are put on trial for procedural blunders or conspiracies, things of that sort."

"You know," Leeza said, "it's sad, really, when you think that all the people who doubted you before now feel the need to call and tell you they knew you were innocent all along."

"We've gotten about twenty calls so far," Madison said.

"It seems like people prefer going with the flow. It's rare that an individual will buck the tide, stand up for someone he or she believes in," Leeza said, looking at Hellman. "Thanks."

"Well, practice was getting boring. I needed something to spice it up. Maybe I should be thanking you."

"So what happens now, to Harding?"

"Well, now that the DNA has been a confirmed match, they're running it through a different method just to make sure. Denton looked bad once; he doesn't intend to look bad twice. He said he wants to go into this trial with as much foolproof ammunition as possible."

"You think the jury will convict her?"

"With everything we've given him, Denton's got enough to make a compelling case of it. I think there's a good chance she'll go down." He looked at Madison, afraid to broach the subject, but realizing he had to, sooner or later. "How would you feel about testifying at her trial?" He couched it as a casual question, as if Madison really had a choice.

"Do you think that's really going to be necessary?"

"Denton thinks so. He asked me to mention it to you."

"Why should I, because he's been such a nice guy to me?"

"He was just doing his job, Phil. Besides, he needs your testimony to establish motive. If he can show that she had a reason to kill, and a reason to frame you with the crime, he's got a case. But without an eyewitness and no established motive, his case is weak to the point of almost being fruitless."

"I thought you just got through saying that the case was compelling," Leeza said.

"With Phil's testimony it is. Without it . . ." He shrugged and tilted his head, as if to say, *Who knows?*

"He's got the DNA in the car," Madison said.

"You don't really want to base the entire case on that. Who's to say that the cans weren't planted there? It's not likely, but that could be what the defense will argue."

"Personally, I'd rather you didn't testify, Phil," Leeza said. "Enough is enough. A minute ago we were talking about putting this episode behind us and moving on, and now you're asking Phil to testify," she said, throwing her napkin onto the table.

"What I'm hearing is that I really don't have much of a choice." He looked at Hellman.

"Afraid not. If you won't agree to testify, Denton will subpoena you."

"This is ridiculous," Leeza said. "Haven't they caused enough—"

"What's your recommendation?" Madison asked Hellman.

"Agree to testify voluntarily. Let's help them make their case and get this whole thing behind us. Permanently," he said, looking over at Leeza, who was staring at him through narrowed eyes.

Madison looked at Leeza. "I don't have a choice, honey. Better to do it voluntarily than to be antagonistic. You never know when you need them on your side. Besides, maybe it'll do me some good to tell my story."

She folded her arms across her chest and shook her head. "You're nicer than I would be, Phil. A week ago, they were preparing to hang you in the town square." She looked hard at Hellman. "I'd tell them to go to hell."

CHAPTER
58

HIS TIE WAS loosened at the neckline, his thinning hair was windblown and uncombed, and he had a five o'clock shadow. Denton looked at Jeffrey Hellman sitting across the desk from him and raked a hand across the stubble on his chin. "No, I can't do that."

Hellman leaned forward in his chair. "Can't or won't?"

"Won't. I won't give Phillip Madison immunity if he testifies. It's as simple as that."

"You need Madison to make your case. He's a key witness."

"If he's innocent, as you've claimed so fervently, why would he want immunity?"

"He isn't asking for it, I am. He doesn't know anything about this conversation. I consider it part of my responsibility to my client—I'd be remiss in my duties if I didn't ask for it."

Denton took a sip of coffee that had been sitting on his desk for several hours. He knew that all good defense attorneys asked for immunity in cases such as this. Depending on the prosecutor and the witness, it was sometimes granted.

"Tim, look at it from my perspective: you were days away from placing him on trial for a double murder he didn't commit. So being truly innocent isn't worth jack shit in my book. I don't have to tell you this wasn't the first time an innocent person was charged with a crime." He paused to size up Denton, who was reclining in his chair, expressionless, listening to Hellman's argument. "Not only that, but my client's going to take the stand and testify against a person who's tried very hard to destroy him by ruining his reputation. The defense attorney is going to try and tee off on him. He'll bring in anything he can possibly get his hands on—true or not—to discredit him. And I won't be there to protect him."

"You have my word that I'll do everything I can to protect his reputation. I don't want to see him get beaten up on the stand. Remember, he's my witness too. He's crucial to my case."

"That's exactly my point. He's crucial to your case. His wife doesn't want him to testify, and he's not exactly keen on the idea either. He's had enough. It's been a very rough six months for them. And it's questionable whether or not he's ever going to be able to put his professional career back together. You don't want your relationship with one of your key witnesses to be adversarial."

"So what's your point?" Denton said, making no attempt to mask his impatience with the conversation.

"Give him immunity and I'll make sure that you have the most cooperative witness you could ask for." Hellman waited for a response; there was none. "Look, you yourself felt that with the new DNA evidence there wasn't enough of a case against Madison. Otherwise, you wouldn't have dismissed the charges."

"But who knows what the future holds? New evidence, a new witness for that matter, could come forward that implicates your client."

"How often does that happen?"

"Not very often," Denton conceded. "But it does happen."

"Yeah, once in a million cases. The same could be said of huge asteroids striking the planet and wiping out all of humanity."

Denton hesitated.

"Of all the cases you've handled, has it ever happened?"

"No," he said, looking down at his desk.

Hellman leaned farther forward. "Phil Madison is bright and articulate and will make a good witness. He also understands when someone is working with him and when someone is out for his own interests."

"Justice is my interest. That's it."

"And my interest is doing what's best for my client. Immunity."

"I still don't see why."

"You know that I never have my clients testify at trial. But now, he's going to testify at Harding's trial, and he could theoretically say things on the stand that you'll then be privy to, on the record, that could be used against him later. And no, I have nothing specific in mind. I promise you that. But I don't want to leave him naked up there when all he's trying to do is help you out. Hell, you could lose this trial against Harding and then turn around and recharge my client again to save face. It was only a week ago that you wanted his skin." Hellman sat down, lowered his voice, softened his tone. "I want immunity. Shit, he *deserves* immunity. He's been through enough. Do it for me, Tim. In all the years we've worked on opposite sides of the system, I've never deliberately done anything that's harmed you. How many defense attorneys can you make that statement about?"

Denton sat up straight in his chair; he stared at Hellman for a moment, poker-faced. "Okay," Denton said, "I'll do it. I hope to God the judge doesn't press me too hard as to why. It's probably got more to do with our relationship than with Phillip Madison."

"Who's the judge assigned to this case?"

Denton smiled. "Calvino."

"You drew Calvino again?"

"Can you believe it? I take it as an omen."

"Oh, it's an omen all right. A bad omen when my client was the defendant."

They laughed a bit, and talked about the order of immunity that Denton was going to draw up to bring before the judge. Hellman stood and extended his hand. "Thanks, Tim. I'll do everything I can to help. If you need something, anything, let me know."

CHAPTER
59

FOLLOWING A WEEK of solid rainfall, many Sacramento area homes in low-lying areas sustained flood damage from overrun creeks and broken levees. The storms were hitting on a rotation basis: one came through and did its damage, while the next was approaching, much in the way an airplane departs the runway while several stacked planes behind it await their turn. With the sun fighting its way through the stratus clouds, the unexpected break in the weather gave homeowners and businesses time to clean up, sandbag, and prepare for the next deluge.

Bill Jennings chuckled as he and Angela Moreno drove toward Brittany Harding's house, arrest warrant in hand. "This is truly the calm before the storm," he quipped. "If this lady is as volatile as we've been hearing, she could bring the next storm on prematurely."

"She seemed pretty meek when we were there for her hair sample."

"Part of that was the shock of the situation. Plus, she wasn't threatened with anything then, except the loss of a few strands of hair and a vial of blood. Now we're coming to take her to jail."

They turned into her driveway and radioed their arrival to dispatch; behind them, a police cruiser pulled in front of the house and parked at the curb. They would transport Harding to the station with Moreno for booking while Jennings searched her home and confiscated evidence listed on the warrant: all pairs of shoes and any materials, binders, or notes she kept during her employment at the Consortium.

The front door opened and revealed Harding, dressed in a smart, tightly tailored suit and ready to walk out the door. "What do you want now?" she asked, an air of defensiveness hardening her face. "I'm on my way to a job interview."

"Miss Brittany Harding," Jennings said, stepping through the open front door, "we have a warrant for your arrest in the murders of Otis Silvers and Imogene Pringle."

"Like hell you do!" she shouted, backpedaling; Jennings reached out for her wrist, but she yanked it back. "Get your goddamn hands off me. This is some sort of joke! How dare you come in here and accuse me of murder?"

Moreno rested a hand on her baton.

"Miss Harding, I'm sure you don't want to make this more difficult than it already is," Jennings said as he advanced on her. "Come peacefully and it'll be easier, for all of us."

She backed against the entryway wall; as Jennings took another step toward her, she kicked him in the groin, doubling him over. Moreno leaped forward and pinned Harding against the wall with the baton shoved beneath her chin. She then spun her around and took her suspect down, face first, onto the tile floor.

Jennings stood up slowly, his brow crumpled in pain. He pulled out his handcuffs and leaned over the suspect's prone body, fastening the cuffs to her forearms with a swift flick of his wrist. He made them exceptionally tight.

"Miss Harding," he said through clenched teeth, "I think we'll add resisting arrest to the charges against you." He proceeded to read her her rights, and while still somewhat stooped over, led her outside where the uniformed officer took her to the waiting patrol car.

THE TRIAL

EIGHT WEEKS LATER
APRIL 20

CHAPTER
60

IN THE PRIVATE SECTOR, the different categories of attorneys are grouped by fields of practice: litigation, criminal defense, real estate, business, estate planning, and the like. In the public defender's office, however, the attorneys are categorized somewhat differently: those whose goal is to gain valuable trial experience, at which time they will leave to join a local firm; those who are superb trial attorneys; those who are mediocre and thus could not land a private position that approached the salary and benefits of their civil service job; and those who are so incompetent that the important, challenging cases are shifted away from them— and replaced with mundane misdemeanors and conservatorships.

When someone is in need of a public defender, as is stated in Miranda, one is assigned. From the accused's perspective, the luck of the draw is worse than a crap shoot—for in a crap shoot, the only thing on the line is money. With respect to the public defender's office, the luck of the draw could be a matter of life and death, depending upon who is assigned to your case.

Brittany Harding drew Wendell Warwick for her defense. Warwick, a fifteen-year veteran of the public defender's office, was generally considered to fit into the mediocre category. He had lost more than his share of cases, but occasionally he would surprise everyone with a sagacious defense. Problem was, such triumphs and flashes of brilliance were few and far between. It was theorized in the office that personal problems suctioned away his ability to devote the time and focus necessary to win important cases consistently.

Harding's case began on an inauspicious note. In keeping with accepted procedure, Warwick made a pretrial motion to challenge Denton's introduction of DNA evidence. However, two days before the Kelly-Frye hearing—a court proceeding to determine whether evidence had scientific validity and reliability—his expert canceled due to illness, and Warwick did a one-eighty, changing his mind on the hearing and deciding to proceed without one. He had his reasons, he explained, and apologized to the court for wasting its time.

The following day, Warwick was due to appear before the judge in chambers, with Denton present, to contest evidence the DA wanted to bring against his client. Denton had requested that this pretrial motion be held in chambers, out of earshot of the press, so as to preserve both Madison's reputation and Harding's privacy. He explained that it would be undesirable to go public with unsubstantiated rape complaints, stories of extortion and clandestine videotapes if there was a chance the judge could deem it all to be inadmissible. Warwick agreed, and shortly before noon they found themselves sitting in Calvino's plush, wood-lined office facing the crotchety man who was staring down at his plate of food.

"Damned restaurant botched my grilled halibut. Dried it to a crisp. But I didn't have time for them to redo the order because I had to get back here for this meeting." Both Warwick and Denton listened intently, as if they were genuinely concerned about the judge's lunch and his misfortune. In fact, they could not care less. Denton laughed inside, realizing that it was probably the last thing he and Warwick would agree on for the rest of the trial. They both ceremoniously apologized to the judge for his spoiled lunch and moved on to the purpose of the hearing.

Calvino nodded to the court reporter to begin her stenography. "So I presume that you have a problem with the evidence that Mr. Denton intends to bring," he said to Warwick.

"Yes, Your Honor. The defense wishes to exclude from trial

any information pertaining to accusations of extortion relative to either Phillip Madison or William Stanton."

"Your Honor," Denton said, "this evidence, and the witnesses who will testify as to the two prior episodes of extortion, are paramount for establishing motive. Harding extorted money from her prior employer with false accusations of sexual harassment—and admitted as much on videotape. She then tried this same tactic on Dr. Madison two years later—but his attorney didn't let her get away with it—"

"Yes, yes, Mr. Denton, I know the story," Calvino said. "Get to the point. Quickly."

"Yes, Your Honor," Denton said, squaring his shoulders and taking a deep breath. "There is a distinct pattern of behavior beginning with a similar episode of extortion two years ago and continuing to the present. When her attempt at extorting Dr. Madison failed, she became enraged and formulated a plan by which she could effect her revenge. She made no attempt at disguising her intentions. She shouted in a public place that she would get even and make him pay. This most definitely goes to motive, and is completely proper in its logical progression from past to present."

As Calvino opened his mouth to speak, Warwick interrupted. "Your Honor, if I may."

Calvino nodded.

"Miss Harding's former employer and her behavior during that supposed videotaped incident have nothing to do with her feelings or motives relative to Phillip Madison. Further, the production of the evidence, particularly the videotape of Miss Harding and Mr. Stanton, is inflammatory and prejudicial, collateral, and definitely inadmissible. Moreover, we have no way of verifying the tape's authenticity or even when it was filmed."

"We have Mr. Stanton himself who will testify that the tape is authentic and he will be able to verify exactly when it was made," Denton said. "And we can subpoena the cameraman— the private investigator who Mr. Stanton's attorney hired to film the event. We can subpoena Stanton's attorney, for that matter, to establish place and time, and obtain a copy of the check written by the attorney to the investigator—"

Calvino held up a hand for Denton to stop. "I get the point, counselor."

Warwick leaned forward. "This doesn't even address the issues of my client being incapable of committing this crime. The DA is, in effect, saying that Miss Harding had access to Madison's vehicle—which Madison will undoubtedly tell you she didn't—so she had to have broken into his garage, stolen his Mercedes, committed the act, planted the beer cans in his car to frame Madison, and then returned his car to the garage. This isn't reasonable. In fact, it's ridiculous."

"Your Honor," Denton said, "we're looking at a pattern of behavior here. We're not looking at a model citizen. Her crimes and accusations became increasingly more complex until the point where her emotions drove her to plan and telegraph what she was going to do. It's all part of a linear continuum, Your Honor."

"A linear continuum," Calvino repeated.

"Ipso facto," Denton said.

Warwick leaned forward. "I disagree. It involves completely unrelated events and information. In fact, it's collateral—we'd have to litigate the other matters as well, just to prove the truth or falsity of the rape allegations. Witnesses will have to be brought in. It'll be, in effect, a mini rape trial—and, therefore, the jury is going to be involved in making collateral decisions, when the issue is simply a matter of whether or not she was guilty of driving Madison's car and killing two people. Therefore, it's completely inappropriate to allow this evidence in, according to sections 1101 and 352 of the California Evidence Code."

Calvino extended an open hand. "Let me see this video-tape Mr. Stanton made."

Denton fished through his attaché case and produced the tape. The judge inserted it into his VCR and watched it. Two minutes later, as it ended, Calvino sighed. "Counselors, I've heard and seen enough. What I'm going to say is going to make one of you pleased and the other pissed as hell. Well, I don't really care one way or the other," he said, looking both of them in the eye. He turned to the stenographer and nodded for her to resume her transcript. "I will say this: you both make compelling arguments, and another judge may see this in a different light. Keep that in mind, Mr. Warwick, for appeal. But I feel that there is sufficient relationship between the various incidents to link them together toward establishing motive." He looked over at Warwick. "Had your client not told everyone and their uncle in that market what she was going to do, I might be ruling differently. However, she said what she said because of the extortion-rape issue, and this was obviously not the first time that she's engaged in this type of behavior. It's her MO, counselor, and I believe there's enough foundation to go forward. I am not going to exclude this evidence."

Denton breathed a sigh of relief as the court reporter slapped away at her steno keys; Warwick did his best to hide his frustration, but his downcast expression spoke volumes.

Additional pretrial motions were made, fought over, and either granted or rejected. Denton and Warwick sparred repeatedly, with Calvino serving as arbiter in his reputedly restive manner. With the trial scheduled to be followed heavily by the media, both sides were gearing up for the onslaught of public interest usually accompanied by the magnifying glass that Warwick despised, and under which Denton thrived.

Madison's preparation with Denton lasted four hours, and delved into private corners of his life that even he did not realize he had. The prosecutor explained that if he had this information, then Warwick might have it as well. He had to be ready for just about anything, Denton cautioned.

Later that evening, Madison reiterated his complaint to Hellman that attorneys left a bad taste in his mouth, present company excluded.

Hellman smiled. "You haven't seen me from the other side's perspective. I'm no better than any of them. With one exception," he said straight-faced; "I'm one of the honest ones."

CHAPTER
61

CHANDLER SAT reclining on the playroom lounger, Coke in hand, watching the New York Mets lose to the Florida Marlins in the ninth inning. "Incredible," he said as he took his last swig from the can. He slammed his fist down as the replay showed the thundering four-hundred-fifty-foot home run disappear behind the blue left-centerfield wall. He squeezed his fist hard, crushing the aluminum can. At one of the folds, there was a sharp point that dug into his pinky. He pulled the crumpled container off his hand, examining the punctured flesh where the metal had stuck him.

As the sportscaster announced that the Marlins had pulled out a miraculous come-from-behind victory, Chandler noticed something where the aluminum had creased. He stared at the can for a long moment, then turned it over and around, several times.

Denise walked into the room with Noah. "They lost?" she asked, staring at the screen where the score was displayed. "They were ahead a couple of minutes ago."

Chandler was not listening; he was on the phone. Denise popped a videotape into the VCR for Noah, then looked at the notes Chandler was scribbling on his pad as he spoke. He thanked the person on the other end of the phone, and hung up.

"What are you doing?"

"Following up on something."

Denise looked at him. "Work? It's Sunday evening. Can't it wait until tomorrow morning?"

"This isn't work. Something on Phil's case."

"What is it?"

Chandler hesitated. "I'm not sure."

CHAPTER
62

THE JURY SELECTION process took three days. Attempting to empanel an impartial group of twelve people who had not seen any of the news reports on television proved more difficult than originally thought. Fortunately, however, much of the pretrial publicity centered around Phillip Madison as a suspect—so, if anything, the bias against Madison was the sticky point for Denton, since the doctor was his prime witness.

Denton's questions during voir dire, the preliminary examination used by the court and attorneys to select a suitable panel of jurors, were therefore directed toward identifying bias against Madison. As Denton saw it, the worst scenario would be ending up with jurors who still harbored ill feelings toward Madison, because they would then be less inclined to believe him when he was called as a witness.

The jury that both attorneys ultimately agreed on consisted of seven women and five men. Along ethnic lines, there was one Asian, five African-Americans, one Hispanic, and five Caucasians. Denton liked the mix, while Warwick accepted it with trepidation; he was concerned about the prominence of both the female and African-American representation on the jury, being that the victims were both black, with one being a single mother. Trying to avoid an environment of excessive pity for the victims, he also wanted to buffer his client from misdirected disgust leveled by the jury against the suspect who was accused of the crime. The jury should not convict simply because his client was the one chosen and charged by the prosecutor—and because *someone* had to pay for the heinous crime that was going to be presented to them.

The jury empaneled and pretrial motions disposed of, Judge Calvino turned toward Denton and nodded; Denton stood and buttoned his suit coat. He had delivered hundreds of opening statements over the years, and was adept at driving home his point by commanding the jury's undivided attention as he told them with undaunted confidence he was going to prove beyond a reasonable doubt the suspect before them was guilty. Although Madison's removal as the accused dulled the high-profile nature of the case, it was still full of controversy and interest; as a result, members of the press filled the courtroom. Denton knew this, and if butterflies could truly be present in one's stomach, he would have a flock inside his own at the moment.

"That woman—Brittany Harding," Denton shouted, pointing his finger at her, "is accused of murdering two people. Two innocent people who were unfortunate enough to become unwitting pawns in a plan of cold, calculated revenge. A plan of revenge that was carried out by Brittany Harding against a prominent surgeon, a pillar of the community.

"Ladies and gentlemen of the jury, I'm Timothy Denton, the prosecutor, and I represent the People of the State of California." Denton strode toward the jury box, his hair freshly trimmed and his face glowing from a recent session at the local tanning salon. His neatly primped appearance, which included a new double-breasted navy blue suit, signaled the importance of this trial to both him and the state. He had begun with intensity chiseled into his brow, but now, as he approached the jurors, his features were softer, his demeanor inviting. They seemed to receive him well, watching him closely as he kept his hands clasped in front of him and focused all of their attention on the content of his opening argument.

"My job is to present the facts to you, evidence that a crime has been committed. You'll listen to the evidence, and then you'll deliberate amongst yourselves. In the end, the twelve of you will collectively decide whether or not the defendant is guilty of this crime. It's an important assignment—but one I'm confident you'll handle with professionalism and responsibility."

He threw a glance at the defendant, then looked back at the jurors. "That woman," Denton said, again pointing a short and stubby finger at Harding, who looked away, "is accused of murdering two people in cold blood. But the story does not begin there. Let's go back to late August of last year. Brittany Harding was a recently hired assistant for a nonprofit organization whose president was Dr. Phillip Madison, a prominent surgeon in the community. When the organization's administrative officer became ill, Brittany Harding temporarily took over those duties. Witnesses tell us—as they'll tell you during this trial—that Brittany Harding had difficulty handling these activities. She accused one parent of being responsible for her child's mental retardation, when in fact it was a genetic defect that was the causative agent. Others reported she was 'condescending,' and 'unwilling to help' them," Denton said, reading the quotes from witness statements. "But I acknowledge that there's no crime in being ignorant or rude, is there?" He took a few steps toward the prosecution table, then turned and faced them again.

"When Dr. Madison suggested to Brittany Harding that she submit an employment application for the administrative officer's position, a job that she'd taken for granted would automatically become hers, she felt threatened. She thought she was going to be fired, so she manufactured a story in which she claimed that Dr. Madison raped her in his home. And she took this story to the police. She told them he'd raped her. But she didn't go to the police on the same day that 'the rape' allegedly occurred. In fact, she didn't go a week later. Not two weeks later. Not three weeks later. So when did she make this accusation? *Five weeks later,* ladies and gentlemen. I'm going to show you how she manufactured the entire scenario, and attempted to frame the doctor with rape.

"Oh, the police did their work diligently. They repeatedly interviewed Dr. Madison, but they couldn't gather any evidence to support Miss Harding's claim. *Because no proof of rape existed.* But Brittany Harding would not be stopped there: she leaked her story to the newspaper, and an article was written without specifically naming Phillip Madison as the accused doctor. The tactic worked. It scared him—if his name had been mentioned, it could've destroyed his fine reputation as a surgeon.

"Well, Miss Harding's attorney immediately contacted Dr. Madison's attorney and made a proposal: she would drop the rape complaint against him, in exchange for a modest sum of money: fifty thousand dollars." He strode back toward the jury. "This is called extortion, ladies and gentlemen, and it's against the law. I'm going to show you how she played this same game of extortion with a former employer of hers two years ago. And you'll see a videotape of Brittany Harding admitting to this gentleman that she was extorting him. We'll hear him testify as well.

"But Brittany Harding," he said, looking over at her again, pausing, allowing the jurors to follow his gaze to the defendant, "did not succeed with her plan of extortion against Dr. Madison. Oh, he paid the money, because in the long run, sadly, it was cheaper to pay her than go to trial to defend himself, and it was safer than risking damage to his reputation that the public exposure of her false accusations would certainly have caused.

"So why did her plan fail? Because Brittany Harding was not content to take the money and run. She realized she wanted more. Money was not enough. She needed revenge: she wanted to destroy Dr. Madison's marriage. So she mailed a copy of the payoff check along with a copy of the agreement the two lawyers had drafted, as well as a staged picture that I'll show you during the trial.

"As a result, Brittany Harding had violated the agreement, and Dr. Madison's attorney forced Miss Harding to return the money—all of it—to avoid a lawsuit alleging extortion. Well, she was furious, to say the least. Look at all the trouble she'd gone through to extort the money. Ladies and gentlemen, I'll bet she felt that she'd earned this money! After all, she worked hard for it! But then, suddenly, it was stolen right out from under her nose. So she was angry, enraged. So angry, in fact, that she confronted Dr. Madison in a supermarket and began screaming at him." Denton held up his tightened fist toward the ceiling. "'You'll pay for this! I'll get even!' she yelled, in front of witnesses."

He leaned both hands on the railing in front of the jury box, and looked deeply into their eyes as he spoke. "You'll hear from one of these witnesses, the grocery clerk who checked her food out right after the argument occurred. He'll tell you exactly what she said. You'll hear for yourselves just how angry she was. He'll also testify that she purchased a six-pack of Millstone Premium Draft beer—remember this, because in a moment I'll mention these beer cans again, and you'll see their relevance.

"So what was it that she did in order to get even with Dr. Madison?" Denton folded his hands in front of him again, and stood facing the jurors. "I'm going to show you how Brittany Harding stole the motor vehicle which belongs to Dr. Madison, and then used it to kill two pedestrians, leaving one of them, a single parent, to die slowly in the street on a cold, rainy, winter evening.

"And I'm going to show you that following the hit-and-run, Brittany Harding then planted evidence in the vehicle—the Millstone Premium Draft beer cans that she'd purchased in the market a few days earlier—with the intention of fooling the police into thinking that Dr. Madison had, in a drunken state, run those two people over." Denton began strolling slowly, in front of the jurors. "And for a while the police were fooled. They did think Dr. Madison was the guilty party. After all, it was his car. In fact, I'll freely admit to you that I was ready to go to trial against the good doctor until we discovered two additional pieces of evidence. Two things that convinced me that Brittany Harding had committed these murders . . . two things that will convince *you* that she committed these murders: her motive, and the physical evidence that proves the beer cans belonged to her.

"Now, before I tell you how I'm going to prove that Brittany Harding had a motive, let's first discuss what motive means. In a legal sense, motive is that idea, belief, or emotion that leads the mind to indulge in a criminal act." He stopped, allowing the definition to sink in. "It's the cause or reason that moves the will and induces criminal action on the part of the accused," he said. "Through the testimony of several witnesses, you'll hear what kind of person Brittany Harding is, what type of relationship she had with Dr. Madison, and, just as importantly, how she threatened revenge against him in a local supermarket. When she screamed 'I'll get you for this! You'll pay,' she telegraphed her actions loud and clear. She announced what she was going to do, and then she acted upon her promise. We don't have to *guess* what was in her mind because she told everyone who was in earshot of her in the market what she intended to do. And that makes it really quite simple. If you agree that Brittany Harding's emotions led her to commit a criminal act, then the rest is easy. Everything else will then fall into place for you. It'll look black and white, and a verdict of 'guilty' will merely be a logical conclusion.

"I will do everything I can to make this case as clear-cut and black-and-white as possible. But in general, a juror's job is always difficult, because the defendant's attorney will try and cloud the issues, throw roadblocks and smoke screens, and try to confuse you. Don't be fooled. Don't let him deceive you.

"Once you hear all the evidence, you'll then have to decide which of it is significant. Which facts are important, and which are not. Who is telling the truth, and who is not. Ultimately, you'll have to ask yourself if a person like Brittany Harding, who was capable of extortion on two occasions, who was capable of lying to the police about a rape that never occurred, is someone you can believe when she says she is innocent of murder.

"It's important that each and every one of you work hard until you've accomplished your task. Because there was a real crime committed, ladies and gentlemen. Two real victims, and a whole lot of pain. It's your job to determine if the defendant is going to pay for the crime that was committed. The prosecution is confident it will make its case against Brittany Harding; otherwise, I wouldn't be standing here before you, taking up your valuable time, the judge's time, my time, and the state's resources, to present this case. No, if you look at the facts as pre-sented and listen to the witnesses I will bring, you'll see that there is only one truth. That Brittany Harding committed mur-der in order to carry out an act of revenge. And for that she must be held accountable.

"Thank you." Denton sat down, a bit lightheaded, the per-spiration under his armpits disguised by the cover of his suit coat.

As Denton took his seat, Judge Calvino nodded to the defense table.

Wendell Warwick, the public defender, removed his read-ing glasses. Tall and thin, with a sharp nose and small, beady eyes that appeared to be constantly squinting, he smiled at the jury as he arose and buttoned his suit coat. "'Don't be fooled. Don't let the defendant's attorney deceive you,'" he said mockingly. He stopped and smiled again, extended both of his lanky arms out in front of him, palms up, his back arched slightly backward. "Do I look like I'm here to deceive you, ladies and gentlemen?

"I'm not. I'm here for the same reason as the prosecutor: for justice to be served. But that's where the similarity ends. Mr. Denton wants you to find my client guilty. To him, that is justice. To me, justice means that you will not find an innocent woman guilty and send her to prison for a crime she did not commit. But there is one other very important difference between Mr. Denton and myself. The prosecutor has to *prove* his case against my client. If he fails to make a believable case—that is, if he fails to prove beyond a reason-able doubt that my client is guilty—then you must vote to find her not guilty.

"The prosecution has the burden of proof. They have to prove Miss Harding committed these crimes. As the judge will instruct you at the end of the trial, Miss Harding is inno-cent until proven guilty. Although the state has to prove guilt beyond a reasonable doubt, I do *not* have to prove *innocence*. In fact, I don't have to prove anything.

"But what does reasonable doubt mean? It means that if you have even a small degree of doubt that my client is guilty, then these charges get thrown in the garbage can, where they came from."

He began to walk a little bit as he spoke, starting from one end of the jury box and moving to the other. "Now, there are two types of evidence," he was saying, as if teaching a class. "Direct and circumstantial. Direct evidence is something tangible: what a witness sees—his or her own perceptions. Circumstantial evidence is that type of evidence which requires you to make an inference . . . it means that you have to take the facts that are presented, and then make a leap of logic, to try to connect other circumstances to those facts you accept to be true."

He paused, looking at the confused looks of the people on the jury. He had accomplished exactly what he'd set out to do. Try to make the prosecution's case so contrived and confusing that they will take the easier route: acquittal.

"Confusing, I know . . ." he said, with a slight chuckle. "It confuses me at times too, and I deal with this stuff each and every day." *Relate to me,* he was telling them. *I'm just like one of you.* Trying to get them onto his side. "The state's case is based solely on circumstantial evidence. In fact, they're so desperate for something, anything they can hang their hats on, some form of proof that will show that my client is guilty—that they are trying to tell you that my client had motive. Motive is nothing more than circumstantial evidence.

"Did my client like Phillip Madison? No, she did not. He was rude to her, tried to rape her, and then tried to pay her off to stop her from taking the case public. He had a reputation to protect. A well-known surgeon publicly accused of rape? That would be . . . *detrimental* . . . to his practice," he said, smiling, as if he were sharing a joke with the jury—an incredible understatement. Two jurors smiled back.

"No, he couldn't let her go public. So he offered her some money, and she took it—a mere forty thousand dollars to make the misery of a protracted and humiliating rape trial go away. But yes, she was still angry, and she did send the letter and photo to Phillip Madison's wife. But what was wrong with that? It was nothing less than the truth. There wouldn't have been a problem if Madison had told his wife about the settlement, but he kept it from her, *lied* to her. If Madison chose to lie to his wife and keep certain facts from her, well . . ." he said, smiling again at the jury, "you can't blame my client for that.

"And you can't find her guilty of murder because she merely wanted to avoid the publicity and embarrassment of a high-profile rape trial. Can you, now?" He paused, for effect.

"No, my client, in fact, has nothing to do with these murders. Actually, *Phillip Madison* was the suspect they initially charged. But then, suddenly, a few days before his trial is to begin, the DA lets Madison go and charges Miss Harding. Why, we don't know. Oh, he's said it's because of new evidence that they stumbled upon. I don't buy it. But we'll never know the true reason why he suddenly switched gears. Maybe it was pressure from someone, from the press, from someone else who owed Phillip Madison—"

"Objection!" Denton was on his feet. "Your Honor, this is completely inappropriate and Mr. Warwick knows it. He's accusing my office of impropriety and he has absolutely no proof of such an allegation."

"Approach," said Judge Calvino, whose face was as red as a strawberry. His left eyebrow was twitching fiercely.

The two attorneys walked up to the bench; the judge looked down upon them from his perch and covered the microphone so the jury would not hear. "Mr. Warwick, explain."

"Nothing to explain, Your Honor. I simply felt that there had to be some better reason for the DA to have dropped the charges against—"

"This is contemptible!" Denton said.

"Mr. Warwick," Judge Calvino said between clenched teeth, "let's not get off on the wrong foot in this trial. You know the rules. That was a cheap shot against Mr. Denton. If you do anything of this nature again, I'll hold you in contempt. No more warnings, understand?"

Warwick nodded. "Yes, Your Honor."

Calvino motioned them away with his hands, as if he were shooing away flies.

"Ladies and gentlemen," the judge said, addressing the jury, "Mr. Warwick made inappropriate remarks that have absolutely no basis in fact. I'm instructing you to disregard what you've just heard." He shook his head and glared at Warwick. "Objection sustained."

Warwick paced for a moment in front of the jury box, composing his thoughts, hand on his chin. Reprimand notwithstanding, he had accomplished what he had wanted: a judge can tell a jury to disregard certain remarks, but the fact of the matter was, they heard them—and nothing anyone could say would miraculously erase those comments from their memory.

Warwick stopped pacing and faced the jury. "The DA will attempt to show you that there were cans of beer in the vehicle, and that these cans had traces of saliva on them. They extracted DNA from this saliva, and it showed a pattern of genetic material that supposedly matched that of my client. Whether or not DNA is a legitimate test is not important at this moment. What is important is that it doesn't matter whether or not Miss Harding's DNA is on the beer cans. All it proves, if it proves anything at all, is that at some point in time, those cans were in Miss Harding's possession. It doesn't mean that she was driving the vehicle when it struck the two pedestrians.

"I'll ask you to remember three things throughout this trial. The first is reasonable doubt—if there's an ounce of doubt in your minds that my client is guilty, you must find her *not* guilty. The second thing to keep in mind is the concept of circumstantial evidence. No one saw Miss Harding driving that car. No one saw her kill those people. No one even saw her near Phillip Madison's house either before, or after, she supposedly stole his car. There is no direct evidence of my client's guilt whatsoever.

"The last thing that I want you to remember is that Miss Harding is innocent until proven guilty. I'm telling you now that the DA will fail to make his case. He has the burden of proof, and he will not meet his burden. Remember what I'm telling you, because I'll remind you of it when the trial is over. You must find my client not guilty, because she is . . . Not Guilty. Thank you."

Warwick took his seat. Denton tried to look impassively at the judge, awaiting his next orders. He did not want to look at the jury. Warwick had made a good showing, better than Denton had thought he would, exposing many of the weakest points of the prosecution's case against Harding. And while no DA likes it when the defense, or the judge, belabors the point of reasonable doubt, Warwick did not merely belabor it. He beat it into the ground like a flag, and then saluted it.

Judge Calvino looked down at his watch and declared a recess until after lunch. As everyone prepared to file out of the courtroom, the reporters were still scribbling furiously to get down their final thoughts on the opening arguments. The first person to leave the courtroom was the man who was sitting in the last row, nearest the doors: Jeffrey Hellman.

CHAPTER
63

HELLMAN GRABBED LUNCH with Denton and his assistant prosecutor. He commended them on a strong opening statement, and they discussed the strategies that Denton had outlined for the trial. Hellman felt it was a reasonable and sound approach.

When they returned to court, the jury was brought back in and Denton called his first witness: Detective Bill Jennings, who would establish the sequence of events leading up to his arrival at the crime scene, the collection of evidence by the criminalist, the discovery of the physical evidence on the car, the presence of Millstone beer cans inside it, and the resultant arrest of Phillip Madison. Jennings was brief and to the point. He had been through this many times in the past and knew how to allow Denton to lead him without letting it appear as such. He responded negatively here and there, to give the impression that this was all something new, something they had not rehearsed or discussed.

They went through the interview of the witness, Mr. Hollowes, the homeless gentleman who later identified the Chicago White Sox hat. He described their investigation in broad terms, hitting only the high points and explaining why they chose to drop the case against Madison and charge Harding instead.

On cross-examination, Warwick attempted to paint Jennings as a bumbling fool who was not sure who had committed the crime, but who must have been manipulated into dropping Madison as a suspect. He leaned hard on him, trying to ascertain who it was who had applied the pressure to lay off

Madison. Although Warwick attempted to get in Jennings's face, the detective kept his composure, refusing to allow the attorney to rattle him. He explained that the evidence was clearly more convincing against Harding, and given her tirade in the market, he felt it was "a home run." Warwick successfully had the last remark stricken from the record.

"I'd like to ask you, detective, what you consider to be the most important piece of evidence against my client."

"Objection. Vague and misleading. Overbroad." Denton was on his feet.

"Mr. Denton?" Calvino asked.

"When counsel is asking what's the most important, to what is he referring? How does he frame 'most important'? In terms of what?"

Warwick sighed. "I'll restate my question, if it pleases the court."

"It would," Calvino said.

"What piece of evidence carries the most weight, in your opinion, detective, in leading you to conclude that my client is more guilty than Phillip Madison?"

"I'm going to object," Denton said. "It calls for an opinion that has no relevance to the matter at hand."

"I will show relevance, Your Honor, if counsel will give me an opportunity to proceed."

"Very well. Make it quick, Mr. Warwick. Overruled," he said to Denton.

Warwick looked over at Jennings; the judge instructed him to answer.

"There's a lot of evidence that I would consider important."

"Is there *one thing*, detective," Warwick said, "that you consider to be of greatest importance?"

"In my opinion, the evidence regarding her motive and her statements in the market wherein she declared her intention to take revenge are crucial pieces of evidence."

"And the beer can DNA?"

"Important as well."

"Is it accurate to state that those three pieces of evidence are the three most important?"

"Objection." Denton was on his feet again; Calvino looked irritated. He waved Denton down into his seat with a muffled "Overruled."

"Yes," Jennings said, "I would consider those three to be the most important."

"Thank you," Warwick said, walking back to his seat. "Oh, I'm just curious, detective," he said as he sat down, as if it were an afterthought, "does the fact that my client's saliva and DNA were found on the beer cans in the car prove conclusively that my client was in that vehicle at the time the two people were run down?"

Jennings shifted uncomfortably in his seat. "I wouldn't say conclusively. At least, not by itself. But when you combine it with the other evidence, namely the two other factors I mentioned a minute ago, we see that at some point in time the beer cans belonged to her—"

"Your Honor—" Warwick interrupted.

". . . and if she were trying to frame Dr. Madison," Jennings continued, "then it would follow that she planted these cans—"

"Your Honor!" Warwick shouted, jumping to his feet and leaning forward on the defense table, as if ready to pounce if Calvino did not respond. "Please instruct the witness to merely answer the question that was asked of him, and not to launch into a narrative."

"Detective," Calvino said, "please just answer what's asked of you."

Warwick was flushed in the face, apparently frustrated that Jennings had maneuvered an important defense point into a prosecution advantage. As Warwick approached the witness stand, Jennings landed his final dig. Looking at the judge, he said, "I believe I have answered what was asked of me." His eyes were the size of quarters, like a child pleading his case of having raided the candy jar merely because it was there for the taking.

Warwick was now standing and leaning over the railing, his nose twelve inches from Jennings's face. "I'd like to ask you about former Sacramento Police Officer Ryan Chandler," he said, looking into his adversary's eyes, watching for weakness.

"What d'ya wanna know?" Jennings asked with a singsong tone.

Denton's back muscles tightened; it caught him off guard. He did not think that Warwick knew anything about Jennings and Chandler. How far was Warwick going to go with this? How much did he really know? What about the lab and Palucci—

". . . so you had this 'poor relationship' with him, as you put it, detective. Can you be more specific?" Warwick was asking.

Jennings shrugged his right shoulder. "Nothing much to tell. He and I were involved in a case together fifteen years ago. We disagreed on how to proceed, that's all."

"Oh, I believe there's much more to it than that," Warwick said, smiling, walking back to the defense table. He reached into his attaché case and took out a piece of paper. "I have here a department memo—"

"Objection," Denton said as he arose from his seat. "Where is Mr. Warwick going with this? This is completely irrelevant."

"Mr. Warwick, where *are* you going with this?"

"If the court would give me a little latitude, I believe it will become clear."

The judge nodded him on. "Overruled. For now." As Denton resumed his seat, he was handed a copy of the document by Warwick, who was now strolling confidently in front of the prosecution table, headed back toward Jennings. A shark going in for the kill.

"This memo, signed by your supervisor at the time, Lieutenant Beals, is essentially a reprimand to the file, your personnel file, regarding your conduct during that investigation. He used such words as—"

"Chandler and I had a disagreement," Jennings said. "He wanted to handle it one way, and I felt a different approach was indicated."

Warwick paused for a moment, wondering if he should finish his question, or go on. He chose the latter. "And what was the result of the disagreement you two had?"

"The suspect was ultimately captured."

"Only after another two people were murdered. Your actions caused a delay in apprehending—"

"Objection!" Denton shouted again, on his feet. "This has absolutely nothing to do with the defendant, this case, or the evidence at issue."

"Sustained. Mr. Warwick, your latitude has ended. Let's see a different line of questioning or dismiss the witness."

Warwick nodded, walked over to his attaché, and put the memo back in it. "So, detective, how did this reprimand make you feel?"

"Objection."

"Mr. Warwick, I asked you to pursue a different line of questioning."

"I have, Your Honor. There is pertinence to this, and I will make it clear within the next few questions."

"You have three more and then if I don't see the relevance, you're through," Calvino warned.

Warwick, still standing in front of the defense table, looked over toward Jennings. "Detective, how did you feel toward Ryan Chandler after this incident?"

"Let's just say I wouldn't have invited him over for a barbecue."

Denton clenched his jaw again; he did not want to keep objecting, as it might appear to the jury that he was trying to hide something. He only hoped that Chandler and the crime lab incident did not come up; if anything could confuse a jury, divert them from the real issue, it was impropriety in the procedure of handling evidence. It could set the stage for challenging the saliva and DNA findings later.

"No, I would say not," Warwick was saying. "And now, with Chandler the private investigator on the Madison case, was there even the hint of revenge in your mind, a sense of satisfaction, of enjoyment in arresting his client, Phillip Madison?"

Jennings hesitated a second, looked down at the railing for a moment. "I am a professional, sir. What happened in the past is in the past. I was only concerned with the present and apprehending the right suspect in this case, sir."

Denton spread his hands out in front of him and looked at Calvino.

"Mr. Warwick," Calvino said, "you should take Detective Jennings's advice and leave the past in the past, where it belongs. I believe you're finished with this witness."

"But that was only two questions. You said I had three."

"Math was never my strength, Mr. Warwick. The law was and still is, and I see no relevance to the line of questioning you're pursuing."

To Denton, it was quite clear: Warwick wanted to discredit Jennings in any way possible; he could not break him with direct questioning, so he tried to drag something out of Jennings's past. A skeleton in the closet. Although Calvino said he did not know where Warwick was headed, Denton knew—and he was glad that the judge's command of mathematics was admittedly weak.

Denton's second witness, Stuart Saperstein, was a bit more polished in his delivery than was Jennings. He came off as articulate, thoughtful, and reflective.

Testifying as to the physical evidence found on the Mercedes, he established the fact that it was the car used in the murder of both individuals; further, he described the method by which both victims were struck, where they were most likely located prior to impact, and whether or not it appeared that the position in which the bodies were found was consistent with the mechanism of the suspected impact. Saperstein excelled in all aspects of the direct examination; he was working well with Denton, as they had in the past during numerous other cases in which Saperstein was a key forensic witness.

As time was winding down for the day, Denton asked Saperstein about the baseball cap found at Harding's house.

"And this hat, Mr. Saperstein, do you recognize it?" Denton asked, waving the Chicago White Sox cap.

"Yes I do."

"Where have you seen it before?"

"It was the one that was analyzed at the lab."

"And what did the analysis show?" Denton asked, stepping back from the witness box, allowing the jury an unimpeded view of Saperstein.

"Our analysis demonstrated fibers that were consistent with those found in the carpet of Miss Harding's home. Further, there were hair strands that matched those of the defendant, Miss Harding."

"And just how did you determine this, Mr. Saperstein? Did you hold it up to a light, maybe use a magnifying glass?"

Saperstein gave a little chuckle. They had rehearsed this. "No, not a magnifying glass. We have special high-powered instruments that are specifically built just for fiber and hair analysis, called comparison microscopes. Essentially, the instruments consist of two compound microscopes that are integrated into a binocular lens so that you can place both fibers under separate scopes and compare and integrate them into one image."

"So would you consider this method to be accurate in comparing and identifying fibers?"

"Very accurate."

"Thank you," Denton said. "Now on to more important matters. You performed other tests, tests that were run on the beer cans that were found in the back of the Mercedes, is that right?"

"Yes sir."

"What did you find on the cans?"

"Saliva, apparently from the person who drank the beer."

"Where was the saliva found?"

"Around the opening in the can that you drink from."

"And what else did you find around this opening?"

"We found lip prints."

"And just what are lip prints?"

"Just as each individual has a set of unique fingerprints, each person's lips have patterns of ridges, grooves, and wrinkles that are specific to that person. Distinct and intact lip prints were taken from the beer cans."

"Is this a scientifically accurate method?"

"Most definitely."

"And were those prints identified?"

"They were matched against those obtained from another lip print sample."

Denton took a step forward toward Saperstein, drawing the jurors' attention to his witness. "And what was your conclusion as to whose lip prints were present on the beer cans?"

"It was my opinion that the lip prints matched those of Brittany Harding."

A slight murmur rumbled from the spectator seats in the middle of the courtroom. Calvino looked up and restored order with his stare.

"Those of Brittany Harding," repeated Denton. "Not Phillip Madison. Brittany Harding. Are you sure?"

"Quite sure."

"Were there any other tests that were performed on the saliva that was on the beer cans?"

"Yes."

"What kind of tests were those?"

"We performed a blood group study and a DNA analysis."

"Relative to the blood group, what blood type was found in the saliva?"

"AB," Saperstein said.

"Did you test Dr. Madison's blood type?"

"Yes; it was type O."

"And Brittany Harding's?"

"AB."

Denton raised his eyebrows in mock surprise. "The defendant was AB, and the type found on the beer cans was AB?" he asked, reinforcing the fact, rubbing hand lotion into the jury's collective skin and watching it soak in.

"Yes."

"What percent of the world population is type AB?"

"AB is the rarest blood group that exists. Less than four percent of the population has it."

"What about type O? Just to give us a basis of comparison."

"Approximately forty-five percent of the population is type O."

"So AB is quite rare."

"Yes."

"You also said that you performed DNA testing on this saliva," Denton reminded him, receiving an affirmative nod from Saperstein. "I'm not going to go into the specifics of the testing procedure with you, because we have a witness who'll be testifying in that regard. But can you please tell the court whose DNA was found in the saliva?"

"That of Brittany Harding."

Another mumble from the courtroom, a bit louder than before.

"Quiet, please," ordered Calvino.

"So let me get this straight, Mr. Saperstein," Denton said, placing a hand on his chin. "You testified earlier that the vehicle used to cause the deaths of the two decedents was the Mercedes owned by Dr. Phillip Madison. And now you're saying that the beer cans which were found in the rear of that car did not in fact bear any identification relative to Dr. Madison, but in fact contained lip prints and saliva that were consistent with consumption by Brittany Harding—"

"Objection," Warwick said, standing. "Is there a question here? Or is counsel merely summarizing the witness's testimony, putting words into—"

"I'm not putting words—" Denton said.

Calvino was banging his gavel. "Let's keep this civil, please. Unless you have something constructive to offer, allow me to make my ruling on the objection, Mr. Denton."

"Sorry, Your Honor."

"Objection sustained. Mr. Denton, ask a question or dismiss your witness."

"Yes, Your Honor." He turned to Saperstein. "What certainty would you give the fact that the lip prints belong to Brittany Harding?"

"Ninety-five percent."

"And what's the chance that the DNA profile you obtained could come from someone else other than the defendant?"

"I would say that there is an extremely low probability."

"Can you put that into numbers, Mr. Saperstein?"

"Based upon the testing method used, there is only a one-in-fifty-thousand chance that it is not Brittany Harding's."

"Objection. This gentleman is not listed as an expert on DNA by the prosecution."

"He has a point there, Mr. Denton," Calvino said.

"Your Honor, this gentleman is a senior criminalist who is trained in DNA analysis. I chose to designate a different witness as our DNA expert in order to corroborate the findings of Mr. Saperstein."

"I didn't hear you qualify Mr. Saperstein as an expert on DNA analysis," countered Calvino.

"Very well, Your Honor, I shall do so."

"Mr. Warwick?" Calvino asked.

"I withdraw my objection pending Mr. Denton's qualification."

Denton stepped forward. "Mr. Saperstein, what is your training on DNA analysis?"

"I attended several course offerings at University of California at Berkeley and received certification in DNA handling and analysis nearly two years ago."

"And in how many cases have you performed DNA analysis? Approximately."

"Between one and two hundred, I would estimate."

"Your Honor, I submit Mr. Saperstein to the court as an expert in DNA analysis."

"Mr. Warwick, do you have any objections?"

Warwick frowned. "No, Your Honor."

"Very well, then," Denton said. "Mr. Saperstein, you were quoting us the probability that another person could have the same DNA as that of Brittany Harding."

"Yes. There is a one-in-fifty-thousand chance that another person's DNA would match Miss Harding's DNA, according to the method of analysis we used."

"One in fifty thousand. And we already know that the only other suspect who ever existed in this case—Phillip Madison—his DNA does not match that found on the cans. Is that correct?"

"Yes. We tested Madison's DNA, and the pattern's not even close."

"Thank you, Mr. Saperstein," Denton said as he walked back toward the prosecutor's table; he nodded to Warwick. "Your witness."

"Mr. Saperstein," Warwick said as buttoned his sport coat, "did you perform all of the tests on the evidence gathered at the crime scene?"

"No, I did not. I was ill with ulcerative co—"

"Yes, sir, a simple yes or no would be sufficient. Did you perform the testing that was carried out on the lip print analysis?"

"No."

"I thought you said you did." He looked down at the legal pad he was holding. "I believe when Mr. Denton asked, 'What did you find around the opening on the cans,' you answered, 'We found lip prints.' We, as in yourself and others." He removed his reading glasses and looked at Saperstein.

"That's not what I meant."

"But it is what you said."

"I meant it as the collective 'we,' like those of us in the lab. People, in general."

"In general? Did you, in fact, have anything to do with the lip print comparisons? I'm speaking about you, personally. Not the *collective you,*" he said with a smile.

"No, I did not."

Warwick strolled away from Saperstein, and then stopped. "So this was just a generalization."

"Yes."

"But generalizations are often wrong, Mr. Saperstein. What else did you tell the jury that was inaccurate?"

"Objection."

"Sustained," Calvino said. "Move on, Mr. Warwick."

The public defender nodded, then paused for a moment. "Is it standard procedure for one criminalist to collect the data and evidence and another to conduct the testing?"

"No, not usually."

"I'm curious, Mr. Saperstein, why haven't I heard of lip print analysis before?"

"It's not widely used."

"And why is that?"

"We used to think that there aren't as many occasions where lip prints are left at crime scenes, as opposed to fingerprints, which are quite common due to the handling of material objects. It's kind of like the pinky finger. Prints of the pinky are not recorded in the national databases because they're so seldom left behind by a perpetrator. But we're finding that that's simply not the case with lip prints—there are many instances where they're left at crime scenes. A window, or door, for instance, where the criminal looks inside and holds his face right up to the glass. Not to mention the cases where the suspect has left prints on a glass he drank from, on photographs, letters, envelopes—"

"Is it widely known, this lip print analysis?"

"It's still not commonly practiced, but most criminalists I come into contact with know about it."

"Sort of a trick of the trade?"

Saperstein smiled. "Yes, you might say that."

Denton winced. He knew what was coming.

"So how many other *tricks* do you have in your bag, sir?"

"That's not what I meant—"

"Again? I do wish you'd say what you mean. But allow me to rephrase. How many tricks were used in your analysis of the physical evidence?"

"You're twisting—"

"Well, I withdraw that question; I'll ask you this instead: is this 'trick' one of your so-called scientific methods that we're supposed to believe without questioning its validity?"

"Mr. Warwick, if you'd let me speak—"

"Just a simple yes or no is all I want—"

"Objection, Your Honor," shouted Denton. "He's badgering the witness, and not permitting him the freedom to answer any of his questions."

"Mr. Warwick. Make your point and move on. And please permit Mr. Saperstein proper time to answer your questions."

Warwick nodded at the judge, then turned back to Saperstein. "Yes or no, sir? Is this trick one of the so-called scientific methods that you and your *collective colleagues* used in evaluating this physical evidence?"

"I can't answer your question within the parameters you set forth."

Denton smiled. Saperstein was not going to fall into another trap. He may have made a couple of mistakes, but he was one who learned from his errors and adapted.

"Your Honor," pleaded Warwick with outstretched hands, "please direct the witness to answer."

"Mr. Saperstein, please answer the question."

Saperstein turned to Calvino. "I would like to comply, Your Honor, but I can't answer it in the manner in which Mr. Warwick has requested. He's twisting what I'm saying and attempting to force me into saying something that wouldn't be accurate. Does the court wish me to answer incorrectly, or can I be given the proper opportunity to provide truthful information?"

"Answer the question to the best of your ability, sir," Calvino said.

Denton fought back a smile. Saperstein had squelched a favorite tactic of adversarial attorneys who attempted to elicit certain testimony that appeared to be favorable to their case using the narrow parameters inherent in "yes" or "no" answers.

"There are no tricks or sleight of hand here," Saperstein said. "Everything I do in the lab is based on scientific procedure. The tests I perform are widely accepted in the field of forensics, to the best of my knowledge. The—"

"Your Honor," Warwick said, "would you please instruct the witness not to narrate but to merely answer the question?"

"I am answering the question, Your Honor. He asked me if this was a trick or a scientific method, and I'm explaining what was done."

"You opened the door, Mr. Warwick. Let's hear his answer. Continue, Mr. Saperstein."

"The method of lip print detection is called queiloscopy. It was mentioned in the literature as far back as 1902, and discussed in more detail in 1950 by a medicolegal consultant working on a case here in the Sacramento area. It wasn't used as a means of personal identification until I believe 1960, when Dr. Santos of Brazil devised a system for classifying the differences in individuals' lip prints. At the same time, Japanese Professors Suzuki and Tsuchiahashi developed their own method of identification—"

"I have that paper right here," Warwick said, tossing a few stapled pages onto the banister of the witness stand. "Is this what you're basing your analysis on?"

"That is part of what's accepted as baseline research in the field—"

"Read the highlighted portion, Mr. Saperstein," Warwick said, pointing toward the article he had tossed at the witness.

Saperstein picked up the pages and read the portion Warwick requested. "Lip prints were collected from two hundred eighty individuals, consisting of one hundred fifty males and one hundred thirty females, aged six to fifty-seven years."

"So, Mr. Saperstein, this 'scientific method' you are so intent on using against my client is based on a research study of only two hundred eighty people? I would think that it would be more *scientific*—and therefore more reliable—if the study involved thousands of test subjects. Wouldn't it, sir?"

Saperstein took a breath and let it out slowly. "Is that a question you would like me to respond to, or do you want to answer that one yourself as well?"

Calvino scowled. "Mr. Saperstein, lose the attitude."

Saperstein nodded apologetically at Calvino and turned back to Warwick, who was enjoying the moment of admonition. "Yes, Mr. Warwick, that study is what I'm basing my opinions on. That study as well as the follow-up study performed by the same researchers eight years later, in which one thousand four hundred people were evaluated. And the research involving one thousand five hundred people in the 1980s, conducted at the Department of Criminalistics of Civic Militia Headquarters in Poland. In that study, the patterns of the lines in the red part of lips were categorized, utilizing a ten-millimeter portion of the middle part of the lower lip—a section that's almost always visible in a print. Several linear characteristics were identified: bifurcation, reticular, linear, and indeterminate. After the patterns were analyzed, nearly half a million individual properties were counted amongst the four hundred prints. This gave an average of over one thousand individual characteristics per lip print. By comparison, we get only one hundred individual characteristics per *finger*print."

As Saperstein continued, it became evident that Warwick had not performed a complete international journal search for lip print studies; most of the information and research on lip print analysis had come from abroad and had been published in lesser-known journals.

"In our lab," Saperstein continued, "Miss Harding's sample lip print pattern was enlarged in a five-to-one ratio, traced, and then reduced back to its original size and scanned into the computer. The same process was completed for the evidentiary lip print found on the beer cans at the crime scene. Then, points of identification were marked for each of the samples and compared visually by both the analyst and the computer. In general, if we don't get an exact computer match, we look for at least seven different points that visually match. So in summary, Mr. Warwick, this was *pure scientific method*. No tricks or mirrors were involved." Saperstein looked into Warwick's eyes, which were narrow with anger.

"I have nothing further for this witness," Warwick said.

"Redirect," Denton said.

Calvino nodded.

"Why didn't you personally perform the testing on the physical evidence relative to the Mercedes?"

"I was in the hospital. I was suffering from what was diagnosed as ulcerative colitis."

"Who did the testing of the physical evidence in your absence?"

"Kurt Gray."

"And who is Kurt Gray?"

"He's a criminalist."

"With the same training that you possess in forensic science?"

"Yes, sir."

"So therefore he is qualified to run the tests which he conducted."

"Objection. Mr. Saperstein cannot qualify another witness."

"Sustained."

"In your opinion, then, Mr. Saperstein, would you allow Mr. Gray to run tests on a case that involved you or your family?"

"Yes."

"And did you personally perform the DNA testing and analysis?"

"Yes."

"One last question, Mr. Saperstein." Denton walked closer to him and placed both hands on the railing of the witness box. "Whose side are you on?"

Saperstein looked perturbed, as if this question had caught him off guard. "I'm on no one's side. My function is merely to conduct tests in a scientific manner and provide results that are accurate and reproducible."

Perfect answer; Denton smiled. "Thank you, Mr. Saperstein. I have nothing further."

Half an hour after Calvino dismissed the jury for the day, Hellman stopped by Denton's office and knocked on the stippled glass of his door. "Nice job today, Tim," he said.

Denton's tie was loosened and dangling from an unbuttoned collar. "This wool stuff is really comfortable," he said, running a hand along the lapel of his suit coat.

"I've been trying to tell you that for years."

They smiled as Hellman sat down. "It was a good day," Denton said.

"I look forward to many more. You're just getting started."

Denton smiled and stretched. "I'm glad Harding's at the defense table. I feel very comfortable with our case against her."

"Me too. And I'm not just saying that. I think justice will truly be done."

Denton shook his head and sighed. "Tomorrow will be interesting. We've got the DNA expert at leadoff followed by Stanton."

Hellman apologized for not being able to be present due to a trial he was scheduled to begin in the morning, and excused himself. Denton pulled out a crumpled tinfoil mass that was wrapped in a plastic bag: leftovers of his baloney sandwich from yesterday, his dinner for this evening. He had hundreds of pages of documents to review. It was going to be a long night.

CHAPTER
64

LOU PALUCCI WAS laughing, the phone receiver bobbing up and down with the flab on his double chin.

"I'm serious," Chandler said. "I need you to do me a favor."

Palucci reached over and closed his office door. "The last favor I did for you nearly cost me my job. Did you forget already?"

"Last time I checked, you were still in charge of the lab."

"The answer is no, Chandler. Absolutely not."

"You don't even know what I need."

"The very point," Palucci said, "is that *you* need something. And that means that I can't help you. I work for the state, not Ryan Chandler."

Chandler took a deep breath. "Lou, this is no big deal, but you're the only one who can do it."

"I don't like the sound of it already, and I don't even know what 'it' is."

"It's just a few numbers. Lot numbers, on the bottoms of the beer cans found in Phil Madison's car and those confiscated from Harding's house."

"Why do you need those?"

"Don't ask why. Just get them for me. You're not running any tests, you're not spending any state money for private purposes—"

"I'll think about it. I need to let things settle down a bit before I go poking around. I'll call you from home if I have anything for you."

Chandler thanked him and hung up, then slumped in his chair. At this point, there was nothing to do unless Palucci called him back. As he sat there, he thought of a case his father had presided over, a case that first lit the spark in his heart for choosing police work as a career when he was sixteen years old. He smiled at the memory of sitting with his dad on a pier in Bay Shore, going over the forensic evidence that helped put a killer behind bars for life.

Johnny Donnelly's voice echoed through his head. "It's time, Junior . . . it's time . . ."

Chandler picked up the phone, stared at it for a long moment, then dialed his father.

CHAPTER
65

THE FOLLOWING MORNING, with the sun poking through the low-hung sky for the first time in two weeks, Denton called Dr. Leonard Ross to the stand. Dr. Ross, a researcher well schooled in the analysis and typing of DNA, had written a textbook on the topic. As a witness he was presentable, though he did have a tendency to talk above the heads of the jurors at times. At two thousand dollars for a half day of testimony, Denton wanted to make sure Ross's message got through loud and clear to the jurors; he met with his witness on two occasions to go over the testimony and ensure the fact that the words he used were no more than three syllables in length.

Ross testified as to what the prosecution wanted to communicate to the jury: that the evidence was properly handled and preserved with little or no risk of contamination, and the delay in running the DNA testing was of no consequence whatsoever.

He explained the process of DNA analysis, starting with the protein building blocks and moving through genetics in half an hour in a manner that would have had even a ten-year-old nodding comprehension. Denton was quite pleased with how it was presented.

Although Warwick pecked away with information supposedly quoted from his own consultant, namely that the delay could have caused degradation and produced incorrect results, Ross stood by his position. He referred to his text repeatedly, a tactic that was designed to solidify his reputation as the expert and to ground his opinions in fact. "You're arguing with the person who wrote the book," Ross said at one point—which could have been taken as an egotistical comment and turned off the jury. However, it came off instead as his way of defending himself from Warwick's incessant attack that was riddled with desperation tactics and baseless opinions.

"Answer this for me, sir," Warwick asked, getting up close to Ross, "why did the lab use the PCR method as opposed to the RFLP method of analysis?"

"PCR is more sensitive. It also allows typing in situations where it wouldn't have been possible before. We can now type DNA with the smallest of sample sizes. Now, all we require is one-billionth of a gram of DNA. Before, we wouldn't have been able to even begin analysis with RFLP on such a small sample size."

"PCR . . . isn't that the method where photocopies are made of the DNA pattern? Isn't it less accurate than RFLP?"

"Let me answer one question at a time. You mention photocopying. That's a gross simplification to the point of being misleading. PCR is a technique that was developed from the very basis of how DNA strands naturally replicate, or copy themselves, within a cell. The key concept is that an enzyme called DNA polymerase can be stimulated to synthesize, or create, a specific region of DNA. In the same manner, PCR can be used to repeatedly duplicate or *amplify* a strand of DNA many millions of times. So it's not photocopying," he said, talking down to Warwick in a manner in which a teacher reprimands a student who was attempting to show off at the teacher's expense.

"Now to your other question of PCR being less accurate than RFLP," Ross continued. "It used to be that the frequency of occurrence of one of the gene types that is isolated, the DQ alpha gene, is greater than the frequencies typically obtained through the RFLP method. But, a fairly new typing kit known as Polymarker allows the typing of five different genetic markers. When used in combination with DQ alpha, it will produce frequencies of occurrence of less than one in a thousand. In this case, Mr. Saperstein also included the D1S80 marker, which is quite an uncommon marker. In general, the more markers you use, the better the odds are in excluding possible matches from the general population. That's why the odds in this case are one in fifty thousand." Ross paused for a second to take a breath. "So, I personally do not feel that anything significant is lost with the PCR method—in fact, a tremendous amount is gained."

Warwick looked perturbed for a moment. He had committed the cardinal sin in cross-examination: he had asked a question without making sure he knew the answer that was coming. But in fact, there was no way that Warwick could have known that Ross was going to cite cutting-edge research and methodology.

"How big a sample of DNA are we talking about in this particular case against my client?"

"The DNA was obtained from saliva residues on a beer can, so there was more than enough to get an accurate result."

Warwick was aware of that very unfortunate fact for his client. The public defender cocked his head. "How big is a molecule of DNA?"

"It's microscopic."

"So it's nothing we can really see with the naked eye. It's nothing that I or any of the jurors could look at and see for ourselves."

"No. But I assure you it exists and is quite real."

"Uh-huh," he said, as if to mock his last comment. "You said earlier while being questioned by Mr. Denton that DNA can become contaminated?"

"Yes."

"What are some of the ways in which this can occur?"

"DNA can become contaminated by a number of factors or situations."

"Can you name some?"

"Improper handling of the evidence, improper storage conditions, high humidity, excessive dirt, dust, things of that nature."

"What about sneezing? Could that spoil a sample?"

"Yes."

"Coughing?"

"Yes."

"Hmm," Warwick said, pacing away from the witness. The jurors' eyes followed him. "Something as benign as a sneeze could contaminate the sample."

"Yes, but—"

"And how much time elapsed between the time that the evidence was gathered and the actual lifting of the saliva from the cans?"

"As I said earlier, I believe six weeks."

Denton felt pimples of sweat forming on his forehead.

"Six weeks," Warwick said. "And you said dust or even dirt could contaminate the sample?"

"Again, as I said a moment ago, yes. But it would have to be—"

"And when a DNA sample is contaminated, the results that it yields are then no longer considered accurate?"

"I suppose you could say that."

Warwick had stopped and leaned back against the defense table, arms folded across his chest. He looked hard and long at Ross, as if he were pondering what he had just answered. It was no doubt intended as an exclamation point for the jury. "Yes, I suppose I could. Thank you, Dr. Ross. I have nothing further."

"Redirect, Mr. Denton?" Calvino asked.

"Yes, Your Honor." He stood rapidly and walked to the spot in front of the witness stand, facing Ross. "Doctor, was the sample in question contaminated?"

"No. Not to my knowledge."

"Was the evidence properly stored, in a facility where there were no unusual amounts of humidity, direct sunlight, dust, or dirt?"

"From what I've read in the report, standard protocol was followed, and the evidence was properly marked, stored, and handled."

"How does sneezing or coughing contaminate a sample?"

"Contamination occurs because you have someone else's

DNA intermixing with the sample DNA. It's only a concern when you're dealing with a very small sample, which, as I said, is not the case here. However, even if it were, we would be able to separate out the DNA from the person who sneezed or coughed from the DNA of the suspect."

"It sounds very sophisticated."

"It is," Ross said. "Very sophisticated."

"And accurate?"

"Extremely accurate."

"If a DNA sample were contaminated or degraded by dirt or dust, or any such substance, would the tainted analysis come back with results implicating Brittany Harding?"

"No, the results would either be incomplete or unmatchable."

"And that was not the case here?"

"No."

"They clearly matched Brittany Harding's DNA?"

"Yes, they did."

"Is there any reason to believe that the results produced by the DNA analysis in this case were tainted, degraded, contaminated, or otherwise rendered inaccurate?"

"Absolutely none whatsoever."

"Thank you, Dr. Ross."

Denton walked back to the prosecutor's table, threw a look of triumph at Warwick, and sat down. Warwick's strategy of attempting to place doubt in the minds of the jurors was neutralized by Denton's pointedly successful redirect; he was gathering momentum, which was exactly what he wanted as he led into his next witness, William Stanton.

Stanton, impeccably dressed and imposing by way of his wholesome good looks and articulate manner, seduced the jury as he told of Harding's false claims of sexual harassment. As he spoke, Harding, seated at the defense table, rolled her eyes and shook her head. The jury listened intently as he described his conversation with Movis Ehrhardt. Denton inquired about the tape they were about to play. Stanton briefly described why it was made, who made it, the date it was filmed, and the manner in which the filming was accomplished.

Warwick objected again to the showing of the tape for the record, citing its lack of foundation and relevance, and its highly prejudicial nature. Calvino overruled the objection, and the bailiff was instructed to initiate the playback of the video.

As expected, the tape had the same effect on the jury as it had had on everyone else who had viewed it—some of the jurors looked over at Harding afterward, their faces betraying their thoughts: how could someone be so cold and calculating? She looked away to avoid their gazes, as clear an admission of guilt as there was without overtly entering a guilty plea.

Denton extracted from Stanton the reasons for his reluctance to testify, and by the time he finished, he had all the jurors' sympathies . . . while Harding had all their wrath.

To cap off the day, Denton finished with a mere formality: the private investigator who filmed the tape—verifying the date and time when it was created, and what he observed. He flawlessly reiterated Stanton's story. Warwick had no questions for either of them; the damage had been done, and belaboring the subject would only drive home the image of Harding's admission of extortion.

Although Warwick undoubtedly wanted to ignore the repulsive content of the tape and move on, Denton was hoping that it would remain an indelible mark against Harding no matter what her attorney was able to accomplish in the coming days of trial.

CHAPTER

66

THE DAY FOLLOWING Stanton's testimony, Hellman was in Department 12, participating in the trial he had begun a couple of days ago. The judge had recessed early to tend to an unrelated matter of the court, and Hellman stopped in to see how Denton's case was progressing. He arrived at the tail end of the day's testimony pertaining to the accusation of rape against Madison.

One of Denton's last witnesses, who was on the stand when Hellman arrived, was Mary Bender, a police officer trained as a rape counselor. It was her job to meet with the victim upon presentation, and accompany her to the hospital to ensure that the appropriate evidence was properly secured and marked. She was well versed in trials, having testified in over one hundred rape cases as to the nature of the evidence obtained, the type of physical evidence one would expect to find on a victim, and the process by which the evidence was collected.

"So, Officer Bender, please tell the court what evidence one would expect to find following a rape," Denton said.

She leaned forward and used a hand to comb her coarse ash blond locks behind her ears. "We would expect to find seminal constituents in or around the vagina of a rape victim. Physical findings such as bruises or bleeding confirm that a violent act occurred. Sometimes, the transfer of physical evidence, such as blood, semen, hairs, and fibers will occur between assailant and victim.

"Following the act, we take vaginal swabs, and sometimes

oral and anal swabs as well. Pubic combings will be made to check for loose or foreign hairs. Saliva and blood samples are secured, and fingernail scrapings are taken to check for skin that the victim might have scratched from the assailant."

"You've read the report of the investigating officers?"

"Yes, I have."

"And was any of the physical evidence you mentioned a moment ago found in this complaint of rape brought by Ms. Harding?"

"No."

"And why is that?"

"Because Ms. Harding did not come forward until five weeks after the alleged act."

Denton walked back to the jury box, leaned on the railing, and faced his witness. "Now, a moment ago, you mentioned a number of common items of evidence found in rape cases. Have you ever heard of phone calls made from an alleged assailant's home being used as evidence of rape?"

"No."

"What about fingerprints of the alleged assailant on the alleged victim's belt?"

"In and of itself, I wouldn't use that as evidence that a rape occurred. There are obviously a great many explanations for the presence of fingerprints on a belt buckle."

"Objection," interrupted Warwick. "Officer Bender is not an expert on what could or could not be considered evidence in a rape trial."

Calvino looked over to Denton for his response.

"Your Honor," Denton said, turning away from his witness to face the judge, "Ms. Bender is a police officer with special training in rape cases. She often testifies as to the collection of evidence, and the relevance of each piece of that physical evidence. I believe she's eminently qualified to comment—if not from a legal perspective, then from the perspective of a police officer trained in the investigation of rape."

"Overruled, Mr. Warwick."

Denton turned back to Bender. "In your opinion, officer, is there any evidence at all of rape in this case?"

"None. None whatsoever."

"Thank you, officer," Denton said as he turned to take his seat; he caught a glimpse of a smiling Hellman in the back row.

Judge Calvino asked Warwick if his cross-examination could wait until tomorrow; receiving an affirmative response, court was convened for the day and the jury was dismissed. As Denton packed his attaché, Hellman walked over. "Looks good."

Denton smiled. "Yeah, went well. But this is all slam-dunk stuff. This morning I brought on the two rape detectives—Coleman and Valentine."

"Coleman and Valentine, yeah, I remember them," Hellman said, shaking his head in a manner displaying dissatisfaction.

"Don't knock them too hard, they did well for us today. They told how they followed up on all of their leads, and the fact that there was virtually nowhere to go because of the lack of evidence. They discussed the two phone calls made from Madison's house, and Madison's fingerprints on Harding's belt—and explained how both of these pieces of evidence were consistent with Madison's story that he examined Harding when she'd come over complaining of abdominal pain. They told how there were no witnesses, no police report, no medical evidence—and the fact that she waited five weeks before she reported it. It was all relatively straightforward. And Warwick's cross-examination was flat and brief because there wasn't much to challenge." He snapped his attaché shut. "The more difficult part comes when your guy takes the stand."

"He'll be ready," Hellman said. "Any idea when you'll need him?"

"Friday. Tell him to be ready for Friday."

It was Madison who suggested he and Hellman meet for dinner a couple of nights later at Fifth Street Café. He had been unable to go near the place since his distasteful episode with Harding a few months ago; but he thought a positive dining experience now could help him mentally dissociate his favorite restaurant from that disastrous occurrence.

Hellman's escargot sat in front of him; Madison was munching on his duck salad. "It's going well, Phil," Hellman said. "Yesterday, Ronald Norling testified. He was a little rough around the edges, but he did well. Warwick couldn't ruffle him. The kid was tough. At one point, he just looked at Warwick, who was trying to beat him down, and he said, 'Look, man, I'm just telling you what I saw and heard. She said she was going to get even, make him pay. It's as simple as that. I don't know this guy Madison, and I don't know that lady over there. I don't care what happens to either of them. I'm just telling you how it was.' I'll tell you, it really shut Warwick down. He had to back off." Hellman chuckled. "Warwick then tried to attack his background, but the kid put it to him again, telling him that he wasn't a model citizen, and didn't claim to be—he just saw what he saw. Nobody gave him anything for testifying, and he was missing time from his new job back East. So he told him, essentially, to get out of his face. It was beautiful."

Madison was smiling, so mesmerized by what Hellman was relating that he had stopped eating. The main course came before he had finished his salad.

"Denton told me he also had a professional photographer testify that the photo Harding had taken of you and her was staged."

"Yeah, but was he able to prove it?"

"The guy brought a couple of models into court and had them assume similar positions to what you did with Harding, and he snapped a few pictures with a telephoto lens using the same camera angle. They had the film developed over the lunch recess and showed the photos to the jury. According to Denton, they bore a striking resemblance to the picture of you and Harding."

"Gee, what a surprise."

"Warwick was objecting all over the place, renewing the arguments he'd made during his pretrial motion. But the judge allowed it and Denton thinks it only reinforced for the jury what type of person she is."

"If she weren't going to use it against me, why'd she have the picture taken in the first place?"

Hellman nodded acknowledgment. "Denton finished up

with a psychiatrist—a Dr. Hall from the Bay Area—who testified as to an individual's state of mind when driven to prepare a plot seeking revenge. I caught the bulk of his testimony. I think he did a damn good job. Talked about obsessive behavior and how Harding's personality was a good fit. Said something to the effect of her having been driven to revenge by the 'persistence of an irresistible thought or feeling that was associated with anxiety.' Of course, Warwick tried to impeach him by getting Hall to admit that he'd never actually examined Harding—the usual tactic. But I think he left his mark with the jury."

"I've never heard of this guy. Hall, you said?"

"Yeah, from Marin. Came highly recommended. Denton brought him in from the Bay Area to eliminate any accusations that he knew you professionally or personally. He didn't want to give Warwick any ammunition for impeachment due to bias."

"So it's my turn Friday?"

Hellman nodded. "We've gone over the prep. Denton says nothing's changed. Just tell what happened, and no matter what, don't let Warwick rattle you."

"I'm used to hostile attorneys, remember? I've been through all this before."

"Yeah, but this is a little different. You're used to testifying about medical issues. This is your personal life, regarding something that can easily be turned into an attack on you as an individual. He's going to try and bring out all sorts of irrelevant stuff, some of which will be lies and distortions of the truth. My best advice is to remain levelheaded and treat the jury as if they're patients and give them a dose of your sweet bedside manner," Hellman said, speaking more as Madison's attorney than his friend. "But whatever Warwick says to you or about you, just roll with the punches. Don't let him bait you and get you all riled up."

"You know it takes a lot to do that, Jeffrey."

Hellman smiled. He knew, but felt better saying it nonetheless.

CHAPTER
67

THE EVENING TEMPERATURE had been a bone-chilling 26 degrees. While it was not nearly as cold as most winter nights in the East, many people native to the Sacramento area considered the 20s unusually frigid, and fireplaces were burning into the early morning, casting a foglike pall over the moonlit gray sky. The air smelled of smoke, and flakes of ashes lazily rode the gentle breeze through the teeth-chattering night air.

Madison arrived at the Superior Court building at 8:25 Friday morning. Although the police had released his car to him, having examined, videotaped, and photographed it from every conceivable angle, he chose to drive Leeza's van. The thought of arriving at the courthouse in the very car that had been the subject of intense scrutiny during the past few months seemed in bad taste, and only invited more debate and comment—even though the damage to the front end had been repaired.

He was wearing a navy blue suit with a stark white shirt and a silk tie that was emblazoned with a brilliant red paisley pattern. His hair was immaculately styled and his face was clean shaven, lightly bronzed, and taut. It was Leeza's suggestion that he spend yesterday afternoon at a salon getting a tan, followed by a massage, facial, and haircut. It allowed him to collect his thoughts, spruce up for the coming event, and relax.

As he entered the courtroom, the olive-uniformed bailiff led him to the witness chair. He glanced toward the jury. They appeared focused, students with pens and pads poised, as if he were the guest lecturer about to provide answers that were needed for their final exam.

This was the climax of the prosecution's case, the make-or-break point. It was the jury's opportunity to meet the man who was such an integral focus of this case. This was their chance to scrutinize him, to decide whether he was credible, worthy of their vote of confidence against Harding. Both Denton and Hellman had decided that if the jurors believed Madison—particularly if they took a liking to him—they would feel the opposite toward Harding. The verdict would already be decided by the time they sat down to begin their deliberations.

"Dr. Madison," Denton was saying at 9:15, "a few moments ago you outlined your medical credentials, appointments, and accomplishments. A rather long list. I bet you're proud of them."

"I am. I've worked hard for each one of them."

"How about your activities outside of medicine?"

"I have a wife and two young children."

"Doesn't leave much time for anything else, does it?" Denton asked.

"No, it doesn't," Madison said with a chuckle.

"But you have been involved in other things, haven't you?"

"Yes."

"Can you tell us about those activities?"

"I served as president of the American Heart Association for two years, I was a board member for the American Cancer Society and the Sacramento Symphony, and until recently, I served on the River City Theater Company's board of directors. I've been a board member and vice president of the Consortium for Citizens with Mental Retardation. I'm currently president of that same organization."

"Do you get any compensation for any of this?"

"Are you asking me if I get paid for any of this?"

"Yes. Money or other benefits of any sort."

"No. I don't receive anything. Other than the satisfaction of doing something to help others."

"Dr. Madison, do you give money to charitable interests?"

"Yes, I do."

"Approximately, how much did you give to nonprofit causes last year?"

"A little over eighteen thousand dollars."

"Thank you, sir." Denton and Madison had worked on this preamble in advance, and appeared to be in a rhythm together. He proceeded to ask him about his relationship with Brittany Harding, how he came to meet her, his dealings with her, and his conversations with Michael Murphy when it became apparent that she was providing less than a stellar performance as interim administrative officer.

"And how did she react when you suggested to her that she should submit a job application for the position she was temporarily holding?"

"She was angry, surprised."

"Objection," Warwick said from his seat. "The witness couldn't possibly have known my client's state of mind unless he's also a world-class clairvoyant."

"Your Honor," whined Denton.

"Cut the sarcasm, Mr. Warwick. Objection sustained."

"Dr. Madison," Denton said, "*in your opinion,* how did Miss Harding appear to you after informing her that she would have to apply for the position?"

"I thought she looked angry, and surprised."

"Did she ever submit an application?"

"I don't believe she did."

"Let's move on to the rape accusations that she made against you." He took Madison through his side of the story, her unexpected appearance at his house, the examination, her two phone calls.

"And after she left, did you notice anything missing?"

"No, not until some time after that incident, when my wife couldn't find her set of keys to my car."

"Where were they usually kept?"

"On a hook in our kitchen, next to the telephone."

"When was it that she noticed the keys were missing?"

"It was after Brittany Harding was at my house, I don't remember the exact date. They were spare keys, not something my wife used very often. And she was . . . away for a while. I think it was about a week after she got back that she realized the keys were missing."

"Why was your wife away?"

Madison shifted a bit in his seat, leaned forward, glanced over at the jury, then looked back at Denton. "She left me."

"And why was that?"

"It started a couple of days after Miss Harding lost her job at the Consortium. I was outside my house pruning the rose bushes. The defendant drove up, got out of her car, and started screaming at me. Something about my having slept with her, and that she'd get even by going to the police for what I did to her. I didn't know what she was talking about. But my wife saw the entire fiasco."

"Did Miss Harding follow through with her threat?"

"Oh, yes. She filed a complaint with the police, and they investigated me."

"This was, what, five weeks after she alleged the rape to have occurred?"

"Yes. It was obviously an attempt at revenge, at getting back—"

"Objection," Warwick said, jumping up from his seat. "I thought we established the witness isn't telepathic—"

"Sustained. Dr. Madison, please only tell us what you know, and do not speculate on the thoughts of others."

Madison nodded.

"What happened after the police investigated you?"

Madison described his meetings with the two detectives, and related the fact that his attorney was then approached for monetary compensation by Movis Ehrhardt, over the threat of mass media exposure of the alleged rape.

"It was the same thing she did to an ex-employer of hers a couple of years back—extortion."

"Objection!" Warwick shouted.

Calvino looked over at Madison. "Doctor, please refrain from making comments unless it deals with something you have direct knowledge about."

"Doctor," continued Denton, attempting to brush over the admonition. It was crucial that Madison be seen in a favorable light by the jury. "What happened next?"

"I paid her. Unfortunately, it was far less damaging to pay

her the money and stop her from going to the media with this bogus accusation than risk ruining my career." He looked over at Harding, his eyes fixed and his gaze hard. She stared him down. "A couple of days later, my wife received a manila envelope in the mail with a copy of the check I had written to the defendant, as well as a copy of the written agreement outlining the terms of the settlement. There was also a picture of myself and the defendant." He paused and shook his head, out of disbelief. Tears welled up in his eyes. "My wife didn't know about the payment. When she got all this stuff in the mail, she didn't know what to think, and I was away at a surgery conference. She took the kids and left."

Denton paused, giving the jury a moment to reflect on his witness's grief.

A moment later, Madison cleared his throat. "My attorney was able to pressure Mr. Ehrhardt into returning the money because she had broken our agreement."

"Why didn't you tell your wife about the settlement?"

"My friend thought it would upset her, that it wasn't worth dragging her into it. I agreed, at the time. But later, I realized I should've told her about it, discussed it with her."

"Was that the last contact you had with Brittany Harding?"

Madison chuckled sarcastically. "No. It was not. She and I ran into each other in a supermarket. She was irate, started yelling at me. Called me a rapist. Told me that she was going to get even, make me pay."

"Did you notice what she had in her basket?"

"One item in particular."

"And what was that item?"

"A six-pack of Millstone Premium Draft beer."

"And why is it that you noticed that one specific item?"

"I'd turned a corner of an aisle and nearly ran into her basket. That's when I saw the gold- and brown-colored packaging of the Millstone six-pack—before I actually realized that it was her in front of me. In fact, after she started screaming at me, I even said to her, 'Why don't you go home and drown yourself in that beer and stay out of my life.' Something like that."

Madison continued to expound upon the subsequent events, including his interaction with Ronald Norling, the checker, as well as Harding's behavior as he left the market.

"Dr. Madison, how has this entire episode with the defendant affected your life?" Denton asked.

Madison looked down at his lap and paused. When he looked up, his eyes were again glassy. "I wish I'd never met Brittany Harding . . . she's wreaked havoc with my personal and professional lives. My wife and children left me, my practice is a ghost of what it once was, I lost my privileges at the very hospital I helped build, I've been attacked in public in front of my children, my friends stayed away out of fear of association." He stopped, bit his lip. "It's very difficult to describe what I've been through. What my family's been through." He grabbed a tissue from the dispenser on the shelf in front of the witness chair and ran it across his wet eyes. "She just about succeeded in ruining my life. I feel like I've aged ten years in the past several months." He glanced to his right at Harding, who was staring at him. Even from this distance, he could see that her jaw was clenched, her shoulders bunched up toward her ears. Burning anger. Intense hatred.

"Thank you," Denton said, sitting down. "Nothing further."

"Doctor," Calvino said, "do you need a short break to collect yourself?"

Madison pulled his eyes away from Harding and squared his shoulders. "I'm sorry, Your Honor. No, I'll be fine. I'd rather get this over with."

Calvino nodded. "Mr. Warwick, you may begin cross."

"Dr. Madison," Warwick said as he arose and briskly walked toward the witness, "your wife didn't really leave you, now did she?"

"Yes, she did. I didn't know if she was ever going to come back."

"But she did come back, didn't she?"

"Yes, she did."

"Sir, who is Catherine Parker?"

Madison swallowed hard. Denton clenched his jaw and leaned over to his assistant, whispering in his ear, inquiring as to who Catherine Parker was and what significance there could be to the case.

". . . a friend, you say?" Warwick was asking.

"Yes. We go back a long time, to law school. We haven't kept in touch."

"In fact, you were going to marry Miss Parker, isn't that correct?"

"Yes, eighteen years ago."

"And what happened?"

"She married someone else."

"When was the last time that you saw her, doctor?"

"Objection!" Denton was on his feet, waving his hands in the air. "Your Honor, this is completely irrelevant."

Calvino looked down at Warwick, cocking his head as if to ask for a response.

"Your Honor, I will make the relevance clear shortly."

"Remember, counselor, you don't want to get into a situation where I have to count questions."

Warwick managed a smile and nodded.

"Overruled."

"Now, doctor, when was the last time that you spoke with Miss Parker?"

"About two or three months ago."

"And what was the reason for that communication?"

"She contacted me. She'd read about the case in the paper, and read that my wife had left me." He raised his eyebrows. "She was hoping that we could get together and renew our relationship."

"And?"

"And nothing. I told her I wasn't interested, that I still loved my wife. We had dinner, and talked. Caught up on eighteen years of being out of touch."

"Did you have intercourse with Miss Parker that night?"

Madison sat straight up and his face flushed. "Absolutely not. Not that night or any other night. I haven't had relations with Miss Parker in eighteen years."

"Your Honor," Denton said, "I renew my objection to the relevance of this line of questioning."

"I believe it goes to the credibility of the witness."

"What, that he had dinner with an old friend?"

"It was more than that, Your Honor."

"Does counsel have proof?" Denton shot back.

Calvino looked over at Warwick, his eyes tiny and his brow crumpled. "Well, counselor, do you?"

"We're following up some leads as we speak, Your Honor."

"Then I'll take that as a no. Mr. Warwick, you've asked the court for leniency on two occasions and failed to make your case both times. I suggest you stop reaching and stick to the facts. I won't tolerate any more waste of the court's time."

Warwick nodded, walked over to the defense table, and picked up a folder. "Dr. Madison," he said, turning to face the witness, "a while ago you outlined all of the hardships you've had to endure because of your relationship with my client. My heart goes out to you, sir—"

"Objection."

"Sustained. Mr. Warwick—"

"I'll get to a question, Your Honor." He got a nod from Calvino and a wave of a hand to make it quick. "Do you still have your family?"

"Yes."

"Do you still have your big, expensive house?"

"Yes."

"Do you still have your license to practice medicine?"

"Yes."

"Were your hospital privileges reinstated?"

"No."

"Do you expect them to be?"

"I've gotten no assurances, but I hope so."

Warwick began to approach Madison. "And you still have your health. Otis Silvers and Imogene Pringle, the two people who were run over, had nothing. With the exception of a young child, Ms. Pringle had no family. In fact, aside from a few meager possessions, the only thing they had was their lives, and even that was taken away from them."

"Sir, you have no idea how awful I feel that these people were killed—not to mention the fact that my car was used to commit this heinous crime. I've devoted my life to saving people from pain and suffering, to improving their condition. But I can't be responsible for your client's illness. She's a sick individual who in my professional opinion requires treatment—"

"Your Honor, move to strike!"

"So stricken," Calvino said, his voice booming through the speakers in a fit of sudden anger. "Dr. Madison, do not offer medical opinions as to the state of Miss Harding. That is not your purpose here today, and if you do so again, I'm going to have to hold you in contempt of court."

"I'm sorry, Your Honor."

"Jury will disregard that last comment by the witness. Continue, Mr. Warwick."

Warwick paced back over toward the defense table, stood looking down at it for a moment, at a pad of notes; he then turned to Madison. "In order for Miss Harding to have committed this crime, sir, she would've had to break into your garage and steal your car. Isn't that right?"

"No."

"No? Oh, that's right. You said that your wife's set of keys to your car were missing."

"That's correct. Stolen, by the defendant."

"That's a lie!" Harding was standing, her face beet red, her flowing auburn locks tousled. "You're lying. I didn't steal the keys *or* your car—"

"Counselor, get your client under control immediately or I'll have her removed!"

Warwick had already been struggling with her, pushing down on her shoulders, trying to make her sit, his face squarely in front of hers, locking on her eyes. As Harding took her seat, her chest still heaving with anger, the bailiff who was hovering nearby took a few steps backward. Warwick whispered something in her ear and then turned toward Madison again. He glanced down at his notes, took a deep breath, and began again where he had left off.

"You contend that my client had a set of keys to your car. If that's true, how did she get into the garage? Don't you lock it at night?"

"Yes. But my wife's set of keys had a key to the side garage door on it."

Warwick seemed to be caught off guard; even though it was something that he should have anticipated, he apparently did not. "When you realized that the keys had been missing, didn't you have the lock changed as a precaution?"

"As I testified earlier, my wife had left me, and it wasn't until a week after she returned that she realized they were gone. And at that time, my mind was on other things. I didn't think of it."

"Don't you mean that you weren't concerned because the keys were in fact never stolen?"

Madison felt his ire rising; he struggled to contain it. "No, I mean exactly what I said. My mind was on other things." He felt hungry, weak. He had been concentrating hard since he took the stand, and the experience was proving to be emotionally draining. Hellman was right: this was more mentally demanding than testifying about a patient's care.

Warwick began walking toward Madison again. "Do you have an alarm in your house, sir?"

"Yes."

"Does it also protect the garage when you turn it on?"

"Yes."

"When do you usually arm the alarm?"

"Right before we go to bed."

"And at what time had you gone to bed the night of the murders?"

"As I told the detectives, I fell asleep while watching television that night, around eleven o'clock."

"Eleven—"

"So I never set the alarm that night. I awoke around four in the morning when the police came to the door."

Warwick reached the witness box and leaned on the railing, looking down at Madison. "Do you have a car alarm?"

"Yes, I do. But it doesn't arm itself unless I lock the car doors. I don't lock the car when it's parked in the garage because the garage is alarmed. Besides, there's a remote arming device on the same keychain as the spare car key. Without the arming device, the key wouldn't do my wife much good."

Warwick clenched his jaw, moved to his next question. "You have a dog, don't you?"

"Yes."

"Is he a good watchdog?"

"At times."

"I hear that Labs are excellent watchdogs."

"Like with people, generalizations are not always accurate. He's a good watchdog *at times.*"

"And when are those times that he's particularly effective?"

"When he's awake and when he's downstairs or on the second floor. I've got a big house. If he's upstairs and asleep, he usually doesn't hear anything in the garage, which is separate from the house."

Warwick chuckled and turned to face the jury for a moment. "So you're saying that because your dog was asleep, he didn't hear anything. A dog that's a heavy sleeper," he sneered mockingly, shaking his head, as if to say, *Do you believe this?* He turned back to Madison. "Did he awaken you the night of the murders? Had he heard any strange noises?"

"Not that I'm aware of. I don't recall him waking me up."

"So what you're saying, if I may paraphrase—and please stop me if I'm wrong—is that Miss Harding stole your keys, took a chance that your house alarm wasn't armed, stole your car, ran down these two people, planted the beer in the backseat, returned your car to the garage, again risking the fact that the alarm might be set, and then left? And your dog never heard any of it?"

"No."

"No?"

"That's not what I'm saying. That's what the police are saying. I'm not saying anything other than what I've told the police, yourself, and Mr. Denton."

Warwick waved a hand at Madison in disgust. "I have nothing further at this time for this witness. We reserve the right to recall him if additional evidence becomes available."

"Redirect?" the judge asked.

Denton looked up toward Calvino. "Yes, Your Honor. A few questions, if I may." He stood and walked over to Madison.

"Doctor, did you ever tell Brittany Harding that your home has an alarm?"

"No."

"Do you have any of those signs or stickers posted anywhere on your house warning anyone of an alarm?"

"No, my wife thought they were ugly."

"Are there homes in your area that don't have alarms? Please don't answer unless you have direct knowledge," he said, sensing Warwick preparing to pounce like a hungry leopard.

"I have two friends who don't have alarms. One of them lives across the street. Matt Jeffries. The other house belongs to the Fentons, down the block. There may be more, but I don't personally know of any others."

"So, unless the person breaking in knows you personally, or knows someone who knows you personally, the burglar wouldn't know whether or not you have an alarm."

"That's correct."

"Doctor, how many floors are there in your house?"

"Three."

"Which floor is your bedroom on?"

"The third."

"Does your dog usually sleep in the bedroom with you?"

"Yes."

"And was he in the room with you when you fell asleep the night Mr. Silvers and Ms. Pringle were murdered?"

"He was."

"When you were awakened by the police in the middle of the night, was the door to your room open or closed?"

"It was closed."

"Doctor, is your garage part of your house? By that I mean, are they part of the same structure?"

"No, the garage is its own separate building. There's a carport between the garage and the house, and the covering of the carport connects the two buildings."

"So it seems perfectly reasonable that your dog might not

have heard Miss Harding three stories below, in another building, doesn't it, doctor?"

"Objection!"

"Withdrawn," Denton said, moving back to his seat.

Brittany Harding looked at Warwick, her eyes pleading
with him to say something, anything, to help her. But Warwick was busy seething, grinding his teeth, impotently
watching his adversary settle into his chair.

Denton shuffled a few papers, then faced the judge. "The
prosecution rests, Your Honor."

Denton raised a glass and tapped it against Hellman's. "We're
done. Your client did well. Warwick will really have to come
up with something powerful to save Harding."

"I, for one, would like to see her put away, not just for killing
those people, but because she's evil. And I know she'll never
leave Phil alone. She's not only delusional, she's obsessed with
him, fixated on him. I don't know how he's held together as
well as he has."

"Well, please pass along my apologies again to him. I still
feel we did the right thing given our original information.
Even though it made a shambles of his life, he was, at that
time, the most likely suspect. But, shit, nobody's perfect. We
just missed it."

Hellman raised his eyebrows. He felt it was a bit flippant
the way Denton dismissed the hell that he had put Madison
through. Yet, he understood that in fact they were not perfect, and that they were just trying to do a tough job: put the
person responsible for a heinous crime behind bars. "His life
was a shambles before you got involved. Don't get me
wrong—it got worse after his arrest, but at least you realized
the mistake before it was too late."

Denton smiled acknowledgment, raised his glass. "To a
smooth conclusion."

"A smooth conclusion," Hellman said.

CHAPTER
68

IN AN EFFORT to score a few quick and final points to neutral-ize some of the damage done by Madison, Warwick con-cluded his case by calling two witnesses: one was an expert on rape who testified that many women do not come for-ward immediately following the assault because of the embarrassment and grilling they would have to face at trial. It was therefore perfectly understandable, the expert psychol-ogist testified, that Harding did not go to the police earlier. In fact, she pointed out, look what happened when she did decide to file a complaint—no charges were brought and no arrest was made.

On cross-examination, Denton elicited her concession that the reason no charges were filed was not that she came forward as a rape victim, and not that the police did not believe her, but that there was no definitive evidence to sup-port a successful prosecution.

Denton leaned toward the psychologist. "In fact, her quest for money overshadowed her concern for finding justice, didn't it?"

"I don't follow you."

"Well, she hired an attorney to bring a civil case. And once her monetary demands were met, she withdrew the criminal complaint—before the police even had the chance to com-plete their investigation."

"Objection."

"Withdrawn," Denton said, smirking as he walked back to his seat. "Nothing further." Although the comment had been withdrawn from the record, his point had been cemented in the minds of the jury. He viewed this exchange with the psychologist as a victory, but could not help but wonder what the female members of the panel would be thinking relative to Harding's being portrayed as a rape victim. Sympathy to any degree could be deadly when dealing with reasonable doubt.

Warwick's other expert, hastily arranged, testified as to the shortfalls of DNA testing. As soon as Warwick inquired about the weaknesses of PCR analysis, before the researcher could render an opinion, Denton requested a sidebar. Meeting with the judge outside the jury's presence, Denton remarked that if Warwick persisted in this line of questioning, he would request permission to reopen the prosecution's case, as he expected to have the results of the RFLP testing within a day or two. He was confident of the outcome, and he would use the findings as rebuttal testimony. Calvino asked Warwick if he was the gambling type. "Make the perceived weakness of PCR analysis the cornerstone of your case, counselor, and it could be blown clear out of the water should the RFLP test results corroborate the results of the PCR testing."

Warwick mulled it over for a few seconds before choosing to abandon his line of questioning, requesting the right to recall the witness should the RFLP test results support the defense's position. With this granted, the expert's testimony was essentially reduced to harmless rubble and a few impromptu and pointless questions about the dangers of contamination and degradation. Denton promptly fired back the same questions he had asked his own expert, Dr. Ross, about how contamination and degradation could cause the results to match Harding's DNA pattern. The answer was that it could not, and the witness was disposed of harmlessly.

Thus far, much to Denton's satisfaction, there were no surprises during trial. He only hoped that the jury was seeing the events and circumstances as clearly as he viewed them. Although Warwick elected not to put Harding on the stand, a wise move considering her unpredictable and socially abrasive nature, the jury had been force-fed a dose of what she was truly like by the prosecution's witnesses: from delusional nuisance to plotting extortionist to vengeful murderer.

The judge, having nodded to the court recorder, cleared his throat. "Mr. Denton."

Denton smiled at the jurors and remained seated, as was his custom when beginning his closing argument. "This was a gruesome murder of two innocent people, ladies and gentlemen. No one in this courtroom will dispute that. What will be debated, and what has been the subject of this trial, is who did it. Well, we feel that we *know* who did it. And we've presented evidence to you these past couple of weeks showing you who, how—and *why*. We've shown you the character of the person who stands accused over there," he said, throwing out his finger and pointing at Harding, "and we've shown you the events which led up to her eventual action that resulted in the deaths of the two innocent victims. These people didn't die because anyone had anything against them. No, they were true victims in the sense that they had nothing to do with what precipitated the anger that built beyond proportion—and beyond control—in Brittany Harding's mind.

"The aggression in this case was focused against Dr. Phillip Madison, a well-respected surgeon in this community. And what did he do to deserve this aggression? Well, nothing, any reasonable person would conclude. But the defendant took exception to having lost her job due to her own inadequacies, and held it against Dr. Madison. While most of us would simply have gotten angry, maybe yelled a bit, written a nasty letter . . . the defendant sought revenge. She came forward with a bogus rape complaint—you heard the lack of evidence—and when she tried to extort money from him, an attempt which ultimately failed, she cranked up the stakes of revenge a bit more. She tried to turn his wife against him.

"But she didn't stop there. She stole his car and went to the streets of our community in an attempt to commit murder, all the while setting the situation up as if Dr. Madison had done it in a drunken stupor. But she didn't figure on one thing: the fact that our investigative process is largely assisted nowadays by science: in this case, DNA, saliva, and lip print analysis. She didn't know that we would be able to extract her saliva and genetic code—a type of fingerprint, if you will, off the beer cans she planted in his car in an attempt to implicate him.

"She tried to fool the police. She tried to fool me. She tried to fool *you*, ladies and gentlemen. But it didn't work, did it? No, we saw her for who she is, and what she's about.

"I ask you to look carefully at the evidence, at the defendant's state of mind, at her character, at the witnesses who have testified before you under oath. You have to ask yourself: did the defendant have the ability to commit this heinous crime? Let's look at it first from a physical perspective. This crime did not require any unusual amount of strength—just an unusual amount of gall. Leeza Madison noticed that her keys to her husband's car and garage were missing shortly after the defendant was in their home. Dr. Madison testified that he'd fallen asleep watching the evening news—the same statement he'd made to the police when they first began their investigation—so he never did get to arm his house alarm. He didn't bother to set his car alarm because the garage was covered by the house alarm. So I ask you, was it possible for Brittany Harding to walk up to the garage, a semi-attached structure that was on the opposite side of the three-story house from Dr. Madison's bedroom, unlock the door with the key, start his car, and drive off? I believe the answer is obvious. Did she take a chance that the alarm was already set? Most definitely. But did she even know that there *was* an alarm? Her own house doesn't have one—"

"Objection!" shouted Warwick, who was standing and leaning forward on the defense table. "Assumes facts not in evidence."

"Sustained. While I'm not pleased with objections during closing arguments, he does have a point, Mr. Denton. Please stick to the facts of the case, counselor."

Denton was seething. He did not like to be interrupted during his closing statement. As his argument built, so did his momentum. He took a deep breath and squared his shoulders. "Yes, Your Honor."

"Jury will disregard the prosecutor's last statement relative to the defendant not having a home alarm."

Denton faced the jury. "Let's just say that there was no way for the defendant to know if there was an alarm on the garage. At the very least, had she known, she was taking a chance. But that requires levelheaded, prudent, objective thought processes, and I remind you that as the psychiatrist, Dr. Hall, testified, revenge is an act of desperation, and involves obsessive behavior. She was fixated on one goal: revenge against Dr. Madison. So in this instance, it was not just a matter of whether or not she was *able* to kill these two people, it was whether or not the defendant exercised prudence in weighing the reward of revenge against the consequences of getting caught. Clearly, as Dr. Madison and William Stanton, her former employer, testified, she has established a pattern of seeking the reward of revenge over the risk of retribution.

"Then there is the issue of the market incident. Ronald Norling, the grocery clerk, was only interested in telling the truth of what he had seen and heard. He doesn't know Dr. Madison or Miss Harding—he has no ax to grind, no bias, if you will, whatsoever. You heard him tell us what he witnessed. We know why the defendant did what she's accused of doing because, aside from the physical evidence implicating her, *she told us* what she was going to do. She made her intentions quite clear. The last time she threatened to do something—when she accused Dr. Madison of rape and screamed that she was going to go to the police and make him pay—she did just that. And when she screamed at him in a crowded market that she would make him pay and get even with him—she did just that. Or tried to. Ladies and gentlemen, what more do we need? I would submit that we don't need anything more to establish guilt on the part of the defendant.

"But we *do* have more. We have scientific evidence that underscores her involvement in this act of violence. Oh, the defendant's attorney will tell you that just because her genetic fingerprints are on the beer cans found in the car does not mean she was driving it. That's true. But I ask you, who else would have been driving it? Why would the defendant's genetic fingerprints be found on beer cans inside the car if she were not a party to this crime?

"And I remind you that the only eyewitness to the aftermath of this murder said that he saw a Chicago White Sox hat on the driver of the vehicle as it passed by him. Such a hat was found in the defendant's home, because she's a longtime fan of the team. And I remind you, this is not Chicago. There aren't that many White Sox fans in Sacramento, California."

Denton paused, walked a few steps over to the prosecution table. He leaned back against the front edge of it and crossed his arms on his chest. "In my opening statement, I asked you all to concentrate on the facts of the case and on what the witnesses had to say. I told you that if you did that, and did not allow yourselves to be swayed by fantasies, far-reaching theories, or confusing curves that the defense attorney would attempt to throw at you, then the answer to your question of guilt will be black and white. It would be simple, I told you." He stood up straight and began to walk toward them again. "It *is* simple, ladies and gentlemen. I didn't say *easy,* because it's never easy to find someone guilty of murder. But *simple,* because the facts so clearly support it."

He stopped in front of the jury box, rested his hands on the railing. Looked at each of them, making eye contact as he spoke. "Mr. Warwick, in his opening, said that he didn't need to prove anything to you—which is good for him, because he *didn't* prove anything. Because he *couldn't.*" Denton leaned forward. "But we did. We proved our case, met our burden of proof. You must tell everyone in this great nation that murder for revenge will not go unpunished. Ladies and gentlemen, do your duty. Find the defendant guilty, as charged. Thank you."

A low-level murmur erupted from the audience; the reporters were writing furiously, their cellular phones charged and ready. As soon as Warwick finished his statement, the journalists covering the trial for radio would call in and report live, while those handling it for television would choose an appropriate backdrop for filming their remote spot for the early evening news. The local print journalists would head back to their offices to type out their stories, while those from out of town would call in and dictate their copy.

Calvino gave a slight crack of his gavel and asked for quiet. He nodded to Warwick. The lanky public defender stood, buttoned his sportcoat, and approached the jury box. He stopped, and smiled. "Good morning. Ladies and gentlemen of the jury, as you have surmised, we have now reached that part of the case known as closing argument in which each of the lawyers has an opportunity to tell you what his case is about. You've already heard the district attorney's position.

"In my opening, I told you that the evidence that the prosecution had against my client was circumstantial. Not the best type of evidence. In fact, none of it is direct evidence. Because there is no direct evidence linking my client to this crime. No one saw her commit the crime. Oh, yeah, there's a witness who saw someone wearing a White Sox cap. Well, the last time I looked, being a White Sox fan did not make someone a murderer. And we also must remember that based upon this same witness's description, the police arrested a *male* initially, not a *female.*

"Now, ladies and gentlemen, my client is not an angel. She's not a model citizen. I won't insult your intelligence by standing up here and saying that she is. But her past actions were not precursors to murder. Poor judgment, misguided ethics, for sure. But *murder?*" He laughed. "I think not. I *know* not."

He spread his arms out, palms up, pleading his case. "And this incident in the market. My client has what a lot of people call 'verbal diarrhea.' She runs off at the mouth," he clarified, to some stifled laughter. "But again, I ask you . . . does this make her a murderer? No, it does not. She was angry, she was frustrated—whether you feel she was right or justified is irrelevant. But when she came face-to-face with the man who represented her frustrations, she yelled something at him. Did she really mean what she said? Of course not! We all, at one time or another, say things that we regret, that we don't mean. We've all said things that we wish we could take back because they were said in the heat of the moment. The DA wants you to believe that she was announcing to a crowded market her intentions to commit murder. My client may not be an angel, but she is certainly not stupid.

"At the start of this trial, I asked you to remember three things: reasonable doubt, circumstantial evidence, and burden of proof. Burden of proof," Warwick said, walking the length of the jury box and letting his left hand drag along the railing, "means that it is the prosecution's responsibility to make a compelling case against my client. All they did was to throw a bunch of circumstances at you and ask you to make a leap of faith. They gave you nothing concrete about this murder except a bunch of theories. They didn't mean for their case to be so indirect and weak—it's not their fault. They didn't have a choice. But I ask you to ask yourselves," he said slapping his right hand, karate-chop style, into his left palm for emphasis, "did they actually prove anything to you, or did they merely set the stage and ask you to imagine that you've seen the play?

"You have to admit that their case may, in fact, be interesting, but it's not conclusive. Certainly not beyond a reasonable doubt. Which is the standard against which you must judge my client. Reasonable doubt means that if you have any doubts about the innocence or guilt of my client, if there's *something* bothering you about all of this in the back of your mind, something that just doesn't feel right, you must vote not guilty. That's not my invention, it's the law.

"As for Mr. Denton thinking that the matter of imprisoning someone for perhaps the rest of her life is a *simple* decision . . . well, maybe where he comes from, it is. From where you and I come from, it is not. It's never easy to make such drastic decisions regarding another human being's life. I'm sure you feel that in order to do so, you must be *absolutely sure* of the facts!"

As Warwick's voice rose, in the manner that a preacher admonishes his followers, Denton detected the slight nod of the head of two of the jurors.

"I'm not asking you for sympathy for my client. But I *am* asking you for *fairness* for my client. Miss Harding is an innocent person, falsely accused, whose life will never be the same again, even if she is acquitted. Don't reach a verdict of guilty merely because you want to make someone, *anyone*, pay for this horrible crime." He held out his right hand, index finger angled toward the ceiling for emphasis. "Based upon the case that the prosecutor has provided, you *must* find her not guilty.

"Thank you."

Warwick strolled back to the defense table, sat down next to Harding, gave her hand a reassuring squeeze. She sat there, numb, staring straight ahead. She had not heard a word either attorney had said this morning.

As the judge provided his long-winded instructions to the jury, Denton ground his molars so hard he gave himself a splitting headache. He knew what was coming, and he knew there was no way that he could avoid it—the extensive speech by Calvino defining and discussing reasonable doubt. The only positive aspect of his instructions concerned his comments on circumstantial evidence—which were strong and, Denton was sure, unfortunately confusing to the jury at times.

Calvino explained, in an informal manner, that circumstantial evidence was real evidence. "It is to be considered and given weight just as one would give weight to direct evidence. However, the circumstantial evidence must not only point in the direction of guilt, it must also exclude to a moral certainty every reasonable hypothesis *except* guilt." He plowed forward, despite the confused looks of some of the people on the panel. "Further," he said, "every inference you make from the circumstantial evidence needs to arise from facts that were proven beyond a reasonable doubt. Otherwise, the circumstantial evidence could not be considered as evidence of guilt . . ."

After the judge concluded his thirty-minute explanation, the jury was dismissed to its room to begin deliberations. Hellman, who had arrived with Madison and Leeza just prior to the closing statements, stood up and straightened his tie. "Now, we wait," he said.

"How long do you think it'll be?" Leeza asked.

Hellman cocked his head to one side. "You never know. If they're absolutely convinced of her guilt, they'll be back out here in half an hour. If they have issues of conflict, say, if one juror doesn't think the evidence is conclusive enough, it could be days or weeks before they reach a verdict. I've given up trying to read juries. It's not only inaccurate a good portion of the time, it's stressful as all hell."

"Well, I've blocked off the morning from my schedule. God knows I'm not exactly busy these days," Madison said, shaking his head.

"Things will pick up, Phil. It's just a matter of time. People will forget. The other docs will realize they have no one who can do these surgeries as well as you can. They'll start sending cases over again."

"I can just hear it every time I go to testify as an expert witness. 'Doctor, isn't it true that you were once arrested for murder?' It'll be objected to, but I'm sure it'll make a hit with the jury . . . and dredge everything up again. Would you want to hire me as your expert if you knew that question was going to be asked?"

"Why don't we go grab some coffee," Hellman suggested, realizing that this was not going to be a simple issue of reassurance. Leeza urged Madison to go, promising that she'd call him on his portable phone should the jury return while they were away.

They walked out of the courthouse to a Java City café a couple of blocks away. As they walked, Madison took a deep breath, filling his lungs with air that had a brisk, moist chill to it.

"Hopefully, today is the start of something new," Hellman said.

"How did your trial go?"

"We finished closing arguments yesterday," Hellman said. "Jury's still out. Deliberations will go on for a few days, I'm sure. It wasn't as strong a defense as I'd like to have had, especially with the guy facing twenty-five to life. But you take what you have to work with. I think we did okay. Regardless, life goes on. For me, at least."

Madison gave him a look.

"Sorry—just a bit of defense humor."

They ordered decaf lattes and sat at a corner table with a view of the street and sidewalk.

"So is that it? *Life goes on?* Is that how I'm supposed to think?"

Hellman shrugged. "It wouldn't hurt. This past year hasn't been a dream, Phil. As much as you'd like to wake up from it all, you have to accept that it's happened and you have to deal with it. Your life will be changed forever."

"Just move on, that's it."

"That's it. There's not much else you can do. Just be glad that it turned out this way. *You* could just as easily have been sitting in court right now instead of Harding, waiting for the jury to decide your fate."

Madison sat there, shaking his head. "I can't describe what this past year's been like, Jeffrey. I've been to hell and back. I guess I should feel fortunate, but all I feel is numb . . . emotionally spent. I've been on a roller coaster for ten straight months. I've had feelings I've never had in my life. I've done things I've never done, been places I've never been."

Hellman chuckled, tried to lighten the mood. "You can say that again."

"All my life, I've always been liked. Now, people would just as soon spit in my face as shake my hand." He took a sip of his coffee. "Don't get me wrong. I don't mean to say that I've never had conflict in my life—you know I have. But conflict is very different from persistent harassment by a psychotic nut. You never know what she's going to do next. Where she's going to show up, what rumors she's going to spread . . . whether your family is safe when they walk out the door . . ." He shook his head slowly, as if he were reliving a nightmare. "I didn't know where it would lead, Jeffrey, when it would stop. My kids, I was worried about my kids . . ."

"I know, I was there, remember?"

"It just kept building, threatened to consume me. When Leeza left me, everything just . . . fell apart. I couldn't deal with it anymore."

"Look at it this way. In a few days, maybe a week, heck, maybe today, it'll all be over."

Madison took a deep breath, gulped a mouthful of coffee. "And if she's acquitted? What then?"

"First of all, they'll convict. I really believe that. We gave Denton a good case. He had a lot to work with and he did a great job."

"I thought you'd given up trying to guess what juries—"

"That was the attorney side of me talking. Speaking as a friend, my gut tells me she's dead meat." Hellman placed a hand on Madison's shoulder. "And Phil, on the off chance that she's acquitted, I'll get a restraining order. I'll make sure they keep her away from you. We'll do everything within the law to keep you insulated from that nut." He assessed Madison's face, which didn't reveal any signs of relief. "But all this is just meaningless debate. She's going to be convicted."

"After all I've been through . . . I sure hope so."

They finished their lattes, then parted company. Madison stopped by the courthouse to check in with Leeza and learned that the jury had come out to have part of Ronald Norling's testimony read back. They also wanted to hear part of Warwick's cross-examination of Stuart Saperstein. Denton explained to Madison that it was impossible to predict what they were thinking, but he did think it was good that they wanted to hear Norling's testimony again. He was an important link between the establishment of motive and the verbal projection of her intentions.

With Madison due at his office and Leeza leaving to pick up Elliott and Jonah, Denton offered to call him when the jury had reached its verdict. As Madison left the courthouse, he saw the demonstrators carrying signs demanding justice against Harding. He buried his face in the collar of his cashmere overcoat and steered clear of them. While he was no longer the object of the animosity, he did not want to invite recognition or, what's worse, conflict.

CHAPTER
69

CHANDLER ROLLED OVER in bed and fumbled for the phone in the dark. He knocked it off the hook, reached down, and fished along the carpet for the handset. As he found it and pulled it up to his ear, he glanced at the clock. It was 11:45.

"Hello?"

"Junior, did I call too late?"

"Johnny . . . Denise went to bed early. With this pregnancy, she's been turning in around nine-thirty."

"I'm just hitting my stride around nine-thirty."

"I assume you've got info on those lot numbers for me."

"Got a pen?"

Chandler flicked the lamp on and grabbed a pad and pencil from his night table drawer. He jotted down the information, then thanked Johnny. He hung up the phone and lay there, reading his notes.

"Shut the light," Denise moaned.

"Huh? Yeah, okay, in a minute."

"Who was on the phone?"

"Johnny. He got me some info on Phil's case I'd asked him for."

Denise rolled onto her side facing Chandler. "Phil's case? I thought that's done with, at least as far as you're concerned."

Chandler grunted.

"What does that mean? Are you done, or aren't you?"

"It was just a loose end I was following up on."

"What kind of loose end?"

"It's late. I'd rather not go into it now."

"You're not going back out to California, are you?"

"No, nothing like that. It's just . . . the beer cans. The lot numbers stamped on the bottom of the cans they found in Phil's Mercedes don't match one another."

"And this means . . ."

"Nothing. Probably nothing."

She sighed and turned onto her back. "Then shut the light."

"Yeah."

Denise rolled back onto her side facing Chandler. "Ryan, either tell me what's bothering you or shut the damn light."

He sighed, tried to rub the wrinkles from his forehead.

"Something's on your mind," she said, stifling a yawn. "Speak now or forever hold your peace."

He thought of closing his eyes, of trying to go back to sleep. But he was suddenly wide awake. He looked over at Denise, who was staring at him, waiting for a response. "Beer is brewed in fifty-five-thousand-gallon lots; when that lot is canned, the lot number is stamped on the bottom of the can. The lots are then sent to distributors, who deliver them to different retailers. They keep very detailed records, as required by law and as regulated by the state's Department of Alcoholic Beverage Control. The lot numbers on the bottoms of the cans of the six-pack found in Phil's car didn't match. Two cans were from one lot, and the other four were from another. Johnny tracked down the two different lots and found out they were sold at different stores. Are you following me so far?"

Denise shook her head, yawned again. "Yeah."

"Why don't we finish this in the morning. You need your sleep—"

"The cans in his car were from different stores. Don't keep me in suspense. What else?"

"The two cans that matched were the ones that had Harding's saliva on them; that lot was delivered to Food & More, where Phil ran into Harding that night. The other four cans were from another lot, which was delivered to a different retailer—Qual-Mart. When Harding's house was searched, they pulled an unopened can from her refrigerator and an empty can from her recycling bin. Those two cans matched each other—

they had the same lot number. They also had the same lot number as the two cans in Phil's car that had her saliva on them."

Denise was nodding. "Meaning what?"

"Meaning . . . probably nothing."

She looked at him. "Is it nothing, or is it *probably* nothing?"

Chandler rubbed at his forehead again. "It could be argued that someone went by her house and pulled a couple of cans from her recycling bin. And that person could then have taken the cans and planted them in Phil's car along with four cans from a six-pack purchased at Qual-Mart a few days later." He paused, waved a hand at the air. "But it's more likely that Harding bought two different six-packs at different times, and still had a couple of cans left in her refrigerator from the last time she went shopping. Like the eggs in our fridge. You go to the market, buy a dozen eggs, and there's still a few left over from the dozen you bought a couple of weeks ago."

Denise was silent for a moment. "Yeah, but if the egg analogy doesn't apply here," she finally said, "then you're saying that Harding may *not* have done this. Someone could then argue that she was set up or even that Phil did it."

Chandler was shaking his head. "I didn't say that, Denise. I'm convinced Brittany Harding killed those people. Let's not blow this whole thing out of proportion. You know me, I'm a perfectionist. Everything has to fit just right. She just got beer at two different times. There's nothing to it." Chandler rolled over to turn off the light, but Denise grabbed his arm.

"Wait a minute, Ryan."

"What . . ."

"Regardless of your opinion, don't you need to turn this information over to the court?"

"For what?"

"You're supposed to turn over all pertinent information identified during the course of an investigation if it has any ability to aid either the defendant or the State."

"Denise, this isn't anything new, it's just my interpretation of evidence the police already have locked away in their vault."

"So?"

"So both sides have had the opportunity to study the cans, test them, and go over them with a fine-tooth comb."

Denise thought about this for a moment, then shook her head. "I think you're splitting hairs. But let's say for a minute that you're right, and you don't have a legal obligation. What about a moral obligation? Doesn't that count for something?"

"I hate it when you get all self-righteous." He stretched across his pillow toward the lamp switch, flicked it off. "I really don't feel like getting into a debate about this."

"I can't help it. This is what I do all day in law school."

"Well, you're not in law school right now, I'm not one of your professors, and it's almost midnight." He pulled up the covers and let his head fall back onto the pillow. "We'll talk about this in the morning. You need your rest."

"Don't just cut me off like that," she said, turning the night table light back on. "This issue has nothing to do with being self-righteous, and it has nothing to do with being in law school. Besides, I'm already awake, Ryan. I want to finish this discussion."

Chandler blew a long sigh through his lips. "Okay, fine. Try looking at it from a different perspective. Assume for a minute that the defense hasn't thought of this lot number discrepancy. For all I know, they may have. But if they haven't, by bringing it to their attention, I'd be helping Brittany Harding. A lot of the critical evidence against her could be brought into question. The saliva, lip prints, and DNA could be thrown out because the cans would naturally have her identifying marks all over them if someone took them from her recycling bin. At the very least, it could provide just enough reasonable doubt to get her off. If not in this trial, then on appeal. And regardless of what might come up at some later date, they'd never be able to try her again for that crime. Now why would I want to do that? Would justice really be served? Besides, I'd potentially be helping a murderer go free. That's not me."

"But it's not about you. It's about justice. It's not your place to play judge and jury. Do you remember what you used to say? That our judicial system is the best in the world, but that it was full of loopholes?"

"It is. When a judge would let some creep go free on a technicality, I'd head for the bathroom and puke."

"You'd be stressed out, tied up in knots for days. And I took the brunt of it."

"So what's your point?"

"My point is that you had to find a way of dealing with it so it wouldn't tear you apart. You accepted the fact that you had to take our system as it was, and work within its confines until new rules were made. You realized that taking the law into your own hands wouldn't work. Otherwise, where would it leave us? Where would it leave society? If cops had the power to decide who's guilty and who's not on the spot and issue a sentence right there on the street, there'd be chaos. Until something or someone changes the system, the best way—the only way—is to turn over all the evidence and let the court do with it as it sees fit. As twelve impartial people see fit."

"You sound like such a typical law student."

"Actually, I was quoting you. In case you don't remember, it's because of those weaknesses in the system that you pushed me to go to law school."

"I didn't push you."

"You said one way to change the system was for me to do it from the inside."

Chandler sighed and rolled onto his opposite side, away from Denise.

"Turning your back on me isn't the answer." She sat up, leaned on her elbow, and peered over his shoulder. "You need to give them the information, Ryan."

"A *theory* about beer can lot numbers isn't evidence, Denise."

"If you were a defense attorney, wouldn't you try and introduce it as evidence? The judge would decide if it is or it isn't. But if he lets it in, a jury just may listen. You said it yourself: it could be enough to create reasonable doubt."

"Then let her attorney think of it. That's his job. I'm not

going to be the one to give Harding a get-out-of-jail-free card. Especially when she doesn't deserve it."

"But it shouldn't be your decision. It *can't* be your decision, or the system falls apart."

He bit his lip and shook his head.

Denise awaited a response, but Chandler was quiet. Finally, she reached over and picked up the phone. "If you think these are just the ramblings of a green law school student, call Jeffrey Hellman and ask him what he thinks. Or call the DA who's prosecuting the case against Harding and ask him."

Chandler rolled out of bed and walked over to the window to draw the shade. The streetlights of the city lit up the avenue below with an orange luminescence, as if a setting sun were descending behind the tall buildings. "Denise, the Madisons have two young children. Brittany Harding is a sick individual who's done some horrid things. If she went free because of information I gave her attorney, the Madisons wouldn't be safe. Their children wouldn't be safe. If something happened to them, I wouldn't be able to live with myself." He turned to face her. "Think of Noah asleep in the other room. About our child growing inside you right now, as we speak. How would you feel if someone did something that endangered their lives? That's what I'd be doing to Phil's kids."

"So you think the best thing to do is to just let it go. Forget about it, bury it. Be the judge *and* the jury, all by yourself?" She paused and waited for a response. Chandler was silent. "What this comes down to, Ryan, is would you be able to live with yourself if you *don't* turn the information over?"

Chandler shrugged and stared out the window for a long moment. "I don't know, Denise. I just don't know."

Having just left the OR after nearly nine hours of surgery, Madison was exhausted. The case, which had been referred to him just prior to the revocation of his privileges, required a specific procedure that Madison had pioneered a couple of years ago in northern California. Despite their star surgeon's uncertain status with the hospital, John Stevens and the rest of the board agreed that transporting the patient to San Francisco for the operation, or bringing in another surgeon for this one specialized procedure, could be more damaging than granting Madison temporary surgical status. As an aside, Stevens pointed out that with his legal situation having significantly improved, this move was a potential precursor to reinstatement of full privileges.

Madison walked out into the waiting area, still in his surgical garb, and gave his patient's family the good news: the operation went well. After asking a few questions, they thanked him and he trudged off down the hallway toward the lounge. Five chairs were haphazardly arranged around an oval table, with a mini refrigerator sitting atop a counter next to the sink. He entered the small room, grabbed a granola bar from the cabinet, and ripped it open. He realized that he was not only exhausted, he was famished as well.

A moment later, having finished the granola bar, he pulled himself out of the lounge and headed down the hallway toward the locker room to shower and change. Before he could undress, however, a message was handed to him by an orderly who made a quick exit.

Madison stared at the slip of paper: "The jury is returning with a verdict." He felt his chest tightening, the air in the locker room suddenly becoming thin and stale. He snatched his cell phone from the locker and dialed Leeza. The machine snapped on. "It's me, meet me at the courthouse if you get this," he managed to blurt. He struggled for a deep breath, dialed her car phone, and left a voice mail message there as well.

He began to perspire heavily, the weight on his chest squeezing tighter. He stumbled into the rest room five feet away, leaned over the sink and splashed his face with cold water.

The nausea began in waves, his knees feeling like wet noodles. He stumbled backward into a stall and fell onto the toilet.

"I want my life back!" he yelled into the dead air. But John Stevens's voice was echoing in his head . . . *"It's not over . . . it'll never be over . . ."*

He grabbed his hair and pulled, hoping the pain would

overshadow the heightening nausea. Suddenly, a spasm from deep in his neck clamped down on his throat, an uncontrollable urge rising up from his stomach. He whirled off the toilet and, crouching in front of it, heaved, then heaved again, until he filled the bowl with vomit and bile . . . the rough grains of granola scraping the lining of his esophagus as they surged upward through his throat.

He knelt over the toilet, the narrow stall a prison, the confining walls moving in on him. He clamped his eyes shut, brushed the hair back off his face, and tried to breathe deeply. But the pressure on his chest was too great. He stood up, grabbed the door to steady himself, and slipped, falling back onto the toilet.

He tried to take another breath. Tore at his scrubs and ripped open the neck, tearing—clawing—at the material, trying to give himself room to breathe. Reached out, pressed his hands against the walls, the vertigo increasing. Taking rapid gasps of putrid air. Hyperventilating.

Think, Phil, think. Slow your breathing. Relax, get hold of yourself! Can't get to the courthouse like this . . .

He cupped his hands over his mouth and took several deep breaths, each lungful of carbon dioxide slowing his heart rate, decreasing his dizziness, calming his stomach. He slowly stood, opened the stall door, and walked over to the sink. He splashed his face with water, rinsed his mouth out, and leaned on the countertop, staring at his pale reflection in the mirror. *You can do this.*

Feeling stronger, he stood up and squared his shoulders.

He strode back into the locker room to change and saw the crumpled message lying on the floor. He pulled the torn shirt over his head, dressed, and walked out the door.

CHAPTER
70

IT TOOK MADISON ten minutes to drive from Sacramento General to the courthouse. He ran three red lights on the way, narrowly avoiding two broadside collisions. He left his car in the lot and sprinted across the street. As he neared the doors, he felt himself become suddenly short of breath again. He stopped, put his hands on his knees, and panted like a dog, gulping mouthfuls of air. He stood there, hunched over, as several attorneys in dark suits pushed past him.

A moment later, he stood up and wiped the perspiration from his forehead, passed through the metal detectors, and headed for the elevator. He burst through the doors of the courtroom just as the judge looked over toward the foreman of the jury. A few heads turned to the back of the room, where Madison stood looking for a seat. He found one in the last row and quietly slipped into the chair.

"Mr. Foreman, have you reached a verdict?"

"We have, Your Honor." The short, rotund man in his fifties handed a piece of paper to the bailiff, who brought it to the judge.

Madison, still somewhat weak from his panic attack, felt his heart begin to race. There was a hollow sensation in his stomach that he attributed to nerves rather than hunger. He glanced at the members of the jury, trying to read their expressions. Most were staring blankly at the judge, purposely avoiding the gaze of the packed gallery of press and other interested observers. Calvino opened the folded paper and glanced at it.

Madison took a deep, uneven breath, and closed his eyes.

"On count one of the charges, murder in the first degree, how do you find?"

The foreman's attention was cemented on the judge. "We find the defendant guilty."

A roar erupted from the crowd in the packed courtroom; Calvino was banging his gavel and shouting for order. Madison's heart stopped momentarily as dizziness and elation descended upon him simultaneously.

"On count two, murder in the first degree, how do you find?"

"Guilty."

Another uproar could be heard, more gavel banging, hand shaking, and back slapping at the prosecution table. Tears flowed freely from Madison's eyes as he buried his head in his hands and wept.

"Nooo! I'm innocent!" Harding was on her feet, writhing and flailing as one guard restrained her while another slapped handcuffs on her wrists. *"Idiots!"* she shouted at the jury, craning her neck to face them. *"Go to hell, all of you . . ."* she continued to scream as they dragged her away.

Madison felt a hand on his shoulder. He turned, saw Hellman, and buried his face in his friend's chest. And wept uncontrollably.

After taking a few minutes to compose himself, Madison left the courtroom through a back entrance to avoid the press and to find Leeza so he could share the good news with her.

Denton could see the reporters gathered at the courtroom exit. Plastering a broad smile on his face, he made his way toward the throng of camera crews and reporters. Instantly, microphones descended upon him, the news people shoving the handheld devices in front of his face to capture his comments. As he began to answer questions, he spotted Maurice Mather off in the distance, who had just completed a brief interview of Jeffrey Hellman.

"I want to thank all the members of the media for their

support and understanding throughout this long ordeal," Denton said. "I'd also like to thank the jury for their fine work under difficult conditions. And of course, I'm indebted to the district attorney, who again supplied me with the staff and unending support I needed to obtain this victory for the people of the State of California . . ."

CHAPTER
71

THE PARTY THAT FOLLOWED on Friday night was held in the Madisons' home. The children were allowed to sleep in their parents' bedroom, on the third floor, so as to have as quiet an environment as possible. A baby-sitter was hired to care for them for the evening.

Everyone in the medical community who had worked with Madison at one time or another had been invited. A couple of hospital administrators showed up, including John Stevens, as well as friends, neighbors, his parents—and of course Ricky. Music blared from a sound system they had rented for the evening; liquor was flowing freely, as were people's emotions. Drinks were being raised in toast every five minutes, preceded by the clanging of spoon against glass. Following each speech, everyone would drain their beverages and resume their conversations until the next tribute interrupted the chatter.

Streamers were shot off, and even a few fireworks were launched into the cold night air. Choruses of "For He's a Jolly Good Fellow" erupted at various times during the night. As the evening progressed, Madison felt the weight of his troubles drifting away on an ocean of Scotch.

At two in the morning, people began filtering by to offer congratulations on their way out.

Madison raised his glass and banged it hard with a spoon. He swayed a bit to the side, steadied himself on the wall to his right, and looked out amongst his guests. He focused his thoughts and attempted to speak clearly. "I would be remiss if I didn't thank two people who stood beside me and kept me sane during the most difficult and trying time of my life. My wife, Leeza, and my longtime friend, Jeffrey Hellman." A roar went up from the remaining fifty or so guests, some of whom were so blitzed that they would have cheered a toast to the local cow for providing milk.

When the last guest had departed, Madison looked at the clock in his study: it was a few minutes past three in the morning. The place was a mess, with half-empty glasses littering tables, cabinets, bookshelves . . . just about every horizontal surface was occupied.

He took a deep breath, gazed into his own glass, and, in a half-drunken stupor, reflected on the recent turbulence of his life . . . and considered what lay ahead for him in the coming months.

Hellman poked his head in the door and cleared his throat.

"Jeffrey, I thought you left."

"I was getting into my car, but I had to make sure you were okay."

"Come, sit." Madison slumped into his soft leather seat and motioned Hellman to the antique chair in front of his desk. "I'm surprised Chandler didn't make the party. You did call him, didn't you?"

Hellman nodded. "He said he had other plans."

"Other plans? This is a huge feather in his cap. You'd think this would be something he wouldn't want to miss. He'd have been the center of attention."

"He sounded a little distant, but I was about to go into a deposition and I didn't have time to find out what was bugging him. But look at it this way—at least he was here when it counted. I'm glad you made me call him. When you insisted I bring in a guy from New York, I thought you were out of your mind."

"Hell of an investigator. We were lucky to have had him on our team." Madison smiled, his face haggard, the strain of the past nine months etched into his skin like acid on a pane of glass. "And I'm equally fortunate to have you for a friend, Jeffrey. Thanks again. You came through when I needed it most."

"While you're so appreciative, I should hand you my bill."
They both laughed.

Leeza's call from upstairs urging him to come to bed interrupted them. He reached over to the intercom on the wall behind his desk and told her he would join her in a few moments.

"Well, I'd better be going," Hellman said as he rose from the chair.

"You okay to drive? You can stay the night if you want."

"Nah," he said with the wave of a hand. "I'm fine. I'll call you in a couple of days."

Madison started to get up; Hellman motioned him down. "I'll let myself out."

Madison leaned back in the leather chair, resting his feet on the desk. He felt numb as he attempted to sort through his thoughts, his plans for the future. Although it was quiet now in the house, the echoes of the noise from the party still buzzed in his ears.

He lay silently, watching the gentle rise and fall of his chest with each breath, the gleeful alcohol-induced high of only an hour ago becoming a postdrunken depression. He thought of one of his favorite poems: "The Road Not Taken," by Robert Frost. As he lay there, he pondered what his life would have been like had Brittany Harding not crossed his path, had she not accused him of rape, had she not tried to blackmail him, had she not attempted to destroy his marriage. Had she not made him kill those two innocent people.

He began to weep, appraising his hollow victory. Physically free, emotionally imprisoned for life. Held captive by his own horrible secret.

ACKNOWLEDGMENTS

I OWE EXTENSIVE THANKS to Emily Bestler, my editor at Pocket Books, who has the ability to add polish in just the right places to make a novel shine.

Additionally, a book of this nature required input and technical information that could be provided only by those practicing in the field. Sincere thanks goes to **Victor Reeve**, manager of the California Criminalists Institute (CCI), and **Fred Tulleners**, program manager of the CCI, for allowing me extensive use of the Bureau of Forensic Services Library, as well as for permitting me to audit the classes and labs reserved for criminalists, FBI agents, sheriffs, and other law enforcement personnel.

Thanks as well to **Nancy Edralin** of the Department of Justice, Division of Law Enforcement, for helping me establish contacts within the many departments of the Division of Law Enforcement. **Terry Spear** at CCI kindly counseled me on the intricacies of DNA testing. **John Dehaan**, impression and arson analyst at CCI, assisted me with the fine points of lip print analysis. **Chuck Jones**, manager of the Attorney General's Bureau of Investigation Intelligence Operations Unit, provided information on the process involving impropriety and penal code violations relative to the California State Crime Lab. Criminalist **Mike Saggs** assisted me with information on blood alcohol clearance rates.

Thanks also to Special Investigator **John McVey** of the Sacramento County District Attorney's office for his time and information. In New York, police officer **Norene Murray** graciously expounded the workings and structure of the New York City Crime Lab and its forensic investigators.

Extensive assistance was provided by Professor **Joshua Dressler**, McGeorge School of Law, who literally wrote the book(s) on criminal procedure. He was wonderful to work with, and I thank him for the many hours he afforded me. Also at McGeorge, Professor **Joseph Taylor**, the former assistant chief deputy district attorney for Sacramento County and former supervising deputy district attorney for Ventura County, provided valuable insight into the mind of a prosecutor. His patience and prompt, helpful replies to my endless follow-up phone calls and e-mails were very much appreciated. In addition, **Michael Sands**, the school's former director of the Center for Legal Advocacy and a criminal defense attorney with invaluable experience in high-profile cases, helped me view the case from a defendant's perspective. I thank him for the many hours he devoted to this project, including the time he spent reviewing and critiquing the manuscript. Without the assistance of **Don Aron**, Esq., I would never have made the acquaintance of the above professionals.

Paul Joncich, anchor-reporter for KOVR-TV, gave me a no-holds-barred behind-the-scenes look at television news reporting. To a first-class individual and a top-rate newscaster, thank you. Additionally, thanks to **Perry Ginsberg**, Esq., whose concern, lawyerly advice, and friendship I will always value; to **John Lewis**, who stood beside me as only a true friend would; and to **David Altman**, M.D., who without exception made himself available to answer any questions I had at the time.

Thanks as well to those people who have offered their time, contacts, and expertise in helping me navigate the turbulent waters of the publishing world: author **Marion Rosen**, **Fred Bissinger**, **Norman Fassler-Katz**, and **Claude Choquette**. I would like to extend a special thanks to **Robert Youdelman**, Esq., a truly gentle man whose assistance and work on my behalf I will always remember. To **Colin Swift**, thanks for your encouragement and unending support. And to **Steve Gold**, a good friend with a heart like his name . . . a long time ago you tried to expand my horizons—and years later you did so again by sending me my first copy of *Writer's Market* . . . (from all of us at *The Shea*), thanks.

I would like to express my sincere thanks as well to **Justin Manus**, Esq., and Canadian barrister **Timothy S. Ellam**, of McCarthy Tetrault.

All writers need a "sounding board" in whom they can trust and believe. My wife, **Jill**, fills that need and has sat (and sometimes stood over my shoulder) and listened, debated, and insisted at times . . . but I always knew that her only goal was to improve the manuscript. To my soul mate, thanks for being beside, behind, and in front of me. You made it all bearable. Further, all of the material regarding the fictional Consortium for Citizens with Mental Retardation is based upon information provided by Jill, a special-education teacher and resource specialist who holds a masters in education.

And finally, to the other Jill in my life, my agent, **Jillian Manus**, I can only express my heartfelt thanks. Jillian is so full of energy I sincerely believe that if she were an automobile, other cars would be able to run on the fumes she leaves in her wake. It's comforting to know that someone of Jillian's skill and determination is behind me. If most agents go the extra mile for their clients, Jillian goes two.

Errors of fact, if any exist in the book, are strictly my own responsibility, and should not reflect on any of the esteemed professionals noted above. In addition, because this is a work of fiction, any similarity to actual persons or events is purely coincidental.

ABOUT THE AUTHOR

ALAN JACOBSON received his Bachelor of Arts in English Writing from Queens College of the City University of New York, and his doctorate from Palmer College of Chiropractic—West in San Jose, California. He achieved prominence as an Agreed Medical Examiner and was subsequently appointed to the position of Qualified Medical Evaluator by the State of California. He has gained extensive experience testifying as an expert witness, which exposed him to the many strengths and weaknesses of the judicial system. His next novel of suspense, *The Hunted,* will be published in hardcover by Pocket Books. Dr. Jacobson lives with his wife and children in California.

You can e-mail the author at The_Novel_One@hotmail.com.